Born in the Kingdom of Fife in 1960, Ian Rankin graduated from the University of Edinburgh and has since been employed as grape-picker, swineherd, taxman, alcohol researcher, hi-fi journalist and punk musician. His first Rebus novel, *Knots & Crosses*, was published in 1987 and the Rebus books have now been translated into over twenty languages and are increasingly popular in the USA. Ian Rankin has been elected a Hawthornden Fellow, and is a past winner of the prestigious Chandler-Fulbright Award, as well as two CWA short-story 'Daggers' and the 1997 CWA Macallan Gold Dagger for Fiction for *Black & Blue*, which was also shortlisted for the Mystery Writers of America 'Edgar' award for best novel. *Black & Blue*, *The Hanging Garden*, *Dead Souls* and *Mortal Causes* have been televised on ITV, starring John Hannah as Inspector Rebus. *Dead Souls*, the tenth novel in the series, was shortlisted for the CWA Gold Dagger Award in 1999. An Alumnus of the Year at Edinburgh University, he has also been awarded three honorary doctorates, from the University of Abertay Dundee in 1999, from the University of St Andrews in 2001 and in 2003 from the University of Edinburgh. In 2002 Ian Rankin was awarded an OBE for services to literature. In 2004 *Resurrection Men* won the Edgar Award for Best Novel. He lives in Edinburgh with his wife and two sons.

# Ian Rankin

# Beggars Banquet

ORION

An Orion paperback

First published in Great Britain in 2002
by Orion
This paperback edition published in 2003
by Orion Books Ltd,
Orion House, 5 Upper St Martin's Lane,
London WC2H 9EA

Fourth impression 2004

A CIP catalogue record for this book is available
from the British Library.

ISBN 0 75284 959 X

Typeset by Deltatype Ltd, Birkenhead, Merseyside
Printed and bound in Great Britain by
Clays Ltd, St Ives plc

www.orionbooks.co.uk

# Contents

# Introduction

I started off life as a short story writer. Actually, that's not strictly true. I started as a comic-book writer, drawing stick-men cartoons with speech bubbles. I was about seven or eight, and I'd fold sheets of plain paper until I had a little booklet. Then I'd draw my stick-men. They would appear in strips about football, war, and outer space . . . until it was pointed out to me that I couldn't really draw. A potentially glorious career nipped in the bud. It didn't really bother me. By now I was ten or eleven and starting to listen to music. But being an obsessive sort of kid, it wasn't enough just to listen – same as I'd never just been happy as a reader of comics. I did what any sensible person would do – started a band. Problem was, none of my friends shared my interest. It didn't help that I couldn't read music or play an instrument. I didn't need to: the music could be stored in my head, the lyrics written down. So I invented a 'bubble-gum' pop group called The Amoebas, whose roster included Ian Kaput (vocals), Zed 'Killer' Macintosh (bass) and Blue Lightning (guitar). I recall the drummer had a double-barrelled name, but forget what it was. By writing lyrics for this band, I found myself writing poetry – doggerel, admittedly, but poetry all the same, in that the lyrics scanned and had a rhyme scheme. It wasn't such a leap, therefore, to write my first 'proper' poem at around the age of sixteen. The Amoebas were still around then, incidentally, but had shifted from pop to progressive rock.

The thing about my poems was, they told stories. They were about people going to places and the consequences of their actions. I think that's why I started writing short stories. I wrote several while still at school, aided by an English teacher called Mr Gillespie, who seemed to think I had 'something'. At that time, in our English class we were given topics and had to construct a weekly short story. In one instance, Mr Gillespie gave us the phrase 'Dark they were and golden-eyed'. The rest was up to us. My contribution concerned worried parents searching a busy squat for their drug-addict son. A lot of my stories were in this – ahem – vein. At home, I wrote about kids running away from their small-town existences, only to end up committing suicide in London. One longer story took place in my own school, where a poster of Mick Jagger took on devilish powers and persuaded the kids to go on a rampage. (Influenced by *Lord of the Flies*? Maybe more than a smidge . . .)

At university, I wrote poems and short stories both. My first 'proper' short story, about a shipyard closure, came second in a national competition. My next, based on a real family event, won another prize. The first story of mine to appear in a collection was 'An Afternoon'. It was about a seasoned copper patrolling a Hibs football match. (It wasn't good enough for the collection you're about to read, so don't bother looking.)

The stories collected here span a decade or more. Some first appeared on radio, others in American magazines. They comprise my first short story collection since 1992's *A Good Hanging*. Not all of them are Rebus stories. There's a good reason for this: I tend to write short stories in between books, as a way of getting the good Inspector out of my system for a while. This was certainly true of 'A Deep Hole', featured here and one of the collection's most successful stories, in that it won a Dagger for Best Story of the Year, and was also shortlisted for the prestigious Anthony award. The really curious thing about 'A Deep Hole' is that it started life set entirely in Edinburgh. Then an editor called and asked if I had anything set in London for a book he was compiling. I tweaked 'A Deep Hole' and sent it off. Not a bad move, as it turned out. Another story here, 'Herbert in Motion', also won a Dagger for Best Short Story. Its genesis was an off-hand comment by my partner about how government ministers in Whitehall could borrow works of art from various galleries and museums. This is the beauty of the short story: all you need is a single good idea. No convolutions or sub-plots. Well, not many. Not as many as in a novel, certainly. Stories are also good ways of experimenting with narrative voice, structure and methods of economy. I've managed to whittle stories down from 800 words to 200 – a struggle, but useful in that I came to learn just how much it is possible to leave out. There's no place for fat on a story: it has to be lean and fit. 'Glimmer' started life as a novella, until I realised I was indulging myself. Whittling away, I found the real story peering out at me. It's still an indulgence, giving me a chance to create a mythology around one of my favourite Rolling Stones songs, but now it's as lean as it is mean.

A couple of the stories here – 'The Confession' and 'The Hanged Man' – started life as pieces for radio. Another, 'Principles of Accounts', began as a treatment for a TV drama which never came to be. Strangest of all, perhaps, is 'The Only True Comedian', which began as a monologue for radio. Eventually, changed out of all recognition and renamed 'Kings of the Wild Frontier', it appeared as a short TV drama as part of Scottish Television's 'Newfoundland' series. I think I was credited as co-writer, but when I sat down to watch the finished product, I don't think I heard more than two lines which I'd written. The rest had been altered to suit the medium. It seemed to work: the actor picked up an award for his performance. But all told, I was much happier with my short story.

I like short stories. I enjoy reading other people's, as well as writing them myself. For a time, I mistakenly thought it might even be possible to make a living as a short story writer. After all, in this jump-cut, fast-paced, bite-sized urban world, short stories offer convenience – you can start and finish one on a short bus ride or train journey. You can read one in your lunch break. It might even be possible to write one in your lunch break. Look around you. The ideas are out there. Sometimes they're close enough to touch.

In closing, and before you begin I should thank my editor for this collection, Jon Wood. The title *Beggars Banquet* was his idea. A great Stones album. I hope you enjoy tucking into these morsels.

Ian Rankin
Edinburgh

# Trip Trap

## AN INSPECTOR REBUS STORY

Blame it on patience.

Patience, coincidence, or fate. Whatever, Grace Gallagher came downstairs that morning and found herself sitting at the dining table with a cup of strong brown tea (there was just enough milk in the fridge for one other cup), staring at the pack of cards. She sucked cigarette smoke into her lungs, feeling her heart beat the faster for it. This cigarette she enjoyed. George did not allow her to smoke in his presence, and in his presence she was for the best part of each and every day. The smoke upset him, he said. It tasted his mouth, so that food took on a funny flavour. It irritated his nostrils, made him sneeze and cough. Made him giddy. George had written the book on hypochondria.

So the house became a no-smoking zone when George was up and about. Which was precisely why Grace relished this small moment by herself, a moment lasting from seven fifteen until seven forty-five. For the forty years of their married life, Grace had always managed to wake up thirty clear minutes before her husband. She would sit at the table with a cigarette and tea until his feet forced a creak from the bedroom floorboard on his side of the bed. That floorboard had creaked from the day they'd moved into 26 Gillan Drive, thirty-odd years ago. George had promised to fix it; now he wasn't even fit to fix himself tea and toast.

Grace finished the cigarette and stared at the pack of cards. They'd played whist and rummy the previous evening, playing for stakes of a penny a game. And she'd lost as usual. George hated losing, defeat bringing on a sulk which could last the whole of the following day, so to make her life a little easier Grace now allowed him to win, purposely throwing away useful cards, frittering her trumps. George would sometimes notice and mock her for her stupidity. But more often he just clapped his hands together after another win, his puffy fingers stroking the winnings from the table top.

Grace now found herself opening the pack, shuffling, and laying out the cards for a hand of patience, a hand which she won without effort. She shuffled again, played again, won again. This, it seemed, was her morning. She tried a third game, and again the cards fell right, until four neat piles stared back at her, black on red on black on red, all the way from king to ace. She was halfway through a fourth hand, and confident of success, when the floorboard creaked, her name was called, and the day – her real day – began. She made tea (that was the end of the milk) and toast, and took it to George in bed. He'd been to the bathroom, and slipped slowly back between the sheets.

'Leg's giving me gyp today,' he said. Grace was silent, having no new replies to add to this statement. She placed his tray on the bed and pulled open the curtains. The room was stuffy, but even in summer he didn't like the windows open. He blamed the pollution, the acid rain, the exhaust fumes. They played merry hell with his lungs, making him wheezy, breathless. Grace peered out on to the street. Across the road, houses just like hers seemed already to be wilting from the day's ordinariness. Yet inside her, despite everything, despite the sour smell of the room, the heavy breath of her unshaven husband, the slurping of tea, the grey heat of the morning, Grace could feel something extraordinary. Hadn't she won at patience? Won time and time again? Paths seemed to be opening up in front of her.

'I'll go fetch you your paper,' she said.

George Gallagher liked to study racing form. He would pore over the newspaper, sneering at the tipsters' choices, and would come up with a 'super yankee' – five horses which, should they all romp home as winners, would make them their fortune. Grace would take his betting slip to the bookie's on the High Street, would hand across the stake money – less than £1.50 per day – and would go home to listen on the radio as horse after horse failed in its mission, the tipsters' choices meantime bringing in a fair return. But George had what he called 'inside knowledge', and besides, the tipsters were all crooked, weren't they? You couldn't trust them. Grace was a bloody fool if she thought she could. Often a choice of George's would come in second or third, but despite her efforts he refused to back any horse each way. All or nothing, that's what he wanted.

'You never win big by betting that way.'

Grace's smile was like a nail file: *we never win at all.*

George wondered sometimes why it took his wife so long to fetch the paper. After all, the shop was ten minutes' walk away at most, yet Grace would usually be out of the house for the best part of an hour. But there was always the story of a neighbour met, gossip exchanged, a queue in the shop, or the paper not having arrived, entailing a longer walk to the newsagent's further down the road . . .

In fact, Grace took the newspaper to Lossie Park, where, weather permitting, she sat on one of the benches and, taking a ballpoint pen (free with a woman's magazine, refilled twice since) from her handbag, proceeded to attempt the newspaper's crossword. At first, she'd filled in the 'quick' clues, but had grown more confident with the years so that she now did the 'cryptic', often finishing it, sometimes failing for want of one or two answers, which she would ponder over the rest of the day. George, his eyes fixed on the sports pages, never noticed that she'd been busy at the crossword. He got his news, so he said, from the TV and the radio, though in fact Grace had noticed that he normally slept through the television news, and seldom listened to the radio.

If the weather was dreich, Grace would sit on a sheltered bench, where one day a year or so back she had been joined by a gentleman of similar years (which was to say, eight or nine years younger than George). He was a local, a widower, and his name was Jim Malcolm. They talked, but spent most of the time just watching the park itself, studying mothers with prams, boys with their dogs, games of football, lovers' tiffs, and, even at that early hour, the occasional drunk. Every day they met at one bench or another, seeming to happen upon one another by accident, never seeing one another at any other time of the day, or any other location, other than those truly accidental meetings in a shop or on the pavement.

And then, a few weeks back, springtime, standing in the butcher's shop, Grace had overheard the news of Jim Malcolm's death. When her turn came to be served, Grace asked for half a pound of steak mince, instead of the usual 'economy' stuff. The butcher raised an eyebrow.

'Something to celebrate, Mrs Gallagher?'

'Not really,' Grace had said quietly. That night, George had eaten the expensive mince without comment.

Today she completed the crossword in record time. It wasn't that the clues seemed easier than usual; it was more that her brain seemed to be working faster than ever before, catching that inference or this anagram. Anything, she decided, was possible on a day like this. Simply anything. The sun was appearing from behind a bank of cloud. She closed the newspaper, folded it into her bag alongside the pen, and stood up. She'd been in the park barely ten minutes. If she returned home so quickly, George might ask questions. So instead she walked a slow circuit of the playing fields, her thoughts on patience, and crosswords and creaking floorboards, and much more besides.

Blame it on Patience.

Detective Inspector John Rebus had known Dr Patience Aitken for several years, and not once during their working relationship had he been able to refuse her a favour.

Patience seemed to Rebus the kind of woman his parents, if still alive, would have been trying to marry him off to, were he still single. Which, in a sense, he was, being divorced. On finding he *was* divorced, Patience had invited Rebus round to her surprisingly large house for what she had called 'dinner'. Halfway through a home-baked fruit pie, Patience had admitted to Rebus that she was wearing no underwear. Homely but smouldering: that was Patience. Who could deny such a woman a favour? Not John Rebus. And so it was that he found himself this evening standing on the doorstep of 26 Gillan Drive, and about to intrude on private grief.

Not that there was anything very private about a death, not in this part of Scotland, or in any part of Scotland come to that. Curtains twitched at neighbouring windows, people spoke in lowered voices across the divide of a garden fence, and fewer televisions than usual blared out the ubiquitous advertising jingles and even more ubiquitous game show applause.

Gillan Drive was part of an anonymous working-class district on the south-eastern outskirts of Edinburgh. The district had fallen on hard times, but there was still the smell of pride in the air. Gardens were kept tidy, the tiny lawns clipped like army haircuts, and the cars parked tight against the kerbs were old – W and X registrations predominated – but polished, showing no signs of rust. Rebus took it all in in a moment. In a neighbourhood like this, grief was for sharing. Everybody wanted their cut. Still something stopped him lifting the door knocker and letting it fall. Patience Aitken had been vague, wary, ambivalent: that was why she was asking him for a favour, and not for his professional help.

'I mean,' she had said over the telephone, 'I've been treating George Gallagher on and off – more *on* than off – for years. I think about the only complaints I've ever not known him to think he had are beri-beri and elephantiasis, and then only because you never read about them in the "Doc's Page" of the *Sunday Post*.'

Rebus smiled. GPs throughout Scotland feared their Monday morning surgeries, when people would suddenly appear in droves suffering from complaints read about the previous morning in the *Post*. No wonder people called the paper an 'institution' . . .

'And all the while,' Patience Aitken was saying, 'Grace has been by his bedside. Always patient with him, always looking after him. The woman's been an angel.'

'So what's the problem?' Rebus nursed not only the telephone, but a headache and a mug of black coffee as well. (Black coffee because he was dieting; a headache for not unconnected reasons.)

'The problem is that George fell downstairs this morning. He's dead.'

'I'm sorry to hear it.'

There was a silence at the other end of the line.

'I take it,' Rebus said, 'that you don't share my feelings.'

'George Gallagher was a cantankerous old man, grown from a bitter younger man and most probably a fairly unsociable teenager. I don't think I ever heard him utter a civil word, never mind a "please" or a "thank you".'

'Fine,' said Rebus, 'so let's celebrate his demise.'

Silence again.

Rebus sighed and rubbed his temples. 'Out with it,' he ordered.

'He's supposed to have fallen downstairs,' Patience Aitken explained. 'He did go downstairs in the afternoon, sometimes to watch racing on the telly, sometimes just to stare at a different set of walls from the bedroom. But he fell at around eleven o'clock, which is a bit early for him . . .'

'And you think he was pushed?' Rebus tried not to sound cynical.

Her reply was blunt. 'Yes, I do.'

'By this angel who's managed to put up with him all these years?'

'That's right.'

'OK, Doc, so point me to the medical evidence.'

'Well, it's a narrow staircase, pretty steep, about eleven or twelve steps, say. If you weighed around thirteen stone, and happened to slip at the top, you'd sort of be bounced off the sides as you fell, wouldn't you?'

'Perhaps.'

'And you'd try to grab hold of something to stop your fall. There's a banister on one wall. They were waiting for the council to come and fit an extra banister on the other wall.'

'So you'd reach out to grab something, fair enough.' Rebus drained the sour black coffee and studied the pile of work in his in-tray.

'Well, you'd have bruising, wouldn't you?' said Patience Aitken. 'Grazes on your elbows or knees, there'd be marks where you'd clawed at the walls.'

Rebus knew that she was surmising, but could not disagree thus far. 'Go on,' he said.

'George Gallagher only has significant marks on his head, where he hit the floor at the bottom of the stairs, breaking his neck in the process. No real bruising or grazing to the body, no marks on the wall as far as I can see.'

'So you're saying he flew from the top landing with a fair bit of momentum, and the first thing he touched was the ground?'

'That's how it looks. Unless I'm imagining it.'

'So he either jumped, or he was pushed?'

'Yes.' She paused again. 'I know it sounds tenuous, John. And Christ knows I don't want to accuse Grace of anything . . .'

Rebus picked up a ballpoint pen from beside the telephone and scrabbled on the surface of his desk until he found the back of an envelope upon which to write.

'You're only doing your job, Patience,' he said. 'Give me the address and I'll go pay my respects.'

The door of 26 Gillan Drive opened slowly, and a man

peered out at Rebus, then ushered him quickly inside, laying a soft hand on his arm.

'In ye come, son. In ye come. The women are in the living-room. The kitchen's through here.' He nodded his head, then led Rebus through a narrow hallway past a closed door, from behind which came tearful sounds, towards a half-open door at the back of the house. Rebus had not even glanced at the stairs as they'd passed them, the stairs which had faced him at the open front door of the house. The kitchen door was now opened from within, and Rebus saw that seven or eight men had squeezed into the tiny back room. There were stale smells of cooking fat and soup, stew and fruit cake, but above them wafted a more recent smell: whisky.

'Here ye are, son.' Someone was handing him a tumbler with a good inch of amber liquid in it. Everyone else had just such a glass nestling in their hand. They all shuffled from one foot to another, awkward, hardly daring to speak. They had nodded at Rebus's entrance, but now gave him little heed. Glasses were replenished. Rebus noticed the Co-Op price label on the bottle.

'You've just moved into Cashman Street, haven't you?' someone was asking someone else.

'Aye, that's right. A couple of months ago. The wife used to meet Mrs Gallagher at the shops, so we thought we'd drop in.'

'See this estate, son, it was miners' rows once upon a time. It used to be that you lived here and died here. But these days there's that much coming and going . . .'

The conversation continued at the level of a murmur. Rebus was standing with his back to the sink's draining board, next to the back door. A figure appeared in front of him.

'Have another drop, son.' And the inch in his glass rose to an inch and a half. Rebus looked around him in vain, seeking out a relative of the deceased. But these men looked like neighbours, like the sons of neighbours, the male half of the community's heart. Their wives, sisters, mothers would be in the living-room with Grace Gallagher. Closed curtains blocking out any light from what was left of the day: handkerchiefs and sweet sherry. The bereaved in an arm-chair, with someone else perched on an arm of the chair, offering a pat of the hand and well-meant words. Rebus had seen it all, seen it as a child with his own mother, and as a young man with his father, seen it with aunts and uncles, with the parents of friends and more recently with friends themselves. He wasn't so young now. The odd contemporary was already falling victim to the Big C or an unexpected heart attack. Today was the last day of April. Two days ago, he'd gone to Fife and laid flowers on his father's grave. Whether it was an act of remembrance or of simple contrition, he couldn't have said . . .

His guide pulled him back to the present. 'Her daughter-in-law's already here. Came over from Falkirk this after-noon.'

Rebus nodded, trying to look wise. 'And the son?'

Eyes looked at him. 'Dead these past ten years. Don't you know that?'

There was suspicion now, and Rebus knew that he had either to reveal himself as a policeman, or else become more disingenuous still. These people, authentically mourning the loss of someone they had known, had taken him as a mourner too, had brought him in here to share with them, to be part of the remembering group.

'I'm just a friend of a friend,' he explained. 'They asked me to look in.'

It looked from his guide's face, however, as though an interrogation might be about to begin. But then somebody else spoke.

'Terrible crash it was. What was the name of the town again?'

'Methil. He'd been working on building a rig there.'

'That's right,' said the guide knowledgeably. 'Pay night it

was. They'd been out for a few drinks, like. On their way to
the dancing. Next thing . . .'

'Aye, terrible smash it was. The lad in the back seat had to
have both legs taken off.'

Well, thought Rebus, I bet he didn't go to any more hops.
Then he winced, trying to forgive himself for thinking such
a thing. His guide saw the wince and laid the hand back on
his arm.

'All right, son, all right.' And they were all looking at him
again, perhaps expecting tears. Rebus was growing red in
the face.

'I'll just . . .' he said, motioning towards the ceiling with
his head.

'You know where it is?'

Rebus nodded. He'd seen all there was to see downstairs,
and so knew the bathroom must lie upstairs, and upstairs
was where he was heading. He closed the kitchen door
behind him and breathed deeply. There was sweat beneath
his shirt, and the headache was reasserting itself. That'll
teach you, Rebus, it was saying. That'll teach you for taking
a sip of whisky. That'll teach you for making cheap jokes to
yourself. Take all the aspirin you like. They'll dissolve your
stomach lining before they dissolve me.

Rebus called his headache two seven-letter words before
beginning to climb the stairs.

He gave careful scrutiny to each stair as he climbed, and
to the walls either side of each stair. The carpet itself was
fairly new, with a thickish pile. The wallpaper was old, and
showed a hunting scene, horse-riders and dogs with a fox
panting and worried in the distance. As Patience Aitken had
said, there were no scrapes or claw-marks on the paper
itself. What's more, there were no loose edges of carpet. The
whole thing had been tacked down with a professional's
skill. Nothing for George Gallagher to trip over, no threads
or untacked sections; and no smooth threadbare patches for
him to slip on.

He gave special attention to where the upstairs landing

met the stairs. George Gallagher probably fell from here, from this height. Further down the stairs, his chances of survival would have been much greater. Yes, it was a steep and narrow staircase all right. A trip and a tumble would certainly have caused bruising. Immediate death at the foot of the stairs would doubtless have arrested much of the bruising, the blood stilling in the veins and arteries, but bruising there would have been. The post-mortem would be specific; so far Rebus was trading on speculation, and well he knew it.

Four doors led off the landing: a large cupboard (what Rebus as a child would have called a 'press'), filled with sheets, blankets, two ancient suitcases, a black-and-white television lying on its side; a musty spare bedroom, its single bed made up ready for the visitor who never came; the bathroom, with a battery-operated razor lying on the cistern, never to be used again by its owner; and the bedroom. Nothing interested Rebus in either the spare bedroom or the bathroom, so he slipped into the main bedroom, closing the door behind him, then opening it again, since to be discovered behind a closed door would be so much more suspicious than to be found inside an open one.

The sheets, blanket and quilt had been pulled back from the bed, and three pillows had been placed on their ends against the headboard so that one person could sit up in bed. He'd seen a breakfast tray in the kitchen, still boasting the remnants of a morning meal: cups, toast crumbs on a greasy plate, an old coffee jar now holding the remains of some home-made jam. Beside the bed stood a walking-frame. Patience Aitken had said that George Gallagher usually wouldn't walk half a dozen steps without his walking-frame (a Zimmer she'd called it, but to Rebus Zimmer was the German for 'room' . . . ). Of course, if Grace were helping him, he could walk without it, leaning on her the way he'd lean his weight on a stick. Rebus visualised Grace Gallagher coaxing her husband from his bed, telling him he wouldn't be needing his walking-frame, she'd help him down the stairs. He could lean on her . . .

On the bed rested a newspaper, dotted with tacky spots of jam. It was today's paper, and it was open at the racing pages. A blue pen had been used to ring some of the runners – Gypsy Pearl, Gazumpin, Lot's Wife, Castle Mallet, Blondie – five in total, enough for a super yankee. The blue pen was sitting on a bedside table, beside a glass half filled with water, some tablets (the label made out to Mr G. Gallagher), a pair of reading spectacles in their case, and a paperback cowboy novel – large print – borrowed from the local library. Rebus sat on the edge of the bed and flipped through the newspaper. His eyes came to rest on a particular page, the letters and cartoons page. At bottom right was a crossword, a completed crossword at that. The pen used to fill in the squares seemed different to that used for the racing form further on in the paper, and the hand seemed different too: more delicate, more feminine. Thin faint marks rather than the robust lines used to circle the day's favoured horses. Rebus enjoyed the occasional cross-word, and, impressed to find this one completed, was more impressed to find that the answers were those to the cryptic clues rather than the quick clues most people favoured. He began to read, until at some point in his reading his brow furrowed, and he blinked a couple of times before closing the paper, folding it twice, and rolling it into his jacket pocket. A second or two's reflection later, he rose from the bed and walked slowly to the bedroom door, out on to the landing where, taking careful hold of the banister, he started downstairs.

He stood in the kitchen with his whisky, pondering the situation. Faces came and went. A man would finish his drink with a sigh or a clearing of the throat.

'Ay well,' he'd say, 'I suppose I'd better . . .' And with these words, and a bow of the head, he would move out of the kitchen, timidly opening the living-room door so as to say a few words to the widow before leaving. Rebus heard

Grace Gallagher's voice, a high, wavering howl: 'Thanks for coming. It was good of you. Cheerio.'

The women came and went, too. Sandwiches appeared from somewhere and were shared out in the kitchen. Tongue, corned beef, salmon paste. White 'half-pan' bread sliced in halves. Despite his diet, Rebus ate his fill, saying nothing. Though he only half knew it, he was biding his time, not wishing to create a disturbance. He waited as the kitchen emptied. Once or twice someone had attempted to engage him in conversation, thinking they knew him from a neighbouring street or from the public bar of the local. Rebus just shook his head, the friend of a friend, and the enquiries usually ended there.

Even his guide left, again patting Rebus's arm and giving him a nod and a wink. It was a day for universal gestures, so Rebus winked back. Then, the kitchen vacant now, muggy with the smell of cheap cigarettes, whisky and body odour, Rebus rinsed out his glass and stood it end-up on the draining board. He walked into the hallway, paused, then knocked and pushed open the living-room door.

As he had suspected, Grace Gallagher, as frail-looking as he'd thought, dabbing behind her fifties-style spectacles, was seated in an armchair. On the arm of the chair sat a woman in her forties, heavy-bodied but not without presence. The other chairs were vacant. Teacups sat on a dining table, alongside an unfinished plate of sandwiches, empty sherry glasses, the bottle itself, and, curiously, a pack of playing cards, laid out as though someone had broken off halfway through a game of patience.

Opposite the television set sat another sunken armchair, looking as if it had not been sat in this whole afternoon. Rebus could guess why: the deceased's chair, the throne to his tiny kingdom. He smiled towards the two women. Grace Gallagher only half looked towards him.

'Thanks for dropping by,' she said, her voice slightly revived from earlier. 'It was good of you. Cheerio.'

'Actually, Mrs Gallagher,' said Rebus, stepping into the room, 'I'm a police officer, Detective Inspector Rebus. Dr Aitken asked me to look in.'

'Oh.' Grace Gallagher looked at him now. Pretty eyes sinking into crinkly white skin. A dab of natural colour on each cheek. Her silvery hair hadn't seen a perm in quite a while, but someone had combed it, perhaps to enable her to face the rigours of the afternoon. The daughter-in-law – or so Rebus supposed the woman on the arm of the chair to be – was rising.

'Would you like me to . . . ?'

Rebus nodded towards her. 'I don't think this'll take long. Just routine really, when there's been an accident.' He looked at Grace, then at the daughter-in-law. 'Maybe if you could go into the kitchen for five minutes or so?'

She nodded keenly, perhaps a little too keenly. Rebus hadn't seen her all evening, and so supposed she'd felt duty bound to stay cooped up in here with her mother-in-law. She seemed to relish the prospect of movement.

'I'll pop the kettle on,' she said, brushing past Rebus. He watched the door close, waited as she padded down the short hallway, listened until he heard water running, the sounds of dishes being tidied. Then he turned back to Grace Gallagher, took a deep breath, and walked over towards her, dragging a stiff-backed dining chair with him. This he sat on, only a foot or two from her. He could feel her growing uneasy. She writhed a little in the armchair, then tried to disguise the reaction by reaching for another paper hankie from a box on the floor beside her.

'This must be a very difficult time for you, Mrs Gallagher,' Rebus began. He wanted to keep things short and clear cut. He had no evidence, had nothing to play with but a little bit of psychology and the woman's own state of mind. It might not be enough; he wasn't sure whether or not he *wanted* it to be enough. He found himself shifting on the chair. His arm touched the newspaper in his pocket. It felt like a talisman.

'Dr Aitken told me,' he continued, 'that you'd looked after your husband for quite a few years. It can't have been easy.'

'I'd be lying if I said that it was.'

Rebus tried to find the requisite amount of iron in her words. Tried but failed.

'Yes,' he said, 'I believe your husband was, well, a bit *difficult* at times.'

'I won't deny that either. He could be a real bugger when he wanted to.' She smiled, as if in memory of the fact. 'But I'll miss him. Aye, I'll miss him.'

'I'm sure you will, Mrs Gallagher.'

He looked at her, and her eyes fixed on to his, challenging him. He cleared his throat again. 'There's something I'm not absolutely sure about, concerning the accident. I wonder if maybe you can help me?'

'I can try.'

Rebus smiled his appreciation. 'It's just this,' he said. 'Eleven o'clock was a bit early for your husband to be coming downstairs. What's more, he seemed to be trying to come down without his walking-frame, which is still beside the bed.' Rebus's voice was becoming firmer, his conviction growing. 'What's more, he seems to have fallen with a fair amount of force.'

She interrupted him with a snap. 'How do you mean?'

'I mean he fell straight down the stairs. He didn't just slip and fall, or stumble and roll down them. He went flying off the top step and didn't hit anything till he hit the ground.' Her eyes were filling again. Hating himself, Rebus pressed on. 'He didn't fall, Mrs Gallagher. He was helped to the top of the stairs, and then he was helped down them with a push in the back, a pretty vigorous push at that.' His voice grew less severe, less judgmental. 'I'm not saying you meant to kill him. Maybe you just wanted him hospitalised, so you could have a rest from looking after him. Was that it?'

She was blowing her nose, her small shoulders squeezed inwards towards a brittle neck. The shoulders twitched with

sobs. 'I don't know what you're talking about. You think I
. . . How could you? Why would you say anything like that?
No, I don't believe you. Get out of my house.' But there was
no power to any of her words, no real enthusiasm for the
fight. Rebus reached into his pocket and brought out the
newspaper.

'I notice you do crosswords, Mrs Gallagher.'

She glanced up at him, startled by this twist in the
conversation. 'What?'

He motioned with the paper. 'I like crosswords myself.
That's why I was interested when I saw you'd completed
today's puzzle. Very impressive. When did you do that?'

'This morning,' she said through another handkerchief.
'In the park. I always do the crossword after I've bought the
paper. Then I bring it home so George can look at his
horses.'

Rebus nodded, and studied the crossword again. 'You
must have been preoccupied with something this morning
then,' he said.

'What do you mean?'

'It's quite an easy one, really. I mean, easy for someone
who does crosswords like this and finishes them. Where is it
now?' Rebus seemed to be searching the grid. 'Yes,' he said.
'Nineteen across. You've got the down solutions, so that
means the answer to nineteen across must be something R
something P. Now, what's the clue?' He looked for it, found
it. 'Here it is, Mrs Gallagher. "Perhaps deadly in part." Four
letters. Something R something P. Something deadly. Or
deadly in part. And you've put TRIP. 'What were you
thinking about, I wonder? I mean, when you wrote that? I
wonder what your mind was on?'

'But it's the right answer,' said Grace Gallagher, her face
creasing in puzzlement. Rebus was shaking his head.

'No,' he said. 'I don't think so. I think the "in part" means
the letters of "part" make up the word you want. The
answer's TRAP, Mrs Gallagher. "Perhaps deadly in part":
TRAP. Do you see? But you were thinking of something else

when you filled in the answer. You were thinking about how if your husband tripped down the stairs you might be rid of him. Isn't that right, Grace?'

She was silent for a moment, the silence broken only by the ticking of the mantelpiece clock and the clank of dishes being washed in the kitchen. Then she spoke, quite calmly.

'Myra's a good lass. It was terrible when Billy died. She's been like a daughter to me ever since.' Another pause, then her eyes met Rebus's again. He was thinking of his own mother, of how old she'd be today had she lived. Much the same age as this woman in front of him. He took another deep breath, but stayed silent, waiting.

'You know, son,' she said, 'if you look after an invalid, people think you're a martyr. I was a martyr all right, but only because I put up with him for forty years.' Her eyes strayed to the empty armchair, and focused on it as though her husband were sitting there and hearing the truth for the very first time. 'He was a sweet talker back then, and he had all the right moves. None of that once Billy came along. None of that ever again.' Her voice, which had been growing softer, now began hardening again. 'They shut the pit, so he got work at the bottle factory. Then they shut that, and all he could get was part-time chalking up the winners at the bookie's. A man gets gey bitter, Inspector. But he didn't have to take it out on me, did he?' She moved her eyes from the chair to Rebus. 'Will they lock me up?' She didn't sound particularly interested in his answer.

'That's not for me to say, Grace. Juries decide that sort of thing.'

She smiled. 'I thought I'd done the crossword in record time. Trust me to get one wrong.' And she shook her head slowly, the smile falling from her face as the tears came again, and her mouth opened in a near-silent bawl.

The door swung open, the daughter-in-law entering with a tray full of crockery.

'There now,' she called. 'We can all have a nice cup of—' She saw the look on Grace Gallagher's face, and she froze.

'What have you done?' she cried accusingly. Rebus stood up.

'Mrs Gallagher,' he said to her, 'I'm afraid I've got a bit of bad news . . .'

She had known of course. The daughter-in-law had known. Not that Grace had said anything, but there had been a special bond between them. Myra's parting words to Rebus's retreating back had been a vicious 'That bugger deserved all he got!' Net curtains had twitched; faces had appeared at darkened windows. Her words had echoed along the street and up into the smoky night air.

Maybe she was right at that. Rebus couldn't judge. All he could be was fair. So why was it that he felt so guilty? So ashamed? He could have shrugged it off, could have reported back to Patience that there was no substance to her fears. Grace Gallagher had suffered; would continue to suffer. Wasn't that enough? OK, so the law demanded more, but without Rebus there was no case, was there?

He felt right, felt vindicated, and at the same time felt a complete and utter bastard. More than that, he felt as though he'd just sentenced his own mother. He stopped at a late-night store and stocked up on beer and cigarettes. As an afterthought, he bought six assorted packets of crisps and a couple of bars of chocolate. This was no time to diet. Back home, he could conduct his own post-mortem, could hold his own private wake. On his way out of the shop, he bought the final edition of the evening paper, and was reminded that this was 30 April. Tomorrow morning, before dawn, crowds of people would climb up Arthur's Seat and, at the hill's summit, would celebrate the rising of the sun and the coming of May. Some would dab their faces with dew, the old story being that it would make them more beautiful, more handsome. What exactly was it they were celebrating, all the hungover students and the druids and the curious? Rebus wasn't sure any more. Perhaps he had never known in the first place.

Later that night, much later, as he lay along his sofa, the hi-fi blaring some jazz music from the sixties, his eye caught the day's racing results on the paper's back page. Gypsy Pearl had come home first at three-to-one. In the very next race, Gazumpin had won at seven-to-two on. Two races further on, Lot's Wife had triumphed at a starting price of eight-to-one. At another meeting, Castle Mallet had won the two thirty. Two-to-one joint favourite. That left only Blondie. Rebus tried to focus his eyes, and finally found the horse, its name misprinted to read 'Bloodie'. Though three-to-one favourite, it had come home third in a field of thirteen.

Rebus stared at the misspelling, wondering what had been going through the typist's mind when he or she had made that one small but no doubt meaningful slip . . .

# Someone Got to Eddie

They paid me not to make mistakes. Not that I ever made mistakes, that's why I was the man for the job, and they knew it. I was cautious and thorough, discreet and tight-lipped. Besides, I had other qualities which they found quite indispensable.

He was lying on the living-room floor. He'd fallen on his back, head coming to rest against the front of a leather armchair. It looked like it might be one of those reclining armchairs, you know, with a footrest and everything, an expensive item. The TV was expensive too, but then I don't suppose he ever went out much. They don't go out much, people like him. They stay indoors where it's safe. The irony of this being, of course, that they become prisoners in their own homes, prisoners all their lives.

He was still alive, breathing badly through his wet nose, his hand sort of stroking the front of his T-shirt. There was a big damp stain there, and it was all his. His hair had gone grey in the past year or so, and he'd put on a lot of weight. His eyes were dark-ringed from too many late nights.

'Please,' he whispered. 'Please.'

But I was busy. I didn't like interruptions. So I stabbed him again, just the twice, probably in his abdomen. Not deep wounds, just enough to give him the hint. His head slouched floorwards, tiny moaning sounds dribbling from his lips. They didn't want a quick painless death. It was in the contract. They wanted something that was both revenge on him and a message to others. Oh yes, I was the man for the job all right.

I was wearing overalls and gardening gloves and a pair of

old training shoes with the heel coming away from one of them. Disposable, the lot of it, fit for little more than a bonfire. So I didn't mind stepping in the small pools of blood. In fact, that was part of the plan. I'd put the overalls and gloves and trainers on in his bathroom. This was just prior to stabbing him, of course. He'd been surprised to see me coming out of the bathroom looking like that. But of course it hadn't dawned on him till too late. Always watch your back, they say. But the advice I'd give is: always watch your *front*. It's the guy you're shaking hands with, the guy you're talking to who will turn out to be your enemy. There aren't monsters hiding in the bushes. All they hide behind are smiles.

(Don't worry about me, I always ramble on when I'm nervous.)

I got to work. First, I dropped the knife into a plastic bag and placed the package in my holdall. I might need it again, but at this stage I doubted it. He wasn't talking any more. Instead, his mouth opened and closed soundlessly, like a fish in an unaerated aquarium. You hardly knew he was in pain. Pain and shock. His body was going to wave a white flag soon, but the brain was taking a little time to understand. It thought it was still in the foxhole, head down and safe.

Aquariums and foxholes. Funny the things that go through your mind at a time like this. I suppose it's to shut out the reality of the situation. Never mind virtual reality, this was visceral reality.

I was keeping the gloves on for the moment. I walked around the living-room, deciding how the place should look. There was a table in the corner with some bottles and glasses on it. They could go for a start. Hold on though, some music first. There had been no indications that any neighbours were at home – I'd watched outside for an hour, and since coming in had been listening for sounds – but all the same. Besides, music soothed the soul, didn't it?

'What do you fancy?' I asked him. He had a cheap little

midi-system and a couple of dozen CDs and tapes. I switched the system on and opened the drawer of the CD player, slipped in a disc, closed the drawer and pressed 'play'. 'A bit of Mantovani,' I said needlessly as strings swelled from the small speakers. It was a version of the Beatles' 'Yesterday'. Good song that. I turned the volume up a bit, played with the treble and bass, then went back to the corner table and swept all the stuff on to the floor. Not with a flourish or anything, just a casual brush of the forearm. A couple of wine glasses broke, nothing else. And it didn't make much noise either. It looked good, though.

The sofa was next. I thought for a moment, then pulled a couple of the cushions off, letting them drop to the floor. It wasn't much, was it? But the room was looking cluttered now, what with the bottles and cushions and the body.

He wasn't watching any of this, though he could probably hear it. His eyes were staring at the carpet below him. It had been light blue in colour, but was now looking like someone had dropped a mug of tea (no milk) on it. An interesting effect. In the films blood always looks like paint. Yes, but it depends what you mix it with, doesn't it? Red and blue would seem to make tea (no milk). Suddenly I felt thirsty. And I needed the toilet too. There was milk in the fridge. I poured half a carton down my throat and was putting it back in the fridge when I thought, What the hell. I tossed it towards the sink. Milk splattered the work surfaces and poured on to the linoleum floor. I left the fridge door open.

After visiting the toilet, I wandered back into the living-room, took the crowbar from my holdall, and left the house, closing the door after me. Checking that no one was around, I attacked the door jamb, splintering wood and forcing my way back inside. It didn't make any noise and looked pretty good. I closed the door as best I could, tipped the telephone table in the hall on to its side, and returned to the living-room. His face was on the floor now, deathly pale as you might imagine. In fact, he looked worse than a few of the corpses I've seen.

'Not long now,' I told him. I was all but done, but decided maybe I should take a recce upstairs. I opened his bedside cupboard. Inside a wooden box there was a wad of folded banknotes, tens and twenties. I slipped off the rubber band from around them, chucked it and the box on to the bed, and stuffed the money in my pocket. Let's call it a tip. It's not that I wasn't being paid enough, but I knew damned fine that if I didn't pocket it, some dozy young copper first on the scene would do just the same.

It was a pretty sad little room, this bedroom. There were porn mags on the floor, very few decent clothes in the wardrobe, a couple of empty whisky bottles under the bed along with an unused pack of vending-machine condoms. A transistor radio lying on a chair with some dirty laundry. No framed photos of family, no holiday souvenirs, no paintings on the walls.

He'd been on medication. There were four little bottles of pills on the bedside cabinet. Nerves, probably. Informers often suffer from nerves. It comes of waiting for that monster to jump out of the bushes at them. OK, so after they've given their evidence and 'Mr Big' (or more usually 'Mr Middling') has been locked away, they're given 'protection'. They get new identities, some cash up front, a roof over their heads, even a job. All this comes to pass. But they've got to leave the only life they've known. No contact with friends or family. This guy downstairs, whose name was Eddie, by the way, his wife left him. A lot of the wives do. Sad, eh? And these informers, they do all this just to save themselves from a few years in the clink.

The police are good at spotting the weak ones, the ones who might just turn. They work on them, exaggerating the sentences they're going to get, exaggerating the prizes awaiting under the witness protection scheme. ('The Witless Protection Scheme', I've heard it called.) It's all psychology and bullshit, but it sometimes works. Often though a jury will throw the evidence out anyway. The defence counsel's line is always the same: can you rely on the evidence of a man who himself is so heavily implicated in these serious crimes, and who is giving evidence solely to save his own skin?

Like I say, sometimes it works and sometimes it doesn't. I went downstairs and crouched over the body. It *was* a body now, no question of that. Well, I'd let it cool for a little while. Ten or fifteen minutes. Now that I thought of it, I'd broken open the door too soon. Someone might come along and notice. A slight error, but an error all the same. Too late for regrets though. The course was set now, so I went back to the fridge and lifted out what was left of a roast chicken. There was a leg with some meat on it, so I chewed that for a while, standing in the living-room watching through the net curtains as the sun broke from behind some cloud. Want to know what blood smells like? It smells like cold chicken grease. I stuffed the bones into the kitchen bin. I'd stripped them clean. I didn't want to leave behind any teeth-marks, anything the forensic scientists could begin to work with. Not that anyone would be working too hard on this case. People like me, we're seldom caught. After a hit, we just melt into the background. We're as ordinary as you are. I don't mean that we *seem* to be ordinary, that we make a show of looking ordinary, I mean we *are* ordinary. These hit men and assassins you read about in novels, they go around all day and all night like Arnold Schwarzenegger. But in real life that would get them noticed. The last thing you want to be if you're like me is noticed. You want to blend into the scenery.

I'm running on again, aren't I? It was just about time. A final lingering inspection. Another visit to the toilet. I checked myself in the bathroom mirror. I looked fine. I took my clothes back out of the holdall and stripped off the overalls, gloves, trainers. My shoes were black brogues with new soles and heels. I checked myself again in the mirror as I knotted my tie and put on my jacket. No tell-tale flecks of blood on my cheeks or forehead. I washed my hands without using soap (the fragrance might be identifiable) and dried them on toilet paper, which I flushed away. I zipped the holdall shut, picked it up, and walked back through the living-room ('Ciao, Eddie'), into the small hallway, and out of the house.

Potentially, this was the most dangerous part of the whole job. As I walked down the path, I was pretty well hidden from view by the hedge, the hedge Eddie must have considered a comfort, a barrier between him and prying eyes. At the pavement, I didn't pause. There was no one around anyway, no one at all, as I walked briskly around the corner to where I'd parked my car, locked the holdall in the boot, and started the engine.

Later that afternoon I returned to the house. I didn't park on a side street this time. I drew right up to the kerb in front of the hedge. Well, as close as I could get anyway. There were still no signs of activity in any of the other houses. Either the neighbours kept themselves to themselves or else they all had places to be. I gave my engine a final loud rev before turning it off, and slammed the door noisily after me. I was wearing a black leather jacket and cream chinos rather than a suit, and different shoes, plain brown rather than the black brogues. Just in case someone *had* seen me. Often, witnesses saw the clothes, not the face. The real professionals didn't bother with hair dyes, false moustaches and the like. They just wore clothes they wouldn't normally wear.

I walked slowly up the path, studying the terrain either side, then stopped at the door, examining the splintered jamb. The door was closed, but suddenly swung open from inside. Two men looked at me. I stood aside to let them pass, and walked into the house. The telephone table in the hall was still lying on its side, the phone beside it (though someone had replaced the receiver).

The body was where I'd left it. He'd been so surprised to see me at his door. Not wary, just surprised. Visiting the area, I'd explained, thought I'd look in. He'd led me into the living-room, and I'd asked to use his loo. Maybe he

29

wondered why I took the holdall with me. Maybe he didn't. There could have been anything in it, after all. Anything.

There were two men crouching over the body now, and more men in the bathroom, the kitchen, walking around upstairs. Nobody was saying anything much. You can appreciate why. One of the men stood up and stared at me. I was surveying the scene. Bottles and glasses everywhere, cushions where I'd dropped them, a carpet patterned with blood.

'What's happened here?' I asked unnecessarily.

'Well, sir.' The Detective Constable smiled a rueful smile. 'Looks like someone got to Eddie.'

# A Deep Hole

I used to be a road digger, which is to say I dug up roads for a living. These days I'm a Repair Effecter for the council's Highways Department. I still dig up roads – sorry, *highways* – only now it sounds better, doesn't it? They tell me there's some guy in an office somewhere whose job is thinking up posh names for people like me, for the rubbish collectors and street sweepers and toilet attendants. (Usually they manage to stick in the word 'environmental' somewhere.) This way, we're made to feel important. Must be some job that, thinking up posh names. I wonder what job title *he's* given himself. Environmental Title Co-ordination Executive, eh?

They call me Sam the Spade. There's supposed to be a joke there, but I don't get it. I got the name because after Robbie's got to work with the pneumatic drill, I get in about things with the spade and clear out everything he's broken up. Robbie's called 'The Driller Killer'. That was the name of an old horror video. I never saw it myself. I tried working with the pneumatic drill a few times. There's more pay if you operate the drill. You become *skilled* rather than unskilled labour. But after fifteen seconds I could feel the fillings popping out of my teeth. Even now my spine aches in bed at night. Too much sex, the boys say. Ha ha.

Now Daintry, his title would be something like Last Hope Cash Dispensation Executive. Or, in the old parlance, a plain money lender. Nobody remembers Daintry's first name. He shrugged it off some time back when he was a teenager, and he hasn't been a teenager for a few years and some. He's the guy you go to on a Friday or Saturday for a few quid to see you through the weekend. And come the following week's dole cheque (or, if you're one of the fortunate few, pay packet), Daintry'll be waiting while you cash it, his hand out for the money he loaned plus a whack of interest.

While you're only too happy to see Daintry before the weekend, you're not so happy about him still being around *after* the weekend. You don't want to pay him back, certainly not the interest. But you do, inevitably. You do pay him back. Because he's a persistent sort of fellow with a good line in colourful threats and a ready abundance of Physical Persuasion Techniques.

I think the chief reason people didn't like Daintry was that he never made anything of himself. I mean, he still lived on the same estate as his clients, albeit in one of the two-storey houses rather than the blocks of flats. His front garden was a jungle, his window panes filthy, and the inside of his house a thing of horror. He dressed in cheap clothes, which hung off him. He wouldn't shave for days, his hair always needed washing . . . You're getting the picture, eh? Me, when I'm not working I'm a neat and tidy sort of guy. My mum's friends, the women she gossips with, they're always shaking their heads and asking how come I never found myself a girl. They speak about me in the past tense like that, like I'm not going to find one now. On the contrary. I'm thirty-eight, and all my friends have split up with their wives by now. So there are more and more single women my age appearing around the estate. It's only a question of time. Soon it'll be Brenda's turn. She'll leave Harry, or he'll kick her out. No kids, so that's not a problem. I hear gossip that their arguments are getting louder and louder and more frequent. There are threats too, late at night after a good drink down at the club. I'm leaving you, no you're not, yes I am, well get the hell out then, I'll be back for my stuff, on you go, I wouldn't give you the satisfaction, well stay if you like.

Just like a ballet, eh? Well, I think so anyway. I've been

waiting for Brenda for a long time. I can wait a little longer.
I'm certainly a more attractive prospect than Daintry.
Who'd move in with him? Nobody, I can tell you. He's a
loner. No friends, just people he might drink with. He'll
sometimes buy a drink for a few of the harder cases, then
get them to put the frighteners on some late-payer who's
either getting cocky or else talking about going to the police.
Not that the police would do anything. What? Around
here? If they're not in Daintry's pocket, they either don't
care about the place anyway or else are scared to come near.
Daintry did a guy in once inside the club. A Sunday
afternoon too, stabbed him in the toilets. Police came,
talked to everyone in the club – nobody'd seen anything.
Daintry may be a bastard, but he's *our* bastard. Besides,
there's always a reason. If you haven't crossed him, you're
none of his business . . . and *he'd* better not be any of *yours*.

I knew him of course. Oh yeah, we went to school
together, same class all the way from five to sixteen years
old. He was never quite as good as me at the subjects, but he
was quiet and pretty well behaved. Until about fifteen. A
switch flipped in his brain at fifteen. Actually, I'm lying: he
was always better than me at arithmetic. So I suppose he
was cut out for a career as a money lender. Or, as he once
described himself, 'a bank manager with menaces'.

God knows how many people he's murdered. Can't be
that many, or we'd all have noticed. That's why I thought
all the information I used to give him was just part of his
act. He knew word would get around about what he was
asking me for, and those whispers and rumours would
strengthen his reputation. That's what I always thought. I
never took it seriously. As a result, I tapped him for a loan
once or twice and *he never charged me a penny*. He also
bought me a few drinks, and once provided a van when I
wanted to sell the piano. See, he wasn't all bad. He had his
good side. If it hadn't been for him, we'd never have shifted
that piano, and it'd still be sitting there in the living-room
reminding my mother of the tunes Dad used to play on it,

tunes she'd hum late into the night and then again at the crack of dawn.

It seemed strange at first that he'd want to see me. He would come over to me in pubs and sling his arm around my neck, asking if I was all right, patting me and ordering the same again. We'd hardly spoken more than a sentence at a time to one another since leaving school, but now he was smiles and reminiscences and all interested in my job of work.

'I just dig holes.'

He nodded. 'And that's important work, believe me. Without the likes of you, my car's suspension, would be shot to hell.'

Of course, his car's suspension *was* shot to hell. It was a 1973 Ford Capri with tinted windows, an air duct and a spoiler. It was a loser's car, with dark green nylon fur on the dashboard and the door panels. The wheel arches were history, long since eaten by rust. Yet every year without fail it passed its MOT. The coincidence was, the garage mechanic was a regular client of Daintry's.

'I could get a new car,' Daintry said, 'but it gets me from A back to A again, so what's the point?'

There was something in this. He seldom left the estate. He lived there, shopped there, he'd been born there and he'd die there. He never took a holiday, not even a weekend away, and he never ever ventured south of the river. He spent all his free time watching videos. The guy who runs the video shop reckoned Daintry had seen every film in the shop a dozen times over.

'He knows their numbers off by heart.'

He did know lots about movies: running time, director, writer, supporting actor. He was always a hot contender when the club ran its trivia quiz. He sat in that smelly house of his with the curtains shut and a blue light flickering. He was a film junkie. And somehow he managed to spend all his money on them. He must have done, or what else did he do with it? His Rolex was a fake, lighter than air when you picked it up, and probably his gold jewellery was fake too. Maybe somewhere there's a secret bank account with thousands salted away, but I don't think so. Don't ask me why, I just don't think so.

Roadworks. That's the information I passed on to Daintry. That's what he wanted to talk to me about. Roadworks. *Major* roadworks.

'You know the sort of thing,' he'd say, 'anywhere where you're digging a *big* hole. Maybe building a flyover or improving drainage. Major roadworks.'

Sure enough, I had access to this sort of information. I just had to listen to the various crews talking about what they were working on and where they were doing the work. Over tea and biscuits in the canteen, I could earn myself a few drinks and a pint glass of goodwill.

'How deep does that need to be?' Daintry would ask.

'I don't know, eight, maybe ten feet.'

'By what?'

'Maybe three long, the same wide.'

And he'd nod. This was early in the game, and I was slow catching on. You're probably much faster, right? So you know why he was asking. But I was puzzled the first couple of times. I mean, I thought maybe he was interested in the . . . what's it, the infrastructure. He wanted to see improvements. Then it dawned on me: no, what he wanted to see were big holes. Holes that would be filled in with concrete and covered over with huge immovable objects, like bridge supports for example. Holes where bodies could be hidden. I didn't say anything, but I knew that's what we were talking about. We were talking about Human Resource Disposal.

And Daintry knew that I knew. He'd wink from behind his cigarette smoke, using those creased stinging eyes of his. Managing to look a little like his idol Robert de Niro. In *Goodfellas*. That's what Daintry would say. He'd always be making physical comparisons like that. Me, I thought he was much more of a Joe Pesci. But I didn't tell him that. I didn't even tell him that Pesci isn't pronounced pesky.

He knew I'd blab about our little dialogues, and I did, casually like. And word spread. And suddenly Daintry was a man to be feared. But he wasn't really. He was just stupid, with a low flashpoint. And if you wanted to know what sort of mood he was going to be in, you only had to visit the video shop.

'He's taken out *Goodfellas* and *Godfather 3*'. So you knew there was trouble coming. Now you really didn't want to cross him. But if he'd taken out soft-core or a Steve Martin or even some early Brando, everything was going to be all right. He must have been on a gangster high the night he went round to speak with Mr and Mrs McAndrew. In his time, Mr McAndrew had been a bit of a lad himself, but he was in his late seventies with a wife ten years younger. They lived in one of the estate's nicer houses. They'd bought it from the council and had installed a fancy front door, double-glazed windows, you name it, and all the glass was that leaded criss-cross stuff. It wasn't cheap. These days, Mr McAndrew spent all his time in the garden. At the front of the house he had some beautiful flower beds, with the back garden given over to vegetables. In the summer, you saw him playing football with his grandchildren.

'Just like', as somebody pointed out, 'Marlon Brando in *The Godfather*.' This was apt in its way since, like I say, despite the gardening Mr McAndrew's hands were probably cleaner these days than they had been in the past.

How he got to owe Daintry money I do not know. But Daintry, believe me, would have been only too happy to lend. There was McAndrew's reputation for a start. Plus the McAndrews seemed prosperous enough, he was sure to see his money and interest returned. But not so. Whether out of sheer cussedness or because he really couldn't pay, McAndrew had been holding out on Daintry. I saw it as a struggle between the old gangster and the new. Maybe Daintry did too. Whatever, one night he walked into the McAndrews' house and beat up Mrs McAndrew in front of her husband. He had two heavies with him, one to hold

Mr McAndrew, one to hold Mrs McAndrew, either one of them could have dropped dead of a heart attack right then and there.

There were murmurs in the street the next day, and for days afterwards. Daintry, it was felt, had overstepped the mark. He was out of order. To him it was merely business, and he'd gotten the money from McAndrew so the case was closed. But he now found himself shorter of friends than ever before. Which is probably why he turned to me when he wanted the favour done. Simply, he couldn't get anyone else to do it.

'You want me to what?'

He'd told me to meet him in the children's play-park. We walked around the path. There was no one else in the park. It was a battlefield, all broken glass and rocks. Dog shit was smeared up and down the chute, the swings had been wrapped around themselves until they couldn't be reached. The roundabout had disappeared one night, leaving only a metal stump in place. You'd be safer sending your kids to play on the North Circular.

'It's quite simple,' Daintry said. 'I want you to get rid of a package for me. There's good money in it.'

'How much money?'

'A hundred.'

I paused at that. A hundred pounds, just to dispose of a package . . .

'But you'll need a deep hole,' said Daintry.

Yeah, of course. It was *that* kind of package. I wondered who it was. There was a story going around that Daintry had set up a nice little disposal operation which dealt with Human Resource Waste from miles around. Villains as far away as Watford and Luton were bringing 'packages' for him to dispose of. But it was just a story, just one of many.

'A hundred,' I said, nodding.

'All right, one twenty-five. But it's got to be tonight.'

I knew just the hole.

They were building a new footbridge over the North

Circular, over to the west near Wembley. I knew the gang wouldn't be working night-shift: the job wasn't that urgent and who could afford the shift bonus these days? There'd be a few deep holes there all right. And while the gang might notice a big black bin-bag at the bottom of one of them, they wouldn't do anything about it. People were always dumping rubbish down the holes. It all got covered over with concrete, gone and quite forgotten. I hadn't seen a dead body before, and I didn't intend seeing one now. So I insisted it was all wrapped up before I'd stick it in the car-boot.

Daintry and I stood in the lock-up he rented and looked down at the black bin-liner.

'It's not so big, is it?' I said.

'I broke the rigor mortis,' he explained. 'That way you can get it into the car.'

I nodded and went outside to throw up. I felt better after that. Curried chicken never did agree with me.

'I'm not sure I can do it,' I said, wiping my mouth.

Daintry was ready for me. 'Ah, that's a pity.' He stuck his hands in his pockets, studying the tips of his shoes. 'How's your old mum, by the way? Keeping well, is she?'

'She's fine, yeah . . .' I stared at him. 'What do you mean?'

'Nothing, nothing. Let's hope her good health continues.' He looked up at me, a glint in his eye. 'Still fancy Brenda?'

'Who says I do?'

He laughed. 'Common knowledge. Must be the way your trousers bulge whenever you see her shadow.'

'That's rubbish.'

'She seems well enough, too. The marriage is a bit shaky, but what can you expect? That Harry of hers is a monster.' Daintry paused, fingering his thin gold neck-chain. 'I wouldn't be surprised if he took a tap to the skull one of these dark nights.'

'Oh?'

He shrugged. 'Just a guess. Pity you can't . . .' He touched the bin-bag with his shoe. 'You know.' And he smiled.

We loaded the bag together. It wasn't heavy, and was easy enough to manoeuvre. I could feel a foot and a leg, or maybe a hand and arm. I tried not to think about it. Imagine him threatening my old mum! He was lucky I'm not quick to ignite, not like him, or it'd've been broken nose city and hospital cuisine. But what he said about Brenda's husband put thoughts of my mum right out of my head.

We closed the boot and I went to lock it.

'He's not going to make a run for it,' Daintry said.

'I suppose not,' I admitted. But I locked the boot anyway.

Then the car wouldn't start, and when it did start it kept cutting out, like the engine was flooding or something. Maybe a block in the fuel line. I'd let it get very low before the last fill of petrol. There might be a lot of rubbish swilling around in the tank. After a couple of miles it cut out on me at some traffic lights in Dalston. I rolled down my window and waved for the cars behind me to pass. I was content to sit for a few moments and let everything settle, my stomach included. One car stopped alongside me. And Jesus, wouldn't you know it: it was a cop car.

'Everything all right?' the cop in the passenger seat called.

'Yeah, just stalled.'

'You can't sit there for ever.'

'No.'

'If it doesn't start next go, push your car to the side of the road.'

'Yeah, sure.' He made no move to leave. Now the driver was looking at me too, and traffic was building up behind us. Nobody sounded their horn. Everyone could see that a cop car was talking with the driver of another vehicle. Sweat tickled my ears. I turned the ignition, resisting the temptation to pump the accelerator. The engine rumbled, then came to life. I grinned at the cops and started forwards, going through an amber light.

They could probably arrest me for that. It was five

minutes before I stopped staring in the rearview mirror. But I couldn't see them. They'd turned off somewhere. I let all my fear and tension out in a rasping scream, then remembered the window was still rolled down. I wound it back up again. I decided not to go straight to the bridge-site, but to drive around a bit, let all the traffic clear along with my head.

I pulled into a bus-stop just before the North Circular and changed into my work clothes. That way I wouldn't look suspicious. Good thinking, eh? It was my own idea, one Daintry had appreciated. I had a question for him now, and the question was: why wasn't he doing this himself? But he wasn't around to answer it. And I knew the answer anyway: he'd rather pay someone else to do dangerous jobs. Oh yes, it was dangerous; I knew that now. Worth a lot more than a hundred and twenty-five nicker, sixty of which was already in my pocket in the shape of dirty old pound notes. Repayments, doubtless, from Daintry's punters. Grubby money, but still money. I hoped it hadn't come from the McAndrews.

I sat at the bus-stop for a while. A car pulled in behind me. Not a police car this time, just an ordinary car. I heard the driver's door slam shut. Footsteps, a tap at my window. I looked out. The man was bald and middle-aged, dressed in suit and tie. A lower executive look, a sales rep maybe, that sort of person. He was smiling in a friendly enough sort of fashion. And if he wanted to steal my car and jemmy open the boot, well, that was fine too.

I wound down my window. 'Yeah?'

'I think I missed my turning,' he said. 'Can you tell me where we are, roughly?'

'Roughly,' I said, 'roughly we're about a mile north of Wembley.'

'And that's west London?' His accent wasn't quite English, not southern English. Welsh or a Geordie or a Scouser maybe.

'About as west as you can get,' I told him. Yeah, the wild west.

'I can't be too far away then. I want St John's Wood. That's west too, isn't it?'

'Yeah, not far at all.' These poor sods, you came across them a lot in my line of work. New to the city and pleading directions, getting hot and a bit crazy as the signposts and one-ways led them further into the maze. I felt sorry for them a lot of the time. It wasn't their fault. So I took my time as I directed him towards Harlesden, miles away from where he wanted to be.

'It's a short cut,' I told him. He seemed pleased to have some local knowledge. He went back to his car and sounded his horn in thank you as he drove off. I know, that was a bit naughty of me, wasn't it? Well, there you go. That was my spot of devilry for the night. I started my own car and headed back on to the road.

There was a sign off saying 'Works Access Only', so I signalled and drove between two rows of striped traffic cones. Then I stopped the car. There were no other cars around, just the dark shapes of earth-moving equipment and cement mixers. Fine and dandy. Cars and lorries roared past, but they didn't give me a second's notice. They weren't about to slow down enough to take in any of the scene. The existing overpass and built-up verges hid me pretty well from civilisation. Before unloading the package, I went for a recce, taking my torch with me.

And of course there were no decent holes to be found. They'd been filled in already. The concrete was hard, long metal rods poking out of it like the prongs on a fork. There were a few shallow cuts in the earth, but nothing like deep enough for the purpose. Hell's teeth and gums. I went back to the car, thinking suddenly how useful a car-phone would be. I wanted to speak to Daintry. I wanted to ask him what to do. A police car went past. I saw its brake lights glow. They'd noticed my car, but they didn't stop. No, but they might come back round again. I started the car and headed out on to the carriageway.

Only a few minutes later, there was a police car behind me. He sat on my tail for a while, then signalled to overtake, drawing level with me and staying there. The passenger checked me out. They were almost certainly the ones who'd seen me parked back at the bridge-site. The passenger saw that I was wearing overalls and a standard-issue work-jacket. I sort of waved at him. He spoke to the driver, and the patrol car accelerated away.

Lucky for me he hadn't seen the tears in my eyes. I was terrified and bursting for a piss. I knew that I had to get off this road. My brain was numb. I couldn't think of another place to dump the body. I didn't want to think about it at all. I just wanted rid of it. I think I saw the travelling salesman hurtle past, fleeing Harlesden. He was heading out of town.

I came off the North Circular and just drove around, crawling eastwards until I knew the streets so well it was like remote control. I knew exactly where I'd effected repairs, and where repairs were still waiting to be carried out. There was one pot-hole on a sharp bend that could buckle a wheel. That was down as a priority, and would probably be started on tomorrow. I calmed myself a little with memories of holes dug and holes filled in, the rich aroma of hot tarmac, the jokes yelled out by the Driller Killer. I'd never worked out why he'd try telling jokes to someone wearing industrial ear protectors beside a pneumatic drill.

Seeking safety, I came back into the estate. I felt better immediately, my head clearing. I knew what I had to do. I had to face up to Daintry. I'd give him back the money of course, less a quid or two for petrol, and I'd explain that nowhere was safe. Mission impossible. I didn't know what he'd do. It depended on whether tonight was a *Goodfellas* night or not. He might slap me about a bit. He might stop buying me drinks.

He might do something to my mum.

Or to Brenda.

I'd have to talk to him. Maybe we could do a deal. Maybe I'd have to kill him. Yeah, then I'd just have the *two* bodies to worry about. In order to stop worrying about the first, I stopped by the lock-up. This was one of a cul-de-sac of identical garages next to some wasteland which had been planted with trees and was now termed a Conservation Area. The man in the High Street had certainly conserved his energy thinking up that one.

There were no kids about, so I used a rock to break the lock, then hauled the door open with my crowbar. I stopped for a moment and wondered what I was going to do now. I'd meant to leave the body in the garage, but I'd had to break the lock to get in, so now if I left the body there anybody at all could wander along and find it. But then I thought, this is *Daintry's* garage. Everybody knows it, and nobody in their right mind would dare trespass. So I hauled the package inside, closed the door again, and left a rock in front of it. I was confident I'd done my best.

So now it was time to go talk with Daintry. The easy part of the evening was past. But first I went home. I don't know why, I just wanted to see my mum. We used to be on the eleventh floor, but they'd moved us eventually to the third because the lifts kept breaking and Mum couldn't climb eleven flights. I took the stairs tonight, relieved not to find any of the local kids shooting up or shagging between floors. Mum was sitting with Mrs Gregg from along the hall. They were talking about Mrs McAndrew.

'Story she gave her doctor was she fell down the stairs.'

'Well, I think it's a shame.'

Mum looked up and saw me. 'I thought you'd be down the club.'

'Not tonight, Mum.'

'Well, that makes a change.'

'Hallo, Mrs Gregg.'

'Hallo, love. There's a band on tonight, you know.'

'Where?'

She rolled her eyes. 'At the club. Plenty of lovely girls too, I'll bet.'

They wanted rid of me. I nodded. 'Just going to my room. Won't be long.'

I lay on my bed, the same bed I'd slept in since I was . . . well, since before I could remember. The room had been painted and papered in the last year. I stared at the wallpaper, lying on one side and then on the other. This room, it occurred to me, was probably the size of a prison cell. It might even be a bit smaller. What was it, eight feet square? But I'd always felt comfortable enough here. I heard my mum laughing at something Mrs Gregg said, and pop music from the flat downstairs. These weren't very solid flats, thin walls and floors. They'd knock our block down one of these days. I liked it well enough though. I didn't want to lose it. I didn't want to lose my mum.

I decided that I was probably going to have to kill Daintry.

I packed some clothes into a black holdall, just holding back the tears. What would I say to my mum? I've got to go away for a while? I'll phone you when I can? I recalled all the stories I'd heard about Daintry. How some guy from Trading Standards had been tailing him and was sitting in his car at the side of the road by the shops when a sawn-off shotgun appeared in the window and a voice told him to get the hell out of there pronto. Guns and knives, knuckle-dusters and a machete. Just stories . . . just stories.

I knew he wouldn't be expecting *me* to try anything. He'd open his door, he'd let me in, he'd turn his back to lead me through to the living-room. That's when I'd do it. When his back was turned. It was the only safe and certain time I could think of. Anything else and I reckoned I'd lose my bottle. I left the holdall on my bed and went through to the kitchen. I took time at the open drawer, choosing my knife. Nothing too grand, just a simple four-inch blade at the end of a wooden handle. I stuck it in my pocket.

'Just nipping out for some fresh air, Mum.'

'Bye then.'

'See you.'

And that was that. I walked back down the echoing stairwell with my mind set on murder. It wasn't like the films. It was just . . . well, *ordinary*. Like I was going to fetch fish and chips or something. I kept my hand on the knife handle. I wanted to feel comfortable with it. But my legs were a bit shaky. I had to keep locking them at the knees, holding on to a wall or a lamppost and taking deep breaths. It was a five-minute walk to Daintry's, but I managed to stretch it to ten. I passed a couple of people I vaguely knew, but didn't stop to talk. I didn't trust my teeth not to chatter, my jaw not to lock.

And to tell you the truth, I was relieved to see that there was someone standing on the doorstep, another visitor. I felt my whole body relax. The man crouched to peer through the letter box, then knocked again. As I walked down the path towards him, I saw that he was tall and well-built with a black leather jacket and short black hair.

'Isn't he in?'

The man turned his head slowly towards me. I didn't like the look of his face. It was grey and hard like the side of a house.

'Doesn't look like it,' he said. 'Any idea where he'd be?'

He was standing up straight now, his head hanging down over mine. Police, I thought for a second. But he wasn't police. I swallowed. I started to shake my head, but then I had an idea. I released my grip on the knife.

'If he's not in he's probably down the club,' I said. 'Do you know where it is?'

'No.'

'Go back down to the bottom of the road, take a left, and when you come to the shops it's up a side road between the launderette and the chip shop.'

He studied me. 'Thanks.'

'No problem,' I said. 'You know what he looks like?'

45

He nodded in perfect slow motion. He never took his eyes off me.

'Right then,' I said. 'Oh, and you might have to park outside the shops. The car-park's usually full when there's a band on.'

'There's a band?'

'In the club.' I smiled. 'It gets noisy, you can hardly hear a word that's said to you, even in the toilets.'

'Is that so?'

'Yes,' I said, 'that is so.'

Then I walked back down the path and gave him a slight wave as I headed for home. I made sure I walked home too. I didn't want him thinking I was on my way to the club ahead of him.

'Short walk,' Mum said. She was pouring tea for Mrs Gregg.

'Bit cold.'

'Cold?' squeaked Mrs Gregg. 'A lad your age shouldn't feel the cold.'

'Have you seen my knife?' Mum asked. She was looking down at the cake she'd made. It was on one of the better plates and hadn't been cut yet. I brought the knife out of my pocket.

'Here you are, Mum.'

'What's it doing in your pocket?'

'The lock on the car-boot's not working. I'd to cut some string to tie it shut.'

'Do you want some tea?'

I shook my head. 'I'll leave you to it,' I said. 'I'm off to bed.'


It was the talk of the estate the next morning, how Daintry had been knifed to death in a toilet cubicle, just as the band were finishing their encore. They were some sixties four-piece, still performing long past their sell-by. That's what people said who were there. And they'd compensated for a lack of ability by cranking the sound system all the way up.

You not only couldn't hear yourself think, you couldn't *think*.

I suppose they have to make a living as best they can. We all do.

It was the assistant manager who found Daintry. He was doing his nightly check of the club to see how many drunks had managed to fall asleep in how many hidden places. Nobody used the end cubicle of the gents' much; it didn't have any toilet seat. But there sat Daintry, not caring any more about the lack of amenities. Police were called, staff and clientele interviewed, but no one had anything much to say.

Well, not to the police at any rate. But there was plenty of gossip on the streets and in the shops. And slowly a story emerged. Mr McAndrew, remember, had been a lad at one time. He was rumoured still to have a few contacts, a few friends who owed him. Or maybe he just stumped up cash. Whatever, everyone knew Mr McAndrew had put out the contract on Daintry. And, as also agreed, good riddance to him. On a Friday night too. So anyone who'd tapped him for a loan could see the sun rise on Monday morning with a big wide smile.

Meantime, the body was found in Daintry's lock-up. Well, the police knew who was responsible for that, didn't they? Though they did wonder about the broken lock. Kids most likely, intent on burglary but doing a runner when they saw the corpse. Seemed feasible to me too.

Mr McAndrew, eh? I watched him more closely after that. He still looked to me like a nice old man. But then it was only a story after all, only one of many. Me, I had other things to think about. I knew I could do it now. I could take Brenda away from Harry. Don't ask me why I feel so sure, I just do.

# Natural Selection

'Hellish about Anthony.'

'Christ, isn't it? Six years.'

'Six is a long one.'

'The longest,' Thomas agreed. 'I've only ever done two and a half.'

'Three, me,' said Paul. 'My shout then.'

'No, Paul, it's mine,' Philip said.

'Your money's no good today, Philip,' Paul said. 'Hiy, Matthew, give us two spesh, a dark rum, and a vodka.'

Paul was buying. Paul, for a change, had plenty of money.

'Cheers, Paul.'

'Aye, all the best, Paolo.'

'You're quiet, Leonard,' Paul said.

'Eh?'

'Quiet.'

Leonard shrugged. He wasn't usually quiet. But then it wasn't a normal day. 'Just thinking about Anthony.'

'Six years,' said Philip, exhaling.

'Hellish,' said Paul. 'Here, Leonard, have a—'

'No, I'll take it neat.'

'You always have a skoosh of Irn-Bru in your vodka.'

'Not today.'

'What's wrong, Leonardo?'

'Christ, nothing, I just don't . . . look, okay, give me the Irn-Bru.'

'Not if you don't want it.'

'I want it.'

'You've changed your mind?'

'Just give the bottle here.'

'Touchy today, isn't he, Thomasino?'

'A bit, Paul, I'd have to agree with you there.'

'Hell, all I said was . . .'

'Okay, Leonard, no problemo, big man. You take your vodka any way you want your vodka. No big deal. Okay?'

'It's only vodka.'

'A metaphysical statement indeed. So get it down you. Hiy, Philip, how's your spesh?'

'Nothing special.'

Paul laughed. 'Says the same thing every time. Dependable, Philip, that's you. Not like these two.'

'What?'

'Look at you,' Paul told them. 'Leonard usually going twenty to the dozen, Thomas like a deaf mute in a sensory deprivation tank. Roles reversed today, eh?'

'What's a sensory deprivation tank?'

'Well,' said Philip, 'here's to Anthony.'

'Anthony.'

'Cheers.'

'All the best.'

'So . . . a wee skoosh of Irn-Bru after all, eh, Leonard?'

'I thought we weren't going to—'

'You are not wrong, I was out of turn. Sorry, Leonard.'

'Leonard's all right.'

'Why shouldn't I be?'

'One for yourself, Matthew?'

The barman was still waiting to be paid. 'Thanks, Paul, I'll stick one aside for later.' He walked back to his till with the cash.

'Matthew's all right,' Paul said, tucking his wallet back into his pocket.

'Not bad.'

'Keeps himself to himself.'

'Wise in a place like this,' said Thomas, wiping foam from his top lip, 'full of people like us. I'll tell you something, Paul, if I wasn't me, *I* wouldn't drink in here.'

'Where else is there?'

'There's the Last Drop or the World's End.'

'No chance.'

'Well, it's a hell-hole all the same.'

'Ach, you get used to it. I've been drinking here thirty years, man and boy. Come on, Leonard, no slacking.'

'I'm pacing myself.'

'Philip's finished his spesh already, by the way.'

'Thirsty,' Philip explained.

'Whose shout?'

'I mean,' Paul went on, 'this is a big night, a kind of wake. No night to be pacing yourself. Six years: we're drinking for Anthony tonight.'

'That judge . . .'

'And the jury.'

'Ach, it was the evidence though,' said Philip. 'If they've got the evidence, what can you do?'

'You can't scare off every jury.'

'They knew everything.'

'Who did?' Leonard asked.

'Those two cops. How did they know all that?'

'Go on then.'

'What do you say, Leonard?'

'Huh?'

'You're the one with the brains. How did those two cops know?'

'Guesswork? I don't know.'

'Maybe they got lucky,' Philip suggested.

'They can't all be as thick as the ones we know,' Thomas added.

'Or as scared.'

'Anthony'll be all right,' said Paul. 'Whichever nick he goes to, he'll end up running the place.'

'Very true,' said Philip. 'All the same, six years. He'll be out in . . . what? Three? Three years locked up, no fresh air . . .'

'When did that ever bother Anthony?'

'How do you mean, Leonard?'

'Or any of us, come to that,' Leonard went on. 'I mean, at least the screws will make him go for a walk around the yard. That's more fresh air than he ever got sitting in here.'

'You're a cheery bugger,' said Thomas.

'He's probably got a cell bigger than this . . . and better decorated.'

'Leonard, Leonard, where would we be without you, eh? Always joking.'

'Am I?'

'You know you are,' Paul said, lighting a cigarette and passing the pack on. 'We're all gutted, it's a natural reaction.'

'What is?'

'Eh? Good man, Matthew. Put them down there, and chalk up another for yourself.' Paul reached into his pocket for the wallet.

'Where did all that cash come from, by the way?' Leonard asked.

'Never you mind.' Paul winked and handed Matthew another ten. Matthew went back to the till.

'You know,' Paul said quietly, 'I sometimes wonder how much Matthew hears.'

'You mean how much he listens?'

'Yes.'

'Matthew's all right.'

'Well, he knows everything we talk about in here.'

'We never talk jobs.'

'Don't get me wrong, I'm not saying he'd . . . you know.'

'What's going on?' Thomas asked, appearing not to follow things at all.

'Just a natural reaction,' said Philip. He was watching Paul hand out the drinks. 'We're all . . . something like this, it guts you, doesn't it?'

'All right, Thomas,' Paul said, 'get this down you, leave all your troubles behind. Leonard, another wee vodka. There's the Irn-Bru, your decision, okay? You're a free agent. All right there, Thomasino? Cough it up. Good man, now get that down you. Philip, one pint of delicious foaming spesh. Enough to quench the fire, eh?'

'It's never enough.'

'Cheers, Paul.'

'No, but it's only natural, isn't it?' Paul said, not touching his own Black Heart. 'I mean, natural to wonder, to ask yourself how the cops knew. It's a reaction, we'll get over it. Having trouble with that bottle-top, Leonard?'

'You always screw the fucking thing back on too tight.'

'Give it here.'

'No, I can—'

'Here, I'll—'

'*I can do it!*'

'Whoah there, Leonard. Brakes on, pal, no need for this. Look, there it is, the top's off. Amazing how strong you can get when you're angry. Right then, everybody, good health.'

'Cheers.'

'All the best.'

'Aye.'

'Hiy, Matthew,' Thomas called, 'can you no' open a window? It's like a furnace in here.' He turned to Paul. 'Windows, they paint over them, you can't open the things. Never would have happened in the old days. Sloppy these days, decorators. I mean, hot's fine in the winter, but this isn't winter.'

'Hellish hot,' Leonard agreed, calm again. 'It's always too hot in here.'

'You could heat pies without a microwave.'

'One of those ceiling fans would be nice,' Paul said. 'There used to be one, didn't there?'

'Did there?'

'This was before your time, Leonard, before you came here. Up there it was, a big white electric fan.'

'White electric?'

'I mean painted white, run on electric.'

'Right.'

'I don't know how you can put Irn-Bru in that.'

'You want me to drink it neat?'

'Christ, don't be so . . . look, just do what—'

'I like Irn-Bru.'

'Me too,' said Philip.

'Ach, everyone likes Irn-Bru . . . but with vodka?'

'I used to drink it that way at school,' Leonard said. 'I'd steal some voddy from the drinks cabinet and mix it in an Irn-Bru bottle.'

'Drinks cabinet, eh? Your family had class, Leonard.'

'Didn't stop him turning into a criminal at an early age.'

'I was born a criminal.'

'Isn't everybody?' Philip said, deep into his drink.

'No,' said Leonard, 'some people have to learn. Anthony wasn't a born criminal.'

'You don't think so?'

'He told me so. He ran with his big brother's gang. He was okay till he started running with them.'

'His brother Donny?'

'That's the one.'

'You don't see him in here.'

'He's gone away,' said Thomas. 'Been away a while.'

'There's a lot you don't see in here any more.'

'Well, we're here,' said Paul, 'and that's all that matters.'

'Aye, we're always here.'

'For ever and ever, amen.'

'Where *did* you get that money though, Paul?'

Paul winked again. 'Is it bothering you, Leonard?'

'Was it the gee-gees?' Thomas asked. 'Lottery? Dogs? Pools? I'll bet it was a betting thing.'

'You'd lose your money. Now either stop asking, or stop taking drinks off me.'

Thomas laughed. 'Nobody'd be that daft.'

'No? What about you, Leonard?'

'What about me?'

'Nothing,' said Paul.

'No,' Leonard persisted, 'what is it? Something's stuck up your arse and I'd like to know what it is.'

Paul looked amazed. 'Me? There's nothing bothering *me*, pal. What about you, Leonardo?'

'Here we go again,' said Philip. 'Just cool it, compadres.'

'You're right, Philip,' said Paul, 'as ever. How come you're always right? You never lose your rag, do you? You're a calm sort, controlled. Isn't he, lads?' Paul tapped his own brow. There was a sheen of sweat on it. 'But we know there's a lot going on in that head of his.'

'It's the quiet ones you have to watch,' said Thomas.

'Thomas, you'll never say a truer word. Out of the mouths of babes, as they say. Jesus, Philip, are you finished already?'

'It's hot,' Philip said.

'A furnace.'

'This thirst,' Philip added, 'I can't seem to shake it.'

'Christ, Matthew,' Paul called, 'do something, will you?'

'Like what?'

'Open the fridge door or something. Start putting ice in the drinks. *Something*.'

'We're out of ice.'

'You'll be out of a job if we take our custom elsewhere.'

Matthew smiled. 'You four aren't going anywhere.'

'No talking back to the customers, Matthew,' Paul said, pointing a finger. 'Leonard, ready for another?'

'I've two in front of me.'

'Apply yourself to the task. We'll have the same again, Matthew.'

'Not for me,' said Leonard.

'Play the game, Leonardo. Give him another, Matthew.'

The barman walked back to the optics.

'You're wasting your money, Paul.'

'It's my money.'

'You'll be skint again tomorrow.'

'Who cares about tomorrow?'

'Suit yourself.'

'I always do.'

'This is very pleasant,' said Philip.

'It's not meant to be pleasant,' Paul said. 'It's a wake, remember?'

'How can I forget?'

'Levity ill becomes you, Filipi.'

'What's levity?' Thomas asked.

'Lightness,' Leonard explained.

Thomas nodded. 'Like being light in the head?'

'Lot of levity about here,' Paul said, winking.

'Maybe I'm ill,' said Philip, loosening his collar. 'My mouth's parched all day.'

'Could be a lot of reasons for that,' Paul said. 'Could be nerves.'

'Nerves?'

'I saw something yesterday,' Thomas said, 'on the telly. It was about these insects that eat each other. Or maybe it was their babies they ate.'

Paul and Philip looked at one another, the way they did when Thomas said this sort of thing.

'That's not so rare,' Leonard told Thomas, his eyes on Paul.

'You're a smart one, aren't you?' said Paul.

Leonard shook his head, drained one of his vodkas. 'It's all relative,' he said. Then he slipped off his barstool.

'First one tonight,' said Paul, smiling. 'And as usual it's Leonard. Three shorts he's put away, but he's bursting for a piss. You need a bladder transplant, Leonardo.'

Leonard stopped in front of Paul. 'Maybe it's just nerves, Paul,' he said.

Nobody said anything as he left the bar.


The toilet was reeking. There was the constant hiss of a broken ballcock, and names scratched into the paint on the dark red wall. The urinal was a stainless steel trough. It was cooler in here though, damp and cool. Leonard lit a cigarette for himself. He reckoned if it weren't for the smell, this place would be a preferable alternative to the bar itself. Freezing in winter though. Bloody awful pub altogether, why didn't they just leave? Well, as somebody had said, where else was there?

The door creaked open and Matthew came in.

'Matthew.'

'Leonard.'

The barman went to the urinal and unzipped himself loudly. His stare was high up the wall when he spoke.

'They're out for your blood.'

'What?'

'Those three. Well, Paul specifically, but he'll carry the other two. He's buying, after all.'

'What have I done?'

'Come on, Leonard. Paul thinks you shopped Anthony.'

'Then how come he's the one with the money?'

'If it was a cop payoff, he wouldn't be flashing it about. Get out, right now. Just run for it.'

'I've never run in my life.'

'It's up to you.' Matthew zipped himself up. 'But if I was in your shoes, I'd be offski.'

'Where would I go?'

'I don't know.' There was another creak as the door opened. Paul came in first. Philip and Thomas were right behind him. The door closed quietly after them.

'What's that you're saying, Matthew?'

'Nothing, Paul.'

'You're a great one for talking, aren't you?'

'No.'

'A gossip, a right wee sweetie-wife. Talking's in your blood.'

'No.'

'No? This had the look of a snitches' convention when I walked in. Guilty looks all round.'

Matthew tried shaking his head.

'Easy to confuse guilt with fear,' Leonard said quietly.

'Know where that money came from?' Paul said. He

wasn't speaking to any one of them in particular. His eyes were on his shoes, examining the toes. 'I'll tell you, it came from Anthony.'

'Anthony?' Thomas said. 'Why did he give you that much money? I mean, he's usually tight . . . I mean, careful. He's canny with his money.' Thomas's voice died away.

Paul half turned his head and gave Thomas a smile full of sympathy.

'You aren't half going on tonight, Thomasino. Not like you at all. It's not like him at all, is it, Philip?'

Philip was wiping his face with the roller-towel. 'No, it's not,' he said.

'He's usually quiet, isn't he?'

'Quiet as the grave,' Philip agreed.

'And even someone as thick as you sometimes appear to be, Thomas, has got to have an inkling why Anthony would give me a load of cash.' He paused. 'Don't *you* want to know, Philip?'

Philip shrugged. 'You'll tell us when you're ready.'

Paul was smiling. 'You never change, Philip. Always the same face, the same voice. Nothing out of place. I bet you could do away with your granny and we'd never know about it, not by looking at you.' He paused again. 'Except tonight you're sweating. Why is that?'

'I think I'm coming down with something.'

'Well, we'll see to it you get a doctor when this is over.' Matthew started to open the door. '*Shut it!*' Paul smiled. 'Don't want to let the heat in, do we?' He turned to Leonard. 'Anthony gave me the money because he wants someone taken care of. Someone in particular. He told me once I was sure in my mind, I was to start earning the cash. That's what Anthony told me.'

'In other words, he doesn't know?'

'That's right, Leonard.'

'Funny he asked you.'

'He trusts me.'

'But what if he's wrong, Paolo? What if he's wrong about

that?' Leonard looked to the other men in the cramped space – Matthew, Philip, Thomas. 'What if *you* grassed him up, and *we* found out?' They'd all been looking nervous; now they were looking interested. 'What would we do?'

'Yes,' Thomas said quietly, getting it, 'what would we do?'

Philip was nodding slowly, and Matthew straightened his back, adding an inch to his height.

'There's only one guilty party here, Leonard,' Paul was saying.

'You really believe that?'

'I'm not saying it's you.' Paul was staring into Leonard's eyes. He saw red paint reflected from the walls.

'You're saying it's one of us, Paul. The rest of us don't like that.'

Leonard took a step forwards. Paul's hand went to his jacket pocket. Philip was behind him, his arms stretching. Thomas's hands were fists. Matthew leaned against the door, keeping it closed.

Outside it was dark, no streetlight, no traffic. You would bet that it couldn't get any darker, but you'd be wrong. People most often are.

# Facing the Music

## AN INSPECTOR REBUS STORY

An unmarked police car.

Interesting phrase, that. Inspector John Rebus's car, punch-drunk and weather-beaten, scarred and mauled, would still merit description as 'unmarked', despite the copious evidence to the contrary. Oily-handed mechanics stifled grins whenever he waddled into a forecourt. Garage proprietors adjusted the thick gold rings on their fingers and reached for the calculator.

Still, there were times when the old war-horse came in handy. It might or might not be 'unmarked'; unremarkable it certainly was. Even the most cynical law-breaker would hardly expect CID to spend their time sitting around in a breaker's-yard special. Rebus's car was a must for under-cover work, the only problem coming if the villains decided to make a run for it. Then, even the most elderly and infirm could outpace it.

'But it's a stayer,' Rebus would say in mitigation.

He sat now, the driving-seat so used to his shape that it formed a mould around him, stroking the steering-wheel with his hands. There was a loud sigh from the passenger seat, and Detective Sergeant Brian Holmes repeated his question.

'Why have we stopped?'

Rebus looked around him. They were parked by the side of Queensferry Street, only a couple of hundred yards from Princes Street's west end. It was early afternoon, overcast but dry. The gusts of wind blowing in from the Firth of Forth were probably keeping the rain away. The corner of Princes Street, where Fraser's department store and the

Caledonian Hotel tried to outstare one another, caught the winds and whipped them against unsuspecting shoppers, who could be seen, dazed and numb, making their way afterwards along Queensferry Street, in search of coffee and shortcake. Rebus gave the pedestrians a look of pity. Holmes sighed again. He could murder a pot of tea and some fruit scones with butter.

'Do you know, Brian,' Rebus began, 'in all the years I've been in Edinburgh, I've never been called to any sort of a crime on this street.' He slapped the steering-wheel for emphasis. 'Not once.'

'Maybe they should put up a plaque,' suggested Holmes.

Rebus almost smiled. 'Maybe they should.'

'Is that why we're sitting here? You want to break your duck?' Holmes glanced into the tea-shop window, then away again quickly licking dry lips. 'It might take a while, you know,' he said.

'It might, Brian. But then again . . .'

Rebus tapped out a tattoo on the steering-wheel. Holmes was beginning to regret his own enthusiasm. Hadn't Rebus tried to deter him from coming out for this drive? Not that they'd driven much. But anything, Holmes reasoned, was better than catching up on paperwork. Well, just about anything.

'What's the longest time you've been on a stake-out?' he asked, making conversation.

'A week,' said Rebus. 'Protection racket run from a pub down near Powderhall. It was a joint operation with Trading Standards. We spent five days pretending to be on the broo, playing pool all day.'

'Did you get a result?'

'We beat them at pool,' Rebus said.

There was a yell from a shop doorway, just as a young man was sprinting across the road in front of their car. The young man was carrying a black metal box. The person who'd called out did so again.

'Stop him! Thief! Stop him!'

The man in the shop doorway was waving, pointing towards the sprinter. Holmes looked towards Rebus, seemed about to say something, but decided against it. 'Come on then!' he said.

Rebus started the car's engine, signalled, and moved out into the traffic. Holmes was focusing through the windscreen. 'I can see him. Put your foot down!'

' "Put your foot down, *sir*",' Rebus said calmly. 'Don't worry, Brian.'

'Hell, he's turning into Randolph Place.'

Rebus signalled again, brought the car across the oncoming traffic, and turned into the dead end that was Randolph Place. Only, while it was a dead end for cars, there were pedestrian passages either side of West Register House. The young man, carrying the narrow box under his arm, turned into one of the passages. Rebus pulled to a halt. Holmes had the car door open before it had stopped, and leapt out, ready to follow on foot.

'Cut him off !' he yelled, meaning for Rebus to drive back on to Queensferry Street, around Hope Street and into Charlotte Square, where the passage emerged.

' "Cut him off, *sir*",' mouthed Rebus.

He did a careful three-point turn, and just as carefully moved back out into traffic held to a crawl by traffic lights. By the time he reached Charlotte Square and the front of West Register House, Holmes was shrugging his shoulders and flapping his arms. Rebus pulled to a stop beside him.

'Did you see him?' Holmes asked, getting into the car.

'No.'

'Where have you been anyway?'

'A red light.'

Holmes looked at him as though he were mad. Since when had Inspector John Rebus stopped for a red light? 'Well, I've lost him anyway.'

'Not your fault, Brian.'

Holmes looked at him again. 'Right,' he agreed. 'So, back to the shop? What was it anyway?'

'Hi-fi shop, I think.'

Holmes nodded as Rebus moved off again into the traffic. Yes, the box had the look of a piece of hi-fi, some slim rack component. They'd find out at the shop. But instead of doing a circuit of Charlotte Square to take them back into Queensferry Street, Rebus signalled along George Street. Holmes, still catching his breath, looked around disbelieving.

'Where are we going?'

'I thought you were fed up with Queensferry Street. We're going back to the station.'

'*What?*'

'Back to the station.'

'But what about—?'

'Relax, Brian. You've got to learn not to fret so much.'

Holmes examined his superior's face. 'You're up to something,' he said at last.

Rebus turned and smiled. 'Took you long enough,' he said.

But whatever it was, Rebus wasn't telling. Back at the station, he went straight to the main desk.

'Any robberies, Alec?'

The desk officer had a few. The most recent was a snatch at a specialist hi-fi shop.

'We'll take that,' said Rebus. The desk officer blinked.

'It's not much, sir. Just a single item, thief did a runner.'

'Nevertheless, Alec,' said Rebus. 'A crime has been committed, and it's our duty to investigate it.' He turned to head back out to the car.

'Is he all right?' Alec asked Holmes.

Holmes was beginning to wonder, but decided to go along for the ride anyway.

'A cassette deck,' the proprietor explained. 'Nice model, too. Not top of the range, but nice. Top-of-the-range stuff isn't kept out on the shop floor. We keep it in the demonstration rooms.'

Holmes was looking at the shelf where the cassette deck had rested. There were other decks either side of the gap, more expensive decks at that.

'Why would he choose that one?' Holmes asked.

'Eh?'

'Well, it's not the dearest, is it? And it's not even the closest to the door.'

The dealer shrugged. 'Kids these days, who can tell?' His thick hair was still tousled from where he had stood in the Queensferry Street wind-tunnel, yelling against the elements as passers-by stared at him.

'I take it you've got insurance, Mr Wardle?' The question came from Rebus, who was standing in front of a row of loudspeakers.

'Christ yes, and it costs enough.' Wardle shrugged. 'Look, it's okay. I know how it works. Points system, right? Anything under a four-point crime, and you lads don't bother. You just fill out the forms so I can claim from the insurance. What does this rate? One point? Two at the most?'

Rebus blinked, perhaps stunned by the use of the word 'lads' in connection with him.

'You've got the serial number, Mr Wardle,' he said at last. 'That'll give us a start. Then a description of the thief – that's more than we usually get in cases of shop-snatching. Meantime, you might move your stock a bit further back from the door and think about a common chain or circuit alarm so they can't be taken off their shelves. Okay?'

Wardle nodded.

'And be thankful,' mused Rebus. 'After all, it could've been worse. It could have been a ram-raider.' He picked up a CD case from where it sat on top of a machine: Mantovani and his Orchestra. 'Or even a critic,' said Rebus.

Back at the station, Holmes sat fuming like a readying

volcano. Or at least like a tin of something flammable left for too long in the sun.

Whatever Rebus was up to, as per usual he wasn't saying. It infuriated Holmes. Now Rebus was off at a meeting in the Chief Super's office: nothing very important, just routine . . . like the snatch at the hi-fi shop.

Holmes played the scene through in his mind. The stationary car, causing an obstruction to the already slow movement of traffic. Then Wardle's cry, and the youth running across the road, jinking between cars. The youth had half turned, giving Holmes a moment's view of a cheek speckled with acne, cropped spiky hair. A skinny runt of a sixteen-year-old in faded jeans and trainers. Pale blue windcheater with a lumberjack shirt hanging loose below its hemline.

And carrying a hi-fi component that was neither the easiest piece in the shop to steal, nor the dearest. Wardle had seemed relaxed about the whole affair. The insurance would cover it. An insurance scam: was that it? Was Rebus working on some insurance diddle on the q.t., maybe as a favour to some investigator from the Pru? Holmes hated the way his superior worked, like a greedy if talented footballer hogging the ball, dribbling past man after man, getting himself trapped beside the by-line but still refusing to pass the ball. Holmes had known a boy at school like that. One day, fed up, Holmes had scythed the smart-arse down, even though they'd been on the same side . . .

Rebus had known the theft would take place. Therefore, he'd been tipped off. Therefore, the thief had been set up. There was just one big *but* to the whole theory – Rebus had let the thief get away. It didn't make sense. It didn't make any sense at all.

'Right,' Holmes said, nodding to himself. 'Right you are, sir.' And with that, he went off to find the young offender files.

That evening, just after six, Rebus thought that since he was in the area anyway, he'd drop into Mr Wardle's home and report the lack of progress on the case. It might be that, time having passed, Wardle would remember something else about the snatch, some crucial detail. The description he'd been able to give of the thief had been next to useless. It was almost as though he didn't want the hassle, didn't want the thief caught. Well, maybe Rebus could jog his memory.

The radio came to life. It was a message from DS Holmes. And when Rebus heard it, he snarled and turned the car back around towards the city centre.

It was lucky for Holmes, so Rebus said, that the traffic had been heavy, the fifteen-minute journey back into town being time enough for him to calm down. They were in the CID room. Holmes was seated at his desk, hands clasped behind his head. Rebus was standing over him, breathing hard. On the desk sat a matt-black cassette deck.

'Serial numbers match,' Holmes said, 'just in case you were wondering.'

Rebus couldn't quite sound disinterested. 'How did you find him?'

With his hands still behind his head, Holmes managed a shrug. 'He was on file, sir. I just sat there flipping through them till I spotted him. That acne of his is as good as a tattoo. James Iain Bankhead, known to his friends as Jib. According to the file, you've arrested him a couple of times yourself in the past.'

'Jib Bankhead?' said Rebus, as though trying to place the name. 'Yes, rings a bell.'

'I'd have thought it'd ring a whole fire station, sir. You last arrested him three months ago.' Holmes made a show of consulting the file on his desk. 'Funny, you not recognising him . . .' Holmes kept his eyes on the file.

'I must be getting old,' Rebus said.

Holmes looked up. 'So what now, sir?'

'Where is he?'

'Interview Room B.'

'Let him stay there then. Can't do any harm. Has he said anything?'

'Not a word. Mind you, he *did* seem surprised when I paid him a visit.'

'But he kept his mouth shut?'

Holmes nodded. 'So what now?' he repeated.

'Now,' said Rebus, 'you come along with me, Brian. I'll tell you all about it on the way . . .'

Wardle lived in a flat carved from a detached turn-of-the-century house on the south-east outskirts of the city. Rebus pressed the bell on the wall to the side of the substantial main door. After a moment, there was the muffled sound of footsteps, three clicks as locks were undone, and the door opened from within.

'Good evening, Mr Wardle,' said Rebus. I see you're security-conscious at home at least.' Rebus was nodding towards the door, with its three separate keyholes, spy-hole and security chain.

'You can't be too—' Wardle broke off as he saw what Brian Holmes was carrying. 'The deck!'

'Good as new,' said Rebus, 'apart from a few fingerprints.'

Wardle opened the door wide. 'Come in, come in.'

They entered a narrow entrance hall which led to a flight of stairs. Obviously the ground floor of the house did not belong to Wardle. He was dressed much as he had been in the shop: denims too young for his years, an open-necked shirt louder than a Wee Free sermon, and brown moccasins.

'I can't believe it,' he said, leading them towards the stairs. 'I really can't. But you could have brought it round to the shop . . .'

'Well, sir, we were going to be passing anyway.' Rebus closed the door, noting the steel plate on its inner face. The door-surround too was reinforced with metal plates. Wardle turned and noticed Rebus's interest.

'Wait till you see the hi-fi, Inspector. It'll all become clear.'

They could already hear the music. The bass was vibrating each step of the stairs.

'You must have sympathetic neighbours,' Rebus remarked.

'She's ninety-two,' said Wardle. 'Deaf as a post. I went round to explain to her about the hi-fi just after I moved in. She couldn't hear a word I was saying.'

They were at the top of the stairs now, where a smaller hallway led into a huge open-plan living-room and kitchen. A sofa and two chairs had been pushed hard back against one wall, and there was nothing but space between them and the opposite wall, where the hi-fi system sat, with large floor-standing speakers either side of it. One rack comprised half a dozen black boxes, boasting nothing to Rebus's eye but a single red light.

'Amplifiers,' Wardle explained, turning down the music.

'What, all of them?'

'Pre-amp and power supply, plus an amp for each driver.'

Holmes had rested the cassette deck on the floor, but Wardle moved it away immediately.

'Spoils the sound,' he said, 'if there's an extra piece of gear in the room.'

Holmes and Rebus stared at one another. Wardle was in his element now. 'Want to hear something? What's your taste?'

'Rolling Stones?' Rebus asked.

'*Sticky Fingers, Exile, Let It Bleed*?'

'That last one,' said Rebus.

Wardle went over to where a twenty-foot row of LPs was standing against the wall beneath the window.

'I thought those went out with the Ark,' said Holmes.

Wardle smiled. 'You mean with the CD. No, vinyl's still the best. Sit down.' He went over to the turntable and took off the LP he'd been playing. Rebus and Holmes sat. Holmes looked to Rebus, who nodded. Holmes got up again.

'Actually, could I use your loo?' he asked.

'First right out on the landing,' said Wardle. Holmes left the room. 'Any particular track, Inspector?'

' "Gimme Shelter",' stated Rebus. Wardle nodded agreement, set the needle on the disc, rose to his feet, and turned up the volume. 'Something to drink?' he asked. The room exploded into a wall of sound. Rebus had heard the phrase 'wall of sound' before. Well, here he was with his nose pressed against it.

'A whisky, please,' he yelled. Wardle tipped his head towards the hall. 'Same for him.' Wardle nodded and went off towards the kitchen area. Pinned to the sofa as he was, Rebus looked around the room. He had eyes for everything but the hi-fi. Not that there was much to see. A small coffee table whose surface seemed to be covered with arcana to do with the hi-fi system, cleaning-brushes and such like. There were some nice-looking prints on the wall. Actually, one looked like a real painting rather than a print: the surface of a swimming-pool, someone moving through the depths. But no TV, no shelves, no books, no knick-knacks, no family photos. Rebus knew Wardle was divorced. He also knew Wardle drove a Y-registered Porsche 911. He knew quite a lot about Wardle, but not yet enough . . .

A healthy glass of whisky was handed to him. Wardle placed another on the floor for Holmes, then returned to the kitchen and came back with a glass for himself. He sat down next to Rebus.

'What do you think?'

'Fantastic,' Rebus called back.

Wardle grinned.

'How much would this lot cost me?' Rebus asked, hoping Wardle wouldn't notice how long Holmes had been out of the room.

'About twenty-five K.'

'You're joking. My flat didn't cost that.'

Wardle just laughed. But he was glancing towards the living-room door. He looked as though he might be about to say something, when the door opened and Holmes came in, rubbing his hands as though drying them off. He smiled, sat, and toasted Wardle with his glass. Wardle went over to the

amplifier to turn down the volume. Holmes nodded towards
Rebus. Rebus toasted no one in particular and finished his
drink. The volume dipped.

'What was that?' Holmes asked.

'*Let It Bleed*.'

'I thought my ears would.'

Wardle laughed. He seemed to be in a particularly good
mood. Maybe it was because of the cassette deck.

'Listen,' he said, 'how the hell did you get that deck back
so quickly?'

Holmes was about to say something, but Rebus beat him
to it. 'It was abandoned.'

'Abandoned?'

'At the bottom of a flight of stairs on Queen Street,' Rebus
went on. He had risen to his feet. Holmes took the hint and,
eyes twisted shut, gulped down his whisky. 'So you see, sir,
we were just lucky, that's all. Just lucky.'

'Well, thanks again,' said Wardle. 'If you ever want some
hi-fi, drop into the shop. I'm sure a discount might be
arranged.'

'We'll bear that in mind, sir,' said Rebus. 'Just don't
expect me to put my flat on the market . . .'


Back at the station, Rebus first of all had Jib released, then
went to his office, where he spread the files out across his
desk, while Holmes pulled over a chair. Then they both sat,
reading aloud from lists. The lists were of stolen goods,
high-quality stuff stolen in the dead of night by real
professionals. The hauls – highly selective hauls – came
from five addresses, the homes of well-paid middle-class
people, people with things well worth the stealing.

Five robberies, all at dead of night, alarm systems
disconnected. Art objects had been taken, antiques, in one
case an entire collection of rare European stamps. The
house-breakings had occurred at more or less monthly
intervals, and all within a twenty-mile radius of central

Edinburgh. The connection between them? Rebus had explained it to Holmes on their way to Wardle's flat.

'Nobody could see *any* connection, apart from the fact that the five victims worked in the west end. The Chief Super asked me to take a look. Guess what I found? They'd all had smart new hi-fi systems installed. Up to six months before the break-ins. Systems bought from Queensferry Audio and installed by Mr Wardle.'

'So he'd know what was in each house?' Holmes had said.

'And he'd be able to give the alarm system a look-over while he was there, too.'

'Could just be coincidence.'

'I know.'

Oh yes, Rebus knew. He knew he had only the hunch, the coincidence. He had no proof, no evidence of any kind. Certainly nothing that would gain him a search warrant, as the Chief Super had been good enough to confirm, knowing damned well that Rebus would take it further anyway. Not that this concerned the Chief Super, so long as Rebus worked alone, and didn't tell his superiors what he was up to. That way, it was Rebus's neck in the noose, Rebus's pension on the line.

Rebus guessed his only hope was that Wardle had kept some of the stolen pieces, that some of the stuff was still on his premises. He'd already had a young DC go into Queensferry Audio posing as a would-be buyer. The DC had gone in four times in all, once to buy some tapes, then to look at hi-fi, then to spend an hour in one of the demo rooms, and finally just for a friendly chat . . . He'd reported back to Rebus that the place was clean. No signs of any stolen merchandise, no locked rooms or cupboards . . .

So then Rebus had persuaded a uniformed constable to pose as a Neighbourhood Watch supervisor. He had visited Wardle at home, not getting past the downstairs hallway. But he'd been able to report that the place was 'like Fort Knox, metal door and all'. Rebus had had experience of steel-reinforced doors: they were favoured by drug dealers, so that when police came calling with a sledgehammer for invitation, the dealers would have time enough to flush everything away.

But a hi-fi dealer with a steel door . . . Well, that was a new one. True, twenty-five grand's worth of hi-fi was an investment worth protecting. But there were limits. Not that Rebus suspected Wardle of actually doing the breaking and entering himself. No, he just passed the information on to the men Rebus really wanted, the gang. But Wardle was the only means of getting at them . . .

Finally, in desperation, Rebus had turned to Jib. And Jib had done what he was told, meaning Rebus now owed him a large favour. It was all highly irregular; unlawful, if it came to it. If anyone found out . . . well, Rebus would be making the acquaintance of his local broo office. Which was why, as he explained to Holmes, he'd been keeping so quiet about it.

The plan was simple. Jib would run off with something, anything, watched by Rebus to make sure nothing went wrong – such as a daring citizen's arrest by one or more passers-by. Later, Rebus would turn up at the shop to investigate the theft. Then later still, he would arrive at Wardle's flat, ostensibly to report the lack of progress. If a further visit was needed, the cassette deck would be found. But now he had Holmes's help, so one visit only should suffice, one man keeping Wardle busy while the other sniffed around the rooms in the flat.

They sat now, poring over the lists, trying to match what Holmes had seen in Wardle's two bedrooms with what had been reported stolen from the five luxury homes.

'Carriage clock,' read Rebus, 'nineteenth-century Japanese cigar box, seventeenth-century prints of Edinburgh by James Gordon, a Swarbreck lithograph . . .'

Holmes shook his head at the mention of each, then read from one of his own lists. 'Ladies' and gents' Longines watches, a Hockney print, Cartier pen, first-edition set of the Waverley novels, Ming vase, Dresden pieces . . .' He looked up. 'Would you believe, there's even a case of champagne.' He looked down again and read: 'Louis Roederer Cristal 1985. Value put at six hundred pounds. That's a hundred quid a bottle.'

'Bet you're glad you're a lager man,' said Rebus. He sighed. 'Does none of this mean anything to you, Brian?'

Holmes shook his head. 'Nothing like any of this in either of the bedrooms.'

Rebus cursed under his breath. 'Hold on,' he said. 'What about that print?'

'Which one? The Hockney?'

'Yes, have we got a photo of it?'

'Just this,' said Holmes, extracting from the file a page torn from an art gallery's catalogue. He handed it to Rebus, who studied the picture. 'Why?'

'Why?' echoed Rebus. 'Because you sat with this painting in front of your nose on Wardle's living-room wall. I thought it was a real painting, but this is it all right.' He tapped the sheet of paper. 'It says here the print's limited to fifty impressions. What number is the stolen one?'

Holmes looked down the list. 'Forty-four.'

'Right,' said Rebus. 'That should be easy enough to confirm.' He checked his watch. 'What time are you expected home?'

Holmes was shaking his head. 'Never mind that. If you're going back to Wardle's flat, I'm coming too.'

'Come on then.'

It was only as they were leaving the office that Holmes thought to ask: 'What if it isn't the same number on the print?'

'Then we'll just have to face the music,' said Rebus.

But as it turned out, the only one facing the music was Wardle, and he sang beautifully. A pity, Rebus mused later, that he hadn't arranged for a discount on a new hi-fi system first. He'd just have to wait for Queensferry Audio's closing-down sale . . .

# Principles of Accounts

It began as a hobby.

But then quite quickly the hobby became a career, and now he was a professional, taking a professional's care in the details of his craft. True, something had been lost; that was the trouble when a hobby became mere business. But at least he had the consolation of knowing that business was good. He saw himself as a value assessor. He assessed the value of an item, then collected on it, the money being insurance against loss. He had always been good at accounts, economics, business studies. He loved those subjects at school, hardly believing the sheer thrill of balancing books. The sums *always came out the same*, either side of the thick vertical centre line. He used similar skills now when assessing each item: value of item balanced against risk involved.

Not that he ever damaged an item. It hadn't been necessary so far. But he was very good at pretending he would damage them. He could reduce tough fathers to pleas and weeping, and all via the telephone. The telephone was his friend – not any one particular telephone, but *all* phones, spread across the country in a matrix of elegantly anonymous paybooths. He made a point of spending not more than a minute in each phone box he used, timing each call. Single-mindedness was his real strength. Determination of purpose. The sixty-second calls had become his trademark. People knew when they were dealing with the Minute Man.

The media, who had coined the nickname, they too were his friends, stirring up fear, building him into a figure of terror. He rewarded them with increased circulation and viewing figures, while the police held increasingly ineffectual press conferences requesting information, playing tapes they'd made of his voices.

He used several voices, none his own. He hadn't spoken more than six words to any of his four young items, and even then had disguised his voice. Actually, he'd used more than six words with the last one, the one whose value now sat before him on the table. She had been a talker, a good talker, too. She'd recited stories and anecdotes – even when she couldn't be sure he was there. Occasionally he'd asked a question, something to help him get the story straight in his mind. She had given him her stories, and now her father had given him all this money.

Tonight, with an open bottle of cheapish Australian Chardonnay on the floor beside his chair, with his belly full from the meal he'd eaten at the Indian on the High Street, tonight was for reflection. At the top of the hour, he hit the remote to catch the Channel 4 news and saw with some pride that he was the main story. Or rather, the item was.

She blinked a lot. Nervousness, or perhaps the glare of the lights and flashguns. Her hair had been washed, but she wore no make-up, and her face looked pale. She had lost a little weight, her own fault for not eating everything he'd given her.

She'd worked out pretty quickly – they usually did – that the food was laced with tranqs, crushed-up sleeping pills. But like the others, she'd given in and eaten anyway. Sensible, when the only other alternative was force-feeding by rubber tube and plastic funnel.

She stayed on screen only half a minute, refusing to answer the yelled questions. Now she was replaced by a policeman. A caption appeared along the bottom of the screen: Ch. Supt. Thomas Lancaster. Ah yes, Tom Lancaster. He raised his glass, toasting his adversary, even though the police's inefficiency was a constant source of irritation to him.

'. . . and I must praise Miss Webster's calm and her bravery,' Lancaster was saying. 'After her release, she was able to help us compile this composite photograph of her kidnapper.'

He put down his glass. The photo was onscreen now.

'The man we're looking for is five feet seven or eight, stocky, with blue eyes. As you can see, he has a round face, full lips, and thick, slightly curly hair, either black or very dark brown.'

He whooped. He got up and danced. She'd never set eyes on him! He never allowed his items the luxury. He looked at himself in the mirror. He was six feet tall, certainly not stocky. He had brown eyes, short, straight, light-brown hair. Full lips? No. Round face? No. She'd given the police a wholly fictitious account. Tomorrow the photo would be in every newspaper, pinned up outside every police station. This was better than he could ever have imagined . . .

But why had she done it? What was she playing at? He didn't like puzzles, didn't like it when the accounts failed to balance at the bottom. He switched off the TV and put aside his wine. One thing was obvious: she didn't want him caught. Only two people could be certain her description was a fiction: the item, and the Minute Man. He was still deep in thought when ten o'clock came round. He switched on the TV news again, and was thrown into fresh confusion.

'There has been an arrest tonight after the latest Minute Man kidnap victim was released.'

Sitting up, he kicked over the wine bottle. It poured out its contents unchecked.

'A man, believed to be a business acquaintance of Gillian Webster's father, has been taken to Castle Lane police station for questioning. We now go over live to Castle Lane, where Martin Brockman is waiting to speak to us. Martin, any more details?'

Now the reporter was on the screen, looking cold against a damp night-time street, headlamps flashing past him. He wore a sheepskin coat and had one hand pressed to his ear, holding in place the earphone. He began to speak.

'All police will say is that a man is being questioned in connection with the kidnapping of Gillian Webster, who was released unharmed this morning. There's no word yet of whether or not the man will be asked to take part in an identity parade, but rumour has it that the man police are questioning is actually *known* to Miss Webster's father, the millionaire Duncan Webster, and that it was Mr Webster himself who first noticed the resemblance between the photofit and the man police are currently questioning.'

'Let's get this right, Martin, you're saying Mr Webster *identified* his daughter's kidnapper?'

'I don't think we can go that far just yet, but . . .'

But he had switched off the television.

'What's your game, little Gillian?' he said quietly. 'Your game . . . or your father's?' He felt dizzy, confused. There had to be a reason for all of this. The wine was thumping in his head.

'I hate puzzles!' he yelled at the blank TV screen. 'I hate puzzles!'

In Castle Lane police station, Chief Superintendent Tom Lancaster was about to get some sleep. He'd phoned his wife to explain that he wouldn't be home. He kept a fresh suit, shirt, and tie in the office anyway, and now there was a camp bed there too, with an army-quality sleeping bag. Nothing to the comforts of home, but it would have to do. Tomorrow might be even busier than today. He was comforted to know that the press weren't going home either. Some had crawled off to hotels and boarding houses, but others were camping out in cars and vans outside the station.

Lancaster slipped off his clothes and into the chilled sleeping bag. He wriggled for a few seconds, getting warm, then reached to the floor, where several bulging files lay. The transcript of Gillian Webster's conversations with the

Minute Man had been typed up. He read through them again. It was one-way traffic. The Minute Man had said only a couple of dozen words, mostly in the form of abrupt questions.

His second victim, Elaine Chatham, had managed a longer utterance from him. She'd asked if she could have a book of crosswords to pass the time. She'd kept on asking until she'd forced from him a gruff confession (in his Geordie accent this time). Three important little words. Tom Lancaster whispered them to himself.

' "I hate puzzles".'

Then, smiling, he reached for the anglepoise and turned off the light.

It was nearly midday when Mrs Angelo heard the bell tinkling at the front desk.

'Coming!' she called, trying to sound calm. Her husband Tony should have been helping her, but he had the flu and was upstairs asleep. It was his third bout of flu this year; he never wanted the doctor called in. The man standing at the desk carried a sports holdall and a sheaf of the morning papers. He wore a new-smelling sheepskin jacket and a harassed grin.

'I'd like a room, please,' he announced.

'Just the one night, is it?'

'Well . . .'

'You're a journalist,' Mrs Angelo stated. 'You're reporting on that kidnapping, and you don't know how long you'll need the room. Am I right?'

'You could write our astrology column.'

She checked the rack of room keys on the wall. 'Number six has a wash basin, or there's number eleven, but it doesn't. Those are the only two I've got.' She turned to him. 'We're busy all of a sudden.'

'You've already got reporters staying?'

'One's been here all the way through, the others moved

in yesterday. And I've a very nice cameraman and sound-man from the BBC, only they complain because *their* reporter is in some posh hotel. I told them, posh just means expensive. Number six or number eleven?'

'Six, please.'

'Only the best, eh? I dare say you're on expenses.' She unhooked the key, then swivelled the register around for him to sign. 'So which paper are you from?'

He didn't look up from his writing. 'I'm freelance. A few magazines are interested, so I thought I'd . . . you know.'

She swivelled the register back towards her. 'Well, Mr Beattie, let's hope you get your story, eh?'

'Yes,' he agreed, taking the key from her warm, damp fingers. 'Let's hope.'


He threw the papers on to the floor beside the single bed. The mattress was softer than he liked, but the room was clean and fresh. It worried him that there were other reporters here. He didn't want them asking him questions. He unzipped the holdall, taking his Gillian Webster case notes from it. Included in the file was a packet of black and white photographs he'd taken during the weeks leading up to the snatch. He looked through them again.

The Websters lived in a large detached house set in a few acres of rambling grounds. He'd gone out there one Sunday with his camera. He'd been out that way several times before in his car, stopping once with engine trouble near the house. About a hundred yards from the house there was a clump of bushes and saplings, big enough for him to hide in. On that particular Sunday, he'd taken his very best zoom lenses for the Canon camera. Then he went strolling with camera and binoculars and a bird identification book.

What he hadn't expected was that Gillian Webster would not be home. He also had not expected the Websters to be entertaining. They'd invited a dozen or so people for late-afternoon drinks. He was lucky the weather was cool: nobody seemed inclined to wander down into the garden towards where he was hiding. But a veranda ran the length of the back of the house, and some of the guests wandered out on to it; so, occasionally, did the host and hostess. He shot off a single roll of film, concentrating on Webster and his wife. She was younger than her husband by at least ten years; even so, she was showing her age. The skin sagged from her face and neck, and her short blonde hair looked brittle.

Lying on the bed, he paused at one particular photograph. A man had been standing alone on the veranda, then had been joined by Mrs Webster. It looked as though she were greeting the man. They were kissing. The man, who was holding a champagne flute, held Mrs Webster's arm with his free hand, drawing her towards him. The kiss was no perfunctory peck. Their lips met, were maybe even parted. The kiss had seemed to last quite a while. He searched through the other photos for a better one of the man. Yes, here he was with Mr Webster and another guest. They looked serious, as though discussing business. The man was caught face-on. He was shorter than Webster, heavily built, with dark wavy hair just covering his ears. Early on in the party, he had loosened his tie and his shirt collar. Did he merely look serious in this photo, or did he look worried? There were dark bags under his eyes . . .

He lifted a newspaper and stared at the photofit police had issued, the one made up from Gillian Webster's description. It was the guest from the party. He was sure of that.

The local radio station had set up a van in the police station car park, with a tall antenna flexing from its roof. It looked as though the journalists had been made to move into the car park. Probably their cars had been holding up traffic in Castle Lane. As he arrived, they were milling around, drinking beakers of tea, talking into portable phones, reading from sheets of paper.

He looked around. One young man stood apart from the

others. He looked shy and uncomfortable, and was wearing cheap clothes. There were spots around his mouth and on his neck, and he kept pushing slippery glasses back up his nose as he read from his own sheets of paper, glancing up from time to time to see what the other journalists were doing.

He was perfect.

'Local are you, chief?'

The young man looked up in surprise at the man with the south-east accent, the man wearing the expensive jacket.

'Sorry?'

'You look like the local press.'

The young man twitched. 'I'm from the *Post*.'

'Thought so.' The sheets of paper were plucked from the young man's hands. They detailed the morning's media briefing. There would be a conference at three o'clock, and another at seven. Otherwise, the only news was that the man they'd been questioning was to be held for another twenty-four hours.

'What do you think, chief?' The young man looked dazed. 'Come on, you can tell Uncle Des.'

'There's not much *to* think.'

He wrinkled his nose, folding the press release and shoving it into the young man's anorak pocket. 'Don't give me that. That's the *official* line, but this is between you and me. You're *local*, my son, you've got the edge on all of us.' He nodded towards the scattering of journalists, none of whom was taking any notice of this conversation.

'Who are you?'

'I thought I told you, Des Beattie.'

'Beattie?'

'How long you been in this game, son?' He shook his head sadly. 'The Ripper case, I covered it for the *Telegraph*. Freelance now, of course. I can pick and choose my crime stories. A *certain magazine* has asked me to see if there's an angle in all this.' He looked the young man up and down.

'You might be in for half the byline. Could be your ticket out of here, chief. We all had to start somewhere.'

'Stefan's my name, Stefan Duniec.'

'Pleased to meet you, Stefan.' They shook hands. 'What's that, Russian is it?'

'Polish.'

'Well, I'm Des Beattie and I'm from Walthamstow. Only I live in Docklands now.' He winked. 'Handy for the newspaper offices. So what've you got?'

'Well...' Duniec looked around. 'It's not really *my* idea...' Beattie shrugged this aside. There was no copyright on news. 'But I've heard that someone's got a name.'

'For the sod they're questioning?' Duniec nodded. Beattie seemed thoughtful. 'Maybe it'll tie in with my own ideas. What's the name, Stefan?'

'Bernard Cooke.'

Beattie nodded slowly. 'Bernie Cooke. The businessman, right?'

Now Duniec nodded. 'Does it tie in?'

Beattie puckered his mouth. 'Might well do. I need to check a few facts first.'

'I could help.' The kid was keen all right. He didn't want to wear that anorak for ever. Beattie patted his shoulder.

'Stick around here, Stefan. Keep your ears open. I'll go make a couple of calls.' Duniec glanced down at the large pockets of Beattie's sheepskin. Beattie grinned. 'We can't all afford cell phones. Meantime...' He nodded towards the other reporters. 'You might try writing this up. You know, something wry about the long wait. Eight hundred words, who knows, there's always a market for filler. The Sundays are nothing but filler these days.'

'Eight hundred?'

Beattie nodded, then reconsidered. 'Seven-fifty,' he said, heading out of the car park.

A small engineering works on a purpose-built estate.

A helpful sign at the site entrance told him he was

looking for Unit 32, Cooke Engineering Ltd. He drove his rented Fiesta slowly through the narrow winding roads, giving way to lorries and delivery vans. Half a dozen cars were parked outside Unit 32 in tightly marked bays. The building was grey corrugated steel, shared by two companies. Unit 31 manufactured frozen foods. Driving past it, he sized up Unit 32. There was a door which would lead to the reception area or offices, and a loading-bay door near it. Both were closed. Parked in the loading bay was a sporty Ford Sierra, one of the custom jobs. In the driver's seat, a man was talking on a car phone. In the back seat were two more large pasty-faced men. They looked like reporters. Well, if a dolt like Duniec knew about Cooke, the professionals would know too. And though Cooke himself wasn't here, though he was sweating and dog-tired in one of Castle Lane's interview rooms, a team had been sent to stake the place out.

He gnawed at his bottom lip, and decided to take a calculated risk. He drove to the next lot of units, parked, and walked back towards Cooke Engineering. The door he was approaching, having ignored the carful of staring eyes, had OFFICE printed on it. He knocked and entered, closing the door behind him. He'd expected noise: after all, only a partition wall separated this part of the unit from the actual production line. But there was silence, punctuated by the slow clack of fingers on a computer keyboard.

'Can I help you?' She sat behind a desk, but also behind huge red-rimmed spectacles, which magnified her already large eyes. Her tone was hardly welcoming.

'Mr Cooke?' He said nervously. 'Wondered if I could have a—'

'Do you have an appointment?'

'No, well I . . .'

'Are you a reporter?' She examined him, hunched over as he was, shuffling and twitching and awkward. 'You don't look like one.' She sighed. 'No cold calling, reps by appointment only. I take it you *are* a rep?'

'Well, as it happens I—'

'Sorry,' she said, seeming to take pity on this particularly pitiful example of an unlovely breed. 'Mr Cooke's not here anyway.'

He looked around. 'Place looks dead.'

'Dead about sums it up.'

'Business bad.'

'Let's just say you shouldn't look for too many orders.'

'Ah . . .' He seemed to think of something. 'But the cars outside . . . ?'

'We let the guys from the frozen-food place park their excess cars there.'

'Oh dear.' He nodded towards where he assumed the production line would be, just through the wall. 'Then you're not . . . ?'

'We're not producing. So unless you're selling jobs in the light engineering sector, I shouldn't bother.'

He smiled. 'But you're still here.'

'Only till the weekend. No pay by Friday, I'm off.' She went back to her typing, her fingers hammering the keys.

He turned to leave, his back and shoulders more hunched than ever. Then he stopped and half turned. 'What made you think I was a reporter?'

'You'll read about it.'

Only after he'd gone did she pause in her work. She'd seen them all in her time, all the types of rep you could imagine. But she'd never come across one who didn't even bother to bring samples with him . . .

Across from the industrial estate was a recently built pub, doubtless put there by a canny brewing concern who knew there would be plenty of clients from an estate of eighty-odd units.

'That was the idea anyway,' the barman admitted, pouring a pint of beer, 'before times got hard. What gets me is that none of these *financial projections*' – he said the words with distaste – 'ever *projected* hard times ahead. And let me

83

tell you, there's no money-back guarantee with these things.' He had handed over the drink, received a five-pound note, and now pressed a key on the till.

'Accountants aren't all bad,' said the customer.

As the barman handed over the change, the customer asked a question.

'Does a man called Bernard Cooke drink in here?'

There was a snort from further down the bar, where a man on a stool was doing the crossword in the local paper.

'Why do you ask?' asked the barman.

'I was supposed to be seeing him today. Drove all the way down from bloody Lancaster.' The barman didn't seem about to doubt his north-west accent. 'Only there's no bugger about except some right rough types in a car parked outside.'

'Reporters,' said the crossword solver.

'Oh aye?'

'You won't be seeing Cooke for a while.' The crossword solver tipped back the dregs of a half-pint.

'We don't know that,' snapped the barman. 'Don't go jumping to bloody conclusions, Arthur.'

Arthur merely shrugged in compliance, staring down at his paper.

'He's in trouble, is he?' asked the traveller.

'Maybe.'

'Bang goes my bloody contract.'

'You're lucky, then,' said Arthur.'

'How do you mean?' He nodded towards the empty glass. 'Get you another?'

'Thanks, I will.'

The barman refilled the glass, but wouldn't take one himself. Arthur sipped and swallowed. 'I mean,' he said at last, 'Bernie's been in trouble for yonks, money trouble. Chances are, if you were buying from him, you wouldn't have got what you ordered, and if you were selling, you wouldn't have seen the money.'

'Thanks for the tip.'

'I've known for months he was in trouble. Used to be, he'd nip in here Friday lunchtime for something to eat and a couple of brandies. Then it got to be twice a week and four brandies, and three times a week and six. Somebody drinks like that, it's not because they're flush, it's that they're worried.'

'I know what you mean.'

'All *I* know,' chipped in the barman, 'is that he always paid . . . and that's more than some.'

Arthur winked at Beattie. 'That's a dig at me.'

Beattie finished his drink and eased himself off the bar stool.

'Back to Lancaster?'

He shook his head. 'Couple more calls first.'

After he'd gone, the bar was silent a few moments, then Arthur cleared his throat.

'What do you think?'

'Well,' said the barman, 'he wasn't a reporter. I'm not even sure he's in business.'

'How do you make that out?'

'No expense account – didn't ask for a receipt for the drinks.'

'Maybe he doesn't need receipts, Sherlock.'

'Maybe.' The barman lifted away the empty glass and washed it, placing it on the rack to dry. Then he wiped the bartop where the man had been sitting, and put down a fresh beermat. Now there was no sign anyone had ever been there.

'Just be a second,' the barman told Arthur. Then he disappeared into the alcove where the telephone was kept.

At three-forty, the journalists slouched out of the press room carrying the latest news release. They were talkative, if they weren't too busy drawing in cigarette smoke. Some were making calls on their telephones, or going off to their cars to make calls. They squeezed from the police station's double doors and fanned out across the car park. A camera unit had been readied for the TV reporter called Martin Brockman, who was now checking his script while a make-up girl tried to get his hair to stop flying into a vertical peak every time a gust blew.

Stefan Duniec walked slowly across the car park, not heading towards his car – he did not have a car – but just keeping moving, so he looked as busy and important as the other reporters. He was staring down at his notebook and didn't notice the figure blocking his way until he'd practically bumped into it.

'Hello, Mr Beattie, you missed the conference.'

'Couldn't be helped, Stef. Anything to report?'

'I got you a copy of the press release.'

'Good lad.' Beattie started to read from the two stapled sheets. Gillian Webster, he read, had now given a description of the room she'd been kept in during her 'ten-day ordeal'. Not so much a room, more a cupboard, kept in darkness. She could hear distant traffic, as though heavy lorries were passing outside. But she was tied up, mouth taped shut, and couldn't cry out.

Beattie read it again. Well, it was true he'd kept her mouth taped shut occasionally, but everything else was a fabrication, another false account.

'Interesting,' he said. 'Are they still questioning Cooke?' Duniec nodded. 'And I suppose they'll be giving his factory the once-over?'

'How do you mean?'

'Stands to reason, Stef. This cupboard could be in Cooke's factory. I've just come from there. He's been laying off staff. The only person left is a secretary, and I doubt she goes anywhere near the shop floor – she might get her hands mucky.' He glanced again at the paper. 'Lorries going past . . . sounds just like an industrial estate.'

'I suppose it does,' Duniec said quietly.

'And if he's been laying off men, what does that tell you?'

'His company's in trouble.'

'Dead right. So tell me, young Stef, is Cooke wealthy or skint?'

'Skint, I suppose.'

'And desperate.'

'So he kidnaps someone he knows . . . How could he hope to get away with it?'

'All we know is that he knew the parents; we don't know Gillian knew him.'

'But he let her see him,' Duniec protested. 'He must've known she'd give a description – that her father would see it . . .'

Beattie nodded. Precisely. That was just one of the flaws. Would Cooke really have kept her in his factory, with someone else on the premises all day? How could he feed Gillian without the secretary becoming suspicious? Gillian's story was badly flawed. But Beattie wondered if the police would see that. *He* could see what Gillian Webster was doing, and how she was doing it. He just couldn't account for the why. But he had an idea now, a good idea. He only needed to study the photographs again.

Meantime, Stefan had obviously been considering all the flaws too.

'Like you say, he must have been desperate.'

'He was desperate all right, he just wasn't very bright.' He tapped Duniec's shoulder with the rolled-up press release. 'I'll see you later.' He winked. 'Remember the byline.'

'And the seven-fifty words!' Duniec called after him. 'I've already made a start!'

Without looking back, Beattie gave a raised thumbs-up. Duniec watched till he was out of sight, then turned back towards the reporters' cars. Three men were in a huddle next to a red Porsche.

'Excuse me,' he said, interrupting them. One man, the one with a proprietorial hand resting on the Porsche's roof, spoke for all of them.

'What is it?'

'You're Terry Greig, aren't you?'

Greig puffed out his chest. Of course he was Terry Greig, king of the tabloid newsroom, scourge of copy-takers. And here was another tyro looking to make his acquaintance.

'What can I do for you, lad?'

Duniec didn't like that 'lad', but like Beattie's 'Stef' he let it lie. 'Did you see that man I was talking to?' he asked instead. 'In the sheepskin jacket?'

Greig nodded. Little escaped him. 'I saw him earlier,' he confirmed.

'Right,' said Duniec. 'And have you seen him before? I mean, do you know who he is?'

'Don't know him from Adam. Football manager, is he? Third Division? They're the only buggers would wear a coat like that.'

'Except for Brockman,' added one of the other reporters.

'Except for old Brockie,' Greig agreed. Then they all laughed, all except Stefan Duniec. When the laughter had died and they were waiting for him to leave, he turned his gaze once more to Greig.

'He wrote up the Ripper case for the *Telegraph*.'

'No he didn't, not unless he meant the *Belfast Telegraph*.' They all laughed again. Even Duniec's lips were bent slightly in what might have passed for a smile.

'What's it all about, lad?' asked Greig.

'Could we step inside the station, sir?' Duniec said. To anyone standing within earshot, it didn't sound much like a question . . .

The man who called himself Des Beattie was packing his bag.

He tore the ring-pull from another can of McEwan's and gulped from the can. The photographs were lying on the bed. He paused in his packing and studied the photos again. Cooke with Duncan Webster. Cooke with Mrs Webster. Cooke looking *very* comfortable with Mrs Webster. Cooke looking *extremely* uncomfortable with Duncan Webster, looking like maybe he owed the man money, money he couldn't hope to repay. But that wasn't Cooke's problem. No, Cooke's problem was the wife. Look at the two of them: touching, kissing. With Mr Webster, Cooke looked more like a business acquaintance than anything; but with Mrs Webster he looked like a very close friend indeed.

Whether Webster knew or not, he couldn't tell. But the daughter had known. Gillian Webster had found out about Cooke and her mother, about their affair. Christ, and she was Daddy's little daughter, wasn't she? When she'd spoken to him of her home life, hoping to ingratiate herself, hoping he wouldn't harm someone he knew as a *real person* rather than an item (yes, she'd been clever all right), when she had done this, she had spoken always of her father first, her mother second. Daddy, Daddy, Daddy: it had always been Daddy. While Mother had remained just that: 'Mother'.

All those hours she'd been alone, those hours with little to do but struggle against her bonds, little to think about but . . . but how to turn this little adventure to her own advantage. She would set up Bernard Cooke. She must have known his company was in trouble, giving him the motive. Who would suspect she'd lie about something like this? No one, no one would know except three people: Cooke himself, the mother, and the real kidnapper. Cooke would protest his innocence, but it was his word against Gillian's. Mrs Webster . . . what could *she* say without revealing the extent of her ties to Cooke? And as for the kidnapper . . . well, was he going to come forward to help Cooke? Of course not!

It was true, wasn't it? He wasn't going to do anything. He was going to leave this town and never return. With Cooke inside, the heat would be off, the police would stop checking airports and seaports. Yes, a foreign holiday, somewhere sunny and dry, not like this cold miserable island where he worked. He could stop by a travel agent's tomorrow. On the plane out, he'd order champagne and drink to poor Bernard Cooke.

That was that.

He opened another can and picked up the photo, the one of Cooke and Mrs Webster kissing. The more he looked at it, the more he saw that he could be wrong. What if it *was* just a friendly kiss? These types, types like Mrs Webster, they could get overfamiliar. What if it had nothing to do with the mother? What if ... what if it had to do with *Gillian* instead? She'd told him, 'Daddy doesn't like it when I bring home older men.' Could there have been something between Gillian and Bernard Cooke? Maybe he'd broken it off and she was out for his blood ...

Wait, think a bit. If Cooke was single, it wouldn't work. It only worked if he was married and had to hide the relationship. His head began spinning, and he tried to stand up. How could he be sure? How could he be sure that Cooke and Mrs Webster or Cooke and Gillian had been an item?

He caught that word 'item' and smiled. If they'd been an item, people would have seen them together, somewhere they felt safe from Mr Webster. Maybe that was why Cooke started using the pub across from the estate more often; nothing to do with his financial troubles. It should be easy enough to check. He'd go there now, on his way out of town. He thought of Stefan Duniec. Stefan, who probably wasn't fit to report on a flower show, never mind a police inquiry. There were some real thick bastards in the world, when you thought about it.

Jesus, weren't there just.

It was five o'clock when he walked into the bar. As he'd hoped, the shift had changed. The barman was new. What's more, Arthur had moved on. Good: they'd have thought it more than a little off, the Lancastrian returning to ask questions about Cooke and some woman.

The beer he'd drunk in his room had given him a taste, so he ordered a double Armagnac with a half of lager to chase it down. Fuel for the long drive ahead. The bar was medium-busy with workers on their way home from the estate. He sat on the same stool as earlier, and made a show of checking his watch and keeping an eye on the door.

'Waiting on someone?' the new barman dutifully asked.

'Bernard Cooke. I thought we arranged to meet at five.'

The barman tried the name. 'Don't think I know him.'

'He's a lunchtime regular.'

'I never do lunchtime.'

He nodded miserably and finished the Armagnac. It burned him all the way down. One last time then: 'He usually has a woman with him, a bit of posh.'

The barman shrugged and went back to wiping glasses.

'Thanks anyway.' He finished the lager and had another idea. It was a bit late, but worth a try. As he pushed open the door to the outside world, he met resistance. It was Arthur, coming in. Arthur looked surprised. Beattie switched to a north-west accent.

'Hello, Arthur.'

'Thought you were off to the wide blue yonder.'

'Just heading back now. I've been hearing Cooke has a fancy piece.' He winked. 'That's an expensive hobby, no wonder he's gone broke.'

Arthur just stared, as though listening to a ghost. There was almost . . . it wasn't shock, it was more like *fear* in his eyes.

Beattie persisted. 'Nice looker, by the sound of her.'

'Eh?'

'They used to come in here.'

'Did they?'

Was the man pissed? Maybe those crosswords had addled his brain. Beattie felt good and mellow.

'Never mind,' he said. 'See you around.'

Arthur seemed to perk up. 'Oh, right you are. Take care now.'

'I will, Arthur, I will.'

The secretary, having faithfully placed a dustcover over the computer, was putting on her coat when he arrived. She looked daggers at him, and he raised his hands in surrender.

'I'll only take a minute,' he said. He hadn't really expected her to still be here. How much paperwork could an empty factory produce? The reporters had vanished from outside, along with most of the cars on the estate.

'You're persistent,' she said. 'He's not here.'

'It was you I wanted to speak to.'

'Oh?'

He stepped forward and produced the photo from his pocket, the one of Cooke and Mrs Webster kissing.

'Is your boss married?' he asked.

She smiled sourly. 'I knew you weren't a rep.'

'Did I say I was? So what's the answer? A simple yes or no.'

'What business is it of yours?'

He gave a fumey sigh. 'I can find out. It's not difficult.'

'Off you go then and find out.'

'Did you know he was having an affair?'

'It's only an affair if the person's married.'

'Oh? So Cooke's a bachelor then?'

'That's not what I said.'

'Mrs Webster's married though.' He was seeking a reaction, *any* reaction. 'Her daughter's single.'

'Get out.' Her voice was colder than the lager he'd just consumed.

'Let me guess,' he persisted. 'You had the hots for him yourself, maybe he was stringing you along . . .'

She picked up the receiver.

'All right, I'm going.' He put the photo back in his pocket. 'But remember, you don't owe him anything. It's him that owes you. Just give me a yes or no: is he married?'

She started punching telephone buttons, so he left. She was breathing hard, but didn't let it show. She stared at the door, willing it to stay closed. Then she was connected. 'Police?' she said. 'I want to speak to Chief Superintendent Lancaster . . .'

Outside, he sat in his car, thinking about the man called Arthur, the secretary, and Stefan Duniec. Then he got out again and started looking for another car. Any car would do, so long as it had a car phone.

Lancaster put down the receiver and looked towards the two people sitting across the desk from him.

'That was your secretary, Mr Cooke.' Bernard Cooke nodded: he'd gathered as much already. 'Our man has just turned up again, asking if you're married and implying you've been having an affair with Mrs Webster.' He looked at the young woman next to Cooke. 'Or even with you, Gillian.'

Gillian Webster snorted. Lancaster was smiling.

'Looks like it's worked,' he said. *I hate puzzles.* Those three words had set the whole game in motion. And the game was about to end: right result, right team. 'He had a photo with him,' he went on, turning back to Bernard Cooke. 'You and Gillian's mother on the veranda at her home.'

'That Sunday drinks party,' Cooke decided.

'The Minute Man was watching.'

'He thinks Cora and I are lovers?'

'He's putting two and two together and making five, luckily for us. If that photo had just shown the two of you talking, he might not have suspected anything.'

'Whereas as it is . . .'

'He thinks he knows why Gillian's set you up. It couldn't have worked out better.'

Gillian Webster turned to Cooke. 'Kissing my mother on the veranda?'

Cooke tried a nervous smile. Lancaster shifted in his chair. He was nervous for all sorts of reasons. The Minute Man *had* to solve puzzles, even if that meant conjuring an answer out of the thinnest stuff. Lancaster had invented the conundrum, hoping his adversary would be irritated by it . . . and drawn towards it. Someone even suggested the

93

Minute Man might pose as a reporter – a suitable disguise for showing interest in the case . . .

There was a knock at the door, and a young man came in. Lancaster introduced him.

'I don't think either of you has met Detective Constable Duniec.' Duniec nodded a greeting, but Gillian's mind was on the idea of Cooke and her mother. 'Well, Stefan?' Lancaster asked.

The look on Duniec's face was bad news.

'He paid his bill and left over an hour ago.'

Lancaster nodded. 'He's been back to the Forester's, a regular called Arthur just phoned to tell me. And he paid another visit to the factory.'

'We know his car, sir, red Fiesta, there's a call out for it.'

'All exit roads are covered, aren't they?'

Duniec nodded.

'Then all we can do is wait.'

Lancaster tried to look relaxed. Bernard Cooke had been doubtful of the plan at first, but as a friend of Gillian's he'd gone along with it. After all, partly it had been her idea. She was looking pale again. She'd been ordered to rest by the doctors, but had insisted on sticking around. The phone rang again. Lancaster snatched the call.

'Red Fiesta,' he said afterwards. 'Sighted heading for Lower Traherne.' He fixed his eyes on Gillian. 'Looks like he's heading out to your home.' Then he turned to Duniec. 'Get on to it, Stefan.' Duniec nodded and left the room.

This eventuality, too, had been covered. The Websters were in a local hotel, under plainclothes protection. A driver and unmarked car were waiting outside to take Gillian back there. The Minute Man was driving into a trap.

The phone rang yet again, and Lancaster picked it up, glad of something to do. He listened for a moment, a muscle going rigid in his jaw. When he spoke, it was in a dry voice. 'Put him through, will you? And try to get a trace.' He then pushed a button on the telephone and replaced the receiver. A small integral speaker crackled into life. A female voice said, 'You're through, caller.' Lancaster swallowed and spoke.

'Hello?'

'Superintendent Lancaster?'

'Speaking.'

Lancaster watched Gillian. She was staring at the telephone. What little colour she had vanished from her face.

'Don't bother with a trace, Tom. I won't be on long, you know that.'

'We get a dozen cranks a day saying they're the Minute Man.'

'You know who I am, Tom.'

'Why are you phoning?'

'Because you've got the wrong man.'

Lancaster looked to Gillian and Cooke. She looked ready to leap from her seat, while Cooke seemed pinned against the back of his as if by G-force.

'Have we?'

'Yes. She's set him up.'

'Who has?'

'The girl.'

'Why would she do that?'

'He's having an affair with her mother. She wants revenge.'

Lancaster forced a laugh. 'How can you possibly know that?'

'I know. I know all of it now.'

The line went dead.

'Christ,' Cooke said. Lancaster checked with the switchboard, but the Minute Man hadn't been on long enough to give them a chance. In fact, he'd been on the line for scarcely a minute . . .

Lancaster got to his feet. 'I wonder if he still plans to visit Lower Traherne? One way to find out . . .'

'I'm coming too,' said Cooke, rising shakily to his feet. Gillian was still staring at the telephone. Neither man needed confirmation that she had recognised the voice.

When Lancaster touched her shoulder she flinched.

'Come on, Gillian,' he said. 'Let's get you back to the hotel.'

They opened the back door of the car for her and she got in. The engine was running and the car moved off at once, through the car park, past the usual ruck of reporters and cameras, and out of the iron gates of Castle Lane police station. She didn't want to go to the hotel, not really. She wanted to go home, to Lower Traherne. But she doubted the police driver could be persuaded to take her there. She noticed a walkie talkie on the floor by his feet. Or maybe it was a portable phone. Whatever happened at the house, she'd hear of it. He was looking at her in the rearview mirror. When she looked back, he gave her a reassuring smile. Then she noticed they'd passed the regular turning.

'We should have gone left there.'

He was still smiling. The car was building up speed. Gillian felt a lump swell in her throat, the fear nearly choking her.

'I know it all now,' he said quietly. 'The way Lancaster spoke, that confirmed it. Oh yes, that balanced both sides of the ledger quite nicely.'

She swallowed, shifting the blockage. 'Where's the driver?'

'*I'm* the driver.'

'The policeman.'

'You think he's in the boot?' He shook his head. 'I told him his chief wanted him in the press room.'

She was relaxing a little. His voice was calm. It had been calm all the time she'd been his captive. 'Where are we going?' she asked.

'Lower Traherne.'

'What?'

'I'm taking you home, Gillian.'

'But why?'

He shrugged. 'Just to show them I can.'

She thought for a moment. While she was thinking, he spoke again.

'It was good, very good, nearly had me fooled. Except for one scared bloke in a pub . . .'

She felt the words tumble from her mouth, like someone else was speaking. 'They've got the exit roads covered, and there are police at the house, inside and outside. You'll never—'

'It's all right, Gillian. You'll see, both sides will balance.'

'What do you mean, balance?'

So for the rest of the journey, the Minute Man tried to explain to her his own particular theories of the principles of accounts.

# The Only True Comedian

I suppose, looking back, my schooldays were to blame. Or maybe it was my parents' genes, which had left me the smallest boy in my year. The popular boys all seemed to be the tough ones, the sporty ones, the ones who weren't shy, who were good-looking.

I didn't really fit the bill. So instead I became the comedian. Of course, they weren't laughing *with* me – they were laughing *at* me. I knew it even then, as I told my jokes and made my silly faces and did my funny walks. They told me I was off my head, said I was potty. I didn't mind: at least they were talking to me. At least they were noticing me.

Which meant I was allowed to participate in their games, or at least watch from the periphery, which was my favoured spot anyway. Watching them, I was able to learn. I learned which kids and teachers I could make fun of. I'd go for the younger kids, even spottier and uglier than I was, or for one of the unlovely girls who stood by the playground railings, sad looks on their faces. Oh, I was ferocious with anyone who couldn't bite back. It was how I stayed part of the gang.

The other problem was, I wasn't stupid, but when I became a member of Black Alec's gang, I had to pretend to be less clever than I was. And this pretence could only be carried off if I started slipping in class, answering questions wrongly when I knew the right answers, my test marks dropping. The deputy head had a word with me. I think she could see there was a problem, she just couldn't figure out what it was. My parents were summoned to the school for a discussion. *They* started to take notice of me too, helping with homework and revision. Still I refused to fulfil my potential. Sometimes I would slip up, and answer some question which had stumped everyone else. At these times, the teacher would peer at me, wondering what was going on.

Eventually I was taken to hospital for tests on my brain. They glued all these electrodes to my head. Three washings later, my hair still felt sticky, and the results had failed to throw up any incongruities. When the final exams came, I was in a quandary. We'd all have left school by the time the results were posted. So if I wanted to, I could do as well as I liked. But something made me stay in character; maybe it was the thought that though I was leaving school, the gang would still be there, hanging around their favoured street corner, yelling abuse at cars and pedestrians, running down to the park with a carrier-bag of beer. It was a community I understood, and my chosen role made me unique within it. I was 'Joker' or 'The Comedian'. I wasn't expected to take part in the occasional massed battles with other gangs. I proved myself by telling jokes and stories, by deriding other gangs (especially with reference to their personal hygiene and sexual habits), and by improving my range of impressions.

Soon after leaving school, however, I found that a lot of the gang had drifted away. Even Black Alec – our leader and mentor – had gained employment as a car mechanic. The merry band had dwindled to a few losers for whom the daily stint at the street corner had become an unwelcome chore. I thought about resitting my exams, going on to college or university. But Black Alec was my next-door neighbour: how could I tell him my plans? He wouldn't have understood. He'd have asked me to do the walk again, and afterwards his laughter would have had me craving more. More laughter, more acceptance, more of his approval.

Anyway, things didn't work out for him as a mechanic. He became a bouncer instead, working at a discotheque in

Kirkcaldy. He got into trouble, spent a couple of months in jail, and when he came out he told us he'd just paid a visit to the 'University of Life'. From now on, he said, nothing would be beyond him. He'd only be satisfied with 'number one'. At the time, I don't think we really knew what he was talking about, but we found out soon enough.

I went to work in a chicken factory. It wasn't a bad job. The production line was mostly staffed by women, and I kept them smiling. I'd sing a song, do a little dance, whatever it took to please them. They were all married, kept asking me when I'd find a girlfriend. They wore white overalls and green wellies, their hair tucked into white caps. Sometimes, when I met them outside the factory, I wouldn't recognise them. My first Christmas party was a revelation. They were wearing dresses and make-up, having a drink and a laugh. We'd taken over the back room of a pub in Glenrothes. No management, just workers. There was some entertainment. A couple of the women sang songs. One of the foremen got up and told some jokes.

'Get off!' the women yelled at him. 'Our comedian's ten times better than you!' They meant me. I was cajoled, persuaded. I found myself up on the stage, microphone in hand. I cleared my throat, cleared it some more, the sound filling the room. Someone called out for me to get on with it, and then somebody else twigged that I was pretending to be the production supervisor: he was always clearing his throat before he gave you bad news. There was scattered applause and laughter.

'I'm sorry to have to inform you all', I said, 'that Christmas has been cancelled this year. You lot might not be happy, but I've two thousand capons in the back who're over the moon.'

Now everyone understood; they'd all clicked into my act. And it felt wonderful. The hair on my arms was standing up. It seemed I'd been up there a couple of minutes, but I was told afterwards I'd done a twenty-minute set. Women were kissing me, telling me I was the best.

'You should turn professional,' one of them said.

And eventually, plucking up courage, that's just what I did.

I started out at pub talent nights, winning a couple of contests. The publican might then invite me back for a three- or four-week run. I kept up the factory job, but now I had a girlfriend, Emily, who'd sung 'The Night They Drove Old Dixie Down' at one of the talent shows. I'd asked her about the song. She'd no idea what it was all about.

'Just got it from one of my mum's Joan Baez albums.'

We had a laugh together. Emily had a day job, too, in a shoe shop. She came up with the idea of me going full-time pro. She said she'd support me till I got rich and famous. She said it wouldn't take long. Her argument was that with my job, I'd no time to write new material. She was right: I really needed new material. So she became my manager, finding me bookings, and I lay in bed writing jokes and stories.

It all went well for a while. Then we realised I was just treading water. It was still pubs and clubs.

'You need a portfolio,' Emily said. 'Something you can show to agents and the TV companies.'

'What I need are some decent gags,' I replied.

The writing wasn't working. It was never how I'd worked. I was spontaneous, my material came from life. Now that I spent all day mooching around the house, there was nothing for me to write *about*. If the act was going to go anywhere, I needed to take a few risks. And that was what I did. I invested in a tape machine and other electronic stuff, so I could use funny noises and sound effects in my act. Then I got measured for a sharp suit – blue and sparkly, with shirt to match. I looked ridiculous in it, but then that was the point, wasn't it?

I now looked the part. Problem was, none of it came cheap. Emily asked where I'd got the money.

'Savings,' I told her, lying through my teeth. Soon

enough, I knew as I said it, I might not have any teeth left to lie through. Because I'd borrowed the money from Black Alec.

Black Alec had almost fulfilled his ambition of becoming 'number one'. He was now one of the most feared men on the east coast. He ran a string of clubs in Fife, owned two pubs in Edinburgh, and had so many fingers in so many other pies, it was a wonder he could pick his nose. He also ran protection, prostitutes and pornography – or so the rumours said. I'd never worked in any of his clubs – he said they were 'upmarket', 'mostly music-oriented'. He said I was low-class.

But still he loaned me the money. And now, with the act flagging, it was time to start paying it off, beginning with the interest. I knew Emily was broke: the shoe shop had gone bust, and she was on Jobseekers. I knew *I* didn't have any money. And I knew it wouldn't matter to Black Alec that I'd once been his next-door neighbour and personal jester. Nothing mattered to him but repayment and violence against the person. There were those who said he preferred it when people couldn't pay up. That way, Black Alec got to play.

Eventually, I broke down and told Emily. I'd been fobbing Alec's men off as best I could. They'd repossessed the electronics, and soon it would be time for them to start taking possession of my limbs, lungs and lights. So we did what we had to do: went on the run. Thing is, to keep running we needed money, and I only knew one way to make money – keep on with the act, which made it hard for us to stay ahead of the GBH brigade. We'd turn up in a town, and while I tried to hustle a gig, Emily would be checking departure times of buses and trains. I'd do my stint, grab the cash, and we'd make for the station. Up and down the east coast we ran, as far north as Montrose, and south to Eyemouth, finding that the travelling was using up most of the money I made. At this rate, there was no way I was going to be able to pay back Black Alec.

'We'll go to London,' Emily said. 'That's where the agents and TV people are. One spot on Des O'Connor and you could pay Black Alec ten times over.'

'How are we going to get there?'

'First thing is to talk to Des's producer.'

'I mean, how are we going to get to London?'

'We'll hitch,' she told me. 'All we need is a bit of money for food.'

Which meant one last show. There weren't many places left to try. Word was out that Black Alec wanted to see me. Worse still, the rumour was I was washed up, that I stank.

But a pub on Rose Street in Edinburgh was under new management, and looking to kick-start a comedy club. They said they'd give me a fifteen-minute spot. If they liked what they saw, there'd be a twenty in it for me.

Twenty quid: I'd earned more winning talent shows. But I said okay. Of course I said okay.

That night, when I took the stage in my blue sparkly suit, there were about two dozen punters in the place: a smattering at the tables, most of them chatting at the bar. The last thing they wanted was me up there, spoiling their conversation and meaning the jukebox was turned off.

But I kicked off anyway. Nobody was laughing. Emily was in the DJ's booth, supposedly keeping an eye on my mike level so that there was no feedback. Right then, I thought feedback had a better chance of getting a laugh.

And then Black Alec walked in. Someone had tipped him off, and here he came with three of his lads. They took a table right at the front. Alec not taking his eyes off me, a little smile on his face – it was the first smile I'd seen all night, but it didn't exactly cheer me up. A bottle of champagne arrived, and just the one glass. Alec toasted me as he drank. Suddenly, horribly, my mind went blank, not a single joke in my repertoire could I remember. There were slow handclaps from the bar and cries of 'Get off!'

'Does your mum let you out looking like that?' I told the heckler. 'Look at him, face like a bulldog chewing a wasp.'

The heckler's pals laughed at this, and I was on a roll. I knew only one thing: the minute they booed me off, I was in for a doing. I had to stay on that stage, and the only way to do that was to be funny.

And I *was* funny. Inspiration took hold, and the stories started pouring out. I had stories about working in a factory, about shoe shops and working-men's clubs, even stories about schooldays. They clapped and cheered. More punters were coming in, and no one was leaving. I'd been on stage about forty minutes, but the owner wasn't about to signal time-up. The only person in the place not laughing was Black Alec. Even his lads had sniggered at a couple of the routines, but Alec just sat there stony-faced, finishing his champagne.

Eventually, tiredness got the better of me. I could fall back on lame material, or stop while the going was good. I'd have won an audience and be losing my mobility. Alec looked like he was getting impatient. I never liked to keep an old friend waiting.

'Ladies and gentlemen,' I said, 'you've been a great audience, even old bulldog-features over there. This set was dedicated to the one thing I've always enjoyed until this evening, namely good health. Thank you and goodnight.'

I came off to applause, whistles, cheers. I walked right over to Black Alec's table and sat down opposite him. The jukebox came back on. The owner brought me a whisky. So did a couple of punters, congratulating me on the best show they'd seen. The owner wanted to book me a regular slot, maybe hosting the club. And throughout, Alec didn't take his eyes off me.

'So,' he said at last, 'that was your routine?'

'That was it,' I said. I couldn't see Emily. Maybe she'd spotted Alec and done a runner.

'It was good,' he said. 'Really good.'

I looked at him. Was it possible. . . ?

'You can warm an audience up,' he went on. 'I could do with someone like you.'

'You're going to take me to one of your clubs and roast me on a spit?' I guessed.

And he laughed, the way he'd laughed when we were kids. 'I'm offering you work, Comedian. That way, I can keep an eye on you while you pay me what you owe me. How does that sound?'

'It sounds great,' I said, unable to keep the relief out of my voice.

'The same set should do.'

And I nodded, while my insides turned to rubber. The same set? The one I'd improvised? I couldn't remember it, couldn't recall a single blessed punchline. And then Emily was marching towards me, waving a cassette.

'What's that?' I asked.

'I taped you,' she said, leaning down to kiss me. 'Now you've got your portfolio.'

'And my continuing good health,' I said, kissing her back.

I used to think comedy came from wanting acceptance, wanting to be liked. Now I know differently. I know it's all down to fear. Fear, ladies and gentlemen, is the only true comedian in town.

# Herbert in Motion

My choices that day were twofold: kill myself before or *after* the Prime Minister's cocktail party? And if after, should I wear my Armani to the party, or the more sober YSL with the chalk stripe?

The invitation was gilt-edged, too big for the inside pocket of my workaday suit. Drinks and canapés, six p.m. till seven. A minion had telephoned to confirm my attendance, and to brief me on protocol. That had been two days ago. He'd explained that among the guests would be an American visiting London, a certain Joseph Hefferwhite. While not quite spelling it out – they never do, do they? – the minion was explaining why I'd been invited, and what my role on the night might be.

'Joe Hefferwhite,' I managed to say, clutching the receiver like it was so much straw.

'I believe you share an interest in modern art,' the minion continued.

'We share an interest.'

He misunderstood my tone and laughed. 'Sorry, "share an interest" was a bit weak, wasn't it? My apologies.'

He was apologising because art is no mere interest of mine. Art was – is – my whole life. During the rest of our short and one-sided conversation, I stared ahead as though at some startling new design, trying to understand and explain, to make it all right with myself, attempting to wring out each nuance and stroke, each variant and chosen shape or length of line. And in the end there was . . . nothing. No substance, no revelation; just the bland reality of my situation and the simple framing device of suicide.

And the damnation was, it had been the perfect crime.

A dinner party ten years before. It was in Chelsea, deep in the heart of Margaret Thatcher's vision of England. There were dissenters at the table – only a couple, and they could afford their little grumble: it wasn't going to make Margaret Hilda disappear, and their own trappings were safe: the warehouse conversion in Docklands, the BMW, the Cristal champagne and black truffles.

Trappings: the word seems so much more resonant now.

So there we were. The wine had relaxed us, we were all smiling with inner and self-satisfied contentment (and wasn't that the dream, after all?), and I felt just as at home as any of them. I knew I was there as the Delegate of Culture. Among the merchant bankers and media figures, political jobsworths and 'somethings' (and dear God, there was an estate agent there too, if memory serves – *that* fad didn't last long), I was there to reassure them that they were composed of something more lasting and nourishing than mere money, that they had some meaning in the wider scheme. I was there as curator to their sensibilities.

In truth, I was and am a Senior Curator at the Tate Gallery, with special interest in twentieth-century North American art (by which I mean paintings: I'm no great enthusiast of modern sculpture, yet less of more radical sideshows – performance art, video art, all that). The guests at the table that evening made the usual noises about artists whose names they couldn't recall but who did 'green things' or 'you know, that horse and the shadow and everything'. One foolhardy soul (was it the estate agent?) digressed on his fondness for certain wildlife paintings, and trumpeted the news that his wife had once bought a print from Christie's Contemporary Art.

When another guest begged me to allow that my job was 'on the cushy side', I placed knife and fork slowly on plate and did my spiel. I had it down to a fine art – allow the pun, please – and talked fluently about the difficulties my position posed, about the appraisal of trends and talents, the search for major new works and their acquisition.

'Imagine', I said, 'that you are about to spend half a million pounds on a painting. In so doing, you will elevate the status of the artist, turn him or her into a rich and sought-after talent. They may disappoint you thereafter and fail to paint anything else of interest, in which case the resale value of the work will be negligible, and your own reputation will have been tarnished – perhaps even more than tarnished. Every day, every time you are asked for your opinion, your reputation is on the line. Meanwhile, you must propose exhibitions, must plan them – which often means transporting works from all around the world – and must spend your budget wisely.'

'You mean like, do I buy four paintings at half a mil each, or push the pedal to the floor with one big buy at two mil?'

I allowed my questioner a smile. 'In crude economic terms, yes.'

'Do you get to take pictures home?' our hostess asked.

'Some works – a few – are loaned out,' I conceded. 'But not to staff.'

'Then to whom?'

'People in prominence, benefactors, that sort of person.'

'All that money,' the Docklands woman said, shaking her head, 'for a bit of paint and canvas. It almost seems like a crime when there are homeless on the streets.'

'Disgraceful,' someone else said. 'Can't walk along the Embankment without stumbling over them.'

At which point our hostess stumbled into the silence to reveal that she had a surprise. 'We'll take coffee and brandy in the morning room, during which you'll be invited to take part in a murder.'

She didn't mean it, of course, though more than one pair of eyes strayed to the Docklanders, more in hope than expectation. What she meant was that we'd be participating in a parlour game. There had been a murder (her unsmiling

husband the cajoled corpse, miraculously revivified whenever another snifter of brandy was offered), and we were to
look for clues in the room. We duly searched, somewhat in
the manner of children who wish to please their elders.
With half a dozen clues gathered, the Docklands woman
surprised us all by deducing that our hostess had committed
the crime – as indeed she had.

We collapsed thankfully on to the sofas and had our
glasses refilled, after which the conversation came around
to crime – real and imagined. It was now that the host
became animated for the first time that night. He was a
collector of whodunnits and fancied himself an expert.

'The perfect crime,' he told us, 'as everyone knows, is one
where no crime has been committed.'

'But then there *is* no crime,' his wife declared.

'Precisely,' he said. 'No crime . . . and yet a crime. If the
body's never found, damned hard to convict anyone. Or if
something's stolen, but never noticed. See what I'm getting
at?'

I did, of course, and perhaps you do, too.


The Tate, like every other gallery I can think of, has
considerably less wall-space than it has works in its
collection. These days, we do not like to cram our paintings
together (though when well done, the effect can be
breathtaking). One large canvas may have a whole wall to
iself, and praise be that Bacon's triptychs did not start a
revolution, or there'd be precious little work on display in
our galleries of modern art. For every display of gigantism, it
is blessed relief, is it not, to turn to a miniaturist? Not that
there are many miniatures in the Tate's storerooms. I was
there with an acquaintance of mine, the dealer Gregory
Jance.

Jance worked out of Zurich for years, for no other reason,
according to interviews, than that 'they couldn't touch me
there'. There had always been rumours about him, rumours
which started to make sense when one attempted to balance

his few premier-league sales (and therefore commissions) against his lavish lifestyle. These days, he had homes in Belgravia, Manhattan's Upper East Side, and Moscow, as well as a sprawling compound on the outskirts of Zurich. The Moscow home seemed curious until one recalled stories of ikons smuggled out of the old Soviet Union and of art treasures taken from the Nazis, treasures which had ended up in the hands of Politburo chiefs desperate for such things as hard dollars and new passports.

Yes, if even half the tales were true, then Gregory Jance had sailed pretty close to the wind. I was counting on it.

'What a waste,' he said, as I gave him a short tour of the storerooms. The place was cool and hushed, except for the occasional click of the machines which monitored air temperature, light and humidity. On the walls of the Tate proper, paintings such as those we passed now would be pored over, passed by with reverence. Here, they were stacked one against the other, most shrouded in white sheeting like corpses or Hamlet's ghost in some shoddy student production. Identifier tags hung from the sheets like so many items in a lost property office.

'Such a waste,' Jance sighed, with just a touch of melodrama. His dress sense did not lack drama either: crumpled cream linen suit, white brogues, screaming red shirt and white silk cravat. He shuffled along like an old man, running the rim of his panama hat through his fingers. It was a nice performance, but if I knew my man, then beneath it he was like bronze.

Our meeting – *en principe* – was to discuss his latest crop of 'world-renowned artists'. Like most other gallery owners – those who act as agents for certain artists – Jance was keen to sell to the Tate, or to any other 'national' gallery. He wanted the price hike that came with it, along with the kudos. But mostly the price hike.

He had polaroids and slides with him. In my office, I placed the slides on a lightbox and took my magnifier to them. A pitiful array of semi-talent dulled my eyes and my senses. Huge graffiti-style whorls which had been 'in' the previous summer in New York (mainly, in my view, because the practitioners tended to die young). Some neo-cubist stuff by a Swiss artist whose previous work was familiar to me. He had been growing in stature, but this present direction seemed to me an alley with a brick wall at the end, and I told Jance as much. At least he had a nice sense of colour and juxtaposition. But there was worse to come: combine paintings which Rauschenberg could have constructed in kindergarten; some not very clever geometric paintings, too clearly based on Stella's 'Protractor' series; and 'found' sculptures which looked like Nam June Paik on a very bad day.

Throughout, Jance was giving me his pitch, though without much enthusiasm. Where did he collect these people? (The unkind said he sought out the least popular exhibits at art school graduation shows.) More to the point, where did he sell them? I hadn't heard of him making any impact at all as an agent. What money he made, he seemed to make by other means.

Finally, he lifted a handful of polaroids from his pocket. 'My latest find,' he confided. 'Scottish. Great future.'

I looked through them. 'How old?'

He shrugged. 'Twenty-six, twenty-seven.'

I deducted five or six years and handed the photos back. 'Gregory,' I said, 'she's still at college. These are derivative – evidence she's learning from those who have gone before – and stylised, such as students often produce. She has talent, and I like the humour, even if that too is borrowed from other Scottish artists.'

He seemed to be looking in vain for the humour in the photos.

'Bruce McLean,' I said helpfully, 'Paolozzi, John Bellany's fish. Look closely and you'll see.' I paused. 'Bring her back in five or ten years, *if* she's kept hard at it, *if* she's matured, and *if* she has that nose for the difference between genius and sham . . .'

He pocketed the photos and gathered up his slides, his eyes glinting as though there might be some moisture there.

'You're a hard man,' he told me.

'But a fair one, I hope. And to prove it, let me buy you a drink.'

I didn't put my proposition to him quite then, of course, not over coffee and sticky cakes in the Tate cafeteria. We met a few weeks later – casually as it were. We dined at a small place in a part of town neither of us frequented. I asked him about his young coterie of artists. They seemed, I said, quite skilled in impersonation.

'Impersonation?'

'They have studied the greats,' I explained, 'and can reproduce them with a fair degree of skill.'

'Reproduce them,' he echoed quietly.

'Reproduce them,' I said. 'I mean, the influences are there.' I paused. 'I'm not saying they *copy*.'

'No, not that.' Jance looked up from his untouched food. 'Are you coming to some point?'

I smiled. 'A lot of paintings in the storerooms, Gregory. They so seldom see the light of day.'

'Yes, pity, that. Such a waste.'

'When people could be savouring them.'

He nodded, poured some wine for both of us. 'I think I begin to see,' he said. 'I think I begin to see.'

That was the start of our little enterprise. You know what it was, of course. You have a keen mind. You are shrewd and discerning. Perhaps you pride yourself on these things, on always being one step ahead, on knowing things before those around you have perceived them. Perhaps you, too, think yourself capable of the perfect crime, a crime where there is no crime.

There was no crime, because nothing was missing from the quarterly inventory. First, I would photograph the work. Indeed, on a couple of occasions, I even took one of Jance's young artists down to the storeroom and showed her the painting she'd be copying. She'd been chosen because she had studied the minimalists, and this was to be a minimalist commission.

Minimalism, interestingly, proved the most difficult style to reproduce faithfully. In a busy picture, there's so much to look at that one can miss a wrong shade or the fingers of a hand which have failed to curl to the right degree. But with a couple of black lines and some pink waves . . . well, fakes were easier to spot. So it was that Jance's artist saw the work she was to replicate face to face. Then we did the measurements, took the polaroids, and she drew some preliminary sketches. Jance was in charge of finding the right quality of canvas, the correct frame. My job was to remove the real canvas, smuggle it from the gallery, and replace it with the copy, reframing the finished work afterwards.

We were judicious, Jance and I. We chose our works with care. One or two a year – we never got greedy. The choice would depend on a combination of factors. We didn't want artists who were *too* well known, but we wanted them dead if possible. (I had a fear of an artist coming to inspect his work at the Tate and finding a copy instead.) There had to be a buyer – a private collector, who would *keep* the work private. We couldn't have a painting being loaned to some collection or exhibition when it was supposed to be safely tucked away in the vaults of the Tate. Thankfully, as I'd expected, Jance seemed to know his market. We never had any problems on that score. But there was another factor. Every now and then, there would be requests from exhibitions for the loan of a painting – one we'd copied. But as curator, I would find reasons why the work in question had to remain at the Tate, and might offer, by way of consolation, some other work instead.

Then there was the matter of rotation. Now and again – as had to be the case, or suspicion might grow – one of the copies would have to grace the walls of the gallery proper. Those were worrying times, and I was careful to position the works in the least flattering, most shadowy locations, usually with a much more interesting picture nearby, to lure the spectator away. I would watch the browsers. Once or twice, an art student would come along and sketch the copied work. No one ever showed a moment's doubt, and my confidence grew.

But then . . . then . . .

We had loaned works out before, of course – I'd told the dinner party as much. This or that cabinet minister might want something for the office, something to impress visitors. There would be discussions about a suitable work. It was the same with particular benefactors. They could be loaned a painting for weeks or even months. But I was always careful to steer prospective borrowers away from the twenty or so copies. It wasn't as though there was any lack of choice: for each copy, there were fifty other paintings they could have. The odds, as Jance had assured me more than once, were distinctly in our favour.

Until the day the Prime Minister came to call.

This is a man who knows as much about art as I do about home brewing. There is almost a glee about his studious ignorance – and not merely of art. But he was walking around the Tate, for all the world like a dowager around a department store, and not seeing what he wanted.

'Voore,' he said at last. I thought I'd misheard him. 'Ronny Voore. I thought you had a couple.'

My eyes took in his entourage, not one of whom would know a Ronny Voore if it blackballed them at the Garrick. But my superior was there, nodding slightly, so I nodded with him.

'They're not out at the moment,' I told the PM.

'You mean they're in?' He smiled, provoking a few fawning laughs.

'In storage,' I explained, trying out my own smile.

'I'd like one for Number Ten.'

I tried to form some argument – they were being cleaned, restored, loaned to Philadelphia – but my superior was nodding again. And after all, what did the PM know about art? Besides, only one of our Voores was a fake.

'Certainly, Prime Minister. I'll arrange for it to be sent over.'

'Which one?'

I licked my lips. 'Did you have one in mind?'

He considered, lips puckered. 'Maybe I should just have a little look . . .'

Normally, there were no visitors to the storerooms. But that morning, there were a dozen of us posed in front of *Shrew Reclining* and *Herbert in Motion*. Voore was very good with titles. I'll swear, if you look at them long enough, you really can see – beyond the gobbets of oil, the pasted-on photographs and cinema stubs, the splash of emulsion and explosion of colour – the figures of a large murine creature and a man running.

The Prime Minister gazed at them in something short of thrall. 'Is it "shrew" as in Shakespeare?'

'No, sir, I think it's the rodent.'

He thought about this. 'Vibrant colours,' he decided.

'Extraordinary,' my superior agreed.

'One can't help feeling the influence of pop art,' one of the minions drawled. I managed not to choke: it was like saying one could see in Beryl Cook the influence of Picasso.

The PM turned to the senior minion. 'I don't know, Charles. What do you think?'

'The shrew, I think.'

My heart leapt. The Prime Minister nodded, then pointed to *Herbert in Motion*. 'That one, I think.'

Charles looked put out, while those around him tried to hide smiles. It was a calculated put-down, a piece of politics on the PM's part. Politics had decided.

A fake Ronny Voore would grace the walls of Number 10 Downing Street.

I supervised the packing and transportation. It was a busy week for me: I was negotiating the loan of several Rothkos for an exhibition of early works. Faxes and insurance appraisals were flying. American institutions were *very* touchy about lending stuff. I'd had to promise a Braque to one museum – and for three months at that – in exchange for one of Rothko's less inspired creations. Anyway, despite headaches, when the Voore went to its new home, I went with it.

I'd discussed the loan with Jance. He'd told me to switch the copy for some other painting, persisting that 'no one would know'.

'He'll know,' I'd said. 'He wanted a Voore. He knew what he wanted.'

'But why?'

Good question, and I'd yet to find the answer. I'd hoped for a first-floor landing or some nook or cranny out of the general view, but the staff seemed to know exactly where the painting was to hang – something else had been removed so that it could take pride of place in the dining-room. (Or one of the dining-rooms, I couldn't be sure how many there were. I'd thought I'd be entering a house, but Number 10 was a warren, a veritable Tardis, with more passageways and offices than I could count.)

I was asked if I wanted a tour of the premises, so as to view the other works of art, but by that time my head really did ache, and I decided to walk back to the Tate, making it as far as Millbank before I had to rest beside the river, staring down at its sludgy flow. The question had yet to be answered: why did the PM want a Ronny Voore? Who in their right mind wanted a Ronny Voore these days?

The answer, of course, came with the telephone call.

Joe Hefferwhite was an important man. He had been a senator at one time. He was now regarded as a 'senior statesman', and the American President sent him on the occasional high-profile, high-publicity spot of troubleshooting and conscience-salving. At one point in his life, he'd been mooted for president himself, but of course his personal history had counted against him. In younger days, Hefferwhite had been a bohemian. He'd spent time in Paris, trying to be a poet. He'd walked a railway line with Jack Kerouac and Neal Cassady. Then he'd come into enough money to buy his way into politics, and had prospered there.

I knew a bit about him from some background reading I'd done in the recent past. Not that I'd been interested in Joseph Hefferwhite . . . but I'd been *very* interested in Ronny Voore.

The two men had met at Stanford initially, then later on had met again in Paris. They'd kept in touch thereafter, drifting apart only after 'Heff' had decided on a political career. There had been arguments about the hippie culture, dropping out, Vietnam, radical chic – the usual sixties US issues. Then in 1974 Ronny Voore had laid down on a fresh white canvas, stuck a gun in his mouth, and gifted the world his final work. His reputation, which had vacillated in life, had been given a boost by the manner of his suicide. I wondered if I could make the same dramatic exit. But no, I was not the dramatic type. I foresaw sleeping pills and a bottle of decent brandy.

*After* the party.

I was wearing my green Armani, hoping it would disguise the condemned look in my eyes. Joe Hefferwhite had *known* Voore, had seen his style and working practice at first hand. That was why the PM had wanted a Voore: to impress the American. Or perhaps to honour his presence in some way. A political move, as far from aesthetics as one could wander. The situation was not without irony: a man with no artistic sensibility, a man who couldn't tell his Warhol from his Whistler . . . this man was to be my downfall.

I hadn't dared tell Jance. Let him find out for himself afterwards, once I'd made my exit. I'd left a letter. It was sealed, marked *Personal*, and addressed to my superior. I didn't owe Gregory Jance anything, but hadn't mentioned him in the letter. I hadn't even listed the copied works – let them set other experts on them. It would be interesting to see if any *other* fakes had found their way into the permanent collection.

Only of course I wouldn't be around for that.

Number 10 sparkled. Every surface was gleaming, and the place seemed nicely undersized for the scale of the event. The PM moved amongst his guests, dispensing a word here and there, guided by the man he'd called Charles. Charles would whisper a brief to the PM as they approached a group, so the PM would know who was who and how to treat them. I was way down the list apparently, standing on my own (though a minion had attempted to engage me in conversation: it seemed a rule that no guest was to be allowed solitude), pretending to examine a work by someone eighteenth-century and Flemish – not my sort of thing at all.

The PM shook my hand. 'I've someone I'd like you to meet,' he said, looking back over his shoulder to where Joe Hefferwhite was standing, rocking back on his heels as he told some apparently hilarious story to two grinning civil servants who had doubtless been given their doting orders.

'Joseph Hefferwhite,' the PM said.

As if I didn't know; as if I hadn't been avoiding the man for the past twenty-eight minutes. I knew I couldn't leave – would be reminded of that should I try – until the PM had said hello. It was a question of protocol. This was all that had kept me from going. But now I was determined to escape. The PM, however, had other plans. He waved to Joe Hefferwhite like they were old friends, and Hefferwhite broke short his story – not noticing the relief on his listeners' faces – and swaggered towards us. The PM was leading me by the shoulder – gently, though it seemed to me that his grip burned – over towards where the Voore hung. A table separated us from it, but it was an occasional table, and we weren't too far from the canvas. Serving staff moved around with salvers of canapés and bottles of fizz, and I took a refill as Hefferwhite approached.

'Joe, this is our man from the Tate.'

'Pleased to meet you,' Hefferwhite said, pumping my free hand. He winked at the PM. 'Don't think I hadn't noticed the painting. It's a nice touch.'

'We have to make our guests feel welcome. The Tate has another Voore, you know.'

'Is that so?'

Charles was whispering in the PM's ear. 'Sorry, have to go,' the PM said. 'I'll leave you two to it then.' And with a smile he was gone, drifting towards his next encounter.

Joe Hefferwhite smiled at me. He was in his seventies, but extraordinarily well preserved, with thick dark hair that could have been a weave or a transplant. I wondered if anyone had ever mentioned to him his resemblance to Blake Carrington . . .

He leaned towards me. 'This place bugged?'

I blinked, decided I'd heard him correctly, and said I wouldn't know.

'Well, hell, doesn't matter to me if it is. Listen,' he nodded towards the painting, 'that is some kind of sick joke, don't you think?'

I swallowed. 'I'm not sure I follow.'

Hefferwhite took my arm and led me around the table, so we were directly in front of the painting. 'Ronny was my friend. He blew his brains out. Your Prime Minister thinks I want to be *reminded* of that? I think this is supposed to tell me something.'

'What?'

'I'm not sure. It'll take some thinking. You British are devious bastards.'

'I feel I should object to that.'

Hefferwhite ignored me. 'Ronny painted the first version of *Herbert* in Paris, 'forty-nine or 'fifty.' He frowned. 'Must've been 'fifty. Know who Herbert was?' He was studying the painting now. At first, his eyes flicked over it. Then he stared a little harder, picking out that section and this, concentrating.

'Who?' The champagne flute shook in my hand. Death, I thought, would come as some relief. And not a moment too soon.

'Some guy we shared rooms with, never knew his second name. He said second names were shackles. Not like Malcolm X and all that, Herbert was white, nicely brought-up. Wanted to study Sartre, wanted to write plays and films and I don't know what. Jesus, I've often wondered what happened to him. I know Ronny did, too.' He sniffed, lifted a canapé from a passing tray and shoved it into his mouth. 'Anyway,' he said through the crumbs, 'Herbert – he didn't like us calling him Herb – he used to go out running. Healthy body, healthy mind, that was his creed. He'd go out before dawn, usually just as we were going to bed. Always wanted us to go with him, said we'd see the world differently after a run.' He smiled at the memory, looked at the painting again. 'That's him running along the Seine, only the river's filled with philosophers and their books, all drowning.'

He kept looking at the painting, and I could feel the memories welling in him. I let him look. I wanted him to look. It was more his painting than anyone's. I could see that now. I knew I should say something . . . like, 'that's very interesting', or 'that explains so much'. But I didn't. I stared at the painting, too, and it was as though we were alone in that crowded, noisy room. We might have been on a desert island, or in a time machine. I saw Herbert running, saw his hunger. I saw his passion for questions and the seeking out of answers. I saw why philosophers always failed, and why they went on trying despite the fact. I saw the whole bloody story. And the colours: they were elemental, but they were of the city, too. They *were* Paris, not long after the war, the recuperating city. Blood and sweat and the simple, feral need to go on living.

To go on living.

My eyes were filling with water. I was about to say

something crass, something like 'thank you', but Heffer-white beat me to it, leaned towards me so his voice could drop to a whisper.

'It's a hell of a fake.'

And with that, and a pat on my shoulder, he drifted back into the party.

'I could have died,' I told Jance. It was straight afterwards. I was still wearing the Armani, pacing the floor of my flat. It's not much – third floor, two bedrooms, Maida Vale – but I was happy to see it. I could hardly get the tears out of my eyes. The telephone was in my hand . . . I just had to tell *some*body, and who could I tell but Jance?

'Well,' he said, 'you've never asked about the client.'

'I didn't want to know. Jance, I swear to God, I nearly died.'

He chuckled, not really understanding. He was in Zurich, sounded further away still. 'I knew Joe already had a couple of Voores,' he said. 'He's got some other stuff too – but he doesn't broadcast the fact. That's why he was perfect for *Herbert in Motion*.'

'But he was talking about not wanting to be reminded of the suicide.'

'He was talking about *why* the painting was there.'

'He thought it must be a message.'

Jance sighed. 'Politics. Who understands politics?'

I sighed with him. 'I can't do this any more.'

'Don't blame you. I never understood why you started in the first place.'

'Let's say I lost faith.'

'Me, I never had much to start with. Listen, you haven't told anyone else?'

'Who would I tell?' My mouth dropped open. 'But I left a note.'

'A note?'

'For my boss.'

'Might I suggest you go retrieve it?'

Beginning to tremble all over again, I went out in search of a taxi.

The night security people knew who I was, and let me into the building. I'd worked there before at night – it was the only time I could strip and replace the canvases.

'Busy tonight, eh?' the guard said.

'I'm sorry?'

'Busy tonight,' he repeated. 'Your boss is already in.'

'When did he arrive?'

'Not five minutes ago. He was running.'

'Running?'

'Said he needed a pee.'

I ran too, ran as fast as I could through the galleries and towards the offices, the paintings a blur either side of me. Running like Herbert, I thought. There was a light in my superior's office, and the door was ajar. But the room itself was empty. I walked to the desk and saw my note there, still in its sealed envelope. I picked it up and stuffed it into my jacket, just as my superior came into the room.

'Oh, good man,' he said, rubbing his hands to dry them. 'You got the message.'

'Yes,' I said, trying to still my breathing. Message: I hadn't checked my machine.

'Thought if we did a couple of evenings it would sort out the Rothko.'

'Absolutely.'

'No need to be so formal though.'

I stared at him.

'The suit,' he said.

'Drinks at Number Ten,' I explained.

'How did it go?'

'Fine.'

'PM happy with his Voore?'

'Oh yes.'

'You know he only wanted it to impress some American? One of his aides told me.'

'Joseph Hefferwhite,' I said.

'And was he impressed?'

'I think so.'

'Well, it keeps us sweet with the PM, and we all know who holds the purse-strings.' My superior made himself comfortable in his chair and looked at his desk. 'Where's that envelope?'

'What?'

'There was an envelope here.' He looked down at the floor.

I swallowed, dry-mouthed. 'I've got it,' I said. He looked startled, but I managed a smile. 'It was from me, proposing we spend an evening or two on Rothko.'

My superior beamed. 'Great minds, eh?'

'Absolutely.'

'Sit down then, let's get started.' I pulled over a chair. 'Can I let you into a secret? I detest Rothko.'

I smiled again. 'I'm not too keen myself.'

'Sometimes I think a student could do his stuff just as well, maybe even better.'

'But then it wouldn't be *his*, would it?'

'Ah, there's the rub.'

But I thought of the Voore fake, and Joe Hefferwhite's story, and my own reactions to the painting – to what was, when all's said and done, a copy – and I began to wonder . . .

# Glimmer

*This is the way the sixties ends.*

Someone told you Anita's a witch. You can believe it. When you ask her: 'Black or white?' she says: 'Black.' So you don't put any milk in her coffee. She tips some of it on to the carpet, leaving room for a measure of JD. Then she goes to find Keith or Brian. Or somebody.

You screw the top back on the bottle, stepping around the coffee patch. The floor accepts this latest insult, this new recruit to its wash of . . .

Wash of what? Come on, you're the writer here. You need to describe that carpet, keep the metaphor going. 'Recruit' because the floor looks like a battlefield. Original carpet colour: raw liver. Not much of that on view beneath the layered effluvium of trodden crisps, sandwich crusts, paper bags, butt ends, spent matches, roaches, chocolate wrappings. The drinks cans, the bottles, the music papers and magazines, autographed photos, flash-bulbs, envelopes and tape reels.

(How much of this do you need?)

Look there: beside a cigarette packet – three crumpled balls of paper. Lyric sheets. Let's pick up one of those, unravel it. A rough draft, just a few lines really, searching for an internal rhyme. At the top, the words 'Tea and Sympathy' underlined, followed by a double question mark: the song's working title.

The band photo: might be worth something to the groupies outside. Except most of them have gone further: their bodies are their autograph books. They trade stories of scenes they've been part of, tales you'd have to tone down even for the Sunday scandal-sheets. It's four in the morning now, but you can bet there'll still be a huddle outside the studio. Sometimes someone takes pity, gives orders for hot tea to be dispensed, with or without the sympathy. Four o'clock and London feels like a backwater. There's a man seated on the floor in the corner. He's asleep. He was asleep twelve hours ago. Twice now you've checked he's still breathing. Thin grey hair, curdled beard, clothes from California. *He's* a writer too, only he's more famous than you. His first novel made him rich. He's been working eight years on a follow-up. When he was last awake, you interviewed him for your piece.

'This', he told you, 'is the beginning of the negation of a generation. The cusp of devilment, my friend, seizing the day and wringing its neck. All God's children got wings, but only acid has the flight schedule. You have the look of a smoker: give me a cigarette.'

You'd seen him described once as 'a lost generation guru'. More than one meaning there, friend.

Where did they come from, these people? They seemed to attach themselves to the band for hours, days, weeks. They seemed to do so with ease. But the core of the band . . . you've yet to see anyone penetrate *that*. Like there's some inner sanctum, someplace no one else is allowed. That's what you want your piece to penetrate; yours would be the last word, the defining statement. This was the deal you'd made with yourself.

Biography: born working class; local secondary modern; art college and rhythm guitar in a couple of groups. Then you'd written your four angry plays and they'd become a quartet, a success on the London stage, now touring the provinces. Nobody got all the jokes; nobody got all the anger.

The thing is: you're not angry now. But anger is what everyone wants from you. You've written five hundred words on the band, only another four and a half thousand to go. And there are girls outside who would sleep with you for your mere *proximity* to something they can't have. And there's a man asleep in the corner who earns more for a public lecture than you did for your first two plays. And as he told you, he lectures off the top of his head. The head you're itching to kick, but not in an angry way . . .

And here's Anita again, and she's saying: 'You're my chauffeur, darling.' Handing you some keys, she pecks your cheek, her eyes smeared black. You ask her what your name is, and she laughs.

'Chauffeurs don't have names, *liebchen*.'

Then she leads you out to the Bentley.

The girls outside, they don't like Anita. They offer her dark glances. Does Anita have one of those metaphysical backstage passes, the kind marked 'All Areas'? No, you don't think so, and it seems to annoy her. For all her power, all her obvious allure, she lacks that final ticket of admission.

So you're driving through the silent streets, getting further and further away from your story, and she's spread across the back seat. The windows are open and her hair is flying across her face. She's singing the same notes over and over.

'Ooo-ooo; ooo-ooo.'

She asks you what they sound like.

'A train,' you yell into the wind. 'You know, the whistle blowing.'

She smiles. 'You're a romantic.'

'Well, if it's not a train, what is it?'

She sits upright, slides forward so her head is just behind yours. 'Banshees,' she says quietly. 'They're banshees.' Her mouth is close to your ear. 'Ooo-ooo,' she goes. Then she sits back.

You ask her where you're supposed to be going, but she's not listening. You end up driving along the Embankment, thinking maybe she wants dropping off at Cheyne Walk, but she doesn't even recognise the place. A couple of taxis are pulling away from the Houses of Parliament: end of a late-night debate. There's a police car parked at the entrance to Downing Street. You wrote a piece about the government for one of the Sunday papers. Nobody paid much attention. When the tramp back at the studio wrote about JFK's assassination for *Playboy*, they paid him five thousand dollars. And he got to spend the day at Hefner's mansion. You're sure the band have been there, too. Anita probably wasn't invited.

'Christ!' she shrieks, so that you flinch at the steering-wheel. 'I've had the most *amazing* idea!'

She's ordering you to turn the car round, cursing you for taking her so far from the studio. You don't even know whose car it is. But you bend to her urgency, take the Bentley up on to a pavement as you swing back in the direction you've just come. Back to the studio, where Anita *flies* into the recording room.

And now she's back again, gathering everyone together. Even the writer wakes to her spell. There's a French director there, too – Godard, isn't it? He has a film crew with him. He tried to talk to you about anarchy yesterday, but his English and your French conspired against the dialogue. A circle is forming around the microphone. You've all got headphones on, and finally, after instructions from Anita, the track begins to play. Anita leads you all in the dance. Percussion, then the lead vocal with piano accompaniment. On the periphery, you can see the band. They're in the production suite with the engineer. They look tired, indulgent. Maybe just drunk. Then Anita raises her hand. It's just about time.

'Ooo-ooo! Ooo-ooo!'

'Ooo-ooo! Ooo-ooo!'

And you're the banshee in a rock and roll band . . .

Where is this party? The tall windows are draped with black velvet. Candles; red lightbulbs; batik scarves thrown over lampshades. Sweet herbal fug in the air. Drug cocktails a speciality *de la maison*. The host – you've barely spoken with him – is minor aristocracy according to one of your sources, dabbles in the stock market according to another. The food has mostly gone. Guests have been folding up multiple slices of smoked salmon and cramming them into already bloated cheeks.

It's hard to tell because of the lighting, but nobody looks really *well*. Faces are pierrot white, or would be in daylight, in sunshine. Is there sunshine outside? Watches are being removed at the door, taken away and hidden by the host. No clocks. No telephones, radio, TV.

'We're out of time,' he'd said, smiling. 'This party does not exist in time. And we keep on partying till nineteen-seventy.'

You'd felt like asking him how anyone would know when nineteen-seventy arrived, but then someone had passed you a joint and you hadn't asked any questions after that for quite a while.

What was it? Not just hash: hash you can handle. Some altogether weightier matter: a touch of heroin in the mix? A well-toked speedball? There's music playing, and bodies strewn over the floor and the sofas and the scatter-cushions. You were brought here by two of your subjects – you've begun to think of them as 'subjects', not that you're their master, quite the reverse – but now you can't see anyone you know. Jeff the Nose has been and gone. Klein was invited apparently, but no way would he show: rumours of contract difficulties, of money owed. A Beatle . . . did a blessed Beatle drift past your eyeline an hour or more ago? And did he look too mortal?

Kenneth Anger was in town, but declined your request for an interview. He had conversations with your subjects behind closed doors. Some people think Anger is a *magus*. You know who he wants to cast in his next film, *Lucifer Rising*. You know who he thinks would make the perfect Lucifer, the preterperfect Beelzebub.

Everyone knows.

You've been reading a book, *The Master and Margarita*.

Marianne gave it to Mick. Bulgakov's novel gave him notions; hardened up 'Tea and Sympathy', turned it into something stranger and more wonderful. You wonder if it'll get airtime. You didn't just sing backing vocals on that song, you became part of something bigger.

Something you've so far failed to put into words.

A woman is handing you a joint. Her eyelashes are thickened to spider legs. Her long straw-coloured hair has been braided and piled atop her head, looking like coiled snakes.

'Medusa,' you intone. 'Will you turn me to stone?'

She ignores the question, asks you something about Clapton, and you're shaking your head as you inhale.

'Bailey?' she tries. You shake your head again and she moves away, her snakes writhing, but that's all right, because inside your head you can hear percussion and jungle vocals.

Primal: that's the word you've been searching for . . . And now you have it, you don't know what to do with it.

The party is carried along by its own momentum. Guests come and go, but the core group stays, becoming stronger. Then suddenly a decision is made and everyone's groping for jackets and scarves, flouncing out of the flat and down the stairs. It's evening, and the fresh air feels like nothing you've ever experienced. You suck it in, and listen to the traffic. Cars and taxi cabs, everyone's heading somewhere and you're part of the flow. A ten-minute ride, and you're spilling out of the vehicles, scurrying back indoors. A nightclub this time, the Vesuvio. You've been here before, but never in such exalted company.

There's someone tugging at your sleeve. You're wearing the ruffled white shirt which you've been told makes you 'ever so slightly Byronic'. An arm around your shoulder, lips pressed to your ear.

'From now on, sweetcakes,' you hear, 'everything's strictly off the record. Deal?'

Of course it's a deal. And you're in.

Is that McCartney over there? Gifts are being unwrapped: it's Mick's twenty-sixth. Hard to believe, all the history he's made. Christ, anything's possible. It's 1968 and everything's spinning, the world reaching out. Godard – you're sure now it's him – has his arms outstretched. A painted woman falls into them. Is she really naked, or does she just look that way? You're seeing everything through a lens. You're hearing everything in glorious stereophonic. You're ceasing to see the world in terms of *words*, except when they're lyrics.

The DJ announces something very special. That percussive opening again, really cranked up this time. Hairs begin to rise on your arms. People invade the dance floor. They writhe, they squirm. The wine is blood-red and warm. Your knees are refusing to lock. They send you down on to all fours, the glass tumbling and smashing.

'Good dog,' someone says, rubbing your hair. 'Good and faithful servant.'

He's wearing sandals and tight red trousers. You recognise the voice, of course. You force yourself to look up towards his face, but see only radiance.

And the record plays on.

A respectful amount of time later, when the album has finished and the crowd has finished its applause, McCartney hands the DJ something his own band have been working on. The crowd sway and sing along to the chorus. St Jude – patron saint of lost causes. The song seems to go on for ever. And it's so sad, so personal, and emotional, you begin to cry.

A week later, you're still crying.


The album isn't going to be released. Both record companies – UK and US – want the sleeve changed. They don't like toilet humour. You'd made your own humble suggestions about possible graffiti, and managed to feel snubbed when none were taken up.

'Toilet wall,' someone commented. 'Brilliant idea, just

perfect. 'Cos that's where this decade's headed: straight down the shitter.'

You wondered at the time what he was talking about. But the first single, released into a summer of street riots, has already been banned in some American cities. The band is never far from a news story, which is why your magazine has given you so much leeway. Not that they'll give you any more money, but they'll wait another month or so for the *real* commentary, the last word on the drenched hedonism of rock and roll.

Let them wait. The story no longer matters to you. What matters is a sense you have of where things are headed. Which is why you're enraged when Mick makes his film and you're not allowed on the set. He's acting with Anita. There are tensions there to be exploited. Then Marianne loses the baby she's been carrying, and you can't help wondering about signs and portents.

You talk to Brian about it. He's moved into A. A. Milne's old house, and wants to show you around. He says you can feel free to take a dip in the pool, but you refuse. His voice, always a quiet lisp, seems already otherworldly. He has big ideas and a nice sense of betrayal. He tells you again that you can swim any time you like. You were never much of a swimmer, and now you feel like you're sinking. More uppers, more downers, and more of everything in between. The magazine gives up on you, but another shows interest. Everyone thinks you have *access*. Only you know the truth. The access you want, the only access that matters, is the one you'll always be denied. You've captured barely a glimmer of the story.

Your original employer hears about your new employer and decides to sue. Ugly bits of paper fly around your head, full of legalese and figures. Lawyers want your notes and tapes. They want everything you produced. You hand over a single sheet; five hundred words. You lie about everything else, and spend three weeks in your freezing flat, promising your agent (who has promised a West End producer) that you're writing a new play. Another black comedy.

'But angry, yes?' your agent says.

You drop the receiver back into its cradle.

Then you get word of the filming. A TV special, to be recorded over two days. The audience will be in fancy dress. Top acts and circus sideshows. You go along, but are disappointed. On the studio set, you're too obviously a spectator rather than a participant. There's a distance there that you cannot bridge.

You pick up a girl, take her home. She sees your place and immediately becomes less impressed. You play her the record, but there's no way of proving that you were there, that you're part of it. You play her a section from one of your interviews, but the words seem to bore her. She only really perks up when you wheel out the drugs. You owe Jeff the Nose sixty quid for the goods, and only went to him because you owe the others so much they've stopped your supply. Friends aren't as patient as they used to be. You were in a pub in Camden the other night, telling your story, and someone called out: 'Change the fucking record. That one's been played to death.'

Everyone laughed, until you swept your arm across the table, sending the glasses flying.

Your agent is discouraging. 'No one's going to hand over a single halfpenny on the strength of three first-act scenes.'

So you write a fourth.

And then it's 1969. And Brian's out of the group.

And Brian's dead.


You're there for the free concert: just another face in the crowd. The entourage – the powers – know you never finished your article. They think you never will. When the box of butterflies is opened, you're close enough to the stage to see that many of them have already expired. It's July: hotter than hell's fire. Mick looks well. He's heading for

Australia to make another film. You didn't even bother trying for permission to tag along.

But you *have* finished your play. It ended up being performed in Hampstead, didn't transfer to the West End. The critics were scornful, but it got your name back into contention for a little while, and you've been offered some film work, script doctoring in Hollywood. You know a few writers out there, Brits who went for money over sensibility. One novelist who wrote the first two parts of what was going to be England's great postwar trilogy, then legged it at the first sniff of dollars and a nicely tanned coastline. You spoke to him by telephone; he told you to jump at the chance.

You jumped.

Hated Los Angeles. Heard that Marianne had recovered from an overdose. Keith and Anita were in Cheyne Walk, and had created a new magic circle of friends, people who shared their habits. You almost allowed yourself a cruel smile when the money wars became public, Klein the chief suspect. You knew they'd tour: they'd have to. How else to dig themselves out of the financial hole? And you knew they'd hit the west coast. And you knew you'd be waiting.

The script doctors got together to tell stories about past Hollywood prisoners: Faulkner, Fitzgerald, Chandler, all of whom had liked a drink. Alcohol hadn't bothered the moguls. Drugs didn't seem to bother them either – just as long as the work got done. That was your problem: hope and work just didn't mix. You had an apartment in Studio City, but the walls were too close together and the view from your window was a concrete wall. You joked that there was more room in your car, a T-Bird you'd bought from a TV actor who was up on a DUI charge. He was hoping to persuade the court that he was shedding his old life. The consensus was, he'd win his case; he played pretty well to an audience, had some stage work behind him.

You liked to get out of the city, drive up the coast, even when it was hazy. *Especially* when it was hazy. You loved the feeling of driving into something you couldn't see; loved when each curve in the road surprised you. It was like driving into the future. You told a girl about your feelings. She said the image wasn't new, mentioned its use in a novel a few years back.

It was the first novel by the sleepy American. He still hadn't produced a follow-up, and amazingly this had only increased his profile, the non-book taking on heroic status. All he had to do was claim he'd finished another chapter, and it was the talk of the coffee shops.

You saw him once in Haight-Ashbury, stumbling along at the roach-end of the hippy dream. San Francisco had the Airplane and the Dead, but LA had The Doors, and it seemed to you that LA was the true indicator of the way things were going. Nobody much cared when Lennon handed back his MBE. The much greater gesture belonged to Charles Manson and his 'family'. *Everyone* in your circle was talking about that.

Then there was Vietnam, and the Panthers: violence no longer content to bubble beneath the haze. And then the band came to the Los Angeles Forum, riding on the back of hiked ticket prices and rising bad will. The underground press (no longer underground) had the knives out from the start, which didn't stop you paying your $8.50. You made a half-hearted attempt at breaching the backstage defences, but didn't recognise any of the faces.

'Do you have any authority?' one of the security goons asked, and you had to admit to yourself that you did not.

The show itself was okay. They were playing tracks from the new album – your moment of fame was already history. The band had moved on; the new songs seemed obsessed with downfall and mayhem. The last track seemed to you to be waving goodbye to everybody's good times. You doubted the Panthers and the Angels would disagree.

It was typical of the band to want to replicate Woodstock's good feelings. Typical that they misjudged the way the world's mood had travelled since then. Their own free concert was by way of an apology for ticket scams and all that ill-feeling. You knew it wasn't going to be that easy.

For a start, the drugs had moved on. Everything was bad: diluted, cut with poison, lethal. You were a pro; you could probably give Keith lessons on where to score. You had managed to pull yourself away from the siren call of heroin, but the acid seemed to be giving you more bad trips than good ones. Nevertheless, on the day, you took a proffered tab from a complete stranger.

And tripped.

In cold black light, explosions strafing the sky. The sound system consisted of alarm bells and artillery. The crowd was hungry, tired, concussed. They needed everything they weren't getting. The medicos couldn't cope with the trauma victims. Word went around: 'Don't touch any acid you're not sure of.' But you already had. And you'd handed over money for a single sheet of further trips, little purple stars: an ironic comment on the war in Vietnam? Who gave a shit – you were beyond irony by this point.

You had about a week to go before your employers threw you out. You'd added nothing of inspiration to a 'modern western' they'd asked you to pep up; had failed dismally to pitch them a black comedy about the drug scene in LA. You were not justifying their early faith in you. You were on the road out of Tinseltown.

Back to Blighty: a dismal prospect. You'd already traded the T-Bird to pay off a debt which had come with the promise of a switchblade attached. They'd threatened to cut off your eyelids. That was the way things were now. The most potent threat anyone could make was to stop you ceasing to see.

You'd hitched down here with a friend. The traffic had forced you out of the car five miles from the field, and you'd promptly lost your friend in the crowd. Not that he'd be your friend for long: you owed him money, too, and were planning to fly off without making good.

You were way past 'making good'.

You noticed them early on, the Angels. They revved their engines, clearing a path for several dozen hogs, which they parked in front of the stage, creating a security cordon. And then the guest bands started coming on, and it got colder, and trouble flared. Pool cues and motorbike chains. Ugly cries and gashed heads. Pleas from the stage going unheeded, an Angel going up there to pick a fight with a stoned musician.

You were standing next to this black guy when the headliners – your old muckers – finally came on. Your whole body was numb, but your brain was alive with sparks. The air felt malign; the hairs once more rose on your arms. Violence broke out again.

'This is heavy,' the black guy said. You offered him a tab of your acid, showed him the little purple stars.

'I sang backing on this,' you shouted. The black guy nodded. 'In the studio,' you persisted. 'I'm there on the album.'

He nodded again, but you knew he wasn't listening. You were humming now; brimful of brimstone. And up there on the stage they were playing your tune.

'This is it, man,' you yelled at your new friend, slapping him on the back. 'This is us! This is what it's all about! Come on!' And you gave him a push that sent him jogging down to the front, right into the phalanx of guards. You stayed back. You watched. You saw silver flash in the darkness. A gun? A knife? Your friend went down and was swallowed up by denim jackets and leathers. People started screaming, showing bloodied palms to the band on the stage. Over the microphone, a doctor was requested.

*The cusp of devilment, my friend . . .*

You nodded to yourself, jungle drums dying in your ears. The sacrifice had been made. The energy had been earthed. Anger's Lucifer had been appeased.

Or whatever.

And the sky made a song of your cries . . .

# Unlucky in Love, Unlucky at Cards

Unlucky at cards, lucky in love: isn't that how the saying goes?

Which is why Chick Morrison went to the casino the night his wife finally walked out. She'd left a note explaining that she wasn't leaving *him*; it was just that she couldn't stand his habits any longer. He tore her note up. It had taken her several attempts: the rejects were little crumpled balls in the kitchen bin. He lifted each one out and spread them on the table, trying to work out their chronological sequence. It wasn't just a matter of the shortest one being the first attempt: each began on a different tack.

She was leaving him because she felt lost, and had to find herself.

She was leaving him because it would be cruel not to.

She was leaving him – well, he had to admire her for all the effort she'd taken, all the effort she'd felt he merited. Or maybe she just didn't want him going after her. The thing was, he'd already started – started and finished, really. He'd been following her on and off for three weeks, had seen her enter the man's house, had watched her leave, patting her hair back into place. He'd taken to tailing the man, too, not knowing why: wondering, maybe, if he could learn something, something about the kind of man his wife wanted him to be. But all he'd felt was growing tiredness, and, in a moment of sharp lucidity, that he didn't care any more, didn't love her any more.

Which didn't make it any easier to just let her go. He'd wondered about killing her, making ever more convoluted plans. He knew the problem with murder was that the spouse was always first in the frame. So the murder had to be *perfect*. He needed either a cast-iron alibi or to make sure the body was never found. It was a matter of pride, wasn't it? For years, on and off, he'd enjoyed the fantasy of being the one to walk out, the one to make the break. And now she'd beaten him to it: *she* was the one starting the new life; which meant *he* was the one who'd been left in the lurch. He didn't like that. He resolved to do something about it.

What he did was drive into Aberdeen, park the car, and hit the pubs and clubs. And at closing time, as he was being escorted from the final hostelry, he'd seen lights and smoked-glass doors with an illuminated staircase behind them. The casino.

Lucky at cards, unlucky in love. He'd proven the latter; it was time to give the former a chance.

Walked in, watched for a little while, getting a feel for the place. That was what he did, in his line of work: he tried to fit in as quickly as possible, melt into the scenery. The person you didn't notice as you left your hotel assignation or partook of a final embrace in an apparently empty car park. Those were the moments when Chick would catch you with his camera, making sure you were in the frame.

But that night, he felt he wanted to be seen. So he sat in on a card game. Did all right at first, losing a little here, winning a hand or two there. He was not a natural card-player. He knew how to play, knew all about card-counting, but wasn't up to it. He liked to pretend games were all about luck rather than the playing of percentages.

He wrote out a cheque, backed it with his banker's card. The new stack of chips arrived and he began the dogged task of giving them away. His occasional brash bets were whittled away to steady tosses of a single chip into the pot. It was late into the night; most of the tables were quiet. Gamblers who'd finished for the evening were standing around the table, a phalanx which seemed to constrain those still playing. To get up and leave . . . in front of an *audience*. It would have been like walking away from a fight.

He slid another chip across the smooth green cloth, received a card. There were four people playing, but he felt it had become personal between himself and the sweating man opposite. He could smell the man, could feel his heavy breath brushing his cheek and cooling it. The man had an American accent: fat-cat oil-executive-type. So when his opponent won for the umpteenth time, that was enough for Chick. He had found an escape clause, a way to get out without losing face.

He leapt to his feet, accused the man of cheating. People were telling him to calm down. They were *telling* him he was just not a very good player. Saying it wasn't his night, but there'd be others. He was looking around for whoever had said he wasn't any good. His eyes landed on those of the American, who seemed to be smiling as he pulled the chips in with a thick, hairless arm. Chick pointed at the man.

'I'll have you, pal.'

'If you get lucky,' the man said.

Then there were security men on Chick, hauling him out of there as he yelled back at the table, face red from embarrassment, knowing his escape clause had turned sour on him, same as everything else. One of the other players was leaning over to talk to the fat man as Chick was dragged away. He got the idea the man was telling the winner who his opponent had been.

'Chick Morrison!' Chick called out to the room. 'And don't you ever forget it!'

He spent the next couple of days not answering the phone. There was an answering machine behind the sofa, and he'd lie there listening to the messages. Usually, there was horse-racing on TV, which he watched with the sound down, making mental bets which didn't pay out but didn't cost him anything either.

The messages were not important. There was another

machine at his office, and it would be collecting any offers of work. Eventually, he knew he'd go to the office, get back into a routine. He tried telling himself he was enjoying the break. All he ever did in his job was provide photos for suspicious spouses.

There was nothing from his wife. He thought about heading to her new beau's house – wouldn't *that* surprise them? – but didn't. One or two past and potential clients did call him. His home phone number was part of the message they got if they called his office, though it warned them to call his home only in an emergency. The calls he listened to didn't sound like emergencies. A woman who was on her third husband. She'd had him investigate all three. He'd reported back that they were all good and true and faithful, but she didn't sound convinced.

A man who was on the run from his wife. She wanted maintenance payments, money the man said he didn't have. Now he thought she'd hired a private detective, and wanted to hire one of his own to find out.

And how, Chick wondered, was *he* going to get paid, when the man had no money for maintenance . . . ? Some of these people . . .

But then *she* rang. And the sound of her voice made him replay the tape. And on the third play, he found himself reaching for pen and notepad, taking down her number, calling her back.

'I'm glad you could come in at such short notice,' she said.

It was after hours at the car showroom. She'd told him the door would be open, he could let himself in. To get to her office, he'd walked past a gleaming display of supercars. Chick had never been inside the showroom before; knew there was nothing here he'd be able to afford.

She held out her hand and he took it. She was a well-preserved fifty, expensive hair and just the right amount of make-up. He told her he'd always imagined the J. Gemmell of J. Gemmell Motors would be a man. She smiled.

'Surprises a lot of people. The J's for Jacqueline.'

He sat down opposite her, asked what it was he could do for her. She told him she had a repo job.

'That's what they call it, isn't it?'

Chick nodded, though he wasn't sure himself. He took down details as she told him about the car. It was a top-of-the-range Lexus, bought on credit. The last two monthly payments hadn't come through, and the buyer had done a bunk.

'I put word out discreetly,' she told Chick. 'I don't want it getting about that I'm an easy target. That's where you come in.' She told him a garage on the outskirts of Inverness had reported the Lexus stopping for petrol. The driver had told the attendant he was on his way to his holiday place in the hills above Loch Ness. 'I want you to find him, Mr Morrison, and bring my car back here.'

Chick nodded. He was still nodding as she brought a roll of banknotes from her drawer and proceeded to peel off ten fifties.

'I get a lot of cash customers,' she said with a wink. 'Hard to bank the stuff without the taxman taking an interest.'

Chick pocketed the money. Then he asked for the driver's name.

'Jack Grover,' she told him. 'He has a personalised number plate.' As she went on to describe Grover, a smile spread over Chick's face. She saw it and broke off.

'You know him?'

Chick told her he thought he did. He shrugged like it was the most natural thing in the world, and added that knowing people was his job, after all. She looked impressed. As he was leaving, he had a thought.

'Any chance of a test-drive some day?' he asked.

She smiled at him. 'Bring back my Lexus, you can have your pick of the showroom.'

Chick was actually blushing as he left.

He knew a mechanic in Peterhead who showed him the best

way to get into a Lexus and start it up. It took the mechanic about a minute and a half. He told Chick his teenage son could do it in twenty-eight seconds flat.

On the drive west, thoughts raced through Chick's mind. A body could disappear in a loch and never be found. Then there were the Highlands themselves, remote and unvisited. A corpse could lie there for months, becoming unrecognisable. And the roads around Loch Ness were treacherous . . . an accident could have you over the side.

He asked at the tourist board about holiday cottages in the area, got a list. But it might be a private house, so he bought himself an Ordnance Survey map. Each little black dot was a building. He made a triangle of Inverness, Beauly and Urquhart Castle. Somewhere in here, he felt, he would find the Lexus and its driver, Jack Grover, the man who'd beaten him at cards.

The roads were narrow and steep, the land empty except for the occasional croft or recently built bungalow. He stopped to ask questions, not being subtle about it. A man in a big silver car: had anyone seen him? He was living nearby. He spent two days like this, two days of rejection, silence and slow shakes of the head. Two days spent mostly by himself. To save money and the journey back to Inverness, he slept in his Ford Mondeo, parking it on forest tracks. He knew he needed a shave and change of clothes, but those could wait. He wanted the job finished, because now he had a plan of sorts. It was stupid to blame his wife, to think of harming her. Her new man . . . well, that was for the future maybe. But Jack Grover, on the other hand . . . he just *had* to rub *his* nose in it. Just to show him he could.

He was thinking these things when he found the Lexus. It was parked in full view, outside a two-storey house on the outskirts of Milton. Chick stopped his car by the roadside and looked around. The house seemed quiet. He drove into Milton and left his car there – it could be picked up later. Then, taking his camera with him, he walked back to the Lexus, took another look around, and got to work. He was sweating by the time he'd got the door open and started the ignition. He got his camera ready and sounded the horn, wanting Grover to see him making off in the car, wanting a photo of the moment of triumph. But no one came to the door. Chick tried again; still no one came. He felt deflated as he sped out of the driveway and down to the banks of the loch, taking the road back into Inverness.

But as he crossed the Caledonian Canal, he felt the car's steering slip, and a low juddering from beneath. He pulled over and found that he had a puncture. Cursing silently, he kicked the tyre and opened the boot, looking for a jack and spare tyre.

And found instead a body.

Not any old body, but that of the card player, Jack Grover. Chick stumbled backwards and turned his head to be sick on the verge. Trembling, approaching the boot again, he took a handkerchief out to wipe his mouth. The bundle of notes came with it, floating into the boot. He reached in for them . . . beginning to wonder now. Cash in hand, untraceable . . . Gently, he patted the dead man's pockets and reached a hand into one, bringing out a wallet. He thought he could hear a siren in the distance. There were credit cards in the wallet, and the same name on all of them: James Gemmell. The JG on the numberplate stood for James Gemmell, not Jack Grover.

He saw it in a flash: there was no Jack Grover; no stolen Lexus. There was just Jacqueline Gemmell's husband, who had gone home and told his wife about some drunk in the casino who'd been steamed up at him, a private detective of all things . . .

The sirens were closer now. Chick rubbed his jaw, feeling the rasp of his beard, seeing himself dishevelled and dirty, recalling all the witnesses who would say he'd been looking for a man in a Lexus. And the witnesses at the casino – he'd told them to remember his name . . .

Seeing, with absolute clarity, the way he'd been used by Gemmell's wife, who had found for herself the perfect way to get rid of an unwanted spouse. Chick had been wrong: you didn't need an unbreakable alibi or some obscure hiding-place. All you needed was someone like him, unlucky in love, unlucky at cards. Someone you could put in the frame . . .

# Video, Nasty

You know the videos I mean. They get passed around, brought back from trips to Germany or France or the United States. A case of beer and a few mates round while the ladies are elsewhere. You won't see ladies in these videos, except on the covers. Oh yes, the models on the covers are dolls, but on the tape itself . . . well. Once inside, we are talking gynaecology, and the rougher it gets the rougher the women begin to look. When one of the men suggests anal sex, you can be sure a new woman is about to enter the scene, her eyes as tired and heavy as her flesh, all pucker and tattoo and bruise. I wonder about those bruises sometimes, about coercion and persuasion behind the scenes.

I'm always invited to watch these videos. For two reasons: my working knowledge of French and German, and my technical ability with video recorders. These films aren't always compatible with the British VHS players. You can lose colour, sound, or even the picture. But with a few home-made cables and boxes of tricks everything's made hunky-dory, which pleases my friend Maxwell no end.

'What's that he's saying, Kenny?'

'Which one?' I can see at least three men.

'The one who's talking, idiot.'

'He's saying "faster, faster".'

And Maxwell nods. He looks like he's watching a Buñuel film, my translation crucial to his understanding and appreciation of the director's intent. But the film we're watching, along with Andrew, Mark and Jimmy, has the same *dénouement* as the dozen or so others in Maxwell's mews flat. Despite being a bachelor, he keeps these videos tucked away in the wardrobe in his bedroom. I think for him the furtiveness is part of the fun; perhaps even all the fun. I look around at my friends' faces. They are like kids at a birthday party watching Goofy cartoons. They say you can choose your friends, but that's a lie. My life, I am sure, is a closed loop, like the eight-track cartridges you still find at car boot sales, along with Betamax video recorders and broken Rolf Harris Stylophones.

Look at Maxwell. I didn't choose him. On our first day at school we just happened to sit together. The next day, it seemed polite to do the same (and besides, the other desks and chairs were already occupied). We never had much in common. More, certainly, when at school than at university. And more at university than since. Maxwell is still single, has a fabulous job (with attendant car and home in the right part of town), and sees life as a series of challenges. I am married, in a dead-end career, with an ailing automobile and a tenement flat. My life too is a series of challenges. But where Maxwell spends his time trying to work out which gorgeous woman to date next, or where next to go for a sun-drenched holiday, I spend my time worrying over mortgage, overdraft, car insurance and council tax.

One night a week, I slip out from Alice's clutches for the euphemistic 'pint with the lads'. We meet up in the same pub, then visit a new pub where Maxwell will chat up the barmaid, and take carry-out food back to his place where we might watch a video or play cards. Since the videos are all basically the same video, Maxwell attempts variety by trying to freeze-frame the come shot, fast-forward through the humping, or slo-mo the oral sex. I think this irritates the others, not just me. And at the end of it all, Maxwell has the same comment ready for me. A comment whose surface envy disguises a deeper sense of superiority.

'Of course,' he'll say, 'Kenny's the lucky one. He spends all day surrounded by teenage lovelies.'

Of course I do. It's one of the schoolteacher's few perks.

*

You're asking yourself: what does all this have to do with the fact that Alice was eventually put away for murder? And I answer that it's all to do with a video. Because the barmaid reminded me of a model on the cover of one of Maxwell's videos. The video was called 'Asian Brothel Orgy'. No vagueness there. Video titles are seldom open to misinterpretation. You don't look at them and ask yourself, Hm, wonder what that one's about? 'Teenage Dog Orgy' would mean just that, I'm afraid.

Of course, none of 'Asian Brothel Orgy' took place in Asia, and only one model bore any resemblance to someone from that part of the globe. The cover showed a perky blonde and blue-eyed teenager (American, I suppose, like the movie) looking coy and positioned so that, nude, she still showed little of interest to the regular porno customer. She was the tease, the promise of interior revelation.

The back cover of course was a different matter: medical close-ups of penetration and ingestion. The front cover model naturally did not appear in the film. It took me a while to place her. I'm not suggesting that the new lunchtime barmaid did spare-time modelling for porno cassettes, but the two were distinctly similar. I went to the pub most lunchtimes, but seldom paid attention to the staff, being more interested in my beer and the all too occasional presence of Jennie Muir, our French teacher. Actually, it was Jennie's more frequent absences from the pub which put blinkers on me. I'd sit eating crisps, staring into the bag as it emptied, wondering what she'd make of my Friday night translations for Maxwell and the others. 'What's she saying now, Kenny?' 'She's saying "harder harder, faster faster".' When I wanted to watch a video in my own home, I'd try to rent something French, despite Alice's protests that subtitles were too much like hard work. She preferred Steve Martin or Michael Caine over the latest Gallic smash, and had actually unplugged the machine halfway through *Delicatessen*.

'It's anything but delicate,' she'd fumed.

In my short reverie, prior to two crushing hours with the sixth years or an hour of Shakespeare or poetry, I'd stare into the crisp packet and see it as the interior of a nice flat by the river, a small balcony leading to the living-room where Jennie sat on a white leather sofa, sipping Chablis and chuckling àt *Delicatessen*. I proffered more wine, which she accepted. We chinked glasses. Then I folded the crisp packet, tied a knot in it, and tossed it into the ashtray.

It was Frank Marsh who noticed her.

'New barmaid's a smasher,' he said, placing a pint in front of me.

'Really?' Frank taught woodwork. His working knowledge was of planes and drill bits rather than women. He'd been fifty-six years a single man, never having 'seen the point of getting bogged down'. I was a little envious of him. I glanced over my shoulder anyway. 'Christ,' I said, causing Frank to chuckle. She was chatting to a customer, fresh-faced and with a hand resting on one of the beer pumps, slender arms appearing from a baggy white T-shirt. I imagined Jennie Muir having depths of passion and provocation. But there was nothing submerged about the vision in front of me; all was glorious surface.

Inside a few days the lunchtime clientele of our unassuming pub had doubled. Word was getting around. Only later did I equate Donna the barmaid's years, blonde hair and blue eyes with 'Asian Brothel Orgy'. Then I happened to mention it to Maxwell. The biggest mistake of my life, just about.

He turned up one lunchtime with a slap on my shoulder. Startled, I tipped some beer on to my trousers.

'Sorry, Kenny,' he said. 'Here, I'll fetch a cloth.'

When he returned, he already knew her name and her age. 'You were absolutely right,' he told me, watching as I wiped stains from my crotch, 'she's great. And she does look like the bird off the front of the vid.'

'What the hell are you doing here?' I knew Maxwell

worked three miles away from the school and regarded lunch-hours as an anachronism. He shrugged.

'Just passing. My name's Maxwell, by the way.' He shoved a hand out towards Frank Marsh. 'Since Kenny's not going to introduce us.'

Frank blinked towards me. Maxwell was the only one who called me 'Kenny'. At school I was Ken, and to Alice I was always Kenneth. (She managed to make it sound like a rebuke.) I *hated* 'Kenny', and Maxwell knew it. Once or twice I'd responded in kind with Max or even Maxie, but he just smiled fondly and eventually I came back to Maxwell. He'd managed somehow to avoid abbreviations and nicknames at school, while I was (thanks to my parents) already a Kenny when I arrived there. The nearest I got to niggling him was to attempt what I call the 'reverse pun', opening our conversations with the line 'How's Maxwell?' making the 'How's' sound like 'House'. Get it?

'Can I get anyone a drink?' Maxwell asked now. Frank rapidly finished his pint. 'And tell me, do they do food here?' Maxwell stood up. 'No, don't bother. I'll just go ask Donna.'

By this time, you see, Donna had replaced Jennie Muir in my fantasies. Instead of the riverside apartment, there was a stuffy blanketed room, walls painted black and hung with animal skins. Candles flickered on every surface, and in the middle of the floor was a mattress *sans* bedstead. Blood-red wine replaced the chilled Chablis, and there was a frenzy of music on the hi-fi. For nearly two weeks I'd been looking forward to lunchtimes and then going over them again during the subsequent afternoons. I'd broken the ice with Donna, had ascertained that she liked rock and a little bit of jazz, didn't go to watch films but liked 'clubbing' at weekends.

'That's why I work lunchtimes whenever I can, keeps the nights free.' Her pale face surrounded crimson lips. She wore two gold studs in either earlobe. I started to drink a whisky with my beer, just so she'd turn around towards the row of optics, giving me the chance to stare. Her shape seemed near perfect, set off by short hugging skirts and thick black tights. Surface. Everything was *there*. Not like in the videos where the nakedness was so naked that it became clothing in itself.

'I don't know how you can teach in the afternoons,' she said one day. She meant, how could I teach after a couple of pints and a couple of shorts. The answer was: by remote control, literally. I used videos more and more in the classroom, hogging the TV set, showing whatever was vaguely relevant and available. Shakespeare was easy, poetry not. I'd even take a class to the school's video lab – we have some excellent facilities, due to a go-ahead rector who realises that technology is where future jobs lie. (What he doesn't realise is that after hours I often use the video lab's facilities for copying Maxwell's tapes.) I could fill an hour showing the class how to edit films, why the cameraman is so important, and how an editor can make a movie work where the director has failed.

I could do all of this, and still have room in my head for candles and music and animal skins.

Until Maxwell came along. Within a week, he'd fixed a date with Donna, and the first date was followed by a second. One day, I hurried to the pub only to find the manager on reluctant duty.

'She's buggered off,' he informed me. 'Took another job.'

A job Maxwell had found for her, convenient to his own office. When he told me this on the phone that evening, told me while Alice played TV roulette with the remote and ate another packet of crisps, I knew I had to do something. The living-room seemed stuffier than ever, chip fat and salt, blue noise from the television and a sofa full of wife. My life felt horribly scripted, badly acted, its scenes decided long before I'd been cast for the role.

Splice and edit, I thought. Splice and edit. I might not be the director, but I could still save the movie . . .

\*

Just one of those things, I thought to myself. Just one of those crazy things. I couldn't get those two lines out of my head as I stood there over Maxwell's body. I was reassuring myself that I'd only come to his place to talk. To talk about what? That's what the police would ask. To talk about Donna, whom he was dating and I fancied. So you were jealous then, sir?

Officer, I spend most of my life in a state of jealousy.

He'd only fallen down the stairs of course. I'd been apologising as I walked down after him. But he'd lain there very still, and when I hauled him up by the shoulders his head swivelled wildly, neck obviously broken. I checked his pulse anyway, and found nothing.

Only a fall down the stairs . . . except that I pushed him. Oh yes, we'd been arguing. Or rather, I'd been arguing and Maxwell had been laughing at me. We hadn't even got as far as his living-room. I'd been arguing on my way up the stairs, arguing ever since he'd let me in the door. In the hall at the top of the stairs I fairly vented my spleen, until I could feel myself emptying, the anger lessening. Catharsis, I suppose. Or exorcism. But he was still laughing, rocking back on his heels. So I stood there and blinked and then gave him a mighty shove. I only just managed to stop myself tumbling after him. Gripping the banister rail, I watched him sail backwards and begin the thumping descent. It's a steep staircase, uncarpeted, the wood stripped and varnished. I remember the varnish was expensive, but it meant the wood only had to be redone every five years or so.

Just one of those things, I thought to myself. It was lucky Maxwell lived in a mews. Those places are like morgues at the best of times. This one even boasted a dead end, no through traffic. Ground level was all doors and garages, with living-room windows above. Nobody was looking as I dragged Maxwell out of his own door and into the boot of my car. His keys slipped from his trouser pocket, along with some loose change. I scooped it all up and pocketed it.

I was supposed to be fetching fish and chips for our

supper. My excuse to Alice for taking so long was car trouble. I used Maxwell's change to buy the food, parked outside my own flat, and checked the boot was locked. Over supper I'd have a think what to do with Maxwell. Since Alice slept like a horse, I'd have no trouble sneaking out in the dead of night to get rid of the poor bugger. I'd seen enough crime movies to know that I mustn't panic and I must take care. Each take had to be a perfect take, had to be what directors called 'a wrap'. On the way upstairs I unwrapped a hot package and pulled out a chip, dropping it into my mouth. It had a new and vivid flavour.

Not that Alice noticed. If a thing wasn't behind glass and wrapped in Japanese plastic and changeable with one press of the remote, she tended not to see it. She didn't see my heightened colour, or the way I stared at my smeared plate. So passive was she, I almost wanted to blurt out a confession. Just *once* to surprise her. I resisted the temptation of course. As soon as it's out of your mouth, it's in the public domain, and this had to be kept strictly private, strictly between me and God.

It would be interesting, too, to see if I possessed such a thing as a conscience.

By the time we got to bed, I felt I'd explode. I wasn't much nearer working out a plan, my head full of sitcoms and advertising jingles. I cleared my throat.

'Alice, what do you *really* think of Maxwell?'

She was lying on her side, her back to me, one hand supporting her head and the other holding a paperback book.

'Maxwell's all right.' I didn't say anything. 'I feel sorry for him actually.'

'How do you mean?' I was startled. She felt *sorry* for him? She couldn't have surprised me more if she'd said she was carrying his child.

'All that bravado of his, the macho stuff.' She left the explanation at that and returned to her book.

'I don't understand.'

'That, Kenneth, is because you never see things. You and the rest of your cronies.'

'What don't we see?'

'You don't see anything, you don't see anything at all. Now shut up and go to sleep.'

I lay on my back compliantly, wondering whether it was best to feign sleep and wait it out till the wee small hours, or try to get some sleep and trust to my internal alarm clock. I needed to be clear-headed, which suggested sleep. So I closed my eyes and dreamed of a long beach on which I walked for hours and hours, while friends kept swimming ashore as though from some shipwreck.

Alice woke me with a mug of tea and a couple of biscuits. I sat up sluggishly. It had been a long, exhausting night. I looked at the clock: five minutes to eight. My body was stiff, arms aching.

'You look rough,' Alice agreed, starting to dress. I planted my feet on the cold floor and ran fingers through my hair. It took me a while to admit that I'd done nothing about the body in my car-boot.

I'd slept the whole night away.

Over breakfast, I pressed Alice about what she'd said in bed. Her face was grey and puffy like an inmate's. She'd given up looking for a job a year or so ago, and filled her days with shopping, gossip and TV. She gossiped at the shops, often discussing the doings in one or other daytime soap. Her life too was an eight-track cartridge. The sofa had taken her shape, so that I no longer felt comfortable sitting on it. Usually I sat on a beanbag on the floor, reminding myself to get it refilled one of these days. I even ate breakfast (a bowl of cereal) on the beanbag, while Alice sat on the sofa, both of us staring towards breakfast TV with its little onscreen clock in the corner, telling us it would soon be time for work or, in Alice's case, for yet more television.

She ignored my question, so I repeated it.

'What did you mean last night about Maxwell?'

'He's gay.'

'What?'

'Gay.'

I hooted disbelief. 'Who told you that?'

'He did. Well, not in so many words, but women just *know*. The way he talked to me one day . . .'

'When?'

'I don't know, a few months back. He came round, and you'd been kept at school by some meeting.'

'What did he say?'

'He didn't say anything. He sort of talked around it. You had to read between the lines.'

This from someone who didn't even read a newspaper.

'He goes out with loads of women.'

'Exactly,' she said. 'Because he's scared to admit the fact. I bet the reason he's so successful at dating is because his dates are so safe with him.'

'You've been watching too many of those problem-airing programmes.'

She shrugged. But Alice, bless her, had given me an idea. There was a run-down cemetery in the city known to be frequented after dark by gays. What a fine ironic place to dump the body. Then I thought of Donna. If Maxwell *was* gay, I'd killed him needlessly. The whole thing was crazy.

'Why didn't you tell me before?'

'Why should I?' She gave me one of her looks and disappeared into the kitchen. I could hear running water. She was washing her cereal bowl. She hadn't even thought to take mine, empty and on the floor beside me. I stared at the TV. No more porno evenings at Maxwell's flat. No more fucking around with the remote. No reason to leave my own flat on a Friday night . . .

Then, without any warning, the *real* plan leapt into my head, so focused that it seemed like a gift from above.

I took a long detour on my drive to school, stopping at Maxwell's. The lane was as empty as ever. I used his key to let myself in, climbed the stairs quietly and opened his bedroom door. Fingerprints didn't concern me. As a close friend and frequent visitor, my prints would be everywhere anyway. I removed a couple of the videos from Maxwell's wardrobe and while I was there, sniffed around in search of some secret hoard of gay stuff. But I didn't find anything other than some football magazines under the bed.

'Whatever turns you on,' I said to myself as I debated bringing the body back into the flat, but decided against it. I wanted to set everything up before allowing Maxwell to be found. So he stayed in the car-boot all the way to school. I did consider rigor mortis. I wasn't sure about these things, but reckoned he was going to be stiff by the time I got him back to the mews. He'd be all bunched up. I wasn't sure what the police or the pathologist would make of that. TV detectives were infallible, but I had doubts about their real-life counterparts. I hoped my doubts were well founded.

The two free periods before lunch were my real break. There was no one in the video lab, so I could edit to my heart's content. There were three videos in all, two from Maxwell's wardrobe and one from his living-room. This last video was shot at one of his parties. You know the sort of video I mean. The camera is aimed at you, so you open your mouth and eyes wide and wave wildly into the lens, sometimes saying something crass at the same time. Either that or you studiously ignore the contraption, despite the film-maker's enticements. And you still look a prat. Of course, Maxwell being behind the camera most of the time, there were lots of shots of the women in their party dresses, with attendant leg and cleavage, Max calling out a cod director's 'Enthuse, darlings, I want some passion from you!'

After an hour, I had basically what I wanted. It didn't look great. I wasn't at all sure that it looked even halfway persuasive, and I was about to drop the whole scheme, but there was fever in my brain now. It was all or nothing. I was risking all my winnings on another turn of that wheel.

Greedy, that's what I was. Avarice was my sin of the moment.

'To hell with it, it'll do.'

I knew the police wouldn't be watching for clues anyway. They'd be watching for other things, and finding them.

During the lunch-hour, I drove back to the mews, this time pulling Maxwell out of the boot and laying him at the bottom of the stairs. Who could tell, maybe the whole thing would be taken for an accident after all. I didn't put the porn videos back in the wardrobe – they were *en route* to the dump – but I did put my little home-made ensemble in there. Then I sat down in Maxwell's study and switched on his word processor. I'd been thinking about the letter, and it proved easy to write. I read it through and it seemed convincing, so I printed it out. Then I crumpled the sheet of paper and placed it beneath the occasional table at the top of the stairs.

I was back in the study, checking everything was as it should be, when the downstairs door opened. For a hysterical second I thought: It's him! Maxwell's back! How was I going to explain . . . ?

But then I heard a sort of squeal, and a protracted thud. I tiptoed into the hall and looked down. A middle-aged woman was lying inside the door. Maxwell's cleaning lady. I'd never set eyes on her before, but I knew he had a 'Mrs Mop': he never tired of repeating the fact. I crept quickly downstairs and out of the door, and kept my eyes on the rearview mirror all the way back along the mews.

It all moved surprisingly slowly, I thought. In the movies they wrap up these sorts of cases within a good ninety minutes (or occasionally a supremely lousy ninety minutes), but even after we buried Maxwell no one had been asking the obvious questions. Then one evening Mark and Jimmy phoned, one after the other. Both had the same story to tell. They'd been asked to go along to the police station, and there had been shown a video recording. Both said the same thing.

'They told me not to mention anything to you, but I thought . . . you know. You being a mate and all.'

And then there was a ring at the doorbell. Alice answered, and after a few moments came back into the living-room. She didn't look well.

'It's the police,' she said. 'They want to talk to me about Maxwell. Down at the station.'

And indeed there were two grim-faced constables loitering on the stairwell.

'What's going on?' I asked them.

'Nothing to worry about, sir,' said the more loquacious of the pair.

Well, I thought, thank God for that.

I didn't go with Alice. I lay along the sofa, finding it curiously comfortable. The TV wasn't on. I stared at the blank screen until, hours later, there was the sound of a key shivering in the lock. Alice looked exhausted and numb. Without demur she flopped on to the beanbag.

'You won't believe this,' she said. 'They think I had something to do with it.'

I sat up. 'What?'

'They think there was something going on. Between Maxwell and me.'

'What?' This time I stood up. Alice eyed the empty sofa, so I sat back down again. 'They think what?'

So she told me about the interrogation. She called it that, not an interview but an interrogation. A nice WPC who didn't say anything except when the two fat male detectives left the room.

'She asked me if I wanted a cup of tea.'

The whole thing had been tape-recorded. 'They kept on at me about Maxwell, how well I knew him, what he was like, did we ever see one another alone. Christ, he was *your* friend, not mine. Besides, I told them he was gay. One of them smiled. He didn't say anything, but he grinned and shook his head at me.' She looked like she might cry, but only for a moment. Soon enough she was all anger and retribution. She'd talk to our solicitor.

'Solicitor?'

'The one we used to buy this place. I told them, I said I was going to talk to my solicitor.'

'What did they say?'

She swallowed drily. 'They said that might be a good idea.'

The following morning, they came for me.

Not constables this time, but a detective sergeant and another man. The other man drove, while we sat together in the back. The detective sergeant had bloodshot eyes and was overweight. He took me to an interview room where Detective Inspector Claverhouse was waiting. There was a tape recorder on the table between us. On another table sat a TV monitor with a video player built into its base. We had something similar at the school.

It took a lot of questions, some of them about parties I'd attended at Maxwell's flat. Then Inspector Claverhouse rose from his chair.

'There's something we'd like to show you, sir. Just so you can give us an opinion.'

Although they must have watched the video a dozen times, they still drank it in, especially the latter sections. Then they turned to me.

'Well,' I said, 'the first bit . . . with my wife . . .'

'You recognise your wife then?'

'Oh yes,' I said. 'That was her. At a party of Maxwell's. I didn't realise he'd taken so much film of her.' He hadn't, of course. After a while he'd handed the camera to me, and I'd concentrated for a few minutes on Alice, trying to work out if she looked better or worse through a lens. Better was the answer. The distance helped, and she did possess a camera-ready figure.

'And the, er, material after that?' said Inspector Claverhouse.

I raised my eyebrows and exhaled. 'Looks like something home-made,' I replied. 'I know it's said that couples will rent video cameras for a weekend so they can record . . . you know.'

'But they don't need to rent the camera if they already own one,' said Claverhouse.

'True.'

Claverhouse ejected the tape and examined it. 'You couldn't identify the participants?'

I smiled bleakly. 'You didn't exactly see their faces.' Of course you didn't, I'd made sure of that. But I'd also chosen models whose physical shape was at least similar to Maxwell and Alice. I didn't think anyone would notice that part of the way through the male model actually changed identity. By that stage, all you could see was skin and hair. Claverhouse was looking at the spine of the videotape.

'True enough, I just wondered. There's some writing on here, just initials. MG and AB. What do you make of that?'

I stared at him, then at the detective sergeant, and laughed uneasily. 'Come *on*,' I said. 'What are you trying to say?'

'Nothing, sir.'

'You know damned fine MG is Maxwell, and you're implying AB is my wife.'

'Your wife *is* on the tape, sir.'

'Yes, but not . . .' I nodded towards the machine. 'I mean, it's not them doing . . .' My voice died away again. 'It's not,' I said quietly. I did not tell a lie. The two detectives understood. Inspector Claverhouse sat down again.

'There's also a letter, sir,' he said sympathetically. 'It appears to be from Maxwell Gray to someone called Alice. Perhaps you'd care to take a look.' He produced a photocopy of the crumpled sheet for me to read. I read through it twice.

'Alice, there's no easy way to put this. I want out, pure

and simple. It's not your fault, it's mine; or maybe it's neither's fault. I don't know any more. It would break Kenny's heart if he found out, you know that. Not that he would find out, he's too stupid, too guileless. But that just makes me feel all the more guilty. I hope you can understand. I hope we can still be friends. Maxie.'

Two notes jarred. He wouldn't have called himself Maxie, but then the police weren't to know that. It had just been devilment on my part. But neither would he have used a semicolon. Only people like me use semicolons in this day and age. I doubted CID would notice this either. I looked up at Inspector Claverhouse. There were tears in my eyes. Then I broke down altogether.

And still it dragged on.

With Alice under suspicion, I became her champion, protecting her from police and media alike. She didn't understand any of it. How could there be a letter? How could there be a video? It wasn't her on the video, she told Claverhouse. It wasn't. I backed her up. I was sweating about that video. If the police watched it often enough – and I didn't doubt it was required viewing between shifts at the station – maybe they'd begin to see discrepancies. Then again, all they'd want to watch were the dirty bits, and they would be watching for all the wrong reasons. I'd chosen the seediest, most amateurish tapes in Maxwell's collection. They really did look home-made. The police meantime were interviewing more friends of Maxwell's, and his colleagues. Again and again they called us to interview. It was a wearing process.

They knew they were dealing with manslaughter at least. The pathologist had been able to say that Maxwell had fallen with some force, almost certainly not of his own volition. What's more, the body had been moved, then placed back at the foot of the stairs, as if someone had thought to dispose of it, but been unable to. A woman, for example, might not have the weight and power necessary to shift such a load very far.

It turned out, of course, that the police had wanted to prosecute at quite an early stage, but the Crown Office kept pressing for more evidence. At one stage, it seemed that the inquiry was turning more towards me. For a few days I looked like a chief suspect, but by then I was confident the police were just fishing (and *sans* hooks at that). When they'd wheelbarrowed enough information over to the Crown Office, someone must have decided something should happen. Everyone took one step forward. There was to be a trial. A trial not for manslaughter but for murder.

The police produced a witness, a neighbour of Maxwell's who was sure she'd seen a woman of Alice's description going in and out of the flat at irregular intervals. I took a deep breath, and began to view Alice for the first time with suspicion. What if the two of them had *really* been . . . ? And all her talk to me of Maxwell being gay was just to throw me off the scent? Was there to be a brilliant twist right at the end of the film? I asked Alice, but she denied and denied. She'd lost some weight, a lot of weight actually. And the fire had disappeared from her eyes. She wasn't the same woman she'd been. She was obedient to commands, compliant, weepily grateful for my many kindnesses. In other words, she'd been broken. I liked her more than I had in years.

I was almost determined that she should be found not guilty, and put up a firm performance in the witness box. But the looks I got from those in court were still understanding and sympathetic. I was the faithful husband, faithful right to the end. The jury seemed to ignore me altogether, and brought back a verdict of guilty.

The flat seemed so empty, but soon filled with my own choice of music and video viewing. I worked harder than ever at school, but every night I found some space for reminiscence, mostly of the trial. As a witness, I hadn't been able to soak up much of it, but afterwards I'd made it a sort of hobby, a preoccupation. There had been much talk in court of Maxwell's promiscuous lifestyle, his interest in illicit pornography, his affiliations with barmaids, waitresses, secretaries. A little black notebook was produced, detailing names and telephone numbers. Some of the women had appeared in the witness box. None admitted to having sex with Maxwell, but you could see the type of women they were.

I visited Alice when I could. It was always an interesting experience. I'd considered writing her a letter, explaining that I was a weak man who could not live with the shame and the guilty verdict (it was true that at school both pupils and teachers looked at me oddly), and telling her I'd be filing for divorce. I'd considered it, but rejected it almost as quickly. I don't know why exactly. Maybe it had something to do with the evenings I spent going over old photographs of the pair of us, back in the days of foreign travel and fooling around. I still went for a drink some weekends with Andrew, Mark and Jimmy, and even a few times with Frank Marsh. But mostly I stayed home.

Then one night there was a ring at the doorbell. I got the shock of my life when I answered the door. It was Donna, blue-eyed blonde-haired Donna, looking exquisite and smelling of recent perfume. She just needed to talk, to talk with someone who'd known Maxwell like she'd known him. She missed him so much.

'So do I,' I said.

She collapsed into my gentle arms. I smoothed her hair away from one ear, shushing her. Like a friend. Like a friend.

# Talk Show

## AN INSPECTOR REBUS STORY

Lowland Radio was a young but successful station broadcasting to lowland Scotland. It was said that the station owed its success to two very different personalities. One was the DJ on the mid-morning slot, an abrasive and aggressive Shetland Islander, called Hamish MacDiarmid. MacDiarmid hosted a phone-in, supposedly concerning the day's headlines, but in fact these were of relatively minor importance. People did not listen to the phone-in for opinion and comment: they listened for the attacks MacDiarmid made on just about every caller. There were occasional fierce interchanges, interchanges the DJ nearly always won by dint of severing the connection with anyone more intelligent, better informed, or more rational than himself.

Rebus knew that there were men in his own station who would try to take a break between ten-forty-five and eleven-fifteen just to listen. The people who phoned the show knew what they'd get, of course: that was part of the fun. Rebus wondered if they were masochists, but in fact he knew they probably saw themselves as challengers. If they could best MacDiarmid, they would have 'won'. And so MacDiarmid himself became like some raging bull, entering the ring every morning for another joust with the picadors. So far he'd been goaded but not wounded, but who knew how long the luck would last . . . ?

The other 'personality' – always supposing personality could be applied to someone so ethereal – was Penny Cook, the softly spoken, seductive voice on the station's late-night slot. Five nights a week, on her show *What's Cookin'*, she offered a mix of sedative music, soothing talk, and calming advice to those who took part in her own phone-in segment. These were very different people from those who chose to confront Hamish MacDiarmid. They were quietly worried about their lives, insecure, timid; they had home problems, work problems, personal problems. They were the kind of people, Rebus mused, who got sand kicked in their faces. MacDiarmid's callers, on the other hand, were probably the ones doing the kicking . . .

Perhaps it said something about the lowlands of Scotland that Penny Cook's show was said to be the more popular of the two. Again, people at the station talked about it with the fervour usually reserved for TV programmes.

'Did you hear yon guy with the bend in his tackle . . . ?'

'That woman who said her husband didn't satisfy her . . .'

'I felt sorry for that hooker though, wantin' out o' the game . . .'

And so on. Rebus had listened to the show himself a few times, slumped on his chair after closing-time. But never for more than a few minutes; like a bedtime story, a few minutes of Penny Cook sent John Rebus straight to the land of Nod. He'd wondered what she looked like. Husky, comfortable, come-to-bed: the picture of her he'd built up was all images, but none of them exactly physical. Sometimes she sounded blonde and tiny, sometimes statuesque with flowing raven hair. His picture of Hamish MacDiarmid was much more vivid: bright red beard, caber-tossing biceps and a kilt.

Well, the truth would out. Rebus stood in the cramped reception area of Lowland Radio and waited for the girl on the switchboard to finish her call. On the wall behind her, a sign said WELCOME:. That colon was important. This seemed to be Lowland Radio's way of greeting the personalities who'd come to the station, perhaps to give interviews. Today, below the WELCOME:, written in felt tip were the names JEZ JENKS and CANDY BARR. Neither name meant anything to Rebus, though they probably would to his daughter. The receptionist had finished her call.

'Have you come for some stickers?'

'Stickers?'

'Car-stickers,' she explained. 'Only we're all out of them. Just temporary, we'll be getting more next week if you'd like to call back.'

'No, thanks anyway. I'm Inspector Rebus. I think Miss Cook's expecting me.'

'Oh, sorry.' The receptionist giggled. 'I'll see if she's around. It was Inspector . . . ?'

'Rebus.'

She scribbled the name on a pad and returned to her switchboard. 'An Inspector Reeves to see you, Penny . . .'

Rebus turned to another wall and cast an eye over Lowland Radio's small display of awards. Well, there was stiff competition these days, he supposed. And not much advertising revenue to go round. Another local station had countered the challenge posed by Hamish MacDiarmid, hiring what they called 'The Ranter', an anonymous individual who dished out insult upon insult to anyone foolish enough to call his show.

It all seemed a long way from the Light Programme, a long way from glowing valves and Home Counties diction. Was it true that the BBC announcers used to wear dinner jackets? DJs in DJs, Rebus thought to himself and laughed.

'I'm glad somebody's cheerful.' It was Penny Cook's voice; she was standing right behind him. Slowly he turned to be confronted by a buxom lady in her early forties – only a year or two younger than Rebus himself. She had permed light brown hair and wore round glasses – the kind popularised by John Lennon on one hand and the NHS on the other.

'I know, I know,' she said. 'I'm never what people expect.' She held out a hand, which Rebus shook. Not only did Penny Cook sound unthreatening, she *looked* unthreatening.

All the more mysterious then that someone, some anonymous caller, should be threatening her life . . .

*

They walked down a corridor towards a sturdy-looking door, to the side of which had been attached a push-button array.

'Security,' she said, pressing four digits before pulling open the door. 'You never know what a lunatic might do given access to the airwaves.'

'On the contrary,' said Rebus, 'I've heard Hamish MacDiarmid.'

She laughed. He didn't think he'd heard her laugh before. 'Is Penny Cook your real name?' he asked, thinking the ice sufficiently broken between them.

'Afraid so. I was born in Nairn. To be honest, I don't think my parents had heard of Penicuik. They just liked the name Penelope.'

They were passing studios and offices. Loudspeakers placed in the ceiling of the corridor relayed the station's afternoon show.

'Ever been inside a radio station before, Inspector?'

'No, never.'

'I'll show you around if you like.'

'If you can spare the time . . .'

'No problem.' They were approaching one studio outside which a middle-aged man was in quiet conversation with a spiky-headed teenager. The teenager looked sullen and in need of a wash. Rebus wondered if he were the man's son. If so, a lesson in parental control was definitely needed.

'Hi, Norman,' Penny Cook said in passing. The man smiled towards her. The teenager remained sullen: a controlled pose, Rebus decided. Further along, having passed through another combination-lock door, Penny herself cleared things up.

'Norman's one of our producers.'

'And the kid with him?'

'Kid?' She smiled wryly. 'That was Jez Jenks, the singer with Leftover Lunch. He probably makes more a day than you and I make in a good year.'

166

Rebus couldn't remember ever having a 'good year' – the curse of the honest copper. A question came to him.

'And Candy Barr?'

She laughed at this. 'I thought my own name took some beating. Mind you, I don't suppose it's her real name. She's an actress or a comedienne or something. From across the water, of course.'

'Doesn't sound like an Irish name,' Rebus said as Penny Cook held open her office door.

'I wouldn't make jokes around here, Inspector,' she said. 'You'll probably find yourself being signed up for a spot on one of our shows.'

'The Laughing Policeman?' Rebus suggested. But then they were in the office, the door was closed, and the atmosphere cooled appropriately. This was business, after all. Serious business. She sat at her desk. Rebus sat down on the chair across from her.

'Do you want a coffee or anything, Inspector?'

'No thanks. So, when did these calls start, Miss Cook?'

'About a month ago. The first time he tried it, he actually got through to me on-air. That takes some doing. The calls are filtered through two people before they get to me. Efficient people, too. They can usually tell a crank caller from the real thing.'

'How does the system work? Somebody calls in . . . then what?'

'Sue or David takes the call. They ask a few questions. Basically, they want to know the person's name, and what it is they want to talk to me about. Then they take a telephone number, tell the caller to stay by his or her telephone, and if we want to put the person on-air, they phone the caller back and prepare them.'

'Fairly rigorous then.'

'Oh yes. And even supposing the odd crank does get through, we've got a three-second delay on them when they're on-air. If they start cussing or raving, we cut the call before it goes out over the ether.'

'And is that what happened with this guy?'

'Pretty much.' She shook a cassette box at him. 'I've got the tape here. Do you want to hear?'

'Please.'

She started to load a cassette player on the ledge behind her. There were no windows in the office. From the number of steps they'd descended to get there, Rebus reckoned this whole floor of the building was located beneath ground-level.

'So you got a phone number for this guy?'

'Only it turned out to be a phone box in some housing scheme. We didn't know that at the time. We never usually take calls from phone boxes. But it was one of those ones that use the phone cards. No beeps, so nobody could tell.' She had loaded the tape to her satisfaction, but was now waiting for it to rewind. 'After he tried getting through again, we phoned his number. It rang and rang, and then some old girl picked it up. She explained where the box was. That was when we knew he'd tricked us.' The tape thumped to a stop. She hit the play button, and sat down again. There was hiss as the tape began, and then her voice filled the room. She smiled in embarrassment, as if to say: yes, it's a pose, this husky, sultry, late-night me. But it's a living . . .

'And now we've got Peter on line one. Peter, you're through to Penny Cook. How are things with you this evening?'

'Not so good, Penny.'

She interrupted the tape for a moment: 'This is where we cut him off.'

The man's voice had been sleepy, almost tranquillised. Now it erupted. 'I know what you're up to! I know what's going on!' The tape went dead. She leaned back in her chair and switched off the machine.

'It makes me shiver every time I hear it. That anger . . . such a sudden change in the voice. Brr.' She reached into her drawer and brought out cigarettes and lighter. Rebus accepted a cigarette from her.

'Thanks,' he said. Then: 'The name'll be false, of course, but did he give a surname?'

'A surname, an address, even a profession. He said he lived in Edinburgh, but we looked up the street name in the *A to Z* and it doesn't exist. From now on, we check that addresses are real before we call back. His surname was Gemmell. He even spelt it out for Sue. She couldn't believe he was a crank, he sounded so genuine.'

'What did he tell her his problem was?'

'Drinking too much . . . how it was affecting his work. I like that sort of problem. The advice is straightforward, and it can be helping a lot of people too scared to phone in.'

'What did he say his job was?'

'Bank executive. He gave Sue the bank's name and everything, and he kept saying it wasn't to be broadcast.' She smiled, shook her head. 'I mean, this nut really was *good*.'

Rebus nodded. 'He seems to have known the set-up pretty well.'

'You mean he got to the safe without triggering any of the alarms?' She smiled still. 'Oh yes, he's a real pro.'

'And the calls have persisted?'

'Most nights. We've got him tagged now though. He's tried using different accents . . . dialects . . . always a different name and job. But he hasn't managed to beat the system again. When he knows he's been found out, he does that whole routine again. "I know what you've done." Blah, blah. We put the phone down on him before he can get started.'

'And what *have* you done, Miss Cook?'

'Absolutely nothing, Inspector. Not that I know of.'

Rebus nodded slowly. 'Can I hear the tape again?'

'Sure.' She wound it back, and they listened together. Then she excused herself – 'to powder my nose' – and Rebus listened twice more. When she returned, she was carrying two plastic beakers of coffee.

'Thought I might tempt you,' she said. 'Milk, no sugar . . . I hope that's all right.'

'Thank you, yes, that's just the job.'

'So, Inspector, what do you think?'

He sipped the lukewarm liquid. 'I think,' he said, 'you've got an anonymous phone-caller.'

She raised her cup, as though to toast him. 'God bless CID,' she said. 'What would we do without you?'

'The problem is that he's probably mobile, not sticking to the same telephone kiosk every time. That's supposing he's as clever as he seems. We can get BT to put a trace on him, but for that you'd have to keep him talking. Or, if he gives his number, we can trace him from that. But it takes time.'

'And meanwhile he could be slipping off into the night?'

'I'm afraid so. Still, apart from continuing to fend him off and hoping he gets fed up, I can't see what else can be done. You don't recognise the voice? Someone from your past . . . an ex-lover . . . someone with a grudge?'

'I don't make enemies, Inspector.'

Looking at her, listening to her voice, he found that easy to believe. Maybe not personal enemies . . .

'What about the other radio stations? They can't be too thrilled about your ratings.'

Her laughter was loud. 'You think they've put out a contract on me, is that it?'

Rebus smiled and shrugged. 'Just a thought. But yours *is* the most popular show Lowland has got, isn't it?'

'I think I'm still just about ahead of Hamish, yes. But then Hamish's show is just . . . well, Hamish. My show's all about the people themselves, the ones who call in. Human interest, you could say.'

'And there's plenty of interest.'

'Suffering is always interesting, isn't it? It appeals to the voyeur. We *do* get our fair share of crank calls. Maybe that's why. All those lonely, slightly deranged people out there . . .

listening to me. Me, pretending I've got all the answers.' Her smile this time was rueful. 'The calls recently have been getting . . . I don't know whether to say "better" or "worse". Worse problems, better radio.'

'Better for your ratings, you mean?'

'Most advertisers ignore the late-night slots. That's common knowledge. Not a big enough audience. But it's never been a problem on my show. We did slip back for a little while, but the figures picked up again. Up and up and up . . . Don't ask me what sort of listeners we're attracting. I leave all that to market research.'

Rebus finished his coffee and clasped both knees, preparing to rise. 'I'd like to take the tape with me, is that possible?'

'Sure.' She ejected the tape.

'And I'd like to have a word with . . . Sue, is it?'

She checked her watch. 'Sue, yes, but she won't be in for a few hours yet. Night shift, you see. Only us poor disc jockeys have to be here twenty-four hours. I exaggerate, but it feels like it sometimes.' She patted a tray on the ledge beside the cassette player. The tray was filled with correspondence. 'Besides, I have my fan mail to deal with.'

Rebus nodded, glanced at the cassette tape he was now holding. 'Let me have a think about this, Miss Cook. I'll see what we can do.'

'OK, Inspector.'

'Sorry I can't be more constructive. You were quite right to contact us.'

'I didn't suppose there was much you could—'

'We don't know that yet. As I say, give me a little time to think about it.'

She rose from her chair. 'I'll see you out. This place is a maze, and we can't have you stumbling in on the *Afternoon Show*, can we? You might end up doing your Laughing Policeman routine after all . . .'

As they were walking down the long, hushed corridor,

Rebus saw two men in conversation at the bottom of the stairwell. One was a beefy, hearty-looking man with a mass of rumpled hair and a good growth of beard. His cheeks seemed veined with blood. The other man proved a significant contrast, small and thin with slicked-back hair. He wore a grey suit and white shirt, the latter offset by a bright red paisley-patterned tie.

'Ah,' said Penny Cook quietly, 'a chance to kill two birds. Come on, let me introduce you to Gordon Prentice – he's the station chief – and to the infamous Hamish MacDiarmid.'

Well, Rebus had no trouble deciding which man was which. Except that, when Penny did make the introductions, he was proved utterly wrong. The bearded man pumped his hand.

'I hope you're going to be able to help, Inspector. There are some sick minds out there.' This was Gordon Prentice. He wore baggy brown cords and an open-necked shirt from which protruded tufts of wiry hair. Hamish MacDiarmid's hand, when Rebus took it, was limp and cool, like something lifted from a larder. No matter how hard he tried, Rebus couldn't match this . . . for want of a better word, *yuppie* . . . couldn't match him to the combative voice. But then MacDiarmid spoke.

'Sick minds is right, and stupid minds too. I don't know which is worse, a deranged audience or an educationally subnormal one.' He turned to Penny Cook. 'Maybe you got the better bargain, Penelope.' He turned back to Prentice. So that's what a sneer looks like, Rebus thought. But MacDiarmid was speaking again. 'Gordon, how about letting Penny and me swap shows for a day? She could sit there agreeing with every bigoted caller I get, and I could get stuck in about her social cripples. What do you think?'

Prentice chuckled and placed a hand on the shoulder of both his star DJs. 'I'll give it some thought, Hamish. Penny might not be too thrilled though. I think she has a soft spot for her "cripples".'

*

Penny Cook certainly didn't look 'too thrilled' by the time Rebus and she were out of earshot.

'Those two,' she hissed. 'Sometimes they act like I'm not even there! Men . . .' She glanced towards Rebus. 'Present company excluded, of course.'

'I'll take that as a compliment.'

'I shouldn't be so hard on Gordon actually. I know I joke about being here twenty-four hours a day, but I really think he *does* spend all day and all night at the station. He's here from early morning, but each night he comes into the studio to listen to a bit of my show. Beyond the call of duty, wouldn't you say?'

Rebus merely shrugged.

'I bet,' she went on, 'when you saw them you thought it was Hamish with the beard.'

Rebus nodded. She giggled. 'Everybody does,' she said. 'Nobody's what they seem in this place. I'll let you into a secret. The station doesn't keep any publicity shots of Hamish. They're afraid it would hurt his image if everyone found out he looks like a wimp.'

'He's certainly not *quite* what I expected.'

She gave him an ambiguous look. 'No, well, *you're* not quite what *I* was expecting either.' There was a moment's stillness between them, broken only by some coffee commercial being broadcast from the ceiling: '. . . but Camelot Coffee is no myth, and mmm . . . it tastes *so* good.' They smiled at one another and walked on.

Driving back into Edinburgh, Rebus listened, despite himself, to the drivel on Lowland Radio. Advertising was tight, he knew that. Maybe that was why he seemed to hear the same dozen or so adverts over and over again. Lots of airtime to fill and so few advertisers to fill it . . .

'. . . and mmm . . . it tastes *so* good.'

That particular advert was beginning to get to him. It careered around in his head, even when it wasn't being broadcast. The actor's voice was so . . . what was the word?

It was like being force-fed a tablespoon of honey. Cloying, sickly, altogether too much.

'Was Camelot a myth or is it real? Arthur and Guinevere, Merlin and Lancelot. A dream, or—'

Rebus switched off the radio. 'It's only a jar of bloody coffee,' he told his radio set. Yes, he thought, a jar of coffee . . . and mmm . . . it tastes *so* good. Come to think of it, he needed coffee for the flat. He'd stop off at the corner shop, and whatever he bought it wouldn't be Camelot.

But, as a promotional gimmick, there was a fifty-pence refund on Camelot, so Rebus did buy it, and sat at home that evening drinking the vile stuff and listening to Penny Cook's tape. Tomorrow evening, he was thinking, he might go along to the station to catch her show live. He had an excuse after all: he wanted to speak with Sue, the telephonist. That was the excuse; the truth was that he was intrigued by Penny Cook herself.

*You're not quite what I was expecting.*

Was he reading too much into that one sentence? Maybe he was. Well, put it another way then: he had a *duty* to return to Lowland Radio, a duty to talk to Sue. He wound the tape back for the umpteenth time. That ferocious voice. Sue had been surprised by its ferocity, hadn't she? The man had seemed so quiet, so polite in their initial conversation. Rebus was stuck. Maybe the caller *would* simply get fed up. When it was a question of someone's home being called, there were steps you could take: have someone intercept all calls, change the person's number and keep it ex-directory. But Penny Cook needed her number to be public. She couldn't hide, except behind the wall provided by Sue and David.

Then he had an idea. It wasn't much of an idea, but it was better than nothing. Bill Costain at the Forensic Science Lab was keen on sound recording, tape recorders, all that sort of stuff. Maybe he could do something with Mr Anonymous.

Yes, he'd call him first thing tomorrow. He sipped his coffee, then squirmed.

'Tastes more like camel than Camelot,' he muttered, hitting the play button.

The morning was bright and clear, but Bill Costain was dull and overcast.

'I was playing in a darts match last night,' he explained. 'We won for a change. The amount of drink we put away, you'd think Scotland had just done the Grand Slam.'

'Never mind,' said Rebus, handing over the cassette tape. 'I've brought you something soothing . . .'

'Soothing' wasn't the word Costain himself used after listening to the tape. But he enjoyed a challenge, and the challenge Rebus had laid down was to tell him anything at all about the voice. He listened several times to the tape, and put it through some sort of analyser, the voice becoming a series of peaks and troughs.

Costain scratched his head. 'There's too big a difference between the voice at the beginning and the voice when hysterical.'

'How do you mean?' Costain always seemed able to baffle Rebus.

'The hysterical voice is so much higher than the voice at the beginning. It's hardly . . . natural.'

'Meaning?'

'I'd say one of them's a put-on. Probably the initial voice. He's disguising his normal tone, speaking in a lower register than usual.'

'So can we get back to his *real* voice?'

'You mean can we retrieve it? Yes, but the lab isn't the best place for that. A friend of mine has a recording studio out Morningside way. I'll give him a bell . . .'

They were in luck. The studio's facilities were not in use that morning. Rebus drove them to Morningside and then sat back as Costain and his friend got busy at the mixing console. They slowed the hysteric part of the tape; then managed somehow to take the pitch of the voice down several tones. It began to sound more than slightly unnatural, like a Dalek or something electronic. But then they started to build it back up again, until Rebus was listening to a slow, almost lifeless vocal over the studio's huge monitor speakers.

'I . . . know . . . what . . . you've . . . done.'

Yes, there was life there now, almost a hint of personality. After this, they switched to the caller's first utterance – 'Not so good, Penny' – and played around with it, heightening the pitch slightly, even speeding it up a bit.

'That's about as good as it gets,' Costain said at last.

'It's brilliant, Bill, thanks. Can I get a copy?'

Having dropped Costain back at the lab, Rebus wormed his way back through the lunchtime traffic to Great London Road police station. He played this new tape several times, then switched from tape to radio. Christ, he'd forgotten: it was still tuned to Lowland.

'. . . and mmm . . . it tastes *so* good.'

Rebus fairly growled as he reached for the off button. But the damage, the delirious, wonderful damage, had already been done . . .

The wine bar was on the corner of Hanover Street and Queen Street. It was a typical Edinburgh affair in that though it might have started with wine, quiche and salad in mind, it had reverted to beer – albeit mainly of the 'designer' variety – and pies. Always supposing you could call something filled with chickpeas and spices a 'pie'. Still, it had an IPA pump, and that was good enough for Rebus. The place had just finished its lunchtime peak, and tables were still cluttered with plates, glasses and condiments. Having paid over the odds for his drink, Rebus felt the barman owed him a favour. He gave the young man a name. The barman nodded towards a table near the window. The table's sole occupant looked just out of his teens. He flicked a lock of hair back from his forehead and gazed out of the window. There was a newspaper folded into quarters on his knee. He tapped his teeth with a ballpoint, mulling over some crossword clue.

Without asking, Rebus sat down opposite him. 'It whiles away the time,' he said. The tooth-tapper seemed still intent on the window. Maybe he could see his reflection there. The modern Narcissus. Another flick of the hair.

'If you got a haircut, you wouldn't need to keep doing that.'

This achieved a smile. Maybe he thought Rebus was trying to chat him up. Well, after all, this was known as an actors' bar, wasn't it? Half a glass of orange juice sat on the table, the ubiquitous ice-cube having melted away to a sliver.

'Aye,' Rebus mused, 'passes the time.'

This time the eyes turned from the window and were on him. Rebus leaned forward across the table. When he spoke, he spoke quietly, confidently.

'I know what you've done,' he said, not sure even as he said it whether he were quoting or speaking for himself.

The lock of hair fell forward and stayed there. A frozen second, then another, and the man rose quickly to his feet, the chair tipping back. But Rebus, still seated, had grabbed at an arm and held it fast.

'Let go of me!'

'Sit down.'

'I said let go!'

'And I said sit down!' Rebus pulled him back on to his chair. 'That's better. We've got a lot to talk about, you and me. We can do it here or down at the station, and by "station" I don't mean Scotrail. OK?'

The head was bowed, the careful hair now almost completely dishevelled. It was that easy . . . Rebus found the tiniest grain of pity. 'Do you want something else to drink?' The head shook from side to side. 'Not even a cup of coffee?'

Now the head looked up at him.

'I saw the film once,' Rebus went on. 'Bloody awful it was, but not half as bad as the coffee. Give me Richard Harris's singing any day.'

Now, finally, the head grinned. 'That's better,' said Rebus. 'Come on, son. It's time, if you'll pardon the expression, to spill the beans.'

The beans spilled . . .

Rebus was there that night for *What's Cookin'*. It surprised him that Penny Cook herself, who sounded so calm on the air, was, before the programme, a complete bundle of nerves. She slipped a small yellow tablet on to her tongue and washed it down with a beaker of water.

'Don't ask,' she said, cutting off the obvious question. Sue and David were stationed by their telephones in the production room; which was separated from Penny's studio by a large glass window. Her producer did his best to calm things down. Though not yet out of his thirties, he looked to be an old pro at this. Rebus wondered if he shouldn't have his own counselling show . . .

Rebus chatted with Sue for ten minutes or so, and watched as the production team went through its paces. Really, it was a two-man operation – producer and engineer. There was a last-minute panic when Penny's microphone started to play up, but the engineer was swift to replace it. By five minutes to eleven, the hysteria seemed over. Everyone was calm now, or was so tense it didn't show. Like troops just before a battle, Rebus was thinking. Penny had a couple of questions about the running order of the night's musical pieces. She held a conversation with her producer, communicating via mikes and headphones, but looking at one another through the window.

Then she turned her eyes towards Rebus, winked at him, and crossed her fingers. He crossed his fingers back at her.

'Two minutes everyone . . .'

At the top of the hour there was news, and straight after the news . . .

A tape played. The show's theme music. Penny leaned towards her microphone, which hung like an anglepoise over her desk. The music faded.

'Hello again. This is Penny Cook, and this is *What's Cookin'*. I'll be with you until three o'clock, so if you've got a problem, I'm just a phone call away. And if you want to ring me the number as ever is . . .'

It was extraordinary, and Rebus could only marvel at it. Her eyes were closed, and she looked so brittle that a shiver might turn her to powder. Yet that voice . . . so controlled . . . no, not controlled; rather, it was as though it were apart from her, as though it possessed a life of its own, a personality . . . Rebus looked at the studio clock. Four hours of this, five nights a week? All in all, he thought, he'd rather be a policeman.

The show was running like clockwork. Calls were taken by the two operators, details scribbled down. There was discussion with the producer about suitable candidates, and during the musical interludes or the commercials – '. . . and mmm . . . it tastes *so* good' – the producer would relay details about the callers to Penny.

'Let's go with that one,' she might say. Or: 'I can't deal with that, not tonight.' Usually, her word was the last, though the producer might demur.

'I don't know, it's quite a while since we covered adultery . . .'

Rebus watched. Rebus listened. But most of all, Rebus waited . . .

'OK, Penny,' the producer told her, 'it's line two next. His name's Michael.'

She nodded. 'Can somebody get me a coffee?'

'Sure.'

'And next,' she said, 'I think we've got Michael on line two. Hello, Michael?'

It was quarter to midnight. As usual, the door of the production room opened and Gordon Prentice stepped into the room. He had nods and smiles for everyone, and seemed especially pleased to see Rebus.

'Inspector,' he said shaking Rebus's hand. 'I see you take

your work seriously, coming here at this hour.' He patted the producer's shoulder. 'How's the show tonight?'

'Been a bit tame so far, but this looks interesting.'

Penny's eyes were on the dimly lit production room. But her voice was all for Michael.

'And what do you do for a living, Michael?'

The caller's voice crackled out of the loudspeakers. 'I'm an actor, Penny.'

'Really? And are you working just now?'

'No, I'm what we call "resting".'

'Ah well, they say there's no rest for the wicked. I suppose that must mean you *haven't* been wicked.'

Gordon Prentice, running his fingers through his beard, smiled at this, turning to Rebus to see how he was enjoying himself. Rebus smiled back.

'On the contrary,' the voice was saying. 'I've been really quite wicked. And I'm ashamed of it.'

'And what is it you're so ashamed of, Michael?'

'I've been telephoning you anonymously, Penny. Threatening you. I'm sorry. You see, I thought you knew about it. But the policeman tells me you don't. I'm sorry.'

Prentice wasn't smiling now. His eyes had opened wide in disbelief.

'Knew about what, Michael?' Her eyes were staring at the window. Light bounced off her spectacles, sending flashes like laser beams into the production room.

'Knew about the fix. When the ratings were going down, the station head, Gordon Prentice, started rigging the shows, yours and Hamish MacDiarmid's. MacDiarmid might even be in on it.'

'What do you mean, rigging?'

'Kill it!' shouted Prentice. 'Kill transmission! He's raving mad! Cut the line someone. Here, I'll do it—'

But Rebus had come up behind Prentice and now locked his own arms around Prentice's. 'I think you'd better listen,' he warned.

'Out of work actors,' Michael was saying, the way he'd

told Rebus earlier in the day. 'Prentice put together a . . . you could call it a cast, I suppose. Half a dozen people. They phone in using different voices, always with a controversial point to make or some nice juicy problem. One of them told me at a party one night. I didn't believe her until I started listening for myself. An actor can tell that sort of thing, when a voice isn't quite right, when something's an act rather than for real.'

Prentice was struggling, but couldn't break Rebus's hold. 'Lies!' he yelled. 'Complete rubbish! Let go of me, you—'

Penny Cook's eyes were on Prentice now, and on no one but Prentice.

'So what you're saying, Michael, if I understand you, is that Gordon Prentice is rigging our phone-ins so as to boost audience figures?'

'That's right.'

'Michael, thank you for your call.'

It was Rebus who spoke, and he spoke to the producer. 'That'll do.'

The producer nodded through the glass to Penny Cook, then flipped a switch. Music could be heard over the loudspeakers. The producer started to fade the piece out. Penny spoke into her microphone.

'A slightly longer musical interlude there, but I hope you enjoyed it. We'll be going back to your calls very shortly, but first we've got some commercials.'

She slipped off her glasses and rubbed the bridge of her nose.

'A private performance,' Rebus explained to Prentice. 'For our benefit only. The listeners were hearing something else.' Rebus felt Prentice's body soften, the shoulders slump. He was caught, and knew it for sure. Rebus relaxed his hold on the man: he wouldn't try anything now.

The Camelot Coffee ad was playing. It had been easy really. Recognising the voice on the commercial as that of the phone caller, Rebus had contacted the ad agency involved, who had given him the name and address of the actor concerned: Michael Barrie, presently resting and to be found most days in a certain city-centre wine bar . . .

Barrie knew he was in trouble, but Rebus was sure it could be smoothed out. But as for Gordon Prentice . . . ah, that was different altogether.

'The station's ruined!' he wailed. 'You must know that!' He pleaded with the producer, the engineer, but especially with the hate-filled eyes of Penny Cook who, behind glass, could not even hear him. 'Once this gets out, you'll *all* be out of a job! All of you! That's why I—'

'Back on in five seconds, Penny,' said the producer, as though it was just another night on *What's Cookin'*. Penny Cook nodded, resting her glasses back on her nose. The stuffing looked to have been knocked out of her. With one final baleful glance towards Prentice, she turned to her microphone.

'Welcome back. A change of direction now, because I'd like to say a few words to you about the head of Lowland Radio, Gordon Prentice. I hope you'll bear with me for a minute or two. It shouldn't take much longer than that . . .'

It didn't, but what she said was tabloid news by morning, and Lowland Radio's licence was withdrawn not long after that. Rebus went back to Radio Three for when he was driving, and no radio at all in his flat. Hamish MacDiarmid, as far as he could ascertain, went back to a croft somewhere, but Penny Cook stuck around, going freelance and doing some journalism as well as the odd radio programme.

It was very late one night when the knock came at Rebus's door. He opened it to find Penny standing there. She pretended surprise at seeing him.

'Oh, hello,' she said. 'I didn't know you lived here. Only, I've run out of coffee and I was wondering . . .'

Laughing, Rebus led her inside. 'I can let you have the best part of a jar of Camelot,' he said. 'Or alternatively we could get drunk and go to bed . . .'

They got drunk.

# Castle Dangerous

## AN INSPECTOR REBUS STORY

Sir Walter Scott was dead.

He'd been found at the top of his namesake's monument in Princes Street Gardens, dead of a heart attack and with a new and powerful pair of binoculars hanging around his slender, mottled neck.

Sir Walter had been one of Edinburgh's most revered QCs until his retirement a year ago. Detective Inspector John Rebus, climbing the hundreds (surely it must be hundreds) of spiralling steps up to the top of the Scott Monument, paused for a moment to recall one or two of his run-ins with Sir Walter, both in and out of the courtrooms on the Royal Mile. He had been a formidable character, shrewd, devious and subtle. Law to him had been a challenge rather than an obligation. To John Rebus, it was just a day's work.

Rebus ached as he reached the last incline. The steps here were narrower than ever, the spiral tighter. Room for one person only, really. At the height of its summer popularity, with a throng of tourists squeezing through it like toothpaste from a tube, Rebus reckoned the Scott Monument might be very scary indeed.

He breathed hard and loud, bursting through the small doorway at the top, and stood there for a moment, catching his breath. The panorama before him was, quite simply, the best view in Edinburgh. The castle close behind him, the New Town spread out in front of him, sloping down towards the Firth of Forth, with Fife, Rebus's birthplace, visible in the distance. Calton Hill . . . Leith . . . Arthur's Seat . . . and round to the castle again. It was breathtaking, or would have been had the breath not already been taken from him by the climb.

The parapet upon which he stood was incredibly narrow; again, there was hardly room enough to squeeze past someone. How crowded did it get in the summer? Dangerously crowded? It seemed dangerously crowded just now, with only four people up here. He looked over the edge upon the sheer drop to the gardens below, where a massing of tourists, growing restless at being barred from the monument, stared up at him. Rebus shivered.

Not that it was cold. It was early June. Spring was finally late-blooming into summer, but that cold wind never left the city, that wind which never seemed to be warmed by the sun. It bit into Rebus now, reminding him that he lived in a northern climate. He looked down and saw Sir Walter's slumped body, reminding him why he was here.

'I thought we were going to have another corpse on our hands there for a minute.' The speaker was Detective Sergeant Brian Holmes. He had been in conversation with the police doctor, who himself was crouching over the corpse.

'Just getting my breath back,' Rebus explained.

'You should take up squash.'

'It's squashed enough up here.' The wind was nipping Rebus's ears. He began to wish he hadn't had that haircut at the weekend. 'What have we got?'

'Heart attack. The doctor reckons he was due for one anyway. A climb like that in an excited state. One of the witnesses says he just doubled over. Didn't cry out, didn't seem in pain . . .'

'Old mortality, eh?' Rebus looked wistfully at the corpse. 'But why do you say he was excited?'

Holmes grinned. 'Think I'd bring you up here for the good of your health? Here.' He handed a polythene bag to Rebus. Inside the bag was a badly typed note. 'It was found in the binocular case.'

Rebus read the note through its clear polythene window:

GO TO TOP OF SCOTT MONUMENT. TUESDAY MID-
DAY. I'LL BE THERE. LOOK FOR THE GUN.

'The gun?' Rebus asked, frowning.

There was a sudden explosion. Rebus started, but Holmes
just looked at his watch, then corrected its hands. One
o'clock. The noise had come from the blank charge fired
every day from the castle walls at precisely one o'clock.

'The gun,' Rebus repeated, except now it was a statement.
Sir Walter's binoculars were lying beside him. Rebus lifted
them – 'He wouldn't mind, would he?' – and fixed them on
the castle. Tourists could be seen walking around. Some
peered over the walls. A few fixed their own binoculars on
Rebus. One, an elderly Asian, grinned and waved. Rebus
lowered the binoculars. He examined them. 'These look
brand new.'

'Bought for the purpose, I'd say, sir.'

'But what exactly *was* the purpose, Brian? What was he
supposed to be looking at?' Rebus waited for an answer.
None was forthcoming. 'Whatever it was,' Rebus went on,
'it as good as killed him. I suggest we take a look for
ourselves.'

'Where, sir?'

Rebus nodded towards the castle. 'Over there, Brian.
Come on.'

'Er, Inspector . . . ?' Rebus looked towards the doctor,
who was upright now, but pointing downwards with one
finger. 'How are we going to get him down?'

Rebus stared at Sir Walter. Yes, he could see the problem.
It would be hard graft taking him all the way back down the
spiral stairs. What's more, damage to the body would be
unavoidable. He supposed they could always use a winch
and lower him straight to the ground . . . Well, it was a job
for ambulancemen or undertakers, not the police. Rebus
patted the doctor's shoulder.

'You're in charge, Doc,' he said, exiting through the door
before the doctor could summon up a protest. Holmes
shrugged apologetically, smiled, and followed Rebus into

the dark. The doctor looked at the body, then over the edge, then back to the body again. He reached into his pocket for a mint, popped it into his mouth, and began to crunch on it. Then he, too, made for the door.

Splendour was falling on the castle walls. Wrong poet, Rebus mused, but right image. He tried to recall if he'd ever read any Scott, but drew a blank. He thought he might have picked up *Waverley* once. As a colleague at the time had said, 'Imagine calling a book after the station.' Rebus hadn't bothered to explain; and hadn't read the book either, or if he had it had left no impression . . .

He stood now on the ramparts, looking across to the Gothic exaggeration of the Scott Monument. A cannon was almost immediately behind him. Anyone wanting to be seen from the top of the monument would probably have been standing right on this spot. People did not linger here though. They might wander along the walls, take a few photographs, or pose for a few, but they would not stand in the one spot for longer than a minute or two.

Which meant, of course, that if someone *had* been standing here longer, they would be conspicuous. The problem was twofold: first, conspicuous to whom? Everyone else would be in motion, would not notice that someone was lingering. Second, all the potential witnesses would by now have gone their separate ways, in tour buses or on foot, down the Royal Mile or on to Princes Street, along George the Fourth Bridge to look at Greyfriars Bobby . . . The people milling around just now represented a fresh intake, new water flowing down the same old stream.

Someone wanted to be seen by Sir Walter, and Sir Walter wanted to see him – hence the binoculars. No conversation was needed, just the sighting. Why? Rebus couldn't think of a single reason. He turned away from the wall and saw Holmes approaching. Meeting his eyes, Holmes shrugged his shoulders.

'I've talked to the guards on the gate. They don't

remember seeing anyone suspicious. As one of them said, "All these bloody tourists look the same to me."'

Rebus smiled at this, but then someone was tugging at his sleeve, a small handbagged woman with sunglasses and thick lipstick.

'Sorry, could I ask you to move over a bit?' Her accent was American, her voice a nasal sing-song. 'Lawrence wants a picture of me with that gorgeous skyline behind me.'

Rebus smiled at her, even made a slight bow, and moved a couple of yards out of the way, Holmes following suit.

'Thanks!' Lawrence called from behind his camera, freeing a hand so that he could wave it towards them. Rebus noticed that the man wore a yellow sticker on his chest. He looked back to the woman, now posing like the film star she so clearly wasn't, and saw that she too had a badge, her name – Diana – felt-tipped beneath some package company's logo.

'I wonder . . .' Rebus said quietly.

'Sir?'

'Maybe you were asking the wrong question at the gate, Brian. Yes, the right idea but the wrong question. Come on, let's go back and ask again. We'll see how eagle-eyed our friends really are.'

They passed the photographer – his badge called him Larry rather than Lawrence – just as the shutter clicked.

'Great,' he said to nobody in particular. 'Just one more, sweetheart.' As he wound the film, Rebus paused and stood beside him, then made a square from the thumb and forefinger of both hands and peered through it towards the woman Diana, as though assessing the composition of the picture. Larry caught the gesture.

'You a professional?' he asked, his tone just short of awe.

'Only in a manner of speaking, Larry,' said Rebus, turning away again. Holmes was left standing there, staring at the photographer. He wondered whether to shrug and smile again, as he had done with the doctor. What the hell. He shrugged. He smiled. And he followed Rebus towards the gate.

Rebus went alone to the home of Sir Walter Scott, just off the Corstorphine Road near the zoo. As he stepped out of his car, he could have sworn he detected a faint wafting of animal dung. There was another car in the driveway, one which, with a sinking heart, he recognised. As he walked up to the front door of the house, he saw that the curtains were closed in the upstairs windows, while downstairs, painted wooden shutters had been pulled across to block out the daylight.

The door was opened by Superintendent 'Farmer' Watson.

'I thought that was your car, sir,' Rebus said as Watson ushered him into the hall. When he spoke, the superintendent's voice was a whispered growl.

'He's still up there, you know.'

'Who?'

'Sir Walter, of course!' Flecks of saliva burst from the corners of Watson's mouth. Rebus thought it judicious to show not even the mildest amusement.

'I left the doctor in charge.'

'Dr Jameson couldn't organise a brewery visit. What the hell did you think you were doing?'

'I had . . . *have* an investigation on my hands, sir. I thought I could be more usefully employed than playing undertaker.'

'He's stiff now, you know,' Watson said, his anger having diminished. He didn't exactly know why it was that he could never stay angry with Rebus; there was something about the man. 'They don't think they can get him down the stairs. They've tried twice, but he got stuck both times.'

Rebus pursed his lips, the only way he could prevent them spreading into a wide grin. Watson saw this and saw, too, that the situation was not without a trace of humour.

'Is that why you're here, sir? Placating the widow?'

'No, I'm here on a personal level. Sir Walter and Lady Scott were friends of mine. That is, Sir Walter was, and Lady Scott still is.'

Rebus nodded slowly. Christ, he was thinking, the poor bugger's only been dead a couple of hours and here's old Farmer Watson already trying to ... But no, surely not. Watson was many things, but not callous, not like that. Rebus rebuked himself silently, and in so doing missed most of what Watson was saying.

'—in here.'

And a door from the hallway was being opened. Rebus was being shown into a spacious living-room – or were they called drawing-rooms in houses like this? Walking across to where Lady Scott sat by the fireside was like walking across a dance hall.

'This is Inspector Rebus,' Watson was saying. 'One of my men.'

Lady Scott looked up from her handkerchief. 'How do you do?' She offered him a delicate hand, which he lightly touched with his own, in place of his usual firm handshake. Lady Scott was in her mid fifties, a well-preserved monument of neat lines and precise movements. Rebus had seen her accompanying her husband to various functions in the city, had come across her photograph in the paper when he had received his knighthood. He saw, too, from the corner of his eye, the way Watson looked at her, a mixture of pity and something more than pity, as though he wanted at the same time to pat her hand and hug her to him.

Who would want Sir Walter dead? That was, in a sense, what he had come here to ask. Still the question itself was valid. Rebus could think of adversaries – those Scott had crossed in his professional life, those he had helped put behind bars, those, perhaps, who resented everything from his title to the bright blue socks that had become something of a trademark after he admitted on a radio show that he wore no other colour on his feet ...

'Lady Scott, I'm sorry to intrude on you at a time like this. I know it's difficult, but there are a couple of questions . . .'

'Please, ask your questions.' She gestured for him to sit on the sofa – the sofa on which Farmer Watson had already made himself comfortable. Rebus sat down awkwardly. This whole business was awkward. He knew the chess player's motto: if in doubt, play a pawn. Or as the Scots themselves would say, ca' canny. But that had never been his style, and he couldn't change now. As ever, he decided to sacrifice his queen.

'We found a note in Sir Walter's binocular case.'

'He didn't own a pair of binoculars.' Her voice was firm.

'He probably bought them this morning. Did he say where he was going?'

'No, just out. I was upstairs. He called that he was "popping out for an hour or two", and that was all.'

'What note?' This from Watson. What note indeed. Rebus wondered why Lady Scott hadn't asked the same thing.

'A typed note, telling Sir Walter to be at the top of the Scott Monument at midday.' Rebus paused, his attention wholly on Sir Walter's widow. 'There have been others, haven't there? Other notes?'

She nodded slowly. 'Yes. I found them by accident. I wasn't prying, I'm not like that. I was in Walter's office – he always called it that, his "office", never his study – looking for something, an old newspaper I think. Yes, there was an article I wanted to reread, and I'd searched high and low for the blessed paper. I was looking in Walter's office, and I found some . . . letters.' She wrinkled her nose. 'He'd kept them quiet from me. Well, I suppose he had his reasons. I never said anything to him about finding them.' She smiled ruefully. 'I used to think sometimes that the unsaid was what kept our marriage alive. That may seem cruel. Now he's gone, I wish we'd told one another more . . .'

She dabbed at a liquid eye with the corner of her handkerchief, wrapped as it was around one finger, her free hand twisting and twisting the corners. To Rebus, it looked as if she were using it as a tourniquet.

'Do you know where these other notes are?' he asked.

'I don't know. Walter may have moved them.'

'Shall we see?'

The office was untidy in the best legal tradition: any available flat surface, including the carpet, seemed to be fair game for stacks of brown folders tied with ribbon, huge bulging manilla envelopes, magazines and newspapers, books and learned journals. Two walls consisted entirely of bookcases, from floor to near the ornate but flaking ceiling. One bookcase, glass-fronted, contained what Rebus reckoned must be the collected works of the other Sir Walter Scott. The glass doors looked as though they hadn't been opened in a decade; the books themselves might never have been read. Still, it was a nice touch – to have one's study so thoroughly infiltrated by one's namesake.

'Ah, they're still here.' Lady Scott had slid a concertina-style folder out from beneath a pile of similar such files. 'Shall we take them back through to the morning-room?' She looked around her. 'I don't like it in here . . . not now.'

Her Edinburgh accent, with its drawn vowels, had turned 'morning' into 'mourning'. Either that, thought Rebus, or she'd said 'mourning-room' in the first place. He would have liked to have stayed a little longer in Sir Walter's office, but was compelled to follow. Back in her chair, Lady Scott untied the ribbon around the file and let it fall open. The file itself was made up of a dozen or more compartments, but only one seemed to contain any paperwork. She pulled out the letters and handed them to Watson, who glanced through them wordlessly before handing them to Rebus.

Sir Walter had taken each note from its envelope, but had paper-clipped the envelopes to the backs of their respective notes. So Rebus was able to ascertain that the notes had been posted between three weeks and one week ago, and all bore a central London postmark. He read the three notes slowly to himself, then reread them. The first came quickly to its point.

I ENCLOSE A LETTER. THERE ARE PLENTY MORE WHERE IT CAME FROM. YOU WILL HEAR FROM ME AGAIN.

The second fleshed out the blackmail.

I HAVE ELEVEN MORE LETTERS. IF YOU'D LIKE THEM BACK, THEY WILL COST £2,000. GET THE MONEY.

The third, posted a week ago, finalised things.

PUT THE MONEY IN A CARRIER BAG. GO TO THE CAFE ROYAL AT 9 P.M. FRIDAY. STAND AT THE BAR AND HAVE A DRINK. LEAVE THE BAG THERE AND GO MAKE A PHONE CALL. SPEND TWO MINUTES AWAY FROM THE BAR. WHEN YOU COME BACK, THE LETTERS WILL BE THERE.

Rebus looked up at Lady Scott. 'Did he pay?'

'I've really no idea.'

'But you could check?'

'If you like, yes.'

Rebus nodded. 'I'd like to be sure.' The first note said that a letter was enclosed, obviously a letter concerning Sir Walter – but what kind of letter? Of the letter itself there was no sign. Twelve apparently incriminating or embarrassing letters for £2,000. A small price to pay for someone of Sir Walter's position in society. What's more, it seemed to Rebus a small price to *ask*. And if the exchange had taken place as arranged, what was the point of the last note, the one found in Sir Walter's binocular case? Yes, that was a point.

'Did you see the mail this morning, Lady Scott?'

'I was first to the door, yes.'

'And was there an envelope like these others?'

'I'm sure there wasn't.'

Rebus nodded. 'Yes, if there had been, I think Sir Walter would have kept it, judging by these.' He shook the notes – all with envelopes attached.

'Meaning, John?' Superintendent Watson sounded puzzled. To Rebus's ears, it was his natural voice.

'Meaning,' he explained, 'that the last note, the one we found on Sir Walter, was as it arrived at the house. No envelope. It must have been pushed through the letterbox. I'd say sometime yesterday or this morning. The blackmail started in London, but the blackmailer came up here for the payoff. And he or she is still here – or was until midday. Now, I'm not so certain. If Sir Walter paid the money' – he nodded towards Lady Scott – 'and I *would* like you to check on that, please, today if possible. *If*, as I say, Sir Walter paid, *if* he got the letters back, then what was this morning's little game all about?'

Watson nodded, arms folded, looking down into his lap as though seeking answers. Rebus doubted they'd be found so close to home. He rose to his feet.

'We could do with finding those letters, too. Perhaps, Lady Scott, you might have another look in your husband's . . . office.'

She nodded slowly. 'I should tell you, Inspector, that I'm not sure I *want* to find them.'

'I can understand that. But it would help us track down the blackmailer.'

Her voice was as low as the light in the room. 'Yes, of course.'

'And in the meantime, John?' Watson tried to sound like a man in charge of something. But there was a pleading edge to his voice.

'Meantime,' said Rebus, 'I'll be at the Castellain Hotel. The number will be in the book. You can always have me paged.'

Watson gave Rebus one of his dark looks, the kind that said: I don't know what you're up to, but I can't let anyone else know that I *don't* know. Then he nodded and almost smiled.

'Of course,' he said. 'Yes, off you go. I may stay on a little longer . . .' He looked to Lady Scott for her assent. But she was busy with the handkerchief again, twisting and twisting and twisting . . .

The Castellain Hotel, a minute's walk from Princes Street, was a chaos of tourists. The large pot-planted lobby looked as though it was on someone's tour itinerary, with one large organised party about to leave, milling about as their luggage was taken out to the waiting bus by hard-pressed porters. At the same time, another party was arriving, the holiday company's representative conspicuous by being the only person who looked like he knew what was going on.

Seeing that a group was about to leave, Rebus panicked. But their lapel badges assured him that they were part of the Seascape Tours package. He walked up to the reception desk and waited while a harassed young woman in a tartan two-piece tried to take two telephone calls at the same time. She showed no little skill in the operation, and all the time she was talking her eyes were on the scrum of guests in front of her. Finally, she found a moment and a welcoming smile for him. Funny how at this time of year there were so many smiles to be found in Edinburgh . . .

'Yes, sir?'

'Detective Inspector Rebus,' he announced. 'I'd like a word with the Grebe Tours rep if she's around.'

'She's a he,' the receptionist explained. 'I think he might be in his room, hold on and I'll check.' She had picked up the telephone. 'Nothing wrong, is there?'

'No, nothing, just want a word, that's all.'

Her call was answered quickly. 'Hello, Tony? There's a gentleman in reception to see you.' Pause. 'Fine, I'll tell him. 'Bye.' She put down the receiver. 'He'll be down in a minute.'

Rebus nodded his thanks and, as she answered another telephone call, moved back into the reception hall, dodging the bags and the worried owners of the bags. There was something thrilling about holidaymakers. They were like children at a party. But at the same time there was something depressing, too, about the herd mentality. Rebus had never been on a package holiday in his life. He mistrusted the production-line cheerfulness of the reps and the guides. A walk along a deserted beach: now *that* was a holiday. Finding a pleasant out-of-the-way pub . . . playing pinball so ruthlessly that the machine 'tilted' . . . wasn't he due for a holiday himself?

Not that he would take one: the loneliness could be a cage as well as a release. But he would never, he hoped, be as caged as these people around him. He looked for a Grebe Tours badge on any passing lapel or chest, but saw none. The Edinburgh Castle gatekeepers had been eagle-eyed all right, or one of them had. He'd recalled not only that a Grebe Tours bus had pulled in to the car park at around half past eleven that morning, but also that the rep had mentioned where the tour party was staying – the Castellain Hotel.

A small, balding man came out of the lift and fairly trotted to the reception desk, then, when the receptionist pointed towards Rebus, trotted over towards him, too. Did these reps take pills? potions? laughing gas? How the hell did they manage to keep it up?

'Tony Bell at your service,' the small man said. They shook hands. Rebus noticed that Tony Bell was growing old. He had a swelling paunch and was a little breathless after his jog. He ran a hand over his babylike head and kept grinning.

'Detective Inspector Rebus.' The grin subsided. In fact, most of Tony Bell's face seemed to subside.

'Oh Jesus,' he said, 'what is it? A mugger, pickpocket, what? Is somebody hurt? Which hospital?'

Rebus raised a hand. 'No need to panic,' he reassured him. 'Your charges are all quite safe.'

'Thank Christ for that.' The grin returned. Bell nodded towards a door, above which was printed the legend Dining-Room and Bar. 'Fancy a drink?'

'Anything to get out of this war zone,' Rebus said.

'You should see the bar after dinner,' said Tony Bell, leading the way, 'now *that's* a war zone . . .'

As Bell explained, the Grebe Tours party had a free afternoon. He checked his watch and told Rebus that they would probably start returning to the hotel fairly soon. There was a meeting arranged for before dinner, when the next day's itinerary would be discussed. Rebus told the rep what he wanted, and Bell himself suggested he stay put for the meeting. Yes, Rebus agreed, that seemed sensible, and meantime would Tony like another drink?

This particular Grebe Tours party was American. They'd flown in almost a month ago for what Bell called the 'Full British Tour' – Canterbury, Salisbury, Stonehenge, London, Stratford, York, the Lake District, Trossachs, Highlands, and Edinburgh.

'This is just about the last stop,' he said. 'For which relief much thanks, I can tell you. They're nice people mind, I'm not saying they're not, but . . . demanding. Yes, that's what it is. If a Brit doesn't quite understand what's been said to him, or if something isn't *quite* right, or whatever, they tend to keep their gobs shut. But Americans . . .' He rolled his eyeballs. 'Americans,' he repeated, as though it explained all.

It did. Less than an hour later, Rebus was addressing a packed, seated crowd of forty American tourists in a room off the large dining-room. He had barely given them his rank when a hand shot into the air.

'Er . . . yes?'

The elderly woman stood up. 'Sir, are you from Scotland Yard?'

Rebus shook his head. 'Scotland Yard's in London.'

She was still standing. 'Now why is that?' she asked. Rebus had no answer to this, but someone else suggested that it was because that part of London was called Scotland Yard. Yes, but why was it called Scotland Yard in the first place? The woman had sat down now, but all around her was discussion and conjecture. Rebus looked towards Tony

Bell, who rose from his own seat and succeeded in quietening things down.

Eventually, Rebus was able to make his point. 'We're interested', he said, 'in a visitor to Edinburgh Castle this morning. You may have seen someone while you were there, someone standing by the walls, looking towards the Scott Monument. He or she might have been standing there for some time. If that means something to anybody, I'd like you to tell me about it. At the same time, it's possible that those of you who took photographs of your visit may have by chance snapped the person we're looking for. If any of you have cameras, I'd like to see the photos you took this morning.'

He was in luck. Nobody remembered seeing anyone suspicious – they were too busy looking at the sights. But two photographers had used polaroids, and another had taken his film into a same-day processor at lunchtime and so had the glossy photographs with him. Rebus studied these while Tony Bell went over the next day's arrangements with the group. The polaroid photos were badly taken, often blurry, with people in the background reduced to matchstick men. But the same-day photos were excellent, sharply focused 35 mm jobs. As the tour party left the room, en route for dinner, Tony Bell came over to where Rebus was sitting and asked the question he knew he himself would be asked more than once over dinner.

'Any joy?'

'Maybe,' Rebus admitted. 'These two people keep cropping up.' He spread five photographs out in front of him. In two, a middle-aged woman was caught in the background, staring out over the wall she was leaning on. Leaning on, or hiding behind? In another two, a man in his late twenties or early thirties stood in similar pose, but with a more upright stance. In one photo, they could both be seen half turning with smiles on their faces towards the camera.

'No.' Tony Bell was shaking his head. 'They might look

like wanted criminals, but they're in our party. I think Mrs Eglinton was sitting in the back row near the door, beside her husband. You probably didn't see her. But Shaw Berkely was in the second row, over to one side. I'm surprised you didn't see him. Actually, I take that back. He has this gift of being innocuous. Never asks questions or complains. Mind you, I think he's seen most of this before.'

'Oh?' Rebus was gathering the photos together.

'He told me he'd been to Britain before on holiday.'

'And there's nothing between him and—?' Rebus was pointing to the photograph of the man and woman together.

'Him and Mrs Eglinton?' Bell seemed genuinely amused. 'I don't know – maybe. She certainly mothers him a bit.'

Rebus was still studying the print. 'Is he the youngest person on the tour?'

'By about ten years. Sad story really. His mother died, and after the funeral he said he just had to get away. Went into the travel agent's and we were offering a reduction for late bookings.'

'His father's dead too, then?'

'That's right. I got his life story one night late in the bar. On a tour, I get everyone's story sooner or later.'

Rebus flipped through the sheaf of photos a final time. Nothing new presented itself to him. 'And you were at the castle between about half past eleven and quarter to one?'

'Just as I told you.'

'Oh well.' Rebus sighed. 'I don't think—'

'Inspector?' It was the receptionist, her head peering around the door. 'There's a call for you.'

It was Superintendent Watson. He was concise, factual. 'Withdrew five hundred pounds from each of four accounts, all on the same day, and in plenty of time for the rendezvous at the Café Royal.'

'So presumably he paid up.'

'But did he get the letters back?'

'Mmm. Has Lady Scott had a look for them?'

'Yes, we've been through the study – not thoroughly, there's too much stuff in there for that. But we've had a look.' That 'we' sounded comfortable, sounded as though Watson had already got his feet under the table. 'So what now, John?'

'I'm coming over, if you've no objection, sir. With respect, I'd like a look at Sir Walter's office for myself . . .'

He went in search of Tony Bell, just so he could say thanks and goodbye. But he wasn't in the musty conference room, and he wasn't in the dining-room. He was in the bar, standing with one foot on the bar rail as he shared a joke with the woman he had called Mrs Eglinton. Rebus did not interrupt, but he did wink at the phone-bound receptionist as he passed her, then pushed his way out of the Castellain Hotel's double doors just as the wheezing of a bus's air brakes signalled the arrival of yet more human cargo.

There was no overhead lighting in Sir Walter Scott's study, but there were numerous floor lamps, desk lamps, and angle-poises. Rebus switched on as many as worked. Most were antiquated, with wiring to match, but there was one newish anglepoise attached to the bookcase, pointing inwards towards the collection of Scott's writings. There was a comfortable chair beside this lamp, and an ashtray on the floor between chair and bookcase.

When Watson put his head around the door, Rebus was seated in this chair, elbows resting on his knees, and chin resting between the cupped palms of both hands.

'Margaret – that is, Lady Scott – she wondered if you wanted anything.'

'I want those letters.'

'I think she meant something feasible – like tea or coffee.'

Rebus shook his head. 'Maybe later, sir.'

Watson nodded, made to retreat, then thought of something. 'They got him down in the end. Had to use a winch. Not very dignified, but what can you do? I just hope the papers don't print any pictures.'

'Why don't you have a word with the editors, just to be on the safe side?'

'I might just do that, John.' Watson nodded. 'Yes, I might just do that.'

Alone again, Rebus rose from his chair and opened the glass doors of the bookcase. The position of chair, ashtray and lamp was interesting. It was as though Sir Walter had been reading volumes from these shelves, from his namesake's collected works. Rebus ran a finger over the spines. A few he had heard of; the vast majority he had not. One was titled *Castle Dangerous*. He smiled grimly at that. Dangerous, all right; or in Sir Walter's case, quite lethal. He angled the light farther into the bookcase. The dust on a row of books had been disturbed. Rebus pushed with one finger against the spine of a volume, and the book slid a good two inches back until it rested against the solid wall behind the bookcase. Two uniform inches of space for the whole of this row. Rebus reached a hand down behind the row of books and ran it along the shelf. He met resistance, and drew the hand out again, now clutching a sheaf of papers. Sir Walter had probably thought it as good a hiding place as any – a poor testament to Scott the novelist's powers of attraction. Rebus sat down in the chair again, brought the anglepoise closer, and began to sift through what he'd found.

There were, indeed, twelve letters, ornately fountain-penned promises of love with honour, of passion until doomsday. As with all such youthful nonsense, there was a lot of poetry and classical imagery. Rebus imagined it was standard private boys' school stuff, even today. But these letters had been written half a century ago, sent from one schoolboy to another a year younger than himself. The younger boy was Sir Walter, and from the correspondence it was clear that Sir Walter's feelings for the writer had been every bit as inflamed as those of the writer himself.

Ah, the writer. Rebus tried to remember if he was still an MP. He had the feeling he had either lost his seat, or else had retired. Maybe he was still on the go; Rebus paid little attention to politics. His attitude had always been: don't vote, it only encourages them. So, here was the presumed scandal. Hardly a scandal, but just about enough to cause embarrassment. At worst a humiliation. But then Rebus was beginning to suspect that humiliation, not financial profit, was the price exacted here.

And not even necessarily public humiliation, merely the private knowledge that someone knew of these letters, that someone had possessed them. Then the final taunt, the taunt Sir Walter could not resist: come to the Scott Monument, look across to the castle, and you will see who has been tormenting you these past weeks. You will know.

But now that same taunt was working on Rebus. He knew so much, yet in effect he knew nothing at all. He now possessed the 'what', but not the 'who'. And what should he do with the old love letters? Lady Scott had said she wasn't sure she wanted to find them. He could take them away with him – destroy them. Or he could hand them over to her, tell her what they were. It would be up to her either to destroy them unread or to discover this silly secret. He could always say: It's all right, it's nothing really . . . Mind you, some of the sentences were ambiguous enough to disturb, weren't they? Rebus read again. 'When you scored 50 n.o. and afterwards we showered . . .' 'When you stroke me like that . . .' 'After rugger practice . . .'

*Ach.* He got up and opened the bookcase again. He would replace them. Let time deal with them; he could not. But in placing his hand back down behind the line of books, he brushed against something else, not paper but stiff card. He hadn't noticed it before because it seemed stuck to the wall. He peeled it carefully away and brought it into the light. It was a photograph, black and white, ten inches by eight and mounted on card. A man and woman on an esplanade, arm in arm, posing for the photographer. The man looked a little pensive, trying to smile but not sure he actually wanted to be caught like this. The woman seemed to wrap both her arms round one of his, restraining him; and she was laughing, thrilled by this moment, thrilled to be with him.

The man was Sir Walter. A Sir Walter twenty years older than the schoolboy of the love letters, mid thirties perhaps. And the woman? Rebus stared long and hard at the woman. Put the photograph down and paced the study, touching things, peering through the shutters. He was thinking and not thinking. He had seen the woman before somewhere . . . but where? She was not Lady Scott, of that he was certain. But he'd seen her recently, seen that face . . . that face.

And then he knew. Oh yes, he knew.

He telephoned the Castellain, half listening as the story was given to him. Taken ill suddenly . . . poorly . . . decided to go home . . . airport . . . flying to London and catching a connection tonight . . . Was there a problem? Well, of course there was a problem, but no one at the hotel could help with it, not now. The blackmail over, Rebus himself had inadvertently caused the blackmailer to flee. He had gone to the hotel hoping – such a slim hope – for help, not realising that one of the Grebe Tours party was his quarry. Once again, he had sacrificed his queen too early in the game.

He telephoned Edinburgh Airport, only to be told that the flight had already taken off. He asked to be rerouted to Security, and asked them for the name of the security chief at Heathrow. He was calling Heathrow when Watson appeared in the hall.

'Making quite a few calls, aren't you, John? Not personal, I hope.'

Rebus ignored his superior as his call was connected. 'Mr Masterson in Security, please,' he said. And then: 'Yes, it is urgent. I'll hold.' He turned to Watson at last. 'Oh, it's personal all right, sir. But it's nothing to do with me. I'll tell you all about it in a minute. Then we can decide what to tell Lady Scott. Actually, seeing as you're a friend of the family and all, *you* can tell her. That'd be best, wouldn't it, sir?

There are some things only your friends can tell you, after all, aren't there?'

He was through to Heathrow Security, and turned away from Watson the better to talk with Masterson. The superintendent stood there, dimly aware that Rebus was going to force him to tell Margaret something she would probably rather not hear. He wondered if she would ever again have time for the person who would tell her . . . And he cursed John Rebus, who was so good at digging yet never seemed to soil his own hands. It was a gift, a terrible, destructive gift. Watson, a staunch believer in the Christian God, doubted Rebus's gift had come down from on high. No, not from on high.

The phone call was ending. Rebus put down the receiver and nodded towards Sir Walter's study.

'If you'll step into the office, sir,' he said, 'there's something I'd like to show you . . .'

Shaw Berkely was arrested at Heathrow, and, despite protestations regarding his health and cries for consular aid, was escorted back to Edinburgh, where Rebus was waiting, brisk and definitive, in Interview Room A of Great London Road Police Station.

Berkely's mother had died two months before. She had never told him the truth about his birth, spinning instead some story about his father being dead. But in sorting through his mother's papers, Shaw discovered the truth – several truths, in fact. His mother had been in love with Walter Scott, had become pregnant by him, but had been, as she herself put it in her journal, 'discarded' in favour of the 'better marriage' provided by Margaret Winton-Addams.

Shaw's mother accepted some money from Scott and fled to the United States, where she had a younger sister. Shaw grew up believing his father dead. The revelation not only that he was alive, but that he had prospered in society after having caused Shaw's mother misery and torment, led to a son's rage. But it was impotent rage, Shaw thought, until he came across the love letters. His mother must at some point have stolen them from Scott, or at least had come out of the relationship in possession of them. Shaw decided on a teasing revenge, knowing Scott would deduce that any blackmailer in possession of the letters was probably also well informed about his affair and the bastard son.

He used the tour party as an elaborate cover (and also, he admitted, because it was a cheap travel option). He brought with him to Britain not only the letters, but also the series of typed notes. The irony was that he had been to Edinburgh before, had studied there for three months as part of some exchange with his American college. He knew now why his mother, though proud of the scholarship, had been against his going. For three months he had lived in his father's city, yet hadn't known it.

He sent the notes from London – the travel party's base for much of its stay in England. The exchange – letters for cash – had gone ahead in the Café Royal, the bar having been a haunt of his student days. But he had known his final note, delivered by hand, would tempt Sir Walter, would lead him to the top of the Scott Monument. No, he said, he hadn't just wanted Sir Walter to see him, to see the son he had never known. Shaw had much of the money on him, stuffed into a money belt around his waist. The intention had been to release wads of money, Sir Walter's money, down on to Princes Street Gardens.

'I didn't mean for him to die . . . I just wanted him to know how I felt about him . . . I don't know. But Jesus' – he grinned – 'I still wish I'd let fly with all that loot.'

Rebus shuddered to think of the ramifications. Stampede in Princes Street! Hundreds dead in lunchtime spree! Biggest *scoor-oot* ever! No, best not to think about it. Instead, he made for the Café Royal himself. It was late morning, the day after Berkely's arrest. The pub was quiet as yet, but Rebus was surprised to see Dr Jameson standing at the bar, fortifying himself with what looked suspiciously like a double whisky. Remembering how he had left the doctor in the lurch regarding Sir Walter's body, Rebus grinned broadly and offered a healthy slap on the back.

'Morning, Doc, fancy seeing you in here.' Rebus leaned his elbows on the bar. 'We mustn't be keeping you busy enough.' He paused. There was a twinkle in his eye as he spoke. 'Here, let me get you a stiff one . . .' And he laughed so hard even the waiters from the Oyster Bar came to investigate. But all they saw was a tall, well-built man leaning against a much smaller, more timid man, and saying as he raised his glass: 'Here's to mortality, to old mortality!'

So all in all it was just another day in the Café Royal.

# The Wider Scheme

It is, of course, by no means unusual to find a solicitor in a police station.

We're called there at all hours of the day and night, sometimes by clients, sometimes by the police themselves. There is something about those stations, something unwholesome, and it leaves its mark on you. Put me in a room full of lawyers, and I'll tell you which ones spend a lot of time in police cells and interview rooms, and hanging around corridors and empty offices, fingers tapping impatiently against briefcases. Those laywers have a tired, drawn look. They look like morticians. They lose colour and smile less than they used to. And they look nervous and cynical at the same time, their eyes flitting over you as if you'd been accused of something.

Today, I was sitting in Detective Inspector Jack Preston's office. He's a friend of mine, insofar as we've been known to share a drink, a meal, a joke. We have met socially at parties full of other CID men and lawyers. That's why he was doing me what he called a 'favour'. We were having a quiet word, the door closed, about a client of mine. Jack was keen to see my client put away, but knew I could mount a reasonable defence. He wanted to do some trading. He would drop a couple of charges if my client changed his plea.

This is the way the law works. It's the only thing that stops the courts blocking up completely. 'Plumbing', Jack calls it. He says we're all plumbers' mates, trying to keep the *merde* flowing.

I was putting the case for my client, not really trying too

hard, just enjoying the exercise, when there was a knock at the door.

'Yes,' Jack called. A head appeared round the door.

'Sorry, sir, I know you didn't want to be disturbed.'

Jack waved the young man inside and introduced him as DC Derek Halliwell.

'What is it, Derek?'

'The eleven o'clock identification,' DC Halliwell said. Jack checked his watch. It was two minutes to eleven.

'Christ,' he said.

I smiled. 'Time flies.' It was true I'd been in his office a while. We'd been chatting, that's all. Some gossip, a few stories, a cup of coffee.

'Do it without me,' Jack said.

'It's not that, sir. We're one short for the lineup.'

'Have you had a look around?'

'Nobody's available.'

Jack thought about it. 'Well, she knows me, I can't do it.' Then he had an idea. He turned to me. I widened my eyes.

'You want *me* to appear in an ID parade?'

'You'd be doing us a big favour, Roddy.'

'Would it take long?'

He smiled. 'You know it wouldn't.'

I sighed, a little theatrically. 'Only too pleased, Inspector, to help police with their inquiries.'

Jack and DC Halliwell had a laugh as I got to my feet.

Most people I know, when they think of an ID parade, they imagine the American system: two-way mirror, the witness hidden from view. But it's not like that here. Here, the witness is face-to-face with the lineup. He or she walks along the line, then walks back along it. It can be distressing for all concerned. When Jack told me which case this present identification was concerned with, I felt pretty distressed myself.

We were standing in the anteroom.

'You might have warned me,' I said.

'I'm telling you now,' Jack said.

It was the Marshall case. Sophie Marshall had been mugged, and had died of her injuries before help could arrive. Her attacker had left her propped against a wall, and had taken only cash and jewellery. The hell of it was, I'd known Sophie Marshall. Well, I'd met her a few times, as had Jack. She'd been a court usher. We'd met her both professionally and at drinks parties. She'd been a good-looking young woman, full of life.

'Thing is,' Jack confided, 'you know and I know that the MO fits Barry Cooke.'

I nodded. Barry Cooke was a young thug of the district who had mugged before and served time. He'd left the victim propped against a wall. I recalled his barrister saying in mitigation that Cooke had left the victim in that position to make him more comfortable. From the moment they found Sophie Marshall, the police suspected Cooke. They took him in for questioning, but he had a good alibi and a keen young solicitor. The evidence against him was circumstantial. It wouldn't hold up in court.

'But now you've got a witness?' I said, interested.

Jack nodded. He seemed nervous. 'A young woman, says she saw somebody near the scene about the time Sophie Marshall was attacked. We've brought Cooke in, see if she can point the finger.' He shrugged. 'That would just about do it.'

'Good,' I said. 'Who is she?'

'The witness?' Jack shrugged again, lighting a cigarette for himself, despite the No Smoking signs on all four walls and above the door. 'Just someone who lives near there. Actually, she lives on the floor above Marshall, but she didn't know her. She's not what you'd call the perfect witness.'

'How do you mean?'

'Wait till you see her: cropped hair, ring through her nose, tattoos. She's Ray Boyd's girlfriend. Know him?' I shook my head. 'He's got a bit of a temper on him. He was in court a couple of days ago for assault. Got off with it though.'

I nodded. 'I think I recall the case.'

The other members of the lineup were milling around, and now the anteroom door opened and Barry Cooke was led in. I didn't look at him. There was a quick briefing from Jack, and we were told to go into the ID room. There, we were arranged into a line. I was wearing a jacket borrowed from DC Halliwell, to make me look more 'casual', and I'd taken off my tie. I still looked a good deal more formal than the others in the lineup, one of whom was a police officer.

I ended up as Number Four. Barry Cooke was right next to me. He was about a foot shorter than me, with thick unkempt hair tied back into a matted ponytail. His mouth was missing a few teeth, and his face was scarred with acne. I tried to look straight ahead of me, but of course he knew who I was.

'You're a lawyer, aren't you?' he said.

'No talking!' one of the policemen ordered.

Then the witness was brought into the room. Jack was with her, along with Cooke's solicitor, an upstart called Tony Barraclough. Barraclough recognised me, but didn't let it show. He'd probably been forewarned by Jack.

The witness was about Cooke's height and age. It struck me that they might know one another, but then this parade wouldn't have been necessary. She was an ugly little thing, except for her eyes. Her eyes were pretty, the way she'd once been pretty all over. But she'd scraped and savaged herself, pierced herself. She wore her underclass like a uniform.

She stopped in front of Number One, then passed Two and Three and stopped in front of me. I stared straight ahead, and she moved on to Barry Cooke. But she walked right past him to Number Six. I could see hope fade from Jack's face. His shoulders sagged. Eventually, she walked past us again. I thought this time she was going to stop at Cooke, but she was standing in front of me.

Then she reached up and tapped my shoulder.

'That's him,' she said, 'that's the bastard.'

Jack shuffled his feet. 'Are you sure?'

'Oh, I'm sure all right. Definitely him. *Bastard!*' And she slapped me hard across the face.

Two uniformed officers led her away, still screaming. Everyone looked a bit shaken up. I rubbed my cheek where it stung. Barry Cooke was watching me intently. Jack was having a quiet word with Tony Barraclough. Jack was smiling, Barraclough nodding. Then the lineup was dismissed, Cooke went off with Barraclough, and Jack came over to me.

'Sorry about that,' he said.

'Do you think I should press a charge for assault?'

'What do you reckon?'

I shrugged. 'You say her boyfriend's often in trouble?'

'Not often.'

'Maybe she's seen me in the courts.'

'Yes, that's possible. Decided to have a go at you. That makes sense. Otherwise . . . well, I mean, you and Cooke, you're chalk and cheese.'

'Further apart than that, I think.'

'Well, anyway, sorry.' He pointed to my cheek. 'I can see the outline of her fingers.'

I rubbed the cheek again. 'I hope it fades before I go home.'

'I didn't know your wife was the jealous type.' Jack put a hand on my shoulder. 'Roddy, these identity parades work less often than you'd think. I've been picked out myself once or twice.'

'No problem,' I said, trying to smile.

But I was worried, all the same.

The shock wore off, and I found I had an idea.

I wanted to see if it was possible that Ray Boyd himself could have been Sophie Marshall's attacker. I knew from Jack that Boyd had a temper, that he'd been in court for assault. It didn't take me too long to find what I was looking for in the court records. But his previous arrests were for assaults on men, not women. They usually took place in the form of one-sided fights outside pubs. Boyd was a good fighter, by all accounts, in that he tended to lose his head and become a whirlwind, all arms and attitude, feet and ferocity. He didn't care if you hit him back. He shrugged blows off and kept on pummelling. On the last occasion, it had taken several bystanders to drag him off his cowed opponent.

There was no mention of a girlfriend, and I didn't want to ask Jack about her. I didn't want him involved, not at this stage. But I had Boyd's address, so I drove myself out there, thanking God I hadn't yet got rid of my Ford Sierra and traded up to the Mercedes or BMW which I'd been promising myself. Where Ray Boyd lived, even a newish Sierra turned heads.

It was a mazy block of flats, eight storeys high and the colour of old dishwater. I parked my car in a bay and sat for a while, wondering what to do next. Fortunately, my wife is a birdwatcher. Her own car having been out of action last weekend, she'd borrowed mine so she and her fellow 'twitchers' could drive to some godforsaken spot to stare at a rare Siberian visitor. Her binoculars were still in the car. They were her second-best pair, compact in size and sheathed in green rubber. I scanned the tiers of the tower block. On the other side of the block, there were only anonymous windows, but I was parked in a kind of inner arena. This side, there were long walkways and front doors, liftshafts and stairwells. Boyd's flat was 316, which I soon realised meant floor 3, flat 16.

Scanning what third-floor doors I could see, I eventually picked out flat 16. It looked no better or worse than its neighbours. I put the binoculars away and sat there, keeping an eye on it, pretending to read a newspaper. Even the paper, I realised, was wrong for this part of town. Not many broadsheets around here.

'You make a lousy detective,' I told myself.

A few children playing with a ball came to look at me. I don't know who they thought I was but they were properly mistrustful of authority, and soon went away again. I could have been a policeman, a debt collector, or anyone. It struck me how ridiculous this was, me sitting here. But I wanted to get a look at Ray Boyd; to size him up, as it were.

When his flat door opened, Boyd came out accompanied by the witness. I wished I knew her name, but at least I knew where she stayed, Jack had told me. Boyd and his girlfriend were walking. I tried following them in the car but they were walking too slowly for this to be feasible, so I parked by the side of the road and followed on foot. After a quarter of a mile, I reckoned I knew where they were headed: the girlfriend's flat on the Horseshoe Estate, where Sophie Marshall had lived. I'd seen enough; I headed back to my car. A policeman had already ticketed it.

Barry Cooke himself was next.

Again, I used the court records. I even had a quiet word with his solicitor. Meeting casually, we spoke of the identity parade, and laughed about it. Then I asked him about Barry Cooke. Barraclough didn't seem surprised or suspicious that I was asking. We were just two lawyers, enjoying a bit of a chat.

The more I looked at Barry Cooke, the more feasible it all seemed. A mugging gone wrong. Violence taken too far. And the MO fitted his own: I knew that already. All he had on his side were his alibi, his protestation of innocence, and the fact that the witness had singularly failed to identify him. He was still the chief suspect. However, the police had no reason to disbelieve the witness, to suspect that she was playing some game. Not unless it could be shown that she was. I had a picture in my head: an apparent witness who has come forward not to assist the inquiry but to ensure it takes a wrong turn. That she picked me out was an accident; it could have been anybody ... anybody but the actual culprit. I liked this picture and wondered if Jack could see it too.

As I was leaving the court, I saw a figure dart round a corner. I went to my car and sat in it for a moment, pretending to look for something in my briefcase, but really keeping an eye on my wing mirror. The figure reappeared, seeking me out.

It was Barry Cooke.

I drove out of the car park and a couple of hundred yards down the road to a burger restaurant, where I pulled in. I waited, but there was no sign of a following car. Now that I thought about it, I'd read in one of the court reports that Barry Cooke could not drive. It was on his side in the Marshall case, for as Barraclough had said, Cooke's alibi was that he was at a party four miles away from where Sophie Marshall's body had been found. No way could he have walked that distance and back. Someone would have to have driven him there, which, as Barraclough said with a smile, was most unlikely.

Still, Barry Cooke had been to court several times. So had Ray Boyd. And so, in all probability, had Boyd's girlfriend. Any one of them might have seen Sophie Marshall before. Maybe she'd been picked out . . .

None of which got me any further. Proof was the thing. The police needed proof. I waited, but there was no sign of Barry Cooke, so I started the car again and drove home to my wife.

Next morning, as I parked the car outside my offices, I saw him again. He was good at being furtive, but solicitors deal with furtive people all the time, and I spotted him straightaway. I locked the car and started towards him. At first, I thought he was going to run for it, but he decided instead to stand his ground. He put his hands in his pockets and waited for me.

'Are you following me?' I asked.

Barry Cooke shook his head. 'Got a right to be here, haven't I?'

'I saw you yesterday, skulking.'

He shrugged. 'So?'

'So why are you following me?'

He considered a response. Bad liars usually take their time. 'That witness picked you out,' he eventually said.

'Yes?'

'But the coppers are still hassling *me*.'

'You want me to do something about it?'

He frowned. 'No, I just . . . that witness picked you out.'

'Don't be ridiculous. She made a mistake, that's all.' I paused. 'Maybe she was paid to make a mistake.'

He narrowed his eyes. 'How do you mean?'

But I just shrugged. 'Now,' I said, 'are you going to stop following me, or must I call DI Preston?'

He screwed up his face. 'Preston, that bastard. You're all in it together, you lot. All matey, all favours and stuff.'

'I don't know what you mean.'

He just made another face and walked away. I watched him go. Then, trembling a little, I went into my office and opened a fresh bottle of brandy.

I knew I had to talk to the witness. The problem was: Would she talk to me?

It was difficult. I was finding it harder to get things straight in my mind. I knew I was in dangerous territory, and that things might get worse still. I spent all the rest of that day watching for Barry Cooke, but I never saw him. Maybe my warning was enough; maybe he was keeping his distance for reasons of his own. But someone did scratch my car. I phoned my wife and told her about it, explaining that after work I was going to get respray estimates from a couple of garages.

Then I headed out to Sophie Marshall's estate.

I parked at a distance and had to walk down the very alley where she'd been attacked. It was a dreary spot, a narrow corridor bordered by high brick walls covered in graffiti. There was a railway line nearby, trains thundering past. A terrible place to die. I had to stop for a moment and control my breathing. But I went on.

It is difficult, more difficult than I'd imagined, to hang about on these estates while remaining inconspicuous. People came to their windows, and children stopped playing to stare at me. So I climbed the stairwell and walked about a bit outside the lines of flats, looking like I knew where I was going.

It was hopeless. After a nervous half-hour, I decided to return to my car. I was sitting in the driver's seat, hands clutching the steering wheel, trying to calm myself down, when I saw her. She walked on loud high-heeled boots, spiky things, as spiky as she herself was. She wore tight black denims, ripped at the knees, and a baggy black T-shirt. She hadn't brought Boyd with her, thank God. I didn't want to have to deal with Boyd, not if I could help it. She had her head down, either sullenly or just to avoid eye contact with other pedestrians. Standard practice these days, sad to say.

She passed within feet of my car, but didn't so much as glance at it. I gave her half a minute to walk down the alley, then got out of the car, locked it, and followed. I was giving her plenty of time. By the time I got to the far end of the alley, she had already crossed the quadrangle and was somewhere in the block. Then I saw her appear on the third floor. She walked to the fourth door from the stairs, and opened it with a key.

I followed.

I stood outside her door for the best part of a minute, then bent down to look through her letterbox. I could hear music, probably a radio. But no voices, no other sounds. I stood up again and looked at the nameplate on the door. It was a piece of cheap lined paper, stuck to the paintwork with tape. AFFLICK, it said. I knocked a four-beat rhythm, a friendly knock, then waited.

There was no spy hole, so when she came to the door she

opened it. No security chain either. I pushed the door open wide and went in.

'Hoi,' she said, her voice a squeal, 'what the hell—?'

Her voice died as she recognised me. Her cheeks went red.

'I just want to talk, that's all. Five minutes of your time.'

'I'll yell bloody murder,' she said.

I smiled. 'I don't doubt it. Look, I wouldn't have come here, but I need to speak to you.'

'What about?'

'I think you know. Can we sit down?'

She took me into the living-room, which was little more than a hovel. She went straight to the fireplace, switched off the radio, opened a packet of cigarettes, and lit one for herself. She never took her eyes off me. She looked scared. I cleared a space and sat down on the sofa. I crossed my legs, trying to look relaxed, hoping she wouldn't see me as a threat. I didn't want that.

'What do you want?' she said.

'Do you know a young man called Barry Cooke?'

'Never heard of him,' she said defiantly.

'No? He was on that lineup with me. He was standing right next to me. Short, hair tied back, scruffy.'

'You've got a nerve coming here.'

She had pulled herself together. I'll give her that; she was strong-willed.

'Barry Cooke', I continued, 'is the man the police think killed Sophie Marshall. They were hoping you'd identify him.'

'I identified *you*. It was you I saw.'

I smiled and looked at the floor between us. 'The police are trying to pin down Barry Cooke.'

'So what?'

'So . . . you could help them.'

'What?'

'You could remember something about the man you saw that night. You could . . . change your mind.' I reached into my jacket pocket and brought out an envelope.

'What's that?' she said, curious now.

'Money, a lot of it. A one-off payment for your cooperation.'

'You want Cooke convicted?'

'I want *someone* convicted, and it may as well be him.'

Well, hadn't I left Sophie's body that way on purpose, remembering Cooke's MO? Hadn't I taken her money and jewellery? But I hadn't counted on Cooke having such a strong alibi. I hadn't counted on there being a witness.

'Look,' I said, 'take the money.'

'But it was *you* I saw that night.'

'That doesn't matter,' I said, feeling this to be the truth. What did it matter, a brief affair gone badly wrong? A threat to tell wife and colleagues? A chase through an alley? What did any of it matter in the wider scheme?

'You killed her.'

'I didn't mean to.'

'But you did, and now you want to fit up Cooke.'

'What I want,' I said quietly, 'is to give you some money. What have you got to lose? The police didn't believe you when you pointed me out at the lineup. They'll never believe you. You might as well take the money and tell them some other story.'

She came towards me, her eyes on the envelope. I handed it up to her. She took it and placed it on the mantelpiece. 'Barry Cooke,' she said quietly.

'Short,' I said, 'grubby, with a ponytail and spots and a few missing teeth. He's mugged women before. You'd be doing society a favour.'

She stared at me. 'Right,' she said sourly. 'A favour.'

I stood up and buttoned my jacket. 'I think we understand one another,' I said. Then I walked out into her hall. I was opening the front door when she called to me. I turned. She was standing in the living-room doorway. She had the cigarette in her mouth, her eyes slitted against the smoke, and she was hauling at the hem of her T-shirt with both hands, tugging it up. I didn't realise what she was doing. Then I saw. There were strips of tape on her stomach, and a thin snaking black wire attached to a black transmitter. She was bugged.

I yanked open the front door and Jack Preston was standing there in front of me.

'Hello, Roddy,' he said.

We sat in Interview Room A, having a chat.

Jack explained it all quite quickly. How Gayle Afflick *had* seen me in the courts, the day her boyfriend Ray was up for assault, and how she had recognised me as the man she'd seen that night. Her boyfriend told her I was a solicitor, and this worried her. Who would take her word against that of a solicitor? She knew one decent copper, someone who *might* believe her: DI Jack Preston.

That time in Jack's office, it had been a setup, neatly played by Jack and Halliwell to get me into a lineup, where Gayle Afflick could identify me. Jack wanted to see how I'd react, what I'd do. He had a good idea I'd want to talk to the witness afterwards.

It all fitted, as far as he was concerned. There were rumours around the court that Sophie Marshall had been seeing a married man. It figured that this man most probably knew her from her professional life. (She didn't have much of a social one.) When Jack found that my car had been ticketed on a road near the Horseshoe Estate, a long way off my usual patch, he knew he was on to something.

So he'd had Gayle Afflick tailed, and had her wired up too, taking the whole thing carefully, nice and slow, because he knew how easy it would be to lose me. But he hadn't lost me. He had it all now, the whole story. And he had me. He asked if I wanted a solicitor.

'Of course I want a solicitor.'

'I hear Tony Barraclough's good,' Jack said.

## The Wider Scheme

That smell was in my nostrils, that police station smell. There were, I decided suddenly, worse smells, far worse smells, in the wider scheme of things.

# Unknown Pleasures

Nelly sat with his head in his hands. He could feel the sweat, except it was more viscous than sweat, more like a sheen of cooking oil. The tenement stairwell smelt of deep-fried tomcat, and the cold step beneath him was stained and scuffed. Over the years, thousands of pairs of feet must have pulled themselves up here, tired or drunk or ailing. But no one in the whole history of the tenement had ever come near to feeling as bad as he did right now. Eleven o'clock, an hour shy of the millennium, and the only way he was going to make it was if he got some stuff. Hunter was mean at the best of times, doubly mean at this festive period. 'Reverse goodwill' he called it. Chimes outside. Nelly counted eleven. The crowds would be gathering in Princes Street, laser shows and live bands promised, then the fireworks. He could have some fireworks of his own, here on the stairwell, but only if he got some stuff. Which was why he'd climbed the three flights to Mrs McIver's flat. He knew she was out: Cormack's Bar every night, eight till eleven. She was in her seventies, wouldn't swap her eyrie for a retirement home with a lift and ramp. In her seventies and well pickled. Rum and black. When she laughed, her tongue was an inky tentacle. He'd nothing against her, only he'd figured her door would be easiest, so he'd shouldered it and kicked it and shouldered it again. Nothing. She'd morticed it, even though she was only round the corner.

So now he sat with his head in his hands. Soon as the pain got to him, he'd top himself, couldn't see any other way. He'd leave a note grassing up Hunter: revenge from the grave and all that. There was nothing in his flat worth hawking, and nobody to hawk it to at this time of night, this night of all nights. Everyone was on the outside. Hunter and

Sheila and Dickie and his mum and gran, part of the party that was Edinburgh, kissing strangers and wishing Happy New Years less than an hour from now. Should auld acquaintance be forgot.

His acquaintance was the big H, and no way was it letting him forget it.

Methadone was a joke. He sold his. Some chemists had started taking the junkies in ten at a time, shutting up shop while each dose was dispensed. Standing in a line like cub scouts or something. One wee plastic cup . . . With jellies hard to come by, what was the alternative?

There is no alternative, that's what heroin would have said. It wasn't true it would kill you. It was the crap they cut it with did that. Anybody who could afford a good, big habit of the nice stuff, they could go on for ever. Look at Keef. Learned to ski, used to whip Jagger at tennis, made *Exile on Main Street* – skagged out the whole time. Skagged out and playing *tennis*. Nelly started to laugh. He was still laughing when the sound of the tenement door closing came crashing up the stairwell. Slow, steady steps. He rubbed tears from his eyes. His shoulder hurt where it had connected with Mrs McIver's door. And here she was now, climbing towards him.

'What's the joke, Nelly?'

He stood up to let her past. She was getting her keys out of her bag. Big canvas bag with *Las Vegas* painted on the side in loopy red writing. Looked like big red veins to Nelly. He could see a newspaper and a library book and a purse.

'Nothing really, Mrs McIver.' A purse.

'What're you doing up here anyway?'

'Thought I heard something. Wanted to check you were all right.'

'You must be hearing things. I thought you'd be out on the town, night like this.'

'I was just heading out.' He stepped on to her landing. She had her key in the door. 'Eh, Mrs McIver . . . ?'

As she turned her head, his fist caught her on the cheek.

*

Johnny Hunter was holding court in his local. He was in his favourite corner seat, both arms draped round the necks of the blondes he'd chatted up at Chapters on Boxing Day evening. He'd given them champagne, driven them around in his Saab convertible, keeping the top down even though it was cold. He'd told them they needed fur coats, said he'd measure them up. They'd laughed. The littler one, Margo, he'd told her that was the name of an expensive wine. The other one, Juliet, was quieter. A bit stuck-up maybe, but not about to duck out, not with The Hunter throwing his money and his weight around. He'd done a few deals tonight, nothing cataclysmic. The punters wanted speed to keep them going, coke to lend an air of celebration to the new beginning. He'd steered a couple of them towards smack instead. Fashion was cyclical, whether it was hemlines or recreational drugs. Heroin was back in style. That was his pitch.

'And it's safe,' he'd tell them. 'Just follow the instructions on the box.' And with a wink he'd be off, rearranging the lines of his Armani jacket, eyes open to the possibilities around him. Margo seemed to be cosying into him, maybe to get away from Panda, who was seated next to her. Panda was the scariest thing in the pub, which was the whole point of him. He was paid to be a deterrent, and also did the deals outside. The Hunter didn't touch the goods if he could help it. The cops had come after him three times already this year, never enough for a prosecution. And now he had a pair of ears in the Drugs Squad: a hundred a week just for the odd phone call. Cheap insurance, Caldwell had agreed when Hunter had told him about it. Cheap for Caldwell, at any rate.

Hunter didn't know how much Caldwell was making. Ten, fifteen grand a week, had to be. House down in the Borders apparently, more a castle than a house. Six cars, each one better than the Saab. Hunter wanted to be Caldwell. He knew he *could* be Caldwell. He was good enough. But Caldwell had the contacts . . . and the money

. . . and the muscle. Caldwell had made people disappear. And if Hunter didn't keep business moving, he might find himself on the wrong end of his boss. There were other dealers out there: younger, just as hungry, and edging on the desperate, which meant reckless. All of them would like Hunter's power, and his clothes and car, his women and money. They all wanted his money. And now Nelly of all runts was giving him grief – just by his very existence. Caldwell's goons making sure Hunter knew what had to be done, making him acknowledge just how low he was on the ladder.

'It'll be you takes the fall,' one of them had said. 'You or him, so make it clean.'

Oh, he'd make it clean, if that was what it took. He knew he'd no choice, much as he liked Nelly.

'Are we clubbing or what?'

Billy Bones talking: skinny as a wisp of smoke, seated the other side of Juliet, whose legs he'd been staring at for the past half-hour.

'One more,' Hunter said. The pub was heaving, table service impossible. There were a dozen empty glasses on the table. Hunter reached out an arm and swept them to the floor.

Patrick Caldwell examined himself in his bathroom's full-length mirror. He was casually dressed: brogues, chinos, yellow shirt, and a Ralph Lauren red V-necked sweater. Nearing fifty, he was pleased that he still possessed a good head of hair, and that the only grey was provided by touches at either temple. His face was tanned, and his eyes sparkled with self-satisfaction. It had, in the words of the song, been a very good year: less merchandise apprehended by the authorities; demand steady in some areas, increasing in others. A very satisfactory year. But still something niggled him. The more money he made, the more contented he should be: wasn't that the dream? But the things he really wanted seemed still intangible. Seemed further away than ever, yet so close he could almost taste them . . .

He turned out the light and headed back downstairs, where his guests were waiting. The cheeseboard was being placed on the table. A huge log fire crackled and spat in the hearth. The room was wood-panelled and fifty feet long, a devil to heat. But nobody looked uncomfortable. The whiskies and champagnes and wines had done their trick. Armagnac still to come, and the best champagne kept for midnight itself. On his way to his chair, he leaned down and kissed his wife's head, which drew smiles from the guests. Eight of them, all but two staying the night. His driver would take these two home – that way they could both drink.

'I'll have no sobersides tonight,' he'd told them.

His guests were all professional people, wealthy in their own right, and as far as they were concerned Caldwell made his pile in a variety of property deals, security transactions and foreign investments. The Tomkinsons – Ben and Alicia – were seated nearest Caldwell. Ben had made his money early in life, a communications company in the City. He'd been a lowly BT engineer before founding his company, taking his one big risk in life. Now, twenty years on, he had homes in Kent, Scotland and Barbados, and liked to talk too readily about fishing. But Caldwell's wife got on well with Alicia, ten years younger than Ben and a real beauty.

Jonathan Trent had been an MP for two years, resigning finally (and famously) because the hours were too long, the pay laughable. He'd returned to his merchant bank, and was these days one of Caldwell's many advisers. Trent didn't mind where Caldwell's money came from, didn't ask too many questions. His first piece of advice to his client: get the best accountants money can buy. These days Caldwell was shielded as much by his small army of legal people and moneymen as by his hulking Mercedes and bodyguard. Even tonight Crispin was on duty, somewhere on the property, revealing himself only to any unwelcome visitors.

Caldwell glanced at Trent's wife, who was as usual putting away double the drinks her husband was. Not that she couldn't hold the stuff, but it was always quantity over quality with Stella, and this irked Caldwell. Put the finest Burgundy in front of her and she slugged it like it was off the bottom shelf at Thresher's. He'd seated Parnell Wilson next to her, in the hope that the racing driver's tanned good looks would take Stella's mind off grain and grape. But Wilson was too obviously besotted with his girlfriend, Fran, who sat directly opposite him. From their looks, Caldwell knew they were playing some provocative game of footsie under the table. And why not? Fran was like all Wilson's conquests: tiny and gorgeous and leaping out of what dress there was, naked skin the only cloth that would really suit her.

Caldwell had a large share in the syndicate which owned Wilson's racing team. Not that Caldwell enjoyed the sport: frankly, he could see no point to it. But he did enjoy the travelling – Italy, Brazil, Monte Carlo – and he always met interesting people, some of whom turned into useful contacts.

Final guests: Sir Arthur Lorimer and his museum-piece of a wife. Lorimer was a judge and near-neighbour, and it pleased Caldwell to have the old soak here. Cultivate the Establishment: Trent's second piece of advice. His reasoning: if you're ever found out, it reflects badly on them, and as a result they'll try to ignore what misdemeanours they can. Caldwell hoped he'd never have to put this to the test. But that might be up to Hunter.

There'd been a phone call earlier from Franz in Dortmund, just to wish him a happy and prosperous new year. 'With your help, Franz,' Caldwell had said. They never said very much on the phone. You never knew who was listening, even at Hogmanay. It was all codes and intermediaries.

'Your party's tonight?'

'In full flow. I'm sorry you couldn't make it.'

'Business so often interrupts my pleasures. But I'm sending a little token, Patrick. A gift for the millennium.'

'Franz, you needn't have.'

'Oh, but it's nothing really. I look forward to seeing you soon, my friend. And enjoy what's left of your party.'

*Enjoy what's left.*

They were on dessert when the doorbell rang. Caldwell decided to answer it himself, thinking of Franz's gift.

A man was standing on the porch. He was dressed all in black, smiling, pointing a gun directly at Caldwell's heart.

Franz knew he was going to have to head up to Denmark. Those damned Hell's Angels and their little squabbles. All that tribalism was so bad for business. Not that they cared much about business, all they cared about was themselves. They reminded him of nothing so much as feuding families in some American cartoon book, a face-off between two mountain shacks. It had started as a question of territory – almost always his business disputes were to do with encroachment. That was why meetings were so important, so lines of demarcation could be drawn. But these bikers . . . put them in a room together and the hate was like some fug in the air, sucking out oxygen and replacing it with toxic gas.

He needed couriers to Denmark, and the Angels were good at their job. But they lacked *dedication*. And he definitely didn't need a war starting up between rival chapters. He needed that like he needed a hole in the head.

He thought of Caldwell's gift and allowed himself a smile. No visitors to Franz's home this night. Few visitors on that day of the year. He conducted business from an office in the city, and travelled often. But here, in this fortress he had constructed, spending the best part of DM300,000 on security alone, here he felt safe, felt a certain tranquillity at times. These were the moments when his thinking was at its best, when he could plan and debate. Beloved Mozart on the stereo, and tonight not the Requiem – not on a night that should be a blossoming of hope and fresh intentions.

His second fresh intention: after the diplomatic trip to Denmark, a further trip to Afghanistan. He'd heard worrying reports of depleted harvests, and of crops and fields being burned by suddenly efficient soldiers. He'd asked an associate in Chicago what the hell they thought was going on.

'Blame our fucking dick-dipping President. He's trying the same shit he pulled in South America. "Be my friend," he tells them. "Let me loan you money, billions of dollars of clean government money. Use it to rebuild your infrastructure or line your private Zurich bank vault. But just get rid of all the shit you grow." It's all politics, as usual.'

The voice from Chicago was distorted – a side-effect of the scrambler. At least no one would be listening in.

'I don't understand,' Franz had said – though he did. 'I thought we had arranged for friends to be placed where they could help us.'

'What can they do? CBS go prime-time on a field of burning poppies, then up pops the Prez to say he did it. His ratings jump a couple of points, Franz, this guy would do his dear departed grandma in the ass for a couple of points.'

End of conversation.

Sad really, to think that decisions taken a continent away could affect one so much, but thrilling too. Because Franz saw himself as part of a network which embraced the globe, and felt his importance, his *place* in the scheme of things. If they ever set up colonies in space, *he* wanted to be supplying them. Dealer to the universe, by appointment to infinity . . .

Mozart silent now. He hadn't realised, but midnight had come and gone. Then a buzzer sounding: the guardroom, one of his men informing him of intruders entering the compound.

It was not yet quite dawn, and Kejan lay in the darkness, as he had for the preceding five hours, his eyes staring, ears attuned to his wife's light breathing. Three of their children slept in the room with them. Hama, the youngest, coughed and turned, made a slight moan before relaxing again. Kejan didn't know if he'd ever relax again in his life, ever sleep again on this earth. Would the soldiers fulfil their promise and return to torch the shacks by the side of what had once been fields full of crops? Those fields had been Kejan's future. Not that he'd owned them: the owner was a brutal man, a slave-driver. But Kejan had mouths to feed, and what other work was there? Now, with the fields reduced to cinders, he could only wait and wonder: would the soldiers drive the families away? Or would the Bossman chase them off his land, now that there was no work for them?

It was a matter of time. It was for the future.

He tried to envisage a future for his wife, his three children. He had more than once caught the Bossman staring at his wife, running his tongue over his bottom lip. And talking to her once, too, though she would not even admit it, kept her eyes on the ground as she denied and denied.

Kejan had slapped her then, the bruise a lasting smudge against her cheekbone. It didn't seem to want to go away.

There were so many things Kejan didn't understand.

The soldiers passed around lighted torches. Their commander, arguing with the Bossman. The Bossman saying that he always paid, that he always kept everyone sweet. The commander not listening, the Bossman persistent. Soldiers fingering their weapons, noting that the Bossman's men were better armed with newer, gleaming automatics.

'Orders,' the commander kept saying. And: 'Just let us get on with it for now.'

'For now': meaning things might be okay later, that this had some deeper meaning which the commander felt unable to share.

But later . . . later there would be other workers, willing

workers. New people could always be found later. *Now* was what mattered to Kejan. He lived from moment to moment in this dark, overcrowded room. He waited for the moment he knew was coming, when the future would become the present and he would be consigned to the road with his family.

Or perhaps – please, no – without them. He had hit his wife. The Bossman had smiled at her. The Bossman would take her, and Kejan couldn't be sure she wouldn't go. Would she take his children? Would the Bossman want them? Would he treat them right?

His wife's breathing, so shallow. The room a little lighter now, so he could see the outline of her neck, the way it was angled against the stem-filled sack she used as a pillow.

Slender neck. Brittle neck. Kejan touched it with the tips of his fingers, heard a child cough and pulled his fingers away like they'd been too close to a torch.

He sat up then, looked down on the dark, curved shape. Twisted his own body around so that it was easier to reach down with both hands.

And heard the sound of lorries on the rough track outside, coming closer.

An aggrieved Hell's Angel sat in Franz's study, and it was all Franz could do not to reach into his desk drawer for the pistol and blow the man's brains all over the walls. Defilement: that was what it felt like. Engine oil and cigarette smoke had invaded his most private space, and even when the man had gone, those taints would remain.

The rest of the gang was outside. One on one: Franz had demanded it, and the leader had agreed. A dozen of them. They'd scaled the perimeter wall. A dozen of them armed, and Franz with only three guards on duty. But now more were on their way: calls had been made. And meantime the three guards faced off the leather-clad bandits, while their leader and Franz sat with only the antique rosewood desk between them.

'Nice place,' the Angel said. His name was Lars. Well over six feet tall, hair stretched back into a thin ponytail. Denim waistcoat – all-important 'colours' – worn over leather jacket. And his jackboots up on Franz's desk.

He'd grinned when Franz had stopped short of telling him to take his feet off the desk. But Franz was biding his time, waiting for his other men to arrive, and wanting to rise above all this, to be the diplomat. So he'd offered Lars a drink, and Lars now rested a bottle of beer against his crotch, and looked relaxed.

'You're financing our rivals,' the gang leader said, getting down to business.

'In what way?'

'We're in a war, no room for neutrals. And you're funding their side of things.'

'I pay them to act as my couriers, that's all. I'm not financing any conflict.'

'But it's *your* money they're using when they buy guns and ammo.'

Franz shrugged. 'And whose money are *you* using, my friend? Are your mortal enemies at this very moment confronting *your* employer?' He smiled. 'Do you see the absurdity of the situation? I'm not happy, because here you are invading my privacy, and I don't suppose your employer will be feeling any different. I'm a businessman. I *am* neutral: business always is. What you're doing, right this second, is fucking with my business. My instinct naturally is to get out, which is what you want, yes?'

He had lost the biker, who nodded slowly.

'Exactly. But what if the same thought is going through *your* employer's mind? Where does that leave you? With no money, no prospects.' Franz shook his head. 'My friend, the best thing you can do for all our sakes is to begin discussions with your rivals, settle this thing, then we can all get back to what we want to be doing: making money.'

Franz reached into a drawer, held one hand up to let Lars

know nothing tricky was coming. He produced a fat bundle of Deutschmarks and tossed it to the gang-leader.

'See?' he said. 'Now I'm funding both of you. Does that make me neutral?'

Lars studied the notes, stuffed them into a zippered pocket.

'Let me set up a meeting,' Franz went on blandly, 'get all sides together, anyone who has an interest. That's the way business works.'

'You're full of bullshit,' the biker said, but he was grinning.

'Should your employer ever wish to dispense with your services,' Franz continued, 'you may wish to contact me.' He wrote a number on a sheet of paper, ripped it from the pad. 'This is my private line. Maybe next time you're thinking of coming to see me, we could arrange an appointment?'

A nice big smile. Lars slid his feet from the corner of the desk. His heels had left marks on the woodwork. As he reached for the paper, Franz snatched it back.

'One thing, my friend. Try something like this again *without* an appointment, and I'll destroy you. Is that clear between us?'

Lars laughed and took the number, stuck it in the same pocket as the money.

Franz's mobile phone rang. It was in the desk drawer, and he opened the drawer again, shrugging, telling Lars there was no rest for the wicked.

'Hello?'

A hushed voice, one he knew. 'We've got every one of those dirty fuckers in our sights.'

'Fine,' Franz said, making to replace the phone in its drawer, bringing out the pistol in its place. Lars was already reaching across the desk. He'd pulled a combat knife from one boot. Franz was leaning back to take aim when the gunfire started outside.

\*

Caldwell was in the library. He'd locked the door, and when his wife had come knocking, saying the judge and his wife were thinking of leaving, he'd hissed at her to fuck off.

He sat in a burgundy leather chair, hands on his knees, while his visitor stood four feet away, the gun steady in his left hand.

'My bodyguard?' Caldwell asked.

'Tied up outside. Let's hope someone releases him before hypothermia sets in. It's a bitter night. We wouldn't want any unnecessary deaths.'

'You've come from Franz?'

The man nodded. His accent was English. He had a heavy body, thick at the neck, and cropped hair. Ex-forces, Caldwell presumed.

'With a message,' the man said.

A typical gesture by Franz: he always had to show his *puissance*. Caldwell thought he knew now what this was about, and felt a mixture of emotions: the thrill of fear, fury at Franz's little game; embarrassment that his guests would be wondering what the hell was going on.

'Everything's set,' Caldwell told the man.

'Really?'

'Does Franz have any reason to doubt me?'

'That's what I'm here to find out. It's nearly midnight. Everything was supposed to be finalised by midnight.'

'Everything *is*.' Caldwell made to rise from his chair, but the gun waved him back down again.

'Links in a chain, Mr Caldwell. That's all we are. The weakest links have to be taken out, the strong ones reconnected.'

'You think I'd put myself on the line for a little turd like that?'

'I think you like to operate at a distance.'

'And Franz doesn't?'

'He always uses the best people. I'm not sure Hunter falls into that category.'

'Hunter'll do as he's told.'

'Will he? I've heard he might have a personal stake in all of this.'

Caldwell frowned. 'How do you mean?' His wife knocked at the door again, her voice artificially bright.

'Darling, Sir Arthur and Lady Lorimer are leaving. I've asked Foster to bring the Bentley round.'

Her voice grated. It always had. The way she spoke now, like she'd been to elocution classes, like she'd been saying 'Darling' and 'Sir This' and 'Lady That' all her life. And all she was was a piece of crumpet he'd picked up early on in his travels through life. Too early on. He could have done better for himself. Still could, given the chance. Send her off with a settlement, or bring some mistress into the equation. It seemed to Caldwell that he hadn't really started living yet.

'Apologise, will you?' he called. 'I'm on the phone. Important business.' He lowered his voice again, mind half on his life to come, half on the gun in front of him. 'How do you mean?' he repeated.

'You see,' the man said, 'that's the difference between my employer and you. *He* takes the trouble to know things, to know *people*. He's a thousand miles away, and he knows more about your operation here than you do.'

'What does he know?' There was a slight tremble in Caldwell's hands. Why would Franz be so interested in Caldwell's territory? Unless he was planning some incursion, or to move in some new operator. Unless he thought Caldwell wasn't his best bet any more . . .

'Hunter,' the gunman was saying. 'He's tough, but just how tough? I mean, that's what we'll find out tonight, isn't it? If things go the way they're supposed to.'

'Nelly's just a runt. Hunter won't have any trouble with him.'

'No?' The man got right into Caldwell's face. 'What if I tell you something about Nelly?'

'Such as?' Caldwell's voice nearly failed him.

'His surname's Hunter, you fucking idiot. He's Johnny Hunter's kid brother.'

\*

Hunter was in the club, chain-smoking, eyes everywhere. He didn't feel like dancing. The bass was like God's heartbeat, the lights His eyes shining down across the little world. Hunter's right knee was pounding, speed working its way to his fingertips and toes. He sat alone at the table, Panda not six feet away, just standing there so nobody'd bother his boss unless the boss wanted to be bothered. He hadn't much left to sell. Not much at all.

His friends were whooping on the dance-floor, waving to him occasionally. They probably thought he was cool, sitting the dances out, smoking his smokes. He rattled a cube of ice into his mouth and crunched down on it. Another drink replaced the empty glass. Fast service in the club, because he owned thirty per cent. Thirty per cent of all of it. But he knew that fifty-one was the only percentage that mattered.

Fifty-one meant control.

He was waiting for Nelly, hoping not to see him, knowing he'd come here eventually. Hunter could have gone elsewhere, but what did it matter? Nelly would always find him. It was like the guy had a homing instinct.

Nelly: young and whacked out and terminally stupid.

Hunter had always tried to keep things between them strictly business. He could have refused to deal with Nelly, but then Nelly would have gone elsewhere, maybe gotten into worse trouble. But Hunter had never done him any favours. No dope better than anyone else was getting; no discounts for family.

Strictly business.

Only tonight, Nelly was going to get better dope. He was going to get the best stuff going. Caldwell's orders.

'Hey, Hunter!' A girl he knew: short skirt, any tighter and you'd have to call it skin. Waving him on to the floor. He waved back in the negative. She blew him a kiss anyway. Margo and Juliet were off somewhere: maybe at the ladies', or whisked away by other raptors. They were meat, the window-dressing in a butcher's shop. Hunter didn't give a fuck about them.

He didn't give a fuck about anyone but himself. Number One. Looking out for.

Ah, shit, Nelly . . .

Hunter punched the table with his fist. It was all about the future, about Nelly's versus his. No contest, was it? Nelly all fucked over anyway, while Hunter was just starting out. There was never going to be any contest. But all the same, he hoped the crowds outside, the swoop and swirl of this millennial midnight, would keep Nelly away. Maybe the tide would wash him down on to Princes Street, and he'd score there. Or maybe the cops would grab him, spot him at last for the one they wanted. Which was just what Caldwell didn't want. No telling who Nelly would grass up. No telling where the trail would lead. So instead there was to be a deal. There was to be the purest heroin going, stuff that would stop your heart dead.

Caldwell's orders. And Caldwell was acting on orders, too. And the person *above* Caldwell – Hunter had the idea it was some German or Dutch guy – *that* was who Hunter had to impress. Because he had to make a name for himself pronto, had to get ahead of the game, had to stake his place as Caldwell's replacement.

Had to make contact.

Had to make good.

'Yo!'

His chest tightened. Lanky and dripping sweat, unlikely ever to be let in by the bouncers if they didn't know he was Hunter's brother, here came Nelly, nodding towards Panda, sliding into the booth and tipping the remains of someone's lager down his neck.

'Thought I was never going to find you, man.'

Hunter gazed at his brother, couldn't find any words.

'Happy New Year, 'n' 'at,' Nelly said.

'It's not midnight yet. Another couple of minutes.'

'Oh, right.' Nelly nodding, not really giving a toss about

any of this conversation, or any emotions his brother might be feeling. Only needing a taste.

'Dosh,' Nelly said, sliding the money across.

'You know the score, Nelly. Panda takes care of that.'

Panda: standing there with one packet in his pocket exclusively for Nelly. Hunter's orders. And when Nelly OD'd, Panda would know Hunter had balls.

Everyone would know. Nobody'd ever try to screw him. The word would be made flesh. Suicide a small price to pay for that big bright future.

Nelly was already thinking of getting to his feet. He had no business now with Hunter. His business, his most urgent and necessary business, was with Panda. But he had to make a bit more conversation, pretend he'd a bit more respect for Hunter than was the case.

'Eh, man, just to say . . .' Nelly twitched. 'Like, sorry about the kid.'

'Are you?'

'Christ, man, how was I to know he'd take the whole shot? I didn't know he was a virgin.'

'But you sold him your methadone, right?'

'Needed the dosh, man.'

'And he was fourteen?'

Nelly twitched again. 'It's going to be cool though? I mean, the police and the newspapers are going apeshit looking for—'

'I've got friends, Nelly. They'll take care of it.'

Nelly's face brightened. 'You're the best, Johnny.' On his feet now. 'Don't let any of the bastards tell you different.'

Hunter got up. They hugged, wished one another Happy New Year as the siren in the club sounded, releasing balloons. The DJ put on 'Auld Lang Syne', and it was like they were kids again, getting to stay up late this one night of the year, ginger cordial and madeira cake. Sneaking into the kitchen for swigs of whisky and brandy, giggling at each new pleasure revealed to them.

And when Hunter let his brother go, and watched him

put an arm around Panda, and saw them vanish into the haze in front of his eyes, he felt a stab of terror for what he would have to become in this new millennium, and for all the things he would do, and the pleasures he would of necessity forgo.

# In the Frame

## AN INSPECTOR REBUS STORY

Inspector John Rebus placed the letters on his desk.

There were three of them. Small, plain white envelopes, locally franked, the same name and address printed on each in a careful hand. The name was K. Leighton. Rebus looked up from the envelopes to the man sitting on the other side of the desk. He was in his forties, frail-looking and restless. He had started talking the moment he'd entered Rebus's office, and didn't seem inclined to stop.

'The first one arrived on Tuesday, last Tuesday. A crank, I thought, some sort of malicious joke. Not that I could think of anyone who might do that sort of thing.' He shifted in his seat. 'My neighbours over the back from me . . . well, we don't always see eye to eye, but they wouldn't resort to this.' His eyes glanced up towards Rebus for a second. 'Would they?'

'You tell me, Mr Leighton.'

As soon as he'd said this, Rebus regretted the choice of words. Undoubtedly, Kenneth Leighton *would* tell him. Rebus opened the first envelope's flap, extracted the sheet of writing-paper and unfolded it. He did the same with the second and third letters and laid all three before him.

'If it had been only the one,' Kenneth Leighton was saying, 'I wouldn't have minded, but it doesn't look as though they're going to stop. Tuesday, then Thursday, then Saturday. I spent all weekend worrying about what to do . . .'

'You did the right thing, Mr Leighton.'

Leighton wriggled pleasurably. 'Well, they always say you should go to the police. Not that I think there's anything

238

serious. I mean, *I've* not got anything to hide. My life's an open book . . .'

An open book and an unexciting one, Rebus would imagine. He tried to shut out Leighton's voice and concentrated instead on the first letter.

*Mr Leighton,*
*We've got photos you wouldn't want your wife to see, believe us. Think about it. We'll be in touch.*

Then the second:

*Mr Leighton,*
*£2,000 for the photos. That seems fair, doesn't it? You really wouldn't want your wife to see them. Get the money. We'll be in touch.*

And the third:

*Mr Leighton,*
*We'll be sending one reprint to show we mean business. You'd better get to it before your wife does. There are plenty more copies.*

Rebus looked up, and caught Leighton staring at him. Leighton immediately looked away. Rebus had the feeling that if he stood behind the man and said 'boo' quite softly in his ear, Leighton would melt all down the chair. He looked like the sort of person who might make an enemy of his neighbours, complaining too strenuously about a noisy party or a family row. He looked like a crank.

'You haven't received the photo yet?'

Leighton shook his head. 'I'd have brought it along, wouldn't I?'

'And you've no idea what sort of photo it might be?'

'None at all. The last time somebody took my picture was at my niece's wedding.'

239

'And when was that?'

'Three years ago. You see what I'm saying, Inspector? This doesn't make any sense.'

'It must make sense to at least one person, Mr Leighton.' Rebus nodded towards the letters.

They had been written in blue ball-point, the same pen which had been used to address the envelopes. A cheap blue ball-point, leaving smears and blots of ink. It was anything but professional-looking. The whole thing looked like a joke. Since when did blackmailers use their own handwriting? Anyone with a rudimentary education in films, TV cop shows and thriller novels knew that you used a typewriter or letters cut out of newspapers, or whatever; anything that would produce a dramatic effect. These letters were too personal to look dramatic. Polite, too: that use of 'Mr Leighton' at the start of each one. A particular word caught Rebus's attention and held it. But then Leighton said something interesting.

'I don't even have a wife, not now.'

'You're not married?'

'I was. Divorced six years ago. Six years and one month.'

'And where's your wife now, Mr Leighton?'

'Remarried, lives in Glenrothes. I got an invite to the wedding, but I didn't go. Can't remember what I sent them for a present . . .' Leighton was lost in thought for a moment, then collected himself. 'So you see, if these letters are written by someone I know, how come they *don't* know I'm divorced?'

It was a good question. Rebus considered it for a full five seconds. Then he came to his conclusion.

'Let's leave it for now, Mr Leighton,' he said. 'There's not much we can do till this photo arrives . . . *if* it arrives.'

Leighton looked numb, watching Rebus fold the letters and replace them in their envelopes. Rebus wasn't sure what the man had expected. Fingerprints lifted from the envelopes by forensic experts? A tell-tale fibre leading to an arrest? Handwriting identified . . . saliva from the stamps and the envelope-flaps checked . . . psychologists analysing the wording of the messages themselves, coming up with a profile of the blackmailer? It was all good stuff, but not on a wet Monday morning in Edinburgh. Not with CID's case-load and budget restrictions.

'Is that it?'

Rebus shrugged. That was it. We're only human, Mr Leighton. For a moment, Rebus thought he'd actually voiced his thoughts. He had not. Leighton still sat there, pale and disappointed, his mouth set like the bottom line of a balance sheet.

'Sorry,' said Rebus, rising.

'I've just remembered,' said Leighton.

'What?'

'Six wine glasses, that's what I gave them. Caithness glass they were too.'

'Very nice I'm sure,' said Rebus, stifling a post-weekend yawn as he opened the office door.

But Rebus was certainly intrigued.

No wife these past six years, and the last photograph of Leighton dated back three years to a family wedding. Where was the material for blackmail? Where the motive? Means, motive and opportunity. Means: a photograph, apparently. Motive: unknown. Opportunity . . . Leighton was a nobody, a middle-aged civil servant. He earned enough, but not enough to make him blackmail material. He had confided to Rebus that he barely had £2,000 in his building society account.

'Hardly enough to cover their demand,' he had said, as though he were considering actually paying off the black-mailers, even though he had nothing to hide, nothing to fear. Just to get them off his back? Or because he *did* have something to hide? Most people did, if it came to it. The guilty secret or two (or more, many more) stored away just below the level of consciousness, the way suitcases were stored under beds. Rebus wondered if he himself were blackmail material. He smiled: was the Pope a Catholic? Was the Chief Constable a Mason? Leighton's words came back to him: *Hardly enough to cover their demand*. What sort of civil servant was Leighton anyway? Rebus sought out the day-time telephone number Leighton had left along with his home address and phone number. Seven digits, followed by a three-figure extension number. He punched the seven digits on his receiver, waited, and heard a switchboard operator say, 'Good afternoon, Inland Revenue.' Rebus replaced the receiver with a guilty silence.

On Tuesday morning, Leighton phoned the station. Rebus got in first.

'You didn't tell me you were a taxman, Mr Leighton.'

'What?'

'A taxman.'

'What does it matter?'

What did it matter? How many enemies could one taxman make? Rebus swallowed back the question. He could always use a friend in Her Majesty's Inland Revenue, for personal as well as strictly professional use . . .

'I know what you're thinking,' Leighton was saying, though Rebus doubted it. 'And it's true that I work in the Collector's office, sending out the demands. But my name's never on the demands. The Inspector of Taxes might be mentioned by name, but I'm a lowly cog, Inspector.'

'Even so, you must write to people sometimes. There might be somebody out there with a grudge.'

'I've given it some thought, Inspector. It was my *first* thought. But in any case I don't deal with Edinburgh.'

'Oh?'

'I deal with south London.'

Rebus noted that, phoning from his place of work, Leighton was less nervous-sounding. He sounded cool, detached. He sounded like a tax collector. South London: but the letters had local postmarks – another theory sealed under cover and posted into eternity, no return address.

'The reason I'm calling,' Leighton was saying, 'is that I had another letter this morning.'

'With a photo?'

'Yes, there's a photo.'

'And?'

'It's difficult to explain. I could come to the station at lunchtime.'

'Don't bother yourself, Mr Leighton. I'll come to the tax office. All part of the service.'

Rebus was thinking of back-handers, gifts from grateful members of the public, all the pubs where he could be sure of a free drink, chip shops that wouldn't charge for a feed, all the times he'd helped out for a favour, the way those favours accumulated and were paid off . . . Tax forms asked you about tips received. Rebus always left the box blank. Had he always been accurate about amounts of bank interest? More crucially, several months ago he had started renting his flat to three students while he lived rent-free with Dr Patience Aitken. He had no intention of declaring . . . well, maybe he would. It helped to know a friendly taxman, someone who might soon owe him a favour.

'That's very good of you, Inspector,' Leighton was saying.

'Not at all, sir.'

'Only it all seems to have been a mistake anyway.'

'A mistake?'

'You'll see when I show you the photograph.'

Rebus saw.

He saw a man and a woman. In the foreground was a coffee table, spread with bottles and glasses and cans, an ashtray full to overflowing. Behind this, a sofa, and on the sofa a man and a woman. Lying along the sofa, hugging one another. The photographer had caught them like this, their faces just beginning to turn towards the camera, grinning and flushed with that familiar mix of alcohol and passion. Rebus had been to these sorts of party, parties where the alcohol was necessary before there could be any passion.

Behind the couple, two men stood in animated conversation. It was a good clear photo, the work of a 35mm camera with either a decent flash-gun or else no necessity for one.

'And here's the letter,' said Leighton. They were seated on an uncomfortable, spongy sofa in the tax office's reception area. Rebus had been hoping for a sniff behind the scenes, but Leighton worked in an open-plan office with less privacy even than the reception area. Few members of the public ever visited the building, and the receptionist was at the other end of the hallway. Staff wandered through on their way to the coffee machine or the snack dispenser, the toilets or the post-room, but otherwise this was as quiet as it got.

'A bit longer than the others,' Leighton said, handing the letter over.

> *Mr Leighton,*
> *Here is the photo. We have plenty more, plus negatives. Cheap at £2,000 the lot, and your wife will never know. The money should be in fives and tens, nothing bigger. Put it in a William Low's carrier-bag and go to Greyfriars Kirkyard on Friday at 3 p.m. Leave the bag behind Greyfriars Bobby's gravestone. Walk away. Photos and negatives will be sent to you.*

'Not exactly the quietest spot for a handover,' Rebus mused. Although the actual statue of Greyfriars Bobby, sited just outside the kirkyard, was more popular with tourists, the gravestone was a popular enough stop-off. The idea of leaving a bagful of money there surreptitiously was almost laughable. But at least now the extortion was serious. A time and place had been mentioned as well as a sum, a sum to be left in a Willie Low's bag. Rebus more than ever doubted the blackmailer's professionalism.

'You see what I mean?' Leighton said. 'I can only think that if it isn't a joke, then it's a case of mistaken identity.'

True enough, Leighton wasn't any of the three men in the photo, not by any stretch of the will or imagination. Rebus concentrated on the woman. She was small, heavy, somehow managing to fit into a dress two sizes too small for her. It was black and short, rumpled most of the way to her bum, with plenty of cleavage at the other end. She also wore black tights and black patent-leather shoes. But somehow Rebus didn't think he was looking at a funeral.

'I don't suppose', he said, 'this is your wife?'

Leighton actually laughed, the sound of paper shredding.

'Thought not,' Rebus said quietly. He turned his attention to the man on the sofa, the man whose arms were trapped beneath the weight of the smirking woman. There was something about that face, that hairstyle. Then it hit Rebus, and things started to make a little more sense.

'I didn't recognise him at first,' he said, thinking out loud.

'You mean you know him?'

Rebus nodded slowly. 'Only I've never seen him smile before, that's what threw me.' He studied the photo again, then stabbed it with a finger. The tip of his finger was resting on the face of one of the other men, the two behind the sofa. 'And I know him,' he said. 'I can place him now.' Leighton looked impressed. Rebus moved his finger on to the recumbent woman. 'What's more, I know her too. I know her quite well.'

Leighton didn't look impressed now, he looked startled, perhaps even disbelieving.

'Three out of four,' Rebus said. 'Not a bad score, eh?' Leighton didn't answer, so Rebus smiled reassuringly. 'Don't you worry, sir. I'll take care of this. You won't be bothered any more.'

'Well . . . thank you, Inspector.'

Rebus got to his feet. 'All part of the service, Mr Leighton. Who knows, maybe *you'll* be able to help *me* one of these days . . .'

Rebus sat at his desk, reading the file. Then, when he was satisfied, he tapped into the computer and checked some details regarding a man who was doing a decent stretch in

Peterhead jail. When he'd finished, there was a broad grin on his face, an event unusual enough in itself to send DC Siobhan Clarke sauntering over in Rebus's direction, trying not to get too close (fear of being hooked), but close enough to register interest. Before she knew it, Rebus was reeling her in anyway.

'Get your coat,' he said.

She angled her head back towards her desk. 'But I'm in the middle of—'

'You're in the middle of *my* catchment, Siobhan. Now fetch your coat.'

Never be nosy, and always keep your head down: somehow Siobhan Clarke hadn't yet learned those two golden rules of the easy life. Not that anything was easy when John Rebus was in the office. Which was precisely why she liked working near him.

'Where are we going?' she said.

Rebus told her on the way. He also handed the file to her so she could read it through.

'Not guilty,' she said at last.

'And I'm Robbie Coltrane,' said Rebus. They were both talking about a case from a few months before. A veteran hard man had been charged with the attempted armed hold-up of a security van. There had been evidence as to his guilt – just about enough evidence – and his alibi had been shaky. He'd told police of having spent the day in question in a bar near his mother's home in Muirhouse, probably the city's most notorious housing scheme. Plenty of witnesses came forward to agree that he had been there all day. These witnesses boasted names like Tam the Bam, Big Shug, the Screwdriver, and Wild Eck. The look of them in the witness-box, police reasoned, would be enough to convince the jury of the defendant's guilt. But there had been one other witness . . .

'Miss June Redwood,' quoted DC Clarke, rereading the casenotes.

'Yes,' said Rebus, 'Miss June Redwood.'

An innocent, dressed in a solemn two-piece as she gave her evidence at the trial. She was a social worker, caring for the most desperate in Edinburgh's most desperate area. Needing to make a phone call, and sensing she'd have no luck with Muirhouse's few public kiosks, she had walked into the Castle Arms, probably the first female the regulars had seen in the saloon bar since the landlord's wife had walked out on him fifteen years before. She'd asked to use the phone, and a man had wandered over to her from a table and, with a wink, had asked if she'd like a drink. She'd refused. She could see he'd had a few – more than a few. His table had the look of a lengthy session about it – empty pint glasses placed one inside another to form a leaning tower, ashtray brimming with butts and empty packets, the newspaper's racing page heavily marked in biro.

Miss Redwood had given a quietly detailed account, at odds with the loud, confident lies of the other defence witnesses. And she was sure that she'd walked into the bar at 3 p.m., five minutes before the attack on the security van took place. The prosecution counsel had tried his best, gaining from the social worker the acknowledgement that she knew the accused's mother through her work, though the old woman was not actually her client. The prosecutor had stared out at the fifteen jury members, attempting without success to plant doubt in their minds. June Redwood was a rock-solid witness. Solid enough to turn a golden prosecution case into a verdict of 'not guilty'. The accused had walked free. Close, as the fairground saying went, but definitely no goldfish.

Rebus had been in court for the verdict, and had left with a shrug and a low growl. A security guard lay in hospital suffering from shotgun wounds. Now the case would have to be looked at again, if not by Rebus then by some other poor bugger who would go through the same old steps, knowing damned fine who the main suspect was, and knowing that he was walking the streets and drinking in pubs, and chuckling at his luck.

Except that it wasn't luck: it was planning, as Rebus now knew.

DC Clarke finished her second reading of the file. 'I suppose you checked on Redwood at the time?'

'Of course we did. Not married, no boyfriends. No proof – not even the faintest rumour – that she knew Keith.'

Clarke looked at the photo. 'And this is her?'

'It's her, and it's him – Keith Leyton.'

'And it was sent to . . . ?'

'It was addressed to a Mr K. Leighton. They didn't get the spelling right. I checked in the phone book. Keith Leyton's ex-directory. Either that or he doesn't have a phone. But our little tax collector is in there under K. Leighton.'

'And they sent the letters to him by mistake?'

'They must know Keith Leyton hangs out in Muirhouse. His mum lives in Muirhouse Crescent.'

'Where does Kenneth Leighton live?'

Rebus grinned at the windscreen. 'Muir*wood* Crescent – only it's not in Muirhouse, it's in Currie.'

Siobhan Clarke smiled too. 'I don't believe it,' she said.

Rebus shrugged. 'It happens. They looked in the phone book, thought the address looked right, and started sending the letters.'

'So they've been trying to blackmail a criminal . . .'

'And instead they've found a taxman.' Now Rebus laughed outright. 'They must be mad, naïve, or built like a hydro-electric station. If they'd *really* tried this bampot caper on with Leyton, he'd have dug a fresh grave or two in Greyfriars for them. I'll give them one thing, though.'

'What's that?'

'They know about Keith's wife.'

'His wife?'

Rebus nodded. 'She lives near the mum. Big woman. Jealous. That's why Keith would keep any girlfriend secret – that's why he'd *want* to keep her a secret. The blackmailers must have thought that gave them a chance that he'd cough up.'

Rebus stopped the car. He had parked outside a block of flats in Oxgangs. The block was one of three, each one shaped like a capital H lying on its face. Caerketton Court: Rebus had once had a fling with a school-dinner lady who lived on the second floor . . .

'I checked with June Redwood's office,' he said. 'She's off sick.' He craned his neck out of the window. 'Tenth floor apparently, let's hope the lift's working.' He turned to Siobhan. 'Otherwise we'll have to resort to the telephone.'

The lift was working, though barely. Rebus and Siobhan ignored the wrapped paper parcel in one corner. Neither liked to think what it might contain. Still, Rebus was impressed that he could hold his breath for as long as the lift took to crackle its way up ten flights. The tenth floor seemed all draughts and high-pitched winds. The building had a perceptible sway, not quite like being at sea. Rebus pushed the bell of June Redwood's flat and waited. He pushed again. Siobhan was standing with her arms folded around her, shuffling her feet.

'I'd hate to see you on a football terrace in January,' said Rebus.

There was a sound from inside the door, then the door itself was opened by a woman with unwashed hair, a tissue to her nose, and wrapped in a thick dressing-gown.

'Hello there, Miss Redwood,' said Rebus brightly. 'Remember me?' Then he held up the photograph. 'Doubtless you remember him too. Can we come in?'

They went in. As they sat in the untidy living-room, it crossed Siobhan Clarke's mind that they had no way of proving *when* the photo was taken. And without that, they had nothing. Say the party had taken place after the trial – it could well be that Leyton and June Redwood had met then. In fact, it made sense. After his release, Leyton probably *would* want to throw a party, and he would certainly want to invite the woman who had been his saviour. She hoped

Rebus had thought of this. She hoped he wasn't going to go too far . . . as usual.

'I don't understand,' said June Redwood, wiping her nose again.

'Come on, June,' said Rebus. 'Here's the proof. You and Keith together in a clinch. The man you claimed at his trial was a complete stranger. Do you often get this comfortable with strangers?'

This earned a thin smile from June Redwood.

'If so,' Rebus continued, 'you must invite me to one of your parties.'

Siobhan Clarke swallowed hard. Yes, the Inspector was going to go too far. Had she ever doubted it?

'You'd be lucky,' said the social worker.

'It's been known,' said Rebus. He relaxed into his chair. 'Doesn't take a lot of working out, does it?' he went on. 'You must have met Keith through his mum. You became . . . friends, let's call it. I don't know what his wife will call it.' Blood started to tinge June Redwood's neck. 'You look better already,' said Rebus. 'At least I've put a bit of colour in your cheeks. You met Keith, started going out with him. It had to be kept secret though. The only thing Keith Leyton fears is *Mrs* Keith Leyton.'

'Her name's Joyce,' said Redwood.

Rebus nodded. 'So it is.'

'I could know that from the trial,' she snapped. 'I wouldn't have to know him to know that.'

Rebus nodded again. 'Except that you were a witness, June. You weren't in court when Joyce Leyton was mentioned.'

Her face now looked as though she'd been lying out too long in the non-existent sun. But she had a trump card left. 'That photo could have been taken any time.'

Siobhan held her breath: yes, this was the crunch. Rebus seemed to realise it too. 'You're right there,' he said. 'Any time at all . . . up to a month before Keith's trial.'

The room was quiet for a moment. The wind found a gap

somewhere and rustled a spider-plant near the window, whistling as though through well-spaced teeth.

'What?' said June Redwood. Rebus held the photograph up again.

'The man behind you, the one with long hair and the tattoo. Ugly-looking loon. He's called Mick McKelvin. It must have been some party, June, when bruisers like Keith and Mick were invited. They're not exactly your cocktail crowd. They think a canapé's something you throw over a stolen car to keep it hidden.' Rebus smiled at his own joke. Well, someone had to.

'What are you getting at?'

'Mick went inside four weeks before Keith's trial. He's serving three years in Peterhead. Persistent B and E. So you see, there's no way this party could have taken place *after* Keith's trial. Not unless Peterhead's security has got a bit lax. No, it had to be before, meaning you *had* to know him before the trial. Know what that means?' Rebus sat forward. June Redwood wasn't wiping her nose with the tissue now; she was hiding behind it, and looking frightened. 'It means you stood in the witness-box and you lied, just like Keith told you to. Serious trouble, June. You might end up with your own social worker, or even a prison visitor.' Rebus's voice had dropped in volume, as though June and he were having an intimate tête-à-tête over a candlelit dinner. 'So I really think you'd better help us, and you can start by talking about the party. Let's start with the photograph, eh?'

'The photo?' June Redwood looked ready to weep.

'The photo,' Rebus echoed. 'Who took it? Did he take any other pics of the two of you? After all, at the moment you're looking at a jail sentence, but if any photos like this one get to Joyce Leyton, you might end up collecting signatures.' Rebus waited for a moment, until he saw that June didn't get it. 'On your plaster casts,' he explained.

'Blackmail?' said Rab Mitchell.

He was sitting in the interview room, and he was

nervous. Rebus stood against one wall, arms folded, examining the scuffed toes of his black Dr Martens shoes. He'd only bought them three weeks ago. They were hardly broken in – the tough leather heel-pieces had rubbed his ankles into raw blisters – and already he'd managed to scuff the toes. He knew how he'd done it too: kicking stones as he'd come out of June Redwood's block of flats. Kicking stones for joy. That would teach him not to be exuberant in future. It wasn't good for your shoes.

'Blackmail?' Mitchell repeated.

'Good echo in here,' Rebus said to Siobhan Clarke, who was standing by the door. Rebus liked having Siobhan in on these interviews. She made people nervous. Hard men, brutal men, they would swear and fume for a moment before remembering that a young woman was present. A lot of the time, she discomfited them, and that gave Rebus an extra edge. But Mitchell, known to his associates as 'Roscoe' (for no known reason), would have been nervous anyway. A man with a proud sixty-a-day habit, he had been stopped from lighting up by a tutting John Rebus.

'No smoking, Roscoe, not in here.'

'What?'

'This is a non-smoker.'

'What the f— what are you blethering about?'

'Just what I say, Roscoe. No smoking.'

Five minutes later, Rebus had taken Roscoe's cigarettes from where they lay on the table, and had used Roscoe's Scottish Bluebell matches to light one, which he inhaled with great delight.

'Non-smoker!' Roscoe Mitchell fairly yelped. 'You said so yourself!' He was bouncing like a kid on the padded seat. Rebus exhaled again.

'Did I? Yes, so I did. Oh well . . .' Rebus took a third and final puff from the cigarette, then stubbed it out underfoot, leaving the longest, most extravagant stub Roscoe had obviously ever seen in his life. He stared at it with open mouth, then closed his mouth tight and turned his eyes to Rebus.

'What is it you want?' he said.

'Blackmail,' said John Rebus.

'Blackmail?'

'Good echo in here.'

'Blackmail? What the hell do you mean?'

'Photos,' said Rebus calmly. 'You took them at a party four months ago.'

'Whose party?'

'Matt Bennett's.'

Roscoe nodded. Rebus had placed the cigarettes back on the table. Roscoe couldn't take his eyes off them. He picked up the box of matches and toyed with it. 'I remember it,' he said. A faint smile. 'Brilliant party.' He managed to stretch the word 'brilliant' out to four distinct syllables. So it really had been a good party.

'You took some snaps?'

'You're right. I'd just got a new camera.'

'I won't ask where from.'

'I've got a receipt.' Roscoe nodded to himself. 'I remember now. The film was no good.'

'How do you mean?'

'I put it in for developing, but none of the pictures came out. Not a one. They reckoned I'd not put the film in the right way, or opened the case or something. The negatives were all blank. They showed me them.'

'They?'

'At the shop. I got a consolation free film.'

Some consolation, thought Rebus. Some swap, to be more accurate. He placed the photo on the table. Roscoe stared at it, then picked it up the better to examine it.

'How the–?' Remembering there was a woman present, Roscoe swallowed the rest of the question.

'Here,' said Rebus, pushing the pack of cigarettes in his direction. 'You look like you need one of these.'

*

Rebus sent Siobhan Clarke and DS Brian Holmes to pick up Keith Leyton. He also advised them to take along a back-up. You never could tell with a nutter like Leyton. Plenty of back-up, just to be on the safe side. It wasn't just Leyton after all; there might be Joyce to deal with too.

Meantime, Rebus drove to Tollcross, parked just across the traffic lights, tight in at a bus stop, and, watched by a frowning queue, made a dash for the photographic shop's doorway. It was chucking it down, no question. The queue had squeezed itself so tightly under the metal awning of the bus shelter that vice might have been able to bring them up on a charge of public indecency. Rebus shook water from his hair and pushed open the shop's door.

Inside it was light and warm. He shook himself again and approached the counter. A young man beamed at him.

'Yes, sir?'

'I wonder if you can help,' said Rebus. 'I've got a film needs developing, only I want it done in an hour. Is that possible?'

'No problem, sir. Is it colour?'

'Yes.'

'That's fine then. We do our own processing.'

Rebus nodded and reached into his pocket. The man had already begun filling in details on a form. He printed the letters very neatly, Rebus noticed with pleasure.

'That's good,' said Rebus, bringing out the photo. 'In that case, you must have developed this.'

The man went very still and very pale.

'Don't worry, son, I'm not from Keith Leyton. In fact, Keith Leyton doesn't know anything about you, which is just as well for you.'

The young man rested the pen on the form. He couldn't take his eyes off the photograph.

'Better shut up shop now,' said Rebus. 'You're coming down to the station. You can bring the rest of the photos with you. Oh, and I'd wear a cagoule, it's not exactly fair, is it?'

'Not exactly.'

'And take a tip from me, son. Next time you think of blackmailing someone, make sure you get the right person, eh?' Rebus tucked the photo back into his pocket. 'Plus, if you'll take my advice, don't use words like "reprint" in your blackmail notes. Nobody says reprint except people like you.' Rebus wrinkled his nose. 'It just makes it too easy for us, you see.'

'Thanks for the warning,' the man said coolly.

'All part of the service,' said Rebus with a smile. The clue had actually escaped him throughout. Not that he'd be admitting as much to Kenneth Leighton. No, he would tell the story as though he'd been Sherlock Holmes and Philip Marlowe rolled into one. Doubtless Leighton would be impressed. And one day, when Rebus was needing a favour from the taxman, he would know he could put Kenneth Leighton in the frame.

# The Confession

'It was Tony's idea,' he says, shifting in his seat. 'Tony's my brother, a couple of years younger than me, but he was always the brainy one. It was all his idea. I just went along with it.'

He's still trying to get comfortable. It's not easy to get comfortable in the interview room. The CID man could tell him that. He could tell him that the chair he's wriggling in has been modified ever so slightly, a quarter-inch taken off its front legs. The chair isn't designed with rest and relaxation in mind.

'So Tony says to me one day, he says: "Ian, this is one plan that cannot fail." And he tells me about it. We spend a bit of time bouncing it around, you know, me trying to pick holes in it. I have to admit, it looked pretty good. Well, that's the problem really. That's why I'm here. It was just too bloody good all round . . .'

He looks around again, studying the walls, as if expecting two-way mirrors, secret listening devices. The one thing he's not been expecting is the quietness. It's eleven-thirty on a weekday night. The police station is like a ghost town. He wants to see lots of activity, lots of uniforms. Yet again in his life, he's being let down.

Tony had noticed the slip-road. He drove from Fife to Edinburgh most Saturday nights, taking a carful of friends. They went to pubs and clubs, danced, chatted up women. A late-night pizza and maybe a couple of espressos before home. Tony didn't drink. He didn't mind staying sober while everyone around him had a skinful. He always liked to be in control. On the A90 south of the Forth Road Bridge,

he'd seen the signpost for the slip-road. He'd seen it before –
must've passed it a hundred times – but this one night
something about it bothered him. The next morning, he
headed back. The sign said: *Department of Transport Vehicle
Check Area Only*. He took the slip-road, found himself at a
sort of roundabout in the middle of nowhere. He stopped
his car and got out. There was grass growing in the middle
of the road. He didn't think the place got used much. A hut
nearby, and a metal ramp that might have been a weigh-
bridge. Another slip-road led back down on to the A90. He
stood there for a while, listening to the rush of traffic below
him, an idea slowly forming in his head.

'See,' Ian went on, 'Tony had worked for a time as a
security guard, and he still had a couple of uniforms
hanging in his wardrobe. He's always had the idea of
robbing someplace, always knew those uniforms would
come in handy. One of his pals, guy called Malc, he works –
I should say worked – in a printing shop. So Tony brought
Malc in, said we could trust him. Have you got a cigarette?'

The detective points to the No Smoking sign, but then
relents, hands over a packet of ten and some matches.

'Thanks. So you see,' lighting up, exhaling noisily, 'it was
all Tony's idea, and Malc had a certain expertise, too. *I*
didn't have anything. It was just that I was family, so Tony
knew he could trust me. I haven't worked in eight years.
Used to be in heavy engineering up in Leven, got laid off in
the slump. If somebody could do something about the
manufacturing industry in this country, there'd be a lot less
crime. Bit of advice there, free of charge.' He flicks ash into
the ashtray, brushes some stray flecks from his trousers. 'I'm
not saying I didn't play a part. Obviously, I wouldn't be here
otherwise. I just want it on record that I wasn't the brains of
the operation.'

'I think I can go along with that,' the detective says. Ian
asks him if he shouldn't be taking notes or something.
'We're trained, lad. Elephant's memory.'

So Ian nods, goes on with his story. The interview room is

small and airless. It carries the aromas of every person who's ever been through it, all of them telling their stories. A few of them even turning out to be true . . .

'So we make a few recces, and never once do we see the place being used. We stopped the car on the slip-road a few nights. Plenty of lorries steaming past, but nobody so much as notices us or asks what we're up to. This is what Tony wanted to know. We set the thing up for last Wednesday.'

'Why a Wednesday?' the detective asks.

Ian just shrugs. 'Tony's idea,' he says. 'All I did was go along with him. He was the mastermind: that's the word I've been wanting. Mastermind.' He shifts again in his chair, stares at the walls again, remembering Wednesday night.

Tony and Ian were dressed in the uniforms. Tony had a friend with a haulage truck. It had been easy to borrow it for the night. The story was, they were helping someone move house. Malc had come up with IDs for them: they'd had their photos taken at a passport booth, and the laminated cards, each in its own wallet, looked authentic. They took the truck up to the roundabout, left the car near the bottom of the slip-road. Malc was dressed in a leather jacket and baseball cap. He was supposed to be a truck driver. Tony would head back down the ramp and use a torch to signal a lorry on to the slip-road. Then he'd ask the driver to go to the test area, where Ian would be apparently interviewing another lorry-driver. This was so the real driver wouldn't suspect anything.

'It worked,' Ian says. 'That's what's so unbelievable. First lorry he stopped, the driver brought it up to the round-about, stopped it and got out. Tony comes driving up, gets out of his car. Asks to see the delivery note, then says he wants to check the cargo.'

The detective has a question. 'What if it turned out to be cabbages or fish or something?'

'First thing Tony asked was what they were carrying. If it had been something we couldn't sell, he'd have let them go. But we came up gold at the first attempt. Washing machines, two dozen of them at three hundred quid apiece. Only problem was, by the time we'd squeezed them into our own lorry, we'd no room for anything else, and we were cream-crackered anyway. Otherwise, I think we could have kept going all night.' Ian pauses. 'You're wondering about the driver, aren't you? There were three of us, remember. All we did was tie him up, leave him in his cab. We knew he'd get himself free eventually. Quiet up there, we didn't want him starving to death. And off we went with the haul. We had about fifteen of the machines, and were already thinking of who we could sell them to. Storage was no problem. Tony had a couple of lock-ups. We left them there. There's a local villain, name of Andy Horrigan. He runs a couple of pubs and cafés, so I thought maybe he'd be in the market. We were being careful, see. Once the news was out that someone had boosted a consignment of washer-dryers . . . well, we had to be careful who we sold to.' He pauses. 'Only, we'd already made that one fatal mistake . . .'

One mistake. He asks for another cigarette. His hand is shaking as he lights it. He can't get it out of his head, the insane bad luck of it. Even before he'd had a chance to say anything to Andy Horrigan, Horrigan had something to ask him.

'Here, Ian, heard anything about a heist? Washer-dryers, nicked from the back of a lorry?'

'I didn't see anything in the papers,' Ian had replied. Quite honestly, too: it had surprised them, the way there had been nothing in the press or on the radio and TV. Ian could see Horrigan was bursting to tell him. He knew right away it couldn't be good news, not coming from Horrigan.

'It wasn't in the papers, never will be neither.'

And as he'd gone on to explain it, Ian had felt his life ebb away. He'd run to the lock-up, finding Tony there. Tony already knew: it was written on his face. He knew they had to get rid of the machines, dump them somewhere. But that meant getting another lorry from somewhere.

'Hang on though,' Tony had said, his brain slipping into gear. 'Eddie Hart isn't after the machines, is he? He only wants what's his.'

Eddie Hart: at mention of the name, Ian could feel his knees buckling. 'Steady Eddie' was the Dundee Godfather, a man with an almost mythical status as mover and shaker, entrepreneur, and hammer-wielding maniac. If you crossed Steady Eddie, he got out his carpentry nails. And according to the local word, Eddie was absolutely furious.

He'd probably put a lot of thought into the scheme. He needed to move drugs around, and had hit on the idea of hiding them inside white goods. After all, a lorryload of washer-dryers or fridge-freezers – they could saunter up and down every motorway in the country. All you needed were some fake dockets listing origin and destination. It just so happened that Tony had hit on one of Eddie's drivers. And now Eddie was out for blood.

But Tony was right: if they handed back the dope, got it back to Eddie somehow, maybe they'd be allowed to live. Maybe it would be all right. So they started tearing the packing from the machines, unscrewing the back of each to search behind the drum for hidden packages. And when that failed, they emptied out each machine's complimentary packet of washing powder. They went through both lock-ups, they checked and double-checked every machine. And found nothing.

Ian thought maybe the stuff had been hidden in one of the machines they'd left behind.

'Use your loaf,' his brother told him. 'If that were true, why would he be after us? Wait a minute though . . .'

And he went back, counting the machines. There was one missing. The brothers looked at one another, headed for Tony's car. At Malc's mother's house, Malc had just plumbed the machine in. The old twin-tub was out on the front path, waiting to be junked. Malc's mother was rubbing her hands over the front of her new washer-dryer, telling the neighbours who'd gathered in the kitchen what a good laddie her son was.

'Saved up and bought it as a surprise.'

Even Ian knew that they were in real trouble now. Everyone in town would get to hear about the new washing machine . . . and word would most definitely travel.

They took Malc outside, explained the situation to him. He went back indoors and manoeuvred the machine out of its cubby-hole, explaining that he'd forgotten to remove the transit bolts. His hands were trembling so much, he kept dropping the screwdriver. But at last he had the back of the machine off, and started handing brown-paper packages to Tony and Ian. Tony explained to the neighbours that they were weights, to stop the machine slipping and sliding when it was in the back of the lorry.

'Like bricks?' one neighbour asked, and when he agreed with her, sweat pouring down his face, she added a further question. 'Why cover bricks in brown paper?'

Tony, beyond explanations, put his head in his hands and wept.

The detective brings back two beakers of coffee, one for himself, one for Ian. He's been checking up, using the computer, making a couple of phone calls. Ian sits ready to tell him the last of it.

'We couldn't just hand the stuff back, had to think of a way to do it. So we drove up to Dundee, night before last. Steady Eddie has a nightclub. We put the stuff in one of the skips at the back of the club, then phoned the club and told them where they could find it. Thing is, the club gets its rubbish collected privately, and the company works at night. So that night, the skip got emptied. Well, that wouldn't have mattered, only . . . only it was me made the call . . . and there were two numbers in the phone-book. Instead of the office, I'd got through to the public phone on the wall beside the bar. It must have been some punter who answered. I just said my piece then hung up. I don't know

. . . maybe they nipped outside and got the stuff for themselves. Maybe they didn't hear me, or thought I was drunk or something . . .' His voice is choking; he's close to tears.

'Mr Hart didn't get the stuff?' the detective guesses. Ian nods agreement. 'And now your brother and Malc have gone missing?'

'Eddie got them. He must have done.'

'And you want us to protect you?'

'Witness relocation: you can do that, can't you? I mean, there's a price on my head now. You've *got* to!'

The detective nods. 'We can do it,' he says. 'But what exactly is it you're a witness to? There's no record of a lorry being hijacked. Nobody's reported such a loss. You don't seem to have any evidence linking Mr Hart to anything illegal – much as I'd love it if you did.' The detective draws his chair closer. 'It wasn't a slump that led to you losing your job, Ian. It was threatening your foreman. He didn't like your attitude, and you started spinning him some story about having a brother who's a terrorist, and who'd stick a bomb under his car. You scared the poor man half to death, until he found out the truth. See, I've got all of that in the files, Ian. What I don't have is anything about washing machines, drugs wrapped in brown paper, or missing persons.'

Ian leaps from his seat, begins pacing the room. 'You could send a team out to the dump. If the drugs are there, they'll find them. Or . . . or go to the lock-ups, the washing machines will still be there . . . unless Steady Eddie's taken them. I wouldn't put it past him. Don't you see? I'm the only one left who can testify against him!'

The detective is on his feet now, too. 'I think it's time you were off, son. I'll see you as far as the door.'

'I need protection!'

The detective comes up to him again. Their faces are inches apart.

'Get your brother the terrorist to protect you. His name's

. . . Billy, isn't it? Only you can't do that, can you? Because you haven't got a brother called Billy. Or a brother called Tony, if it comes to that.' The detective pauses. 'You haven't got *anybody*, Ian. You're a nobody. These stories of yours . . . that's all they are, stories. Come on now, it's time you were home. Your mum will be worrying.'

'She got a new washing machine last week,' Ian says softly. 'The man who delivered it, he said sorry for being so late. He'd been stopped at a checkpoint.'

It is quiet in the interview room. Quiet for a long time, until Ian begins weeping, weeping for the brother he's just lost again.

# The Hanged Man

The killer wandered through the fairground.

It was a travelling fair, and this was its first night in Kirkcaldy. It was a Thursday evening in April. The fair wouldn't get really busy until the weekend, by which time it would be missing one of its minor, if well-established, attractions.

He'd already made one recce past the small white caravan with its chalkboard outside. Pinned to the board were a couple of faded letters from satisfied customers. A double-step led to the bead curtain. The door was tied open with baling twine. He didn't think there was anyone in there with her. If there was, she'd have closed the door. But all the same, he wanted to be careful. 'Care' was his by-word.

He called himself a killer. Which was to say that if anyone had asked him what he did for a living, he wouldn't have used any other term. He knew some in the profession thought 'assassin' had a more glamorous ring to it. He'd looked it up in a dictionary, found it was to do with some old religious sect and derived from an old Arabic word meaning 'eater of hashish'. He didn't believe in drugs himself; not so much as a half of lager before the job.

Some people preferred to call it a 'hit', which made them 'hit men'. But he didn't *hit* people; he killed them stone dead. And there were other, more obscure euphemisms, but the bottom line was, he was a killer.

And for today, the fair was his place of work, his hunting ground.

Not that it had taken a magic ball to find the subject. She'd be in that caravan right now, waiting for a punter.

He'd give it ten more minutes, just so he could be sure she wasn't with someone – not a punter necessarily; maybe sharing a cuppa with a fellow traveller. Ten minutes: if no one came out or went in, he'd make himself her next and final customer.

Of course, if she was a real astrologer, she'd know he was coming and would have high-tailed it out of town. But he thought she was here. He *knew* she was.

He pretended to watch three youths on the firing range. They made the elementary mistake of aiming along the barrel. The sights, of course, had been skewed; probably the barrel, too. And if they thought they were going to dislodge one of the moving targets by hitting it . . . well, best think again. Those targets would be weighted, reinforced. The odds were always on the side of the showman.

The market stretched along the waterfront. There was a stiff breeze making some of the wooden structures creak. People pushed hair out of their eyes, or tucked chins into the collars of their jackets. The place wasn't busy, but it was busy enough. He didn't stand out, nothing memorable about him at all. His jeans, lumberjack shirt and trainers were work clothes: at home he preferred a bit more style. But he was a long way from home today. His base was on the west coast, just down the Clyde from Glasgow. He didn't know anything about Fife at all. Kirkcaldy, what little he'd seen of it, wouldn't be lingering in his memory. He'd been to towns all over Scotland and the north of England. In his mind they formed a geography of violence. In Carlisle he'd used a knife, making it look like a drunken Saturday brawl. In Peterhead it had been a blow on the head and strangulation, with orders that the body shouldn't ever be found – a grand and a half to a fishing-boat captain had seen to that. In Airdrie, Arbroath, Ardrossan . . . he didn't always kill. Sometimes all that was needed was a brutal and public message. In those cases he became the postman, delivering the message to order.

He moved from the shooting range to another stall, where

children tried to attach hoops to the prizes on a carousel. They were faring little better than their elders next door. No surprise, with most of the prizes oh-so-slightly exceeding the circumference of each hoop. When he checked his watch, he was surprised to find that the ten minutes had passed. A final look around, and he climbed the steps, tapped at the open door, and parted the bead curtain.

'Come in, love,' she said. Gypsy Rosa, the sign outside called her. Palms read, your fortune foretold. Yet here she was, waiting for him.

'Close the door,' she instructed. He saw that the twine holding it open was looped over a bent nail. He loosed it and closed the door. The curtains were shut – which was ideal for his purpose – and, lacking any light from outside, the interior glowed from the half-dozen candles spaced around it. The surfaces had been draped with lengths of cheap black cloth. There was a black cloth over the table, too, with patterns of sun and moon embroidered into it. And there she sat, gesturing for him to squeeze his large frame into the banquette opposite. He nodded. He smiled. He looked at her.

She was middle-aged, her face lined and rouged. She'd been a looker in younger days, he could see that, but scarlet lipstick now made her mouth look too large and moist. She wore black muslin over her head, a gold band holding it in place. Her costume looked authentic enough: black lace, red silk, with astrological signs sewn into the arms. On the table sat a crystal ball, covered for now with a white handkerchief. The red fingernails of one hand tapped against a tarot deck. She asked him his name.

'Is that necessary?' he asked.

She shrugged. 'It helps sometimes.' They were like blind dates alone in a restaurant, the world outside ceasing to matter. Her eyes twinkled in the candlelight.

'My name's Mort,' he told her.

She repeated the name, seeming amused by it.

'Short for Morton. My father was born there.'

266

'It's also the French for death,' she added.

'I didn't know,' he lied.

She was smiling. 'There's a lot you don't know, Mort. That's why you're here. A palm-reading, is it?'

'What else do you offer?'

'The ball.' She nodded towards it. 'The cards.'

He asked which she would recommend. In turn, she asked if this was his first visit to a psychic healer – that was what she called herself, 'a psychic healer': 'because I heal souls', she added by way of explanation.

'I'm not sure I need healing,' he argued.

'Oh, my dear, we all need some kind of healing. We're none of us *whole*. Look at you, for example.'

He straightened in his chair, becoming aware for the first time that she was holding his right hand, palm upwards, her fingers stroking his knuckles. She looked down at the palm, frowned a little in concentration.

'You're a visitor, aren't you, dear?'

'Yes.'

'Here on business, I'd say.'

'Yes.' He was studying the palm with her, as though trying to read its foreign words.

'Mmm.' She began running the tip of one finger down the well-defined lines which criss-crossed his palm. 'Not ticklish?' she chuckled. He allowed her the briefest of smiles. Looking at her face, he noticed it seemed softer than it had when he'd first entered the caravan. He revised her age downwards, felt slight pressure as she seemed to squeeze his hand, as if acknowledging the compliment.

'Doing all right for yourself though,' she informed him. 'I mean moneywise; no problems there. No, dear, *your* problems all stem from your particular line of work.'

'My work?'

'You're not as relaxed about it as you used to be. Time was, you wouldn't have considered doing anything else. Easy money. But it doesn't feel like that any more, does it?'

It felt warm in the caravan, stuffy, with no air getting in

and all those candles burning. There was the metal weight pressed to his groin, the weight he'd always found so reassuring in times past. He told himself she was using cheap psychology. His accent wasn't local; he wore no wedding ring; his hands were clean and manicured. You could tell a lot about someone from such details.

'Shouldn't we agree a price first?' he asked.

'Why should we do that, dear? I'm not a prostitute, am I?' He felt his ears reddening. 'And besides, you can afford it, we both know you can. What's the point of letting money get in the way?' She was holding his hand in an ever tighter grip. She had strength, this one; he'd bear that in mind when the time came. He wouldn't play around, wouldn't string out her suffering. A quick squeeze of the trigger.

'I get the feeling,' she said, 'you're wondering why you're here. Would that be right?'

'I know exactly why I'm here.'

'What? Here with me? Or here on this planet, living the life you've chosen?'

'Either . . . both.' He spoke a little too quickly, could feel his pulse-rate rising. He had to get it down again, had to be calm when the time came. Part of him said *Do it now*. But another part said *Hear her out*. He wriggled, trying to get comfortable.

'What I meant though,' she went on, 'is you're not sure any more why you do what you do. You've started to ask questions.' She looked up at him. 'The line of business you're in, I get the feeling you're just supposed to do what you're told. Is that right?' He nodded. 'No talking back, no questions asked. You just do your work and wait for payday.'

'I get paid upfront.'

'Aren't you the lucky one?' She chuckled again. 'But the money's not enough, is it? It can never recompense for not being happy or fulfilled.'

'I could have got that from my girlfriend's *Cosmopolitan*.'

She smiled, then clapped her hands. 'I'd like to try you with the cards. Are you game?'

'Is that what that is – a game?'

'You have your fun with words, dear. Euphemisms, that's all words are.'

He tried not to gasp: it was as if she'd read his mind from earlier – all those euphemisms for 'killer'. She wasn't paying him any heed, was busy shuffling the outsized Tarot deck. She asked him to touch the deck three times. Then she laid out the top three cards.

'Ah,' she said, her fingers caressing the first one. '*Le soleil*. It means the sun.'

'I know what it means,' he snapped.

She made a pout with her lips. 'I thought you didn't know any French.'

He was stuck for a moment. 'There's a picture of the sun right there on the card,' he said finally.

She nodded slowly. His breathing had quickened again.

'Second card,' she said. 'Death himself. *La mort*. Interesting that the French give it the feminine gender.'

He looked at the picture of the skeleton. It was grinning, doing a little jig. On the ground beside it sat a lantern and an hourglass. The candle in the lantern had been snuffed out; the sand in the hourglass had all fallen through.

'Don't worry,' she said, 'it doesn't always portend a death.'

'That's a relief,' he said with a smile.

'The final card is intriguing – the hanged man. It can signify many things.' She lifted it up so he could see it.

'And the three together?' he asked, curious now.

She held her hands as if in prayer. 'I'm not sure,' she said at last. 'An unusual conjunction, to be sure.'

'Death and the hanged man: a suicide maybe?'

She shrugged.

'Is the sex important? I mean, the fact that it *is* a man?'

She shook her head.

He licked his lips. 'Maybe the ball would help,' he suggested.

She looked at him, her eyes reflecting light from the candles. 'You might be right.' And she smiled. 'Shall we?' As if they were not prospective lovers now but children, and the crystal ball little more than an illicit dare.

As she pulled the small glass globe towards them, he shifted again. The pistol barrel was chafing his thigh. He rubbed his jacket pocket, the one containing the silencer. He would have to hit her first, just to quiet her while he fitted the silencer to the gun.

Slowly, she lifted the handkerchief from the ball, as if raising the curtain on some miniaturised stage-show. She leaned forward, peering into the glass, giving him a view of crêped cleavage. Her hands flitted over the ball, not quite touching it. Had he been a gerontophile, there would have been a hint of the erotic to the act.

'Don't you go thinking that!' she snapped. Then, seeing the startled look on his face, she winked. 'The ball often makes things clearer.'

'What was I thinking?' he blurted out.

'You want me to say it out loud?'

He shook his head, looked into the ball, saw her face reflected there, stretched and distorted. And floating somewhere within was his own face, too, surrounded by licking flames.

'What do you see?' he asked, needing to know now.

'I see a man who is asking why he is here. One person has the answer, but he has yet to ask this person. He is worried about the thing he must do – rightly worried, in my opinion.'

She looked up at him again. Her eyes were the colour of polished oak. Tiny veins of blood seemed to pulse in the whites. He jerked back in his seat.

'You know, don't you?'

'Of course I know, Mort.'

He nearly overturned the table as he got to his feet,

pulling the gun from his waistband. 'How?' he asked. 'Who told you?'

She shook her head, not looking at the gun, apparently not interested in it. 'It would happen one day. The moment you walked in, I felt it was you.'

'You're not afraid.' It was a statement rather than a question.

'Of course I'm afraid.' But she didn't look it. 'And a little sad, too.'

He had the silencer out of his pocket, but was having trouble coordinating his hands. He'd practised a hundred times in the dark, and had never had this trouble before. He'd had victims like her, though: the ones who accepted, who were maybe even a little grateful.

'You know who wants you dead?' he asked.

She nodded. 'I think so. I may have gotten the odd fortune wrong, but I've made precious few enemies in my life.'

'He's a rich man.'

'Very rich,' she conceded. 'Not all of it honest money. And I'm sure he's well used to getting what he wants.' She slid the ball away, brought out the cards again and began shuffling them. 'So ask me your question.'

He was screwing the silencer on to the end of the barrel. The pistol was loaded, he only had to slide the safety off. He licked his lips again. So hot in here, so dry . . .

'Why?' he asked. 'Why does he want a fortune-teller dead?'

She got up, made to open the curtains.

'No,' he commanded, pointing the gun at her, sliding off the safety. 'Keep them closed.'

'Afraid to shoot me in daylight?' When he didn't answer, she pulled open one curtain, then blew out the candles. He kept the pistol trained on her: a head shot, quick and always fatal. 'I'll tell you,' she said, sliding into her seat again. She motioned for him to sit. After a moment's hesitation, he did

271

so, the pistol steady in his right hand. Wisps of smoke from the extinguished candles rose either side of her.

'We were young when we met,' she began. 'I was already working in a fairground – not this one. One night, he decided there had been enough of a courtship.' She looked deep into his eyes, his own oak-coloured eyes. 'Oh yes, he's used to getting what he wants. You know what I'm saying?' she went on quietly. 'There was no question of consent. I tried to have the baby in secret, but it's hard to keep secrets from a man like him, a man with money, someone people fear. My baby was stolen from me. I began travelling then, and I've been travelling ever since. But always with my ear to the ground, always hearing things.' Her eyes were liquid now. 'You see, I knew a time would come when my baby would grow old enough to begin asking questions. And I knew the baby's father would not want the truth to come out.' She reached out a shaking hand, reached past the gun to touch his cheek. 'I just didn't think he'd be so cruel.'

'Cruel?'

'So cruel as to send his own son – our son – to do his killing.'

He shot to his feet again, banged his fists against the wall of the caravan. Rested his head there and screwed shut his eyes, the oak-coloured eyes – mirrors of her own – which had told her all she'd needed to know. He'd left the pistol on the table. She lifted it, surprised by its weight, and turned it in her hand.

'I'll kill him,' he groaned. 'I swear, I'll kill him for this.'

With a smile, she slid the safety catch on, placed the gun back on the table. When he turned back to her, blinking away tears, she looked quite calm, almost serene, as if her faith in him had been rewarded at last. In her hand, she was holding a Tarot card.

The hanged man.

'It will need to look like an accident,' she said. 'Either that or suicide.'

Outside, the screams of frightened children: waltzers and

big wheel and ghost train. One of his hands fell lightly on hers, the other reaching for his pistol.

'Mother,' he said, with all the tenderness his parched soul could muster.

# Window of Opportunity

## AN INSPECTOR REBUS STORY

Bernie Few's jailbreaks were an art.

And over the years he had honed his art. His escapes from prison, his shrugging off of guards and prison officers, his vanishing acts were the stuff of lights-out stories in jails the length and breadth of Scotland. He was called 'The Grease-Man', 'The Blink', and many other names, including the obvious 'Houdini' and the not-so-obvious 'Claude' (Claude Rains having starred as the original *Invisible Man*).

Bernie Few was beautiful. As a petty thief he was hopeless, but after capture he started to show his real prowess. He wasn't made for being a housebreaker; but he surely did shine as a jailbreaker. He'd stuffed himself into rubbish bags and mail sacks, taken the place of a corpse from one prison hospital, squeezed his wiry frame out of impossibly small windows (sometimes buttering his naked torso in preparation), and crammed himself into ventilation shafts and heating ducts.

But Bernie Few had a problem. Once he'd scaled the high walls, waded through sewers, sprinted from the prison bus, or cracked his guard across the head, once he'd done all this and was outside again, breathing free air and melting into the crowd . . . his movements were like clockwork. All his ingenuity seemed to be exhausted. The prison psychologists put it differently. They said he wanted to be caught, really. It was a game to him.

But to Detective Inspector John Rebus, it was more than a game. It was a chance for a drink.

Bernie would do three things. One, he'd go throw a rock through his ex-wife's living-room window. Two, he'd stand in the middle of Princes Street telling everyone to go to hell (and other places besides). And three, he'd get drunk in Scott's Bar. These days, option one was difficult for Bernie, since his ex-wife had not only moved without leaving a forwarding address but had, at Rebus's suggestion, gone to live on the eleventh floor of an Oxgangs tower block. No more rocks through the living-room window, unless Bernie was handy with ropes and crampons.

Rebus preferred to wait for Bernie in Scott's Bar, where they refused to water down either the whisky or the language. Scott's was a villain's pub, one of the ropiest in Edinburgh. Rebus recognised half the faces in the place, even on a dull Wednesday afternoon. Bail faces, appeal faces. They recognised him, too, but there wasn't going to be any trouble. Every one of them knew why he was here. He hoisted himself on to a barstool and lit a cigarette. The TV was on, showing a satellite sports channel. Cricket, some test between England and the West Indies. It is a popular fallacy that the Scots don't watch cricket. Edinburgh pub drinkers will watch *anything*, especially if England are involved, more especially if England are odds on to get a drubbing. Scott's, as depressing a watering hole as you could ever imagine, had transported itself to the Caribbean for the occasion.

Then the door to the toilets opened with a nerve-jarring squeal, and a man loped out. He was tall and skinny, loose-limbed, hair falling over his eyes. He had a hand on his fly, just checking prior to departure, and his eyes were on the floor.

'See youse then,' he said to nobody, opening the front door to leave. Nobody responded. The door stayed open longer than it should. Someone else was coming in. Eyes flashed from the TV for a moment. Rebus finished his drink and rose from the stool. He knew the man who'd just left the bar. He knew him well. He knew, too, that what had just happened was impossible.

The new customer, a small man with a handful of coins,

had a voice hoarse from shouting as he croakily ordered a pint. The barman didn't move. Instead, he looked to Rebus, who was looking at Bernie Few.

Then Bernie Few looked at Rebus.

'Been down to Princes Street, Bernie?' Rebus asked.

Bernie Few sighed and rubbed his tired face. 'Time for a short one, Mr Rebus?'

Rebus nodded. He could do with another himself anyway. He had a couple of things on his mind, neither of them Bernie Few.

Police officers love and hate surveillance operations in more or less equal measure. There's the tedium, but even that beats being tied to a CID desk. Often on a stakeout there's a good spirit, plus there's that adrenal rush when something eventually happens.

The present surveillance was based in a second-floor tenement flat, the owners having been packed off to a seaside caravan for a fortnight. If the operation needed longer than a fortnight, they'd be sent to stay with relations.

The watchers worked in two-man teams and twelve-hour shifts. They were watching the second-floor flat of the tenement across the road. They were keeping tabs on a bandit called Ribs Mackay. He was called Ribs because he was so skinny. He had a heroin habit, and paid for it by pushing drugs. Only he'd never been caught at it, a state of affairs Edinburgh CID were keen to rectify.

The problem was, since the surveillance had begun, Ribs had been keeping his head down. He stayed in the flat, nipping out only on brief sorties to the corner shop. He'd buy beer, vodka, milk, cigarettes, sometimes breakfast cereal or a jar of peanut butter, and he'd always top off his purchases with half a dozen bars of chocolate. That was about it. There had to be more, but there wasn't any more. Any day now, the operation would be declared dead in the water.

They tried to keep the flat clean, but you couldn't help a

bit of untidiness. You couldn't help nosy neighbours either: everyone on the stairwell wondered who the strangers in the Tully residence were. Some asked questions. Some didn't need to be told. Rebus met an old man on the stairs. He was hauling a bag of shopping up to the third floor, stopping for a breather at each step.

'Help you with that?' Rebus offered.

'I can manage.'

'It wouldn't be any bother.'

'I said I can manage.'

Rebus shrugged. 'Suit yourself.' Then he climbed to the landing and gave the recognised knock on the door of the Tullys' flat.

DC Jamphlar opened the door a crack, saw Rebus, and pulled it all the way open. Rebus nipped inside.

'Here,' he said, handing over a paper bag, 'doughrings.'

'Thank you, sir,' said Jamphlar.

In the cramped living-room, DC Connaught was sitting on a dining chair at the net curtain, peering through the net and out of the window. Rebus joined him for a moment. Ribs Mackay's window was grimy, but you could see through the grime into an ordinary-looking living-room. Not that Ribs came to the window much. Connaught wasn't concentrating on the window. He was ranging between the second-floor window and the ground-floor door. If Ribs left the flat, Jamphlar went haring after him, while Connaught followed Ribs's progress from the window and reported via radio to his colleague.

Initially, there'd been one man in the flat and one in a car at street level. But the man at street level hadn't been needed, and looked suspicious anyway. The street was no main thoroughfare, but a conduit between Clerk Street and Buccleuch Street. There were a few shops at road level, but they carried the look of permanent closure.

Connaught glanced up from the window. 'Afternoon, sir. What brings you here?'

'Any sign of him?' Rebus said.

'Not so much as a tweet.'

'I reckon I know why that is. Your bird's already flown.'

'No chance,' said Jamphlar, biting into a doughring.

'I saw him half an hour ago in Scott's Bar. That's a fair hike from here.'

'Must've been his double.'

But Rebus shook his head. 'When was the last time you saw him?'

Jamphlar checked the notebook. 'We haven't seen him this shift. But this morning Cooper and Sneddon watched him go to the corner shop and come back. That was seven-fifteen.'

'And you come on at eight?'

'Yes, sir.'

'And you haven't seen him since?'

'There's someone in there,' Connaught persisted. 'I've seen movement.'

Rebus spoke slowly. 'But you haven't seen Ribs Mackay, and I have. He's out on the street, doing whatever he does.' He leaned closer to Connaught. 'Come on, son, what is it? Been skiving off? Half an hour down the pub, a bit of a thirst-quencher? Catching some kip on the sofa? Looks comfortable, that sofa.'

Jamphlar was trying to swallow a mouthful of dough which had become suddenly dry. 'We've been doing our job!' he said, spraying crumbs.

Connaught just stared at Rebus with burning eyes. Rebus believed those eyes.

'All right,' he conceded, 'so there's another explanation. A back exit, a convenient drainpipe.'

'The back door's been bricked up,' Connaught said stiffly. 'There's a drainpipe, but Ribs couldn't manage down it.'

'How do you know?'

'I know.' Connaught stared out through the curtain.

'Something else then. Maybe he's using a disguise.'

Jamphlar, still chewing, flicked through the notebook. 'Everyone who comes out and goes in is checked off.'

'He's a druggie,' said Connaught. 'He's not bright enough to fool us.'

'Well, son, that's just what he's doing. You're watching an empty flat.'

'TV's just come on,' said Connaught. Rebus looked out through the curtain. Sure enough, he could see the animated screen. 'I hate this programme,' Connaught muttered. 'I wish he'd change the channel.'

'Maybe he can't,' said Rebus, making for the door.

He returned to the surveillance that evening, taking someone with him. There'd been a bit of difficulty, getting things arranged. Nobody was keen for him to walk out of the station with Bernie Few. But Rebus would assume full responsibility.

'Damned right you will,' said his boss, signing the form.

Jamphlar and Connaught were off, Cooper and Sneddon were on.

'What's this I hear?' Cooper said, opening the door to Rebus and his companion.

'About Ribs?'

'No,' said Cooper, 'about you bringing the day shift a selection of patisseries.'

'Come and take a look,' Sneddon called. Rebus walked over to the window. The light was on in Ribs's living-room, and the blinds weren't shut. Ribs had opened the window and was looking down on to the night-time street, enjoying a cigarette. 'See?' Sneddon said.

'I see,' said Rebus. Then he turned to Bernie Few. 'Come over here, Bernie.' Few came shuffling over to the window, and Rebus explained the whole thing to him. Bernie thought about it, rasping a hand over his chin, then asked the same questions Rebus had earlier asked Jamphlar and Connaught. Then he thought about it some more, staring out through the curtain.

'You keep an eye on the second-floor window?' he asked Cooper.

'That's right.'

'And the main door?'

'Yes.'

'You ever think of looking anywhere else?'

Cooper didn't get it. Neither did Sneddon.

'Go on, Bernie,' said Rebus.

'Look at the top floor,' Bernie Few suggested. Rebus looked. He saw a cracked and begrimed window, covered with ragged bits of cardboard. 'Think anyone lives there?' Bernie asked.

'What are you saying?'

'I think he's done a proper switch on you. Turned the tables, like.' He smiled. 'You're not watching Ribs Mackay. *He's* watching *you*.'

Rebus nodded, quick to get it. 'The change of shifts.' Bernie was nodding too. 'There's that minute or two when one shift's going off and the other's coming on.'

'A window of opportunity,' Bernie agreed. 'He watches, sees the new shift arrive, and skips downstairs and out the door.'

'And twelve hours later,' said Rebus, 'he waits in the street till he sees the next shift clocking on. Then he nips back in.'

Sneddon was shaking his head. 'But the lights, the telly . . .'

'Timer switches,' Bernie Few answered casually. 'You think you see people moving about in there. Maybe you do, but not Ribs. Could just be shadows, a breeze blowing the curtains.'

Sneddon frowned. 'Who *are* you?'

'An expert witness,' Rebus said, patting Bernie Few's shoulder. Then he turned to Sneddon. 'I'm going over there. Keep an eye on Bernie here. And I *mean* keep an eye on him. As in, don't let him out of your sight.'

Sneddon blinked, then stared at Bernie. 'You're Buttery Bernie.'

Bernie shrugged, accepting the nickname. Rebus was already leaving.

He went to the bar at the street's far corner and ordered a whisky. He sluiced his mouth out with the stuff, so that it would be heavy on his breath, then came out of the bar and weaved his way towards Ribs Mackay's tenement, just another soak trying to find his way home. He tugged his jacket over to one side, and undid a couple of buttons on his shirt. He could do this act. Sometimes he did it too well. He got drunk on the method.

He pushed open the tenement door and was in a dimly lit hallway, with worn stone steps curving up. He grasped the banister and started to climb. He didn't even pause at the second floor, but he could hear music from behind Ribs's door. And he saw the door was reinforced, just the kind dealers fitted. It gave them those vital extra seconds when the drug squad came calling, sledgehammers and axes their invitations. Seconds were all you needed to flush evidence away, or to swallow it. These days, prior to a house raid, the drugs squad opened up the sewers and had a man stationed there, ready for the flush . . .

On the top-floor landing, Rebus paused for breath. The door facing him looked hard done by, scarred and chipped and beaten. The nameplate had been hauled off, leaving deep screw holes in the wood. Rebus knocked on the door, ready with excuses and his drunk's head-down stance. He waited, but there was no answer. He listened, then put his eyes to the letterbox. Darkness. He tried the door handle. It turned, and the door swung inwards. When he thought about it, an unlocked door made sense. Ribs would need to come and go in a hurry, and locks took time.

Rebus stepped quietly into the short hallway. Some of the interior doors were open, bringing with them chinks of streetlight. The place smelt musty and damp, and it was cold. There was no furniture, and the wallpaper had peeled from the walls. Long strips now lay in wrinkled piles, like an old woman's stockings come to rest at her ankles. Rebus walked on tiptoe. He didn't know how good the floors were, and he didn't want anyone below to hear him. He didn't want Ribs Mackay to hear him.

He went into the living-room. It was identical in shape to the surveillance living-room. There were newspapers on the floor, a carpet rolled up against one wall. Tufts of carpet lay scattered across the floor. Mice had obviously been taking bits for nesting. Rebus went to the window. There was a small gap where two pieces of cardboard didn't quite meet. Through this gap he had a good view of the surveillance flat. And though the lights were off, the streetlight illuminated the net curtain, so that anyone behind the curtain who moved became a shadow puppet. Someone, Sneddon or Cooper or Bernie Few, was moving just now.

'You clever little runt,' Rebus whispered. Then he picked something up off the floor. It was a single-lens reflex camera, with telephoto lens attached. Not the sort of thing you found lying in abandoned flats. He picked it up and focused on the window across the street. There was absolutely no doubt in his mind now. It was so simple. Ribs sneaked up here, watched the surveillance through the telephoto while they thought they were watching him, and at eight o'clock walked smartly out of the tenement and went about his business.

'You're as good as gold, Bernie,' said Rebus. Then he put the camera back just the way he'd found it and tiptoed back through the flat.

'Where is he?'

Stupid question, considering. Sneddon just shrugged. 'He had to use the bathroom.'

'Of course he did,' said Rebus.

Sneddon led him through to the bathroom. It had a small window high on one wall. The window was open. It led not to the outside, but merely back into the hall near the flat's stairwell door.

'He was in here a while, so I came looking. Banged on the door, no answer, managed to force the thing open, but he wasn't here.' Sneddon's face and neck were red with embarrassment; or maybe it was just the exercise. 'I ran downstairs, but there was no sign of him.'

'I don't believe he could have squeezed out of that window,' Rebus said sceptically. 'Not even Bernie Few.' The window was about twelve inches by nine. It could be reached by standing on the rim of the bath, but the walls were white tile, and Rebus couldn't see any signs of scuff marks. He looked at the toilet. Its lid was down, but didn't sit level with the pan. Rebus lifted the lid and found himself staring at towels, several of them, stuffed down into the pan.

'What the . . . ?' Sneddon couldn't believe his eyes. But Rebus could. He opened the small airing cupboard beneath the sink. It was empty. A shelf had been lifted out and placed upright in the back of the cupboard. There was just about room inside to make for a hiding place. Rebus smiled at the disbelieving Sneddon.

'He waited till you'd gone downstairs.'

'Then what?' said Sneddon. 'You mean he's still in the flat?'

Rebus wondered. 'No,' he said at last, shaking his head. 'But think of what he just told us, about how Ribs was tricking us.'

He led Sneddon out of the flat, but instead of heading down, he climbed up a further flight to the top floor. Set into the ceiling was a skylight, and it too was open.

'A walk across the rooftops,' said Rebus.

Sneddon just shook his head. 'Sorry, sir,' he offered.

'Never mind,' said Rebus, knowing, however, that his boss would.

At seven next morning, Ribs Mackay left his flat and walked jauntily to the corner shop, followed by Sneddon. Then he walked back again, enjoying a cigarette, not a care in the world. He'd shown himself to the surveillance team, and now they had something to tell the new shift, something to occupy them during the changeover.

As usual the changeover happened at eight. And exactly a minute after Jamphlar and Connaught entered the tenement, the door across the street opened and Ribs Mackay flew out.

Rebus and Sneddon, snug in Rebus's car, watched him go. Then Sneddon got out to follow him. He didn't look back at Rebus, but he did wave an acknowledgement that his superior had been right. Rebus hoped Sneddon was better as a tail than he was as a watcher. He hoped they'd catch Ribs with the stuff on him, dealing it out perhaps, or taking delivery from his own supplier. That was the plan. That had been the plan throughout.

He started the ignition and drove out on to Buccleuch Street. Scott's Bar was an early opener, and John Rebus had an appointment there.

He owed Bernie Few a drink.

# The Serpent's Back

This was, mind you, back in 1793 or '94. Edinburgh was a better place then. Nothing ever happens here now, but back then . . . back then *everything* was happening.

Back then a caddie was indispensable if you happened to be visiting the town. If you wanted someone found, if a message needed delivering, if you wanted a bed for the night, fresh oysters, a shirtmaker or the local hoor, you came to a caddie. And if the claret got the better of you, a caddie would see you safely home.

See, the town wasn't safe, Lord no. The streets were mean. The high-falutin' were leaving the old town and crossing the Nor' Loch to the New. They lived in Princes Street and George Street, or did until they could no longer stand the stench. The old loch was an open sewer by that time, and the old town not much better.

I was called Cullender, Cully to my friends. No one knew my first name. They need only say 'Cullender', and they'd be pointed in my direction. That was how it was with young Master Gisborne. He had newly arrived by coach from London, and feared he'd never sit down again . . .

'Are you Cullender? My good friend Mr Wilks told me to ask for you.'

'Wilks?'

'He was here for some weeks. A medical student.'

I nodded. 'I recall the young gentleman particularly,' I lied.

'I shall require a clean room, nothing too fancy, my pockets aren't bottomless.'

285

'How long will you be staying, master?'

He looked around. 'I'm not sure. I'm considering a career in medicine. If I like the faculty, I may enrol.'

And he fingered the edges of his coat. It was a pale blue coat with bright silver buttons. Like Master Gisborne it was overdone and didn't quite fit together. His face was fat like a whelp's, but his physique was lean and his eyes shone. His skin had suffered neither disease nor malnourishment. He was, I suppose, a fine enough specimen, but I'd seen fine specimens before. Many of them stayed, seduced by Edinburgh. I saw them daily in the pungent howffs, or slouching through the narrow closes, heads bowed. None of them looked so fresh these days. Had they been eels, the fishwives would have tossed them in a bucket and sold them to only the most gullible.

The most gullible, of course, being those newly arrived in the city.

Master Gisborne would need looking after. He was haughty on the surface, cocksure, but I knew he was troubled, wondering how long he could sustain the act of worldliness. He had money, but not in limitless supply. His parents would be professional folk, not gentry. Some denizens would gull him before supper. Me? I was undecided.

I picked up his trunk. 'Shall I call a chair?' He frowned. 'The streets here are too narrow and steep for coaches, haven't you noticed? Know why they're narrow?' I sidled up to him. 'There's a serpent buried beneath.' He looked ill at ease, so I laughed. 'Just a story, master. We use chairmen instead of horses. Good strong Highland stock.'

I knew he had already walked a good way in search of me, hauling his trunk with him. He was tired, but counting his money too.

'Let's walk,' he decided, 'and you can acquaint me with the town.'

'The town, master,' I said, 'will acquaint you with itself.'

*

We got him settled in at Lucky Seaton's. Lucky had been a hoor herself at one time, then had been turned to the Moderate movement and now ran a Christian rooming house.

'We know all about medical students, don't we, Cully?' she said, while Gisborne took the measure of his room. 'The worst sinners in Christendom.'

She patted Master Gisborne on his plump cheek, and I led him back down the treacherous stairwell.

'What did she mean?' he asked me.

'Visit a few howffs, and you'll find out,' I told him. 'The medical students are the most notorious group of topers in the city, if you discount the lawyers, judges, poets, boatmen, and Lords this-and-that.'

'What's a howff?'

I led him directly into one.

There was a general fug in what passed for the air. Pipes were being smoked furiously, and there were no windows to open, so the stale fumes lay heavy at eye level. I could hear laughter and swearing and the shrieks of women, but it was like peering through a haar. I saw one-legged Jack, balancing a wench on his good knee. Two lawyers sat at the next table along, heads close together. A poet of minor repute scribbled away as he sat slumped on the floor. And all around there was wine, wine in jugs and bumpers and bottles, its sour smell vying with that of tobacco.

But the most noise came from a big round table in the furthest corner, where beneath flickering lamplight a meeting of the Monthly Club was underway. I led Gisborne to the table, having promised him that Edinburgh would acquaint itself with him. Five gentlemen sat round the table. One recognised me immediately.

'Dear old Cully! What news from the world above?'

'No news, sir.'

'None better than that!'

'What's the meeting this month, sirs?'

'The Hot Air Club, Cully.' The speaker made a toast of the

words. 'We are celebrating the tenth anniversary of Mr Tytler's fight by montgolfier over this very city.'

This had to be toasted again, while I explained to Master Gisborne that the Monthly Club changed its name regularly in order to have something to celebrate.

'I see you've brought fresh blood, Cully.'

'Mr Gisborne,' I said, 'is newly arrived from London and hopes to study medicine.'

'I hope he will, too, if he intends to practise.'

There was laughter, and replenishing of glasses.

'This gentleman,' I informed my master, 'is Mr Walter Scott. Mr Scott is an advocate.'

'Not today,' said another of the group. 'Today he's Colonel Grogg!'

More laughter. Gisborne was asked what he would drink.

'A glass of port,' my hapless charge replied.

The table went quiet. Scott was smiling with half his mouth only.

'Port is not much drunk in these parts. It reminds some people of the Union. Some people would rather drink *whisky* and toast their Jacobite "King O'er the Water".' Someone at the table actually did this, not heeding the tone of Scott's voice. 'But we're one nation now,' Scott continued. That man did like to make a speech. 'And if you'll drink some claret with us, we may yet be reconciled.'

The drinker who'd toasted Bonnie Prince Charlie, another lawyer whose name was Urquhart, now turned to Gisborne with his usual complaint to Englishmen. ' "Rule Britannia",' he said, 'was written by a Scot. John Bull was *invented* by a Scot!'

He slumped back, having to his mind made his point. Master Gisborne looked like he had tumbled into Bedlam.

'Now now,' Scott calmed. 'We're here to celebrate montgolfiers.' He handed Gisborne a stemless glass filled to the brim. 'And new arrivals. But you've come to a dangerous place, sir.'

'How so?' my master enquired.

'Sedition is rife.' Scott paused. 'As is murder. How many is it now, Cully?'

'Three this past fortnight.' I recited the names. 'Dr Benson, MacStay the coffin-maker, and a wretch called Howison.'

'All stabbed,' Scott informed Gisborne. 'Imagine, murdering a coffin-maker! It's like trying to murder Death himself!'

As was wont to happen, the Monthly Club shifted to another howff to partake of a *prix fixe* dinner, and thence to another where Scott would drink champagne and lead a discussion of 'the chest'.

The chest in question had been found when the Castle's crown room was opened during a search for some documents. The crown room had been opened, according to the advocate, by special warrant under the royal sign manual. No one had authority to break open the chest. The crown room was locked again, and the chest still inside. At the time of the union with England the royal regalia of Scotland had disappeared. It was Scott's contention that this regalia – crown, sceptre and sword – lay in the chest.

Gisborne listened in fascination. Somewhere along the route he had misplaced his sense of economy. He would pay for the champagne. He would pay for dinner. A brothel was being discussed as the next destination . . . Luckily, Scott was taking an interest in him, so that Gisborne's pockets were still fairly full, though his wits be empty.

I sat apart, conversing with the exiled Comte d'Artois, who had fled France at the outset of revolution. He retained the habit of stroking his neck for luck, his good fortune being that it still connected his head to his trunk. He had reason to feel nervous. Prompted by events in France, sedition was in the air. There had been riots, and now the ringleaders were being tried.

We were discussing Deacon Brodie, hanged six years

before for a series of housebreakings. Brodie, a cabinet-maker and locksmith, had robbed the very premises to which he'd fitted locks. Respectable by day, he'd been nefarious by night. To the Comte (who knew about such matters) this was merely 'the human condition'.

I noticed suddenly that I was seated in shadow. A man stood over me. He had full thick lips, a meaty stew of a nose, and eyebrows which met at the central divide the way warring forces sometimes will.

'Cullender?'

I shook my head and turned away.

'You're Cullender,' he said. 'This is for you.' He slapped his paw on to the table, then turned and pushed back through the throng. A piece of paper, neatly folded, sat on the wood where his hand had been. I unfolded it and read.

*Outside the Tolbooth, quarter before midnight.*

The note was unsigned. I handed it to the Comte.

'You will go?'

It was already past eleven. 'I'll let one more drink decide.'

The Tolbooth was the city jail where Brodie himself had spent his final days, singing airs from *The Beggar's Opera*. The night was like pitch, nobody having bothered to light their lamps, and a haar rolled through from the direction of Leith.

In the darkness, I had trodden in something I did not care to study, and was scraping my shoe clean on the Tolbooth's cornerstone when I heard a voice close by.

'Cullender?'

A woman's voice; even held to a whisper I knew it for that. The lady herself was dressed top to toe in black, her face deep inside the hood of a cloak.

'I'm Cullender.'

'I'm told you perform services.'

'I'm no minister, lady.'

Maybe she smiled. A small bag appeared and I took it, weighing the coins inside.

'There's a book circulating in the town,' said my new mistress. 'I am keen to obtain it.'

'We have several fine booksellers in the Luckenbooths . . .'

'You are glib, sir.'

'And you are mysterious.'

'Then I'll be plain. I know of only one copy of this book, a private printing. It is called *Ranger's Second Impartial List* . . .'

'*Of the Ladies of Pleasure in Edinburgh.*'

'You know it. Have you seen it?'

'It's not meant for the likes of me.'

'I would like to see this book.'

'You want me to find it?'

'It's said you know everyone in the city.'

'Everyone that matters.'

'Then you can locate it?'

'It's possible.' I examined my shoes. 'But first I'd need to know a little more . . .'

When I looked up again, she was gone.

At The Cross, the caddies were speaking quietly with the chairmen. We caddies had organised ourselves into a company, boasting written standards and a Magistrate of Caddies in charge of all. We regarded ourselves superior to the chairmen, mere brawny Highland migrants.

But my best friend and most trusted ally, Mr Mack, was a chairman. He was not, however, at The Cross. Work was nearly over for the night. The last taverns were throwing out the last soused customers. Only the brothels and cockpits were still active. Not able to locate Mr Mack, I turned instead to a fellow caddie, an old hand called Dryden.

'Mr Dryden,' I said, all businesslike, 'I require your services, the fee to be agreed between us.'

Dryden, as ever, was willing. I knew he would work through the night. He was known to the various brothel-keepers, and could ask his questions discreetly, as I might have done myself had the lady's fee not been sufficient to turn me employer.

Me, I headed home, climbing the lonely stairs to my attic quarters and a cold mattress. I found sleep the way a pickpocket finds his gull.

Which is to say, easily.

Next morning, Dryden was dead.

A young caddie called Colin came to tell me. We repaired to the Nor' Loch where the body still lay, face down in the slime. The Town Guard – 'Town Rats' behind their backs – fingered their Lochaber axes, straightened their tall cocked hats, and tried to look important. One of their number, a red-faced individual named Fairlie, asked if we knew the victim.

'Dryden,' I said. 'He was a caddie.'

'He's been run through with a dagger,' Fairlie delighted in telling me. 'Just like those other three.'

But I wasn't so sure about that . . .

I went to a quiet howff, a drink steadying my humour. Dryden, I surmised, had been killed in such a way as to make him appear another victim of the city's stabber. I knew though that in all likelihood he had been killed because of the questions he'd been asking . . . questions I'd sent him to ask. Was I safe myself? Had Dryden revealed anything to his killer? And what was it about my mistress's mission that made it so deadly dangerous?

As I was thus musing, young Gisborne entered the bar on fragile legs.

'Did I have anything to drink last evening?' he asked, holding his head.

'Master, you drank like it was your last day alive.'

Our hostess was already replenishing my wine jug. 'Kill or cure,' I said, pouring two glasses.

Gisborne could see I was worried, and asked the nature of the problem. I was grateful to tell him. Any listener would have sufficed. Mind, I held back some. This knowledge was proving dangerous, so I made no mention of the lady and her book. I jumped from the messenger to my words with Dryden.

'The thing to do then,' my young master said, 'is to track backwards. Locate the messenger.'

I thought back to the previous evening. About the time the messenger had been arriving, the lawyer Urquhart had been taking his leave of the Monthly Club.

'We'll talk to Urquhart,' I said. 'At this hour he'll be in his chambers. Follow me.'

Gisborne followed me out of the howff and across the street directly into another. There, in a booth, papers before him and a bottle of wine beside them, sat Urquhart.

'I'm pleased to see you,' the lawyer announced. His eyes were bloodshot, his nose like a stoned cherry. His breath I avoided altogether. Aged somewhere in his thirties, Urquhart was a seasoned dissolute. He would have us take a bumper with him.

'Sir,' I began, 'do you recall leaving the company last night?'

'Of course. I'm only sorry I'd to leave so early. An assignation, you understand.' We shared a smile at this. 'Tell me, Gisborne, to which house of ill fame did the gang repair?'

'I don't recollect,' Gisborne admitted.

Urquhart enjoyed this. 'Then tell me, did you awake in a bed or the gutter?'

'In neither, Mr Urquhart. I awoke on the kitchen floor of a house I did not know.'

While Urquhart relished this, I asked if he'd taken a chair from the tavern last night.

'Of course. A friend of yours was front-runner.'

'Mr Mack?' Urquhart nodded. 'You didn't happen to see a grotesque, sir?' I described the messenger to him. Urquhart shook his head.

'I heard a caddie was murdered last night,' Urquhart said. 'We all know the Town Rats can't be expected to bring anyone to justice.' He leaned towards me confidentially. 'Are you looking for justice, Cully?'

'I don't know what I'm looking for, sir.'

Which was a lie. For now, I was looking for Mr Mack.

I left Gisborne with Urquhart, and found Mack at The Cross.

'Yes,' he said, 'I saw that fellow going in. A big fat-lipped sort with eyebrows that met in the middle.'

'Had you seen him before?'

Mack nodded. 'But not here, over the loch.'

'The new town?' Mack nodded. 'Then show me where.'

Mack and his fellow chairman carried me down the steep slope towards the building site. Yes, building site, for though Princes Street and George Street were finished, yet more streets were being artfully constructed. Just now, the builders were busy on what would be called Charlotte Square. We took the simpler route, down past Trinity Hospital and the College Kirk, then along Princes Street itself. There were plans to turn the Nor' Loch into either a canal or formal gardens, but for the moment it was a dumping ground. I avoided looking at it, and tried not to think of poor Dryden. Joining the loch to the old town sat The Mound, an apt name for a treacherous heap of new town rubble.

'All change, eh, Cully?' Mr Mack called to me. 'Soon there'll be no business in the old town for the likes of you and me.'

He had a point. The nobility had already deserted the old town. Their grand lands now housed wheelwrights and hosiers and schoolmasters. They all lived in the new town now, at a general distance from the milling rabble. So here the foundations were being laid, not for the new town alone, but for the death of the old.

We passed into George Street and the sedan chair was brought to rest. 'It was here I saw him,' Mr Mack said. 'He was marching up the street like he owned the place.'

I got out of the chair and rubbed my bruised posterior. Mr

Mack's companions had already spotted another likely fare. I waved them off. I must needs talk to my mistress, and that meant finding her servant. So I sat on a step and watched the workcarts grinding past overloaded with rocks and rubble. The day passed pleasantly enough.

Perhaps two hours had gone by when I saw him. I couldn't be sure which house he emerged from; he was some way along the street. I tucked myself behind some railings and watched him head down towards Princes Street. I followed at a canny distance.

He was clumsy, his gait gangling, and I followed him with ease. He climbed back up to the old town and made for the Luckenbooths. Here he entered a bookshop, causing me to pause.

The shop belonged to a Mr Whitewood, who fancied himself not only bookseller, but poet and author also. I entered the premises quietly, and could hear Whitewood's raised voice. He was towards the back of his shop, reciting to a fawning audience of other *soi-distant* writers and people to whom books were mere fashion.

The servant was pushing his way to the front of the small gathering. Whitewood stood on a low unsteady podium, and read with a white handkerchief in one hand, which he waved for dramatic effect. He needed all the help he could get. I dealt daily with the 'improvers', the self-termed 'literati'. I'll tell you now what an improver is, he's an imp who roves. I'd seen them dragging their carcasses through the gutter, and waylaying hoors, and scrapping with the tourists.

The servant had reached the podium, and the bookseller had seen him. Without pausing mid-stanza, Whitewood passed the wretch a note. It was done in an instant, and the servant turned back towards the door. I slipped outside and hid myself, watching the servant head as if towards the courts.

I followed him into the courthouse. I followed him into one particular court . . . and there was brought up short.

Lord Braxfield, the Hanging Judge, was deciding a case. He sat in his wig at his muckle bench and dipped oatcakes into his claret, sucking loudly on the biscuits as he glared at the accused. There were three of them, and I knew they were charged with sedition, being leaders of a popular convention for parliamentary reform. At this time, only thirty or so people in Edinburgh had the right to vote for the Member of Parliament. These three sad creatures had wanted to change that, and a lot more besides.

I glanced at the jury – doubtless hand-picked by Braxfield himself. The accused would be whipped and sent to Botany Bay. The public gallery was restless. There were guards between the populace and the bench. The servant was nodded through by one of the guards and handed White-wood's note to Braxfield. Then he turned quickly and left by another door. I was set to follow when the Hanging Judge noticed me.

'Cullender, approach the bench!'

I bit my lip, but knew better than to defy Braxfield, even if it meant losing my quarry. The guards let me through. I forbore to look at the accused as I passed them.

'Yes, my lord?'

Braxfield nibbled another of his infernal biscuits. He looked like he'd drunk well, too. 'Cullender,' he said, 'you're one of the least honest and civil men in this town, am I correct?'

'I have competitors, my lord.'

He guffawed, spitting crumbs from his wet lips. 'But tell me this, would you have a man live who committed treason?'

I swallowed, aware of three pairs of eyes behind me. 'I might ask myself about his motives, my lord.'

Braxfield leaned over the bench. He was unquestionably ugly, eyes black as night. In his seventies, he grew increasingly eccentric. He was what passed for the law in this city. 'Then it's as well *I'm* wearing this wig and not you!' he screeched. He wagged a finger, the nail of which was sore in need of a trim. 'You'll see Australia one day, my friend if you're not careful. Now be gone, I've some justice to dispense.'

It had been a long time since Braxfield and 'justice' had been even loosely acquainted.

Outside, the servant was long gone. Cursing my luck and the law courts both, I headed down to the Canongate.

I engaged Mr Mack's services regarding my lady's book, warning him to be extra vigilant and telling him of Dryden's demise. He suggested going to the authorities, then realised what he was saying. The law was as effectual as a scented handkerchief against the pox, and we both knew it.

I sat in a howff and ate a dish of oysters. Having been to look at the university, Master Gisborne joined me.

'It'll be fine when it's finished,' was his opinion.

I supped the last of the juice and put down the platter. 'Remember I told you about the serpent, master?'

His eyes were red-rimmed, face puffy with excess. He nodded.

'Well,' I continued thoughtfully, 'perhaps it's not so far beneath the surface as I thought. You need only scratch and you'll see it. Remember that, even in your cups.'

He looked puzzled, but nodded again. Then he seemed to remember something and reached into his leather bag. He handed me a wrapped parcel.

'Cully, can you keep this somewhere safe?'

'What is it?'

'Just hold it for me a day or so. Will you do that?'

I nodded and placed the parcel at my feet. Gisborne looked mightily relieved. Then the howff door swung inwards and Urquhart and others appeared, taking Gisborne off with them. I finished my wine and made my way back to my room.

Halfway there, I met the tailor whose family lived two floors below me.

'Cully,' he said, 'men are looking for you.'

'What sort of men?'

'The sort you wouldn't have find you. They're standing guard on the stairwell and won't shift.'

'Thanks for the warning.'

He held my arm. 'Cully, business is slow. If you could persuade some of your clients of the quality of my cloth . . . ?'

'Depend on it.' I went back up the brae to The Cross and found Mr Mack.

'Here,' I said, handing him the parcel. 'Keep this for me.'

'What's wrong?'

'I'm not sure. I think I may have stepped in something even less savoury than I thought. Any news of the *List*?'

Mack shook his head. He looked worried when I left him; not for himself, but for me.

I kept heading uphill, towards the Castle itself. Beneath Castle Hill lay the catacombs where the town's denizens used to hide when the place was being sacked. And where the lowest of Edinburgh's wretches still dwelt. I would be safe there, so I made my way into the tunnels and out of the light, averting my face where possible from each interested, unfriendly gaze.

The man I sought sat slouched against one of the curving walls, hands on his knees. He could sit like that for hours, brooding. He was a giant, and there were stories to equal his size. It was said he'd been a seditionary, a rabble-rouser, both pirate and smuggler. He had almost certainly killed men, but these days he lay low. His name was Ormond.

He watched me sit opposite him, his gaze unblinking.

'You're in trouble,' he said at last.

'Would I be here otherwise? I need somewhere to sleep for tonight.'

He nodded slowly. 'That's all any of us needs. You'll be safe here, Cullender.'

And I was.

*

But next morning I was roused early by Ormond shaking me.

'Men outside,' he hissed. 'Looking for you.'

I rubbed my eyes. 'Is there another exit?'

Ormond shook his head. 'If you went any deeper into this maze, you could lose yourself for ever. These burrows run as far as the Canongate.'

'How many men?' I was standing up now, fully awake. 'Four.'

I held out my hand. 'Give me a dagger, I'll deal with them.' I meant it too. I was aching and irritable and tired of running. But Ormond shook his head.

'I've a better plan,' he said.

He led me back through the tunnel towards its entrance. The tunnel grew more populous as we neared the outside world. I could hear my pursuers ahead, examining faces, snarling as each one proved false. Then Ormond filled his lungs.

'The price of corn's to be raised!' he bellowed. 'New taxes! New laws! Everyone to The Cross!'

Voices were raised in anger, and people clambered to their feet. Ormond was raising a mob. The Edinburgh mob was a wondrous thing. It could run riot through the streets, and then melt back into the shadows. There'd been the Porteous riots, anti-Catholic riots, price-rise riots, and pro-Revolution riots. Each time, the vast majority escaped arrest. A mob could be raised in a minute, and could disperse in another. Even Braxfield feared the mob.

Ormond was bellowing in front of me. As for me, I was merely another of the wretches. I passed the men who'd been seeking me. They stood dumbfounded in the midst of the spectacle. As soon as the crowd reached the Lawnmarket, I peeled off with a wave of thanks to Ormond, slipped into an alley and was alone again.

But not for long. Down past the Luckenbooths I saw the servant again, and this time he would not evade me. Down towards Princes Street he went, down Geordie Boyd's footpath, a footpath that would soon be wide enough for carriages. He crossed Princes Street and headed up to George Street. There at last I saw him descend some steps and enter a house by its servants' door. I stopped a sedan chair. Both chairmen knew me through Mr Mack.

'That house there?' one of them said in answer to my question. 'It used to belong to Lord Thorpe before he left for London. A bookseller bought it from him.'

'A Mr Whitewood?' I asked blithely. The chairman nodded. 'I admit I don't know that gentleman well. Is he married?'

'Married aye, but you wouldn't know it. She's seldom seen, is she, Donald?'

'Rarely, very rarely,' the second chairman agreed.

'Why's that? Has she the pox or something?'

They laughed at the imputation. 'How would we know a thing like that?'

I laughed too, and bid them thanks and farewell. Then I approached the front door of the house and knocked a good solid knock.

The servant, when he opened the door, was liveried. He looked at me in astonishment.

'Tell your mistress I wish to speak with her,' I said sharply.

He appeared in two minds at least, but I sidestepped him and found myself in a fine entrance hall.

'Wait in here,' the servant growled, closing the front door and opening another. 'I'll ask my lady if she'll deign to see you.'

I toured the drawing-room. It was like walking around an exhibition, though in truth the only exhibition I'd ever toured was of Bedlam on a Sunday afternoon, and then only to look for a friend of mine.

The door opened and the lady of the house swept in. She had powdered her cheeks heavily to disguise the redness there – either embarrassment or anger. Her eyes avoided mine, which gave me opportunity to study her. She was in her mid twenties, not short, and with a pleasing figure. Her lips were full and red, her eyes hard but to my mind seductive. She was a catch, but when she spoke her voice was rough-hewn, and I wondered at her history.

'What do you want?'

'What do you think I want?'

She picked up a pretty statuette. 'Are we acquainted?'

'I believe so. We met outside the Tolbooth.'

She attempted a disbelieving laugh. 'Indeed? It's a place I've never been.'

'You would not care to see its innards, lady, yet you may if you continue in this manner.'

No amount of powder could have hidden her colouring. 'How dare you come here!'

'My life is in danger, lady.'

This quieted her. 'Why? What have you done?'

'Nothing save what you asked of me.'

'Have you found the book?'

'Not yet, and I've a mind to hand you back your money.'

She saw what I was getting at, and looked aghast. 'But if you're in danger . . . I swear it cannot be to do with me!'

'No? A man has died already.'

'Mr Cullender, it's only a book! It's nothing anyone would kill for.'

I almost believed her. 'Why do you want it?'

She turned away. 'That is not your concern.'

'My chief concern is my neck, lady. I'll save it at any cost.'

'I repeat, you are in no danger from seeking that book. If you think your life in peril, there must needs be some other cause.' She stared at me as she spoke, and the damnation of it was that I believed her. I believed that Dryden's death, Braxfield's threat, the men chasing me, that none of it had anything to do with her. She saw the change in me, and smiled a radiant smile, a smile that took me with it.

'Now get out,' she said. And with that she left the room

and began to climb the stairs. Her servant was waiting for me by the front door, holding it open in readiness.

My head was full of puzzles. All I knew with certainty was that I was sick of hiding. I headed back to the old town with a plan in my mind as half-baked as the scrapings the baker tossed out to the homeless.

I toured the town gossips, starting with the fishwives. Then I headed to The Cross and whispered in the ears of selected caddies and chairmen. Then it was into the howffs and dining establishments, and I was glad to wash my hard work down with a glass or two of wine.

My story broadcast, I repaired to my lodgings and lay on the straw mattress. There were no men waiting for me on the stairwell. I believe I even slept a little. It was dark when I next looked out of the skylight. The story I'd spread was that I knew who'd killed Dryden, and was merely biding my time before alerting the Town Rats. Would anyone fall for the ploy? I wasn't sure. I fell to a doze again, but opened my eyes on hearing noises on the stair.

The steps to my attic were rotten and had to be managed adroitly. My visitor – a lone man, I surmised – was doing his best. I sat up on the mattress and watched the door begin to open. In deep shadow, a figure entered my room, closing the door after it with some finality.

'Good evening, Cully.'

I swallowed drily. 'So the stories were true then, Deacon Brodie?'

'True enough,' he said, coming closer. His face was almost unrecognisable, much older, more careworn, and he wore no wig, no marks of a gentleman. He carried a slender dagger in his right hand.

'I cheated the gibbet, Cully,' he said with his old pride.

'But I was there, I saw you drop.'

'And you saw my men cut me down and haul me away.' He grinned with what teeth were left in his head. 'A wooden collar saved my throat, Cully. I devised it myself.'

I recalled the red silk he'd worn ostentatiously around his throat. A scarf from a female admirer, the story went. It would have hidden just such a device.

'You've been in hiding a long time,' I said. The dagger was inches from me.

'I fled Edinburgh, Cully. I've been away these past five and a half years.'

'What brought you back?' I couldn't take my eyes off the dagger.

'Aye,' Brodie said, seeing what was in my mind. 'The doctor who pronounced me dead and the coffin-maker who was supposed to have buried me. I couldn't have witnesses alive . . . not now.'

'And the others, Dryden and the wretch Howison?'

'Both recognised me, curse them. Then *you* started to snoop around, and couldn't be found.'

'But why? Why are you back?'

The dagger was touching my throat now. I'd backed myself into a corner of the bed. There was nowhere to go. 'I was *tempted* back, Cully. A temptation I could not resist. The crown jewels.'

'What?'

His voice was a feverish whisper. 'The chest in the crown room. I will have its contents, my last and greatest theft.'

'Alone? Impossible.'

'But I'm not alone. I have powerful allies.' He smiled. 'Braxfield for one. He believes the theft of the jewels will spark a Scots revolution. But you know this already, Cully. You were seen watching Braxfield. You were seen in Whitewood's shop.'

'Whitewood's part of it too?'

'You know he is, romantic fool that he is.' The point of the dagger broke my skin. I could feel blood trickle down my throat. If I spoke again, they would be my last words. I felt like laughing. Brodie was so wrong in his surmisings. Everything was wrong. A sudden noise on the stair turned Brodie's head. My own dagger was hidden beneath my thigh. I grabbed it with one hand, my other hand wrestling with Brodie's blade.

When Gisborne opened the door, what he saw sobered him immediately.

Brodie freed himself and turned to confront the young Englishman, dagger ready, but not ready enough. Gisborne had no hesitation in running him through. Brodie stood there frozen, then keeled over, his head hitting the boards with a dull dead sound.

Gisborne was the statue now. He stared at the spreading blood.

I got to my feet quickly. 'Where did you get the blade?' I asked, amazed.

Gisborne swallowed. 'I bought it new today, heeding your advice.'

'You saved my life, young master.' I stared down at Brodie's corpse. 'But why are you here?'

Gisborne came to his senses. 'I heard you were looking for a book.'

'I was. What of it?' We were both staring at Brodie.

'Only to tell you that I am in possession of it. Or I was. The lawyer Urquhart gave it to me. He said I would doubtless find it useful . . . Who was this man?'

I ignored the question and glared at him. '*You* have the book?'

He shook his head. 'I daren't keep it in my room for fear my landlady might find it.'

I blinked. 'That parcel?' Gisborne nodded. I felt a fool, a dumb fool. But there was Brodie's corpse to dispose of. I could see little advantage in reporting this, his second demise, to the authorities. Questions would be asked of Master Gisborne, and a young Englishman might not always receive a fair hearing, especially with Braxfield at the bench. God no, the body must be disposed of quietly.

And I knew just the spot.

Mr Mack helped us lug the guts down to the new town,

propping Brodie in the sedan chair. The slumped corpse resembled nothing so much as a sleeping drunk.

In Charlotte Square we found some fresh foundations and buried the remains of Deacon Brodie within. We were all three in a sweat by the time we'd finished. I sat myself down on a large stone and wiped my brow.

'Well, friends,' I said, 'it is only right and proper.'

'What is?' Gisborne asked, breathing heavily.

'The old town has its serpent, and now the new town does too.' I watched Gisborne put his jacket back on. It was the blue coat with silver buttons. There was blood on it, and dirt besides.

'I know a tailor,' I began, 'might make something fresh for an excellent price . . .'

Next morning, washed and crisply dressed, I returned to my lady's house. I waved the parcel under the servant's nose and he hurried upstairs.

My lady was down promptly, but gave me no heed. She had eyes only for the book. Book? It was little more than a ragged pamphlet, its pages well-thumbed, scribbled marginalia commenting on this or that entry or adding a fresh one. I handed her the tome.

'The entry you seek is towards the back,' I told her. She looked startled. 'You are, I suppose, the Masked Lady referred to therein? A lady for daylight assignations only, and always masked, speaking in a whisper?'

Her cheeks were crimson as she tore at the book, scattering its shreddings.

'Better have the floor swept,' I told her. 'You wouldn't want Mr Whitewood to find any trace. That was your reason all along, was it not? He is a known philanderer. It was only a matter of time before he got to read of the Masked Lady, and became intrigued to meet her.'

Her head was held high, like she was examining the room's cornices.

'I'm not ashamed,' she said.

'Nor should you be.'

She saw I was mocking her. 'I am a prisoner here, with no more life than a doll.'

'So you take revenge in your own particular manner? I understand, lady, but you must understand this. Two men died because of you. Not directly, but that matters not to them. Only one deserved to die. For the other . . .' I jangled the bag of money she'd given me that first night. 'These coins will buy him a burial.'

Then I bade her good day and left the whole shining new town behind me, with its noises of construction and busyness. Let them build all the mighty edifices they would; they could not erase the stain. They could not erase the real town, the old town, the town I knew so intimately. I returned to the howff where Gisborne and Mack awaited me.

'I've decided,' the young master said, 'to study law rather than medicine, Cully.' He poured me a drink. 'Edinburgh needs another lawyer, don't you think?'

The image of Braxfield came unasked into my mind. 'Like it needs another plague, master.'

But I raised my glass to him anyway.

# No Sanity Clause

## AN INSPECTOR REBUS STORY FOR CHRISTMAS

It was all Edgar Allan Poe's fault. Either that or the Scottish Parliament. Joey Briggs was spending most of his days in the run-up to Christmas sheltering from Edinburgh's biting December winds. He'd been walking up George IV Bridge one day and had watched a down-and-out slouching into the Central Library. Joey had hesitated. He wasn't a down-and-out, not yet anyway. Maybe he would be soon, if Scully Aitchison MSP got his way, but for now Joey had a bedsit and a trickle of state cash. Thing was, nothing made you miss money more than Christmas. The shop windows displayed their magnetic pull. There were queues at the cash machines. Kids tugged on their parents' sleeves, ready with something new to add to the present list. Boyfriends were out buying gold, while families piled the food trolley high.

And then there was Joey, nine weeks out of prison and nobody to call his friend. He knew there was nothing waiting for him back in his home town. His wife had taken the children and tiptoed out of his life. Joey's sister had written to him in prison with the news. So, eleven months on, Joey had walked through the gates of Saughton Jail and taken the first bus into the city centre, purchased an evening paper and started the hunt for somewhere to live.

The bedsit was fine. It was one of four in a tenement basement just off South Clerk Street, sharing a kitchen and bathroom. The other men worked, didn't say much. Joey's room had a gas fire with a coin-meter beside it, too expensive to keep it going all day. He'd tried sitting in the kitchen with the stove lit, until the landlord had caught him. Then he'd tried steeping in the bath, topping up the hot. But the water always seemed to run cold after half a tub.

'You could try getting a job,' the landlord had said.

Not so easy with a prison record. Most of the jobs were for security and nightwatch. Joey didn't think he'd get very far there.

Following the tramp into the library was one of his better ideas. The uniform behind the desk gave him a look, but didn't say anything. Joey wandered the stacks, picked out a book and sat himself down. And that was that. He became a regular, the staff acknowledged him with a nod and sometimes even a smile. He kept himself presentable, didn't fall asleep the way some of the old guys did. He read for much of the day, alternating between fiction, biographies and textbooks. He read up on local history, plumbing and Winston Churchill, Nigel Tranter's novels and National Trust gardens. He knew the library would close over Christmas, didn't know what he'd do without it. He never borrowed books, because he was afraid they'd have him on some blacklist: convicted housebreaker and petty thief, not to be trusted with loan material.

He dreamt of spending Christmas in one of the town's posh hotels, looking out across Princes Street Gardens to the Castle. He'd order room service and watch TV. He'd take as many baths as he liked. They'd clean his clothes for him and return them to the room. He dreamt of the presents he'd buy himself: a big radio with a CD player, some new shirts and pairs of shoes; and books. Plenty of books.

The dream became almost real to him, so that he found himself nodding off in the library, coming to as his head hit the page he'd been reading. Then he'd have to concentrate, only to find himself drifting into a warm sleep again.

Until he met Edgar Allan Poe.

It was a book of poems and short stories, among them 'The Purloined Letter'. Joey loved that, thought it was really clever the way you could hide something by putting it right in front of people. Something that didn't look out of place, people would just ignore it. There'd been a guy in Saughton, doing time for fraud. He'd told Joey: 'Three things: a suit, a haircut and an expensive watch. If you've got those, it's amazing what you can get away with.' He'd meant that clients had trusted him, because they'd seen something they were comfortable with, something they expected to see. What they hadn't seen was what was right in front of their noses, to wit: a shark, someone who was going to take a big bite out of their savings.

As Joey's eyes flitted back over Poe's story, he started to get an idea. He started to get what he thought was a very good idea indeed. Problem was, he needed what the fraudster had called 'the start-up', meaning some cash. He happened to look across to where one of the old tramps was slumped on a chair, the newspaper in front of him unopened. Joey looked around: nobody was watching. The place was dead: who had time to go to the library when Christmas was around the corner? Joey walked over to the old guy, slipped a hand into his coat pocket. Felt coins and notes, bunched his fingers around them. He glanced down at the newspaper. There was a story about Scully Aitchison's campaign. Aitchison was the MSP who wanted all offenders put on a central register, open to public inspection. He said law-abiding folk had the right to know if their neighbour was a thief or a murderer – as if stealing was the same as killing somebody! There was a small photo of Aitchison, too, beaming that self-satisfied smile, his glasses glinting. If Aitchison got his way, Joey would never get out of the rut.

Not unless his plan paid off.

John Rebus saw his girlfriend kissing Santa Claus. There was a German Market in Princes Street Gardens. That was where Rebus was to meet Jean. He hadn't expected to find her in a clinch with a man dressed in a red suit, black boots and snowy-white beard. Santa broke away and moved off, just as Rebus was approaching. German folk songs were blaring out. There was a startled look on Jean's face.

'What was that all about?' he asked.

'I don't know.' She was watching the retreating figure. 'I think maybe he's just had too much festive spirit. He came up and grabbed me.' Rebus made to follow, but Jean stopped him. 'Come on, John. Season of goodwill and all that.'

'It's assault, Jean.'

She laughed, regaining her composure. 'You're going to take St Nicholas down the station and put him in the cells?' She rubbed his arm. 'Let's forget it, eh? The fun starts in ten minutes.'

Rebus wasn't too sure that the evening was going to be 'fun'. He spent every day bogged down in crimes and tragedies. He wasn't sure that a 'mystery dinner' was going to offer much relief. It had been Jean's idea. There was a hotel just across the road. You all went in for dinner, were handed envelopes telling you which character you'd be playing. A body was discovered, and then you all turned detective.

'It'll be fun,' Jean insisted, leading him out of the gardens. She had three shopping bags with her. He wondered if any of them were for him. She'd asked for a list of his Christmas wants, but so far all he'd come up with were a couple of CDs by String Driven Thing.

As they entered the hotel, they saw that the mystery evening was being held on the mezzanine floor. Most of the guests had already gathered and were enjoying glasses of cava. Rebus asked in vain for a beer.

'Cava's included in the price,' the waitress told him. A man dressed in Victorian costume was checking names and handing out carrier bags.

'Inside,' he told Jean and Rebus, 'you'll find instructions, a secret clue that only you know, your name, and an item of clothing.'

'Oh,' Jean said, 'I'm Little Nell.' She fixed a bonnet to her head. 'Who are you, John?'

'Mr Bumble.' Rebus produced his name-tag and a yellow woollen scarf, which Jean insisted on tying around his neck.

'It's a Dickensian theme, specially for Christmas,' the host revealed, before moving off to confront his other victims. Everyone looked a bit embarrassed, but most were trying for enthusiasm. Rebus didn't doubt that a couple of glasses of wine over dinner would loosen a few Edinburgh stays. There were a couple of faces he recognised. One was a journalist, her arm around her boyfriend's waist. The other was a man who appeared to be with his wife. He had one of those looks to him, the kind that says you should know him. She was blonde and petite and about a decade younger than her husband.

'Isn't that an MSP?' Jean whispered.

'His name's Scully Aitchison,' Rebus told her.

Jean was reading her information sheet. 'The victim tonight is a certain Ebenezer Scrooge,' he said.

'And did you kill him?'

She thumped his arm. Rebus smiled, but his eyes were on the MSP. Aitchison's face was bright red. Rebus guessed he'd been drinking since lunchtime. His voice boomed across the floor, broadcasting the news that he and Catriona had booked a room for the night, so they wouldn't have to drive back to the constituency.

They were all mingling on the mezzanine landing. The room where they'd dine was just off to the right, its doors still closed. Guests were starting to ask each other which characters they were playing. As one elderly lady – Miss Havisham on her name-tag – came over to ask Jean about Little Nell, Rebus saw a red-suited man appear at the top of the stairs. Santa carried what looked like a half-empty sack. He started making his way across the floor, but was stopped by Aitchison.

'*J'accuse!*' the MSP bawled. 'You killed Scrooge because of his inhumanity to his fellow man!' Aitchison's wife came to the rescue, dragging her husband away, but Santa's eyes seemed to follow them. As he made to pass Rebus, Rebus fixed him with a stare.

'Jean,' he asked, 'is he the same one . . . ?'

She only caught the back of Santa's head. 'They all look alike to me,' she said.

Santa was on his way to the next flight of stairs. Rebus watched him leave, then turned back to the other guests, all of them now tricked out in odd items of clothing. No wonder Santa had looked like he'd stumbled into an asylum. Rebus was reminded of a Marx Brothers line, Groucho trying to get Chico's name on a contract, telling him to sign the sanity clause.

But, as Chico said, everyone knew there was no such thing as Sanity Clause.

Joey jimmied open his third room of the night. The Santa suit had worked a treat. Okay, so it was hot and uncomfortable, and the beard was itching his neck, but it worked! He'd breezed through reception and up the stairs. So far, as he'd worked the corridors all he'd had were a few jokey comments. No one from security asking him who he was. No guests becoming suspicious. He fitted right in, and he was right under their noses.

God bless Edgar Allan Poe.

The woman in the fancy dress shop had even thrown in a sack, saying he'd be wanting to fill it. How true: in the first bedroom, he'd dumped out the crumpled sheets of old newspaper and started filling the sack – clothes, jewellery, the contents of the mini-bar. Same with the second room: a tap on the door to make sure no one was home, then the chisel into the lock and hey presto. Thing was, there wasn't much in the rooms. A notice in the wardrobe told clients to lock all valuables in the hotel safe at reception. Still, he had a few nice things: camera, credit cards, bracelet and necklace. Sweat was running into his eyes, but he couldn't afford to shed his disguise. He was starting to have crazy thoughts: take a good long soak; ring down for room service; find a room that hadn't been taken and settle in for the duration. In the third room, he sat on the bed, feeling dizzy. There was a briefcase open beside him, just lots of paperwork. His stomach growled, and he remembered that his last meal had been a Mars Bar supper the previous day. He broke open a jar of salted peanuts, switched the TV on while he ate. As he put the empty jar down, he happened to glance at the contents of the briefcase. 'Parliamentary briefing . . . Law and Justice Sub-Committee . . .' He saw a list of names on the top sheet. One of them was coloured with a yellow marker.

Scully Aitchison.

The drunk man downstairs . . . That was where Joey knew him from! He leapt to his feet, trying to think. He could stay here and give the MSP a good hiding. He could . . . He picked up the room-service menu, called down and ordered smoked salmon, a steak, a bottle each of best red wine and malt whisky. Then heard himself saying those sweetest words: 'Put it on my room, will you?'

Then he settled back to wait. Flipped through the paperwork again. An envelope slipped out. Card inside, and a letter inside the card.

*Dear Scully*, it began. *I hope it isn't all my fault, this idea of yours for a register of offenders . . .*

'I haven't a clue,' said Rebus.

Nor did he. Dinner was over, the actor playing Scrooge was flat out on the mezzanine floor, and Rebus was as far away from solving the crime as ever. Thankfully, a bar had been opened up, and he spent most of his time perched on a high stool, pretending to read the background notes while taking sips of beer. Jean had hooked up with Miss Havisham, while Aitchison's wife was slumped in one of the armchairs, drawing on a cigarette. The MSP himself was playing ringmaster, and had twice confronted Rebus, calling for him to reveal himself as the villain.

'Innocent, m'lud,' was all Rebus had said.

'We think it's Magwitch,' Jean said, suddenly breathless by Rebus's side, her bonnet at a jaunty angle. 'He and Scrooge knew one another in prison.'

'I didn't know Scrooge served time,' Rebus said.

'That's because you're not asking questions.'

'I don't need to; I've got you to tell me. That's what makes a good detective.'

He watched her march away. Four of the diners had encircled the poor man playing Magwitch. Rebus had harboured suspicions, too . . . but now he was thinking of jail time, and how it affected those serving it. It gave them a certain look, a look they brought back into the world on their release. The same look he'd seen in Santa's eyes.

And here was Santa now, coming back down the stairs, his sack slung over one shoulder. Crossing the mezzanine floor as if seeking someone out. Then finding them: Scully Aitchison. Rebus rose from his stool and wandered over.

'Have you been good this year?' Santa was asking Aitchison.

'No worse than anyone else,' the MSP smirked.

'Sure about that?' Santa's eyes narrowed.

'I wouldn't lie to Father Christmas.'

'What about this plan of yours, the offender register?'

Aitchison blinked a couple of times. 'What about it?'

Santa held a piece of paper aloft, his voice rising. 'Your own nephew's serving time for fraud. Managed to keep that quiet, haven't you?'

Aitchison stared at the letter. 'Where in hell . . . ? How . . . ?'

The journalist stepped forward. 'Mind if I take a look?'

Santa handed over the letter, then pulled off his hat and beard. Started heading for the stairs down. Rebus blocked his way.

'Time to hand out the presents,' he said quietly. Joey looked at him and understood immediately, slid the sack from his shoulder. Rebus took it. 'Now on you go.'

'You're not arresting me?'

'Who'd feed Dancer and Prancer?' Rebus asked.

His stomach full of steak and wine, a bottle of malt in the capacious pocket of his costume, Joey smiled his way back towards the outside world.

# Death Is Not The End

## AN INSPECTOR REBUS STORY

# One

*Is loss redeemed by memory? Or does memory merely swell the sense of loss, becoming the enemy? The language of loss is the language of memory: remembrance, memorial, memento. People leave our lives all the time: some we met only briefly, others we'd known since birth. They leave us memories – which become skewed through time – and little more.*

The silent dance continued. Couples writhed and shuffled, threw back their heads or ran hands through their hair, eyes darting around the dance floor, seeking out future partners maybe, or past loves to make jealous. The TV monitor gave a greasy look to everything.

No sound, just pictures, the tape cutting from dance floor to main bar to second bar to toilet hallway, then entrance foyer, exterior front and exterior back. Exterior back was a puddled alley, full of rubbish bins and a Merc belonging to the club's owner. Rebus had heard about the alley: a punter had been knifed there the previous summer. Mr Merc had complained about the bloody smear on his passenger-side window. The victim had lived.

The club was called Gaitanos, nobody knew why. The owner just said it sounded American and a bit jazzy. The larger part of the clientele had decided on the nickname 'Guisers', and that was what you heard in the pubs on a Friday and Saturday night – 'Going down Guisers later?' The young men would be dressed smart-casual, the women scented from heaven and all stations south. They left the pubs around ten or half past – that's when it would be starting to get lively at Guisers.

Rebus was seated in a small uncomfortable chair which itself sat in a stuffy dimly lit room. The other chair was filled by an audio-visual technician, armed with two remotes. His occasional belches – of which he seemed blissfully ignorant – bespoke a recent snack of spring onion crisps and Irn-Bru.

'I'm really only interested in the main bar, foyer and out front,' Rebus said.

'I could edit them down to another tape, but we'd lose definition. The recording's duff enough as it is.' The technician scratched inside the sagging armpit of his black T-shirt.

Rebus leaned forward a little, pointing at the screen. 'Coming up now.' They waited. The view jumped from back alley to dance floor. 'Any second.' Another cut: main bar, punters queuing three deep. The technician didn't need to be told, and froze the picture. It wasn't so much black and white as sepia, the colour of dead photographs. Interior light, the audio-visual wizard had explained. He was adjusting the tracking now, and moving the action along one frame at a time. Rebus moved in on the screen, bending so one knee rested on the floor. His finger was touching a face. He took out the assortment of photos from his pocket and held them against the screen.

'It's him,' he said. 'I was pretty sure before. You can't go in a bit closer?'

'For now, this is as good as it gets. I can work on it later, stick it on the computer. The problem is the source material, to wit: one shitty security video.'

Rebus sat back on his chair. 'All right,' he said. 'Let's run forward at half-speed.'

The camera stayed with the main bar for another fifteen seconds, then switched to the second bar and all points on the compass. When it returned to the main bar, the crush of drinkers seemed not to have moved. Unbidden, the technician froze the tape again.

'He's not there,' Rebus said. Again he approached the screen, touched it with his finger. 'He should be there.'

'Next to the sex goddess.' The technician belched again.

Yes. Spun silver hair, almost like a cloud of candy-floss, dark eyes and lips. While those around her were either intent on catching the eyes of the bar staff or on the dance floor, she was looking off to one side. There were no shoulders to her dress.

'Let's check the foyer,' Rebus said.

Twenty seconds there showed a steady stream entering the club, but no one leaving. Exterior front showed a queue awaiting admittance by the brace of bouncers, and a few passers-by.

'In the toilet maybe,' the technician suggested. But Rebus had studied the tape a dozen times already, and though he watched just once more he knew he wouldn't see the young man again, not at the bar, not on the dance floor, and not back around the table where his mates were waiting – with increasing disbelief and impatience – for him to get his round in.

The young man's name was Damon Mee and, according to the timer running at the bottom right-hand corner of the screen, he had vanished from the world sometime between 11.44 and 11.45 p.m. on Friday 22 April.

'Where is this place anyway? I don't recognise it.'

'Kirkcaldy,' Rebus said.

The technician looked at him. 'How come it ended up here?'

Good question, Rebus thought, but not one he was about to answer. 'Go back to that bar shot,' he said. 'Take it nice and slow again.'

The technician aimed his right-hand remote. 'Yes, sir, Mr DeMille,' he said.

April meant still not quite spring in Edinburgh. A few sunny days to be sure, buds getting twitchy, wondering if winter had been paid the ransom. But there was snow still hanging in a sky the colour of chicken bones. Office talk: how Rangers were going to retain the championship; why Hearts and Hibs would never win it – was it finally time for the two local sides to become friends, form one team which might – *might* – stand half a chance? As someone said, their rivalry was part and parcel of the city's make-up. Hard to imagine Rangers and Celtic thinking of marriage in the same way, or even of a quick poke on the back stairs.

After years of following football only on pub televisions and in the back of the daily tabloid, Rebus was starting to go to matches again. DC Siobhan Clarke was to blame, coaxing him to a Hibs game one dreary afternoon. The men on the green sward weren't half as interesting as the spectators, who proved by turns sharp-witted, vulgar, perceptive and incorrigible. Siobhan had taken him to her usual spot. Those in the vicinity seemed to know her pretty well. It was a good-humoured afternoon, even if Rebus couldn't have said who scored the eventual three goals. But Hibs had won: the final-whistle hug from Siobhan was proof of that.

It was interesting to Rebus that, for all the barriers around the ground, this was a place where shields were dropped. After a while, it felt like one of the safest places he'd ever been. He recalled fixtures his father had taken him to in the fifties and early sixties – Cowdenbeath home games, and a crowd numbered in the hundreds; getting there necessitated a change of buses, Rebus and his younger brother fighting over who could hold the roll of tickets. Their mother was dead by then and their father was trying to carry on much as before, like they might not notice she was missing. Those Saturday trips to the football were supposed to fill a gap. You saw a lot of fathers and sons on the terraces but not many mothers, and that in itself was reminder enough. There was a boy of Rebus's age who stood near them. Rebus had walked over to him one day and blurted out the truth.

'I don't have a mum at home.'

The boy had stared at him, saying nothing.

Ever since, football had reminded him of those days and of his mother. He stood on the terraces alone these days and followed the game mostly – movements which could be graceful as ballet or as jagged as free association – but sometimes found that he'd drifted elsewhere, to a place not at all unpleasant, and all the time surrounded by a community of bodies and wills.

'I'll tell you how to beat Rangers,' he said now, addressing the whole office.

'How?' Siobhan Clarke offered.

'Clone Stevie Scoular half a dozen times.'

There were murmurs of agreement, and then the Farmer put his head around the door.

'John, my office.'

The Farmer – Chief Superintendent Watson to his face – was pouring a mug of coffee from his machine when Rebus knocked at the open door.

'Sit down, John.' Rebus sat. The Farmer motioned with an empty mug, but he turned down the offer and waited for his boss to get to his chair and the point both.

'My birthday's coming up,' the Farmer said. This was a new one on Rebus, who kept quiet. 'I'd like a present.'

'Not just a card this year then?'

'What I want, John, is Topper Hamilton.'

Rebus let that sink in. 'I thought Topper was Mr Clean these days?'

'Not in my books.' The Farmer cupped his hands around his coffee mug. 'He got a fright last time and, granted, he's been keeping a low profile, but we both know the best villains have got little or no profile at all.'

'So what's he been up to?'

'I heard a story he's the sleeping partner in a couple of clubs and casinos. I also hear he bought a taxi firm from Big Ger Cafferty when Big Ger went into Barlinnie.'

Rebus was thinking back three years to their big push against Topper Hamilton: they'd set up surveillance, used a bit of pressure here and there, got a few people to talk. In the end, it hadn't so much amounted to a hill of beans as to a fart in an empty can. The procurator fiscal had decided not to proceed to trial. But then God or Fate, call it what you like, had provided a spin to the story. Not a plague of boils or anything for Topper Hamilton, but a nasty little cancer which had given him more grief than the whole of the Lothian and Borders Police. He'd been in and out of hospital, endured chemo and the whole works, and had emerged a more slender figure in every sense.

The Farmer – who'd once settled an office argument by reeling off the books in both Old and New Testaments – wasn't yet content that God and life had done their worst to Topper, or that retribution had been meted out in some mysterious divine way. He wanted Topper in court, even if they had to wheel him there on a trolley.

It was a personal thing.

'Last time I looked,' Rebus said now, 'it wasn't illegal to invest in a casino.'

'It is if your name hasn't come up during the vetting procedure. Think Topper could get a gaming licence?'

'Fair point. But I still don't see—'

'Something else I heard. You've got a snitch works as a croupier.'

'So?'

'Same casino Topper has a finger in.'

Rebus saw it all and started shaking his head. 'I made him a promise. He'll tell me about punters, but nothing on the management.'

'And you'd rather keep that promise than give me a birthday present?'

'A relationship like that . . . it's eggshells.'

The Farmer's eyes narrowed. 'You think ours isn't? Talk to him, John. Get him to do some ferreting.'

'I could lose a good snitch.'

'Plenty more bigmouths out there.' The Farmer watched Rebus get to his feet. 'I was looking for you earlier. You were in the video room.'

'A missing person.'

'Suspicious?'

Rebus shrugged. 'Could be. He went up to the bar for a round of drinks, never came back.'

'We've all done that in our time.'

'His parents are worried.'

'How old is he?'

'Twenty-three.'

The Farmer thought about it. 'Then what's the problem?'

# Two

The problem was the past. A week before, he'd received a phone call from a ghost.

'Inspector John Rebus, please.'

'Speaking.'

'Oh, hello there. You probably won't remember me.' A short laugh. 'That used to be a bit of a joke at school.'

Rebus, immune to every kind of phone call, had this pegged a crank. 'Why's that?' he asked, wondering which punchline he was walking into.

'Because it's my name: Mee.' The caller spelt it for him. 'Brian Mee.'

Inside Rebus's head, a fuzzy photograph took sudden shape – a mouth full of prominent teeth, freckled nose and cheeks, a kitchen-stool haircut. 'Barney Mee?' he said.

More laughter on the line. 'Aye, they used to call me Barney. I'm not sure I ever knew why.'

Rebus could have told him: after Barney Rubble in *The Flintstones*. He could have added, because you were a dense wee bastard. But instead he asked how this ghost from his past was doing.

'No' bad, no' bad.' The laugh again; Rebus recognised it now as a sign of nerves.

'So what can I do for you, Brian?'

'Well, me and Janis, we thought . . . Well, it was my mum's idea actually. She knew your dad. Both my mum and dad knew him, only my dad passed away, like. They all used to drink at the Goth.'

'Are you still in Bowhill?'

'Never quite escaped. Ach, it's all right really. I work in

Glenrothes though. Lucky to have a job these days, eh? Mind, you've done well for yourself, Johnny. Do you still get called that?'

'I prefer John.'

'I remember you hated it when anyone called you Jock.' Another wheezing laugh. The photo was even sharper now, bordered with a white edge the way photos always were in the past. A decent footballer, a bit of a terrier, the hair reddish-brown. Dragging his satchel along the ground until the stitching rubbed away. Always with some huge hard sweet in his mouth, crunching down on it, his nose running. And one incident: he'd lifted some nude mags from under his dad's side of the bed and brought them to the toilets next to the Miners' Institute, there to be pored over like textbooks. Afterwards, half a dozen twelve-year-old boys had looked at each other, minds fizzing with questions.

'So what can I do for you, Brian?'

'Like I say, it was my mum's idea. Only, she remembered you were in the police in Edinburgh – saw your name in the paper a while back – and she thought you could maybe help.'

'With what?'

'Our son. I mean, mine and Janis's. He's called Damon.'

'What's he done?' Rebus thought: something minor, and way outside his territory anyway.

'He's vanished.'

'Run away?'

'More like in a puff of smoke. He was in this club with his pals, see, and he went—'

'Have you tried calling the police?' Rebus caught himself. 'I mean Fife Constabulary.'

'Oh aye.' Mee sounded dismissive. 'They asked a few questions, like, sniffed around a bit, then said there was nothing they could do. Damon's twenty-three. They say he's got a right to bugger off if he wants.'

327

'They've got a point. People run away all the time, Brian. Girl trouble maybe.'

'He was engaged.'

'Maybe he got scared?'

'Helen's a lovely girl. Never a raised voice between them.'

'Did he leave a note?'

'Nothing. I went through this with the police. He didn't take any clothes or anything. He didn't have any reason to go.'

'So you think something's happened to him?'

'I know what those buggers are thinking. They say we should give him another week or so to come back, or at least get in touch, but I know they'll only start doing something about it when the body turns up.'

Again, Rebus could have confirmed that this was only sensible. Again, he knew Mee wouldn't want to hear it.

'The thing is, Brian,' he said, 'I work in Edinburgh. Fife's not my patch. I mean, I can make a couple of phone calls, but it's hard to know what else to do.'

The voice was close to despair. 'Well, if you could just do *some*thing. Like, anything. We'd be very grateful. It would put our minds at rest.' A pause. 'My mum always speaks well of your dad. He's remembered in this town.'

And buried there, too, Rebus thought. He picked up a pen. 'Give me your phone number, Brian.' And, almost an afterthought, 'Better give me the address, too.'


That evening, he drove north out of Edinburgh, paid his toll at the Forth Bridge, and crossed into Fife. It wasn't as if he never went there – he had a brother in Kirkcaldy. But though they spoke on the phone every month or so, there were seldom visits. He couldn't think of any other family he still had in Fife. The place liked to call itself 'the Kingdom' and there were those who would agree that it was another country, a place with its own linguistic and cultural currency. For such a small place it seemed almost endlessly complex – had seemed that way to Rebus even when he was growing up. To outsiders the place meant coastal scenery and St Andrew's, or a stretch of motorway between Edinburgh and Dundee, but the west-central Fife of Rebus's childhood had been very different, ruled by coal mines and linoleum, dockyards and chemical plants, an industrial landscape shaped by basic needs, and producing people who were wary and inward-looking with the blackest humour you'd ever find.

They'd built new roads since Rebus's last visit, and knocked down a few more landmarks, but the place didn't feel so very different from thirty-odd years before. It wasn't such a great span of time after all, except in human terms; maybe not even then. Entering Cardenden – Bowhill had disappeared from road signs in the 1960s, even if locals still knew it as a village distinct from its neighbour – Rebus slowed to see if the memories would turn out sweet or sour. Then he caught sight of a Chinese takeaway and thought: both, of course.

Brian and Janis Mee's house was easy enough to find: they were standing by the gate waiting for him. Rebus had been born in a prefab but brought up in a house just like the one he now parked in front of. Brian Mee practically opened the car door for him, and was trying to shake his hand while Rebus was still emerging from his seat.

'Let the man catch his breath!' Janis Mee snapped. She was still standing by the gate, arms folded. 'How have you been, Johnny?'

And Rebus realised that Brian Mee had married Janis Playfair, the only girl in his long and trouble-strewn life who'd ever managed to knock him unconscious.

The narrow, low-ceilinged living-room was full to bursting – not just Rebus and Janis and Brian, but Brian's mother and Mr and Mrs Playfair. Introductions had to be made, and Rebus guided to 'the seat by the fire'. The room was overheated. A pot of tea was produced, and on the table by

Rebus's armchair sat enough slices of cake to feed a football crowd.

'He's a brainy one,' Janis's mother said, handing Rebus a framed photo of Damon Mee. 'Plenty of certificates from school. Works hard. Saving up to get married. The date's set for next August.'

The photo showed a smiling imp, not long out of school. 'Have you got anything more recent?'

Janis handed him a packet of snapshots. 'From last summer.'

Rebus went through them slowly. It saved having to look at the faces around him. He felt like a doctor, expected to produce an immediate diagnosis and remedy. The photos showed a man in his early twenties, still retaining the impish smile but recognisably older. Not careworn exactly, but with something behind the eyes, some disenchantment with adulthood. A few of the photos showed Damon's parents.

'We all went together,' Brian explained. 'Janis's mum and dad, my mum, Helen and her parents.'

Beaches, a big white hotel, poolside games. 'Where is it?'

'Lanzarote,' Janis said, handing him his tea. In a few of the pictures she was wearing a bikini – good body for her age, or any age come to that. He tried not to linger.

'Can I keep a couple of the close-ups?' he asked. Janis looked at him. 'Of Damon.' She nodded and he put the other photos back in their packet.

'We're really grateful,' someone said. Janis's mum? Brian's? Rebus couldn't tell.

'Does Helen live locally?'

'Practically round the corner.'

'I'd like to talk to her.'

'I'll give her a bell,' Brian Mee said, leaping to his feet.

'Damon had been drinking in some club?'

'Guisers,' Janis said, handing round cigarettes. 'It's in Kirkcaldy.'

'On the Prom?'

She shook her head, looking just the same as she had that night of the school dance . . . shaking her head, telling him so far and no further. 'In the town. It used to be a department store.'

'It's really called Gaitanos,' Mr Playfair said. Rebus remembered him, too. He was an old man now.

'Where does Damon work?' Careful to stick to the present tense.

Brian Mee came back into the room. 'Same place I do. I managed to get him a job in packaging. He's been learning the ropes; it'll be management soon.'

Working-class nepotism; jobs handed down from father to son. Rebus was surprised it still existed.

'Helen'll be here in a minute,' Brian added.

'Are you not eating any cake, Inspector?' said Mrs Playfair.


Helen Cousins hadn't been able to add much to Rebus's picture of Damon, and hadn't been there the night he'd vanished. But she'd introduced him to someone who had, Andy Peters. Andy had been part of the group at Gaitanos. There'd been four of them. They'd been in the same year at school and still met up once or twice a week, sometimes to watch Raith Rovers if the weather was decent and the mood took them, other times for an evening session in a pub or club. It was only their third or fourth visit to Guisers.

Rebus thought of paying the club a visit, but knew he should talk to the local cops first, and decided that it could all wait until morning. He knew he was jumping through hoops. He didn't expect to find anything the locals had missed. At best, he could reassure the family that everything possible had been done.

Next morning he made a few phone calls from his office, trying to find someone who could be bothered to answer some casual questions from an Edinburgh colleague. He had one ally – Detective Sergeant Hendry at Dunfermline CID – but only reached him at the third attempt. He asked Hendry for a favour, then put the phone down and got back to his own work. But it was hard to concentrate. He kept thinking about Bowhill and about Janis Mee, née Playfair. Which led him – eventually – guiltily – to thoughts of Damon. Younger runaways tended to take the same route: by bus or train or hitching, and to London, Newcastle, Edinburgh or Glasgow. There were organisations who would keep an eye open for runaways, and even if they wouldn't always reveal their whereabouts to the anxious families, at least they could confirm that someone was alive and unharmed.

But a twenty-three-year-old, someone a bit cannier and with money to hand . . . could be anywhere. No destination was too distant – he owned a passport, and it hadn't turned up. Rebus knew, too, that Damon had a current account at the local bank, complete with cashcard, and an interest-bearing account with a building society in Kirkcaldy. The bank might be worth trying. Rebus picked up the telephone again.

The manager at first insisted that he'd need something in writing, but relented when Rebus promised to fax him later. Rebus held while the manager went off to check, and had doodled half a village, complete with stream, parkland and school, by the time the man came back.

'The most recent withdrawal was from a cash machine in Kirkcaldy. One hundred pounds on the twenty-second.'

'What time?'

'I've no way of knowing.'

'No other withdrawals since then?'

'No.'

'How up-to-date is that information?'

'Very. Of course a cheque – especially if post-dated – would take longer to show up.'

'Could you keep tabs on that account, let me know if anyone starts using it again?'

'I could, but I'd need it in writing, and I might also need Head Office approval.'

'Well, see what you can do, Mr Brayne.'

'It's Bain,' the bank manager said coldly, putting down the phone.

DS Hendry didn't get back to him until late afternoon.

'Gaitanos,' Hendry said. 'I don't know the place personally. Locals call it Guisers. It's a pretty choice establishment. Two stabbings last year, one inside the club itself, the other in the back alley where the owner parks his Merc. Local residents are always girning about the noise when the place lets out.'

'What's the owner's name?'

'Charles Mackenzie, nicknamed "Charmer". He seems to be clean. A couple of uniforms talked to him about Damon Mee, but there was nothing to tell. Know how many missing persons there are every year? They're not exactly a white-hot priority. God knows there are times I've felt like doing a runner myself.'

'Haven't we all? Did the woolly suits talk to anyone else at the club?'

'Such as?'

'Bar staff, punters.'

'No. Someone did take a look at the security video for the night Damon was there, but they didn't see anything.'

'Where's the video now?'

'Back with its rightful owner.'

'Am I going to be stepping on toes if I ask to see it?'

'I think I can cover you. I know you said this was personal, John, but why the interest?'

'I'm not sure I can explain.' There were words – community, history, memory – but Rebus didn't think they'd be enough.

'They mustn't be working you hard enough over there.'

'Just the twenty-four hours every day.'

# Three

Matty Paine could tell a few stories. He'd worked his way round the world as a croupier. Cruise liners he'd worked on, and in Nevada. He'd spent a couple of years in London, dealing out cards and spinning the wheel for some of the wealthiest in the land, faces you'd recognise from the TV and the papers. Moguls, royalty, stars – Matty had seen them all. But his best story – the one people sometimes disbelieved – was about the time he'd been recruited to work in a casino in Beirut. This was at the height of the civil war, bomb sites and rubble, smoke and charred buildings, refugees and regular bursts of small-arms fire. And amazingly, in the midst of it all (or, to be fair, on the edge of it all), a casino. Not exactly legal. Run from a hotel basement with torchlight when the generator failed and not much in the way of refreshments, but with no shortage of punters – cash bets, dollars only – and a management team of three who prowled the place like Dobermanns, since there was no surveillance and no other way to check that the games were being played honestly. One of them had stood next to Matty for a full forty minutes one session, making him sweat despite the air-conditioning. He'd reminded Matty of the gaffers casinos employed to check on apprentices. He knew the gaffers were there to protect *him* as much as the punters – there were professional gamblers out there who'd psych out a trainee, watch them for hours, whole nights and weeks, looking for the flaw that would give them an edge over the house. Like, when you were starting out, you didn't always vary the force with which you span the wheel, or sent the ball rolling, and if they could suss it, they'd get a pretty good idea which quadrant the ball was going to stop in. Good croupiers were immune to this. A really good croupier – one of a very select, very highly thought of group – could master the wheel and get the ball to land pretty well where *they* wanted.

Of course, this might be against the interests of the house, too. And in the end, that's why the checkers were out there, patrolling the tables. They were looking out for the house. In the end it all came down to the house.

And when things had got a wee bit too hot in London, Matty had come home, meaning Edinburgh, though really he was from Gullane – perhaps the only boy ever to be raised there and not show the slightest interest in golf. His father had played – his mother too, come to that. Maybe she still did; he didn't keep in touch. There had been an awkward moment at the casino when a neighbour from Gullane days, an old business friend of his father's, had turned up, a bit the worse for wear and in tow with three other middle-aged punters. The neighbour had glanced towards Matty from time to time, but had eventually shaken his head, unable to place the face.

'Does he know you?' one of the all-seeing gaffers had asked quietly, seeking out some scam against the house.

Matty had shaken his head. 'A neighbour from when I was growing up.' That was all; just a ghost from the past. He supposed his mother *was* still alive. He could probably find out by opening the phone book. But he wasn't that interested.

'Place your bets, please, ladies and gentlemen.'

Different houses had different styles. You either did your spiel in English or French. House rules changed, too. Matty's strengths were roulette and blackjack, but really he was happy in charge of any sort of game – most houses liked that he was flexible, it meant there was less chance of him trying some scam. It was the one-note wonders who tried small, stupid diddles. His latest employers seemed fairly laid back. They ran a clean casino which boasted only the very occasional high roller. Most of the punters were business people, well enough heeled but canny with it. You got husbands and wives coming in, proof of a relaxed atmosphere. There were younger punters too – a lot of those were Asians, mainly Chinese. The money they changed, according to the cashier, had a funny feel and smell to it.

'That's because they keep it in their underwear,' the day boss had told her.

The Asians ... whatever they were ... sometimes worked in local restaurants; you could smell the kitchen on their crumpled jackets and shirts. Fierce gamblers, no game was ever played quickly enough for their liking. They'd slap their chips down like they were in a playground betting game. And they talked a lot, almost never in English. The gaffers didn't like that, never could tell what they might be scheming. But their money was good, they seldom caused trouble, and they lost a percentage same as everyone else.

'Daft bastards,' the night manager said. 'Know what they do with a big win? Go bung it on the gee-gees. Where's the sense in that?'

Where indeed? No point giving your money to a bookmaker when the casino would happily take it instead.

It wasn't really on for croupiers to be friends with the clients, but sometimes it happened. And it couldn't very well not happen with Matty and Stevie Scoular, since they'd been in the same year at school. Not that they'd known one another well. Stevie had been the football genius, also more than fair at the hundred and two hundred metres, swimming and basketball. Matty, on the other hand, had skived off games whenever possible, forgetting to bring his kit or getting his mum to write him notes. He was good at a couple of subjects – maths and woodwork – but never sat beside Stevie in class. They even lived at opposite ends of the town.

At playtime and lunchtime, Matty ran a card game – three-card brag mostly, sometimes pontoon – playing for dinner money, pocket money, sweets and comics. A few of the cards were nicked at the corners, but the other players didn't seem to notice and Matty got a reputation as 'lucky'. He'd take bets on horse races too, sometimes passing the bets on to an older boy who wouldn't be turned away by the local bookmaker. Often though, Matty would simply pocket the money and if someone's horse happened to win, he'd say he couldn't get the bets on in time and hand back the stake.

He couldn't tell you exactly when it was that Stevie had started spending less breaktime dribbling past half a dozen despairing pairs of legs and more hanging around the edges of the card school. Thing about three-card brag, it doesn't take long to pick it up and even a moron can have a stab at playing. Soon enough, Stevie was losing his dinner money with the rest of them, and Matty's pockets were about bursting with loose change. Eventually, Stevie had seemed to see sense, drifted away from the game and back to keepie-up and dribbling. But he'd been hooked, no doubt about it. Maybe only for a few weeks, but a lot of those lunchtimes had been spent cadging sweets and apple cores, the better to stave off hunger.

Even then, Matty had thought he'd be seeing Stevie again. It had just taken the best part of a decade, that was all.

When Stevie Scoular walked into the casino, people looked his way. It was the done thing. He was a sharp dresser, young, usually accompanied by women who looked like models. When Stevie had first walked into the Morvena, Matty's heart had sunk. They hadn't seen one another since school and here Stevie was, local boy made good, a hero, picture in the papers and plenty of money in the bank. Here was a schoolboy dream made flesh. And what was Matty? He had stories he could tell but that was about it. So he'd been hoping Stevie wouldn't grace his table, or if he did that he wouldn't recognise him. But Stevie had seen him, seemed to know him straight off and come bouncing up.

'Matty!'

'Hello there, Stevie.'

It was flattering really. Stevie hadn't become big-headed or anything. He took the whole thing – the way his life had gone – as a bit of a joke really. He'd made Matty promise to meet him for a drink when his shift was over. All through their conversation, Matty had been aware of gaffers hovering and when Stevie wandered off to another table one of them muttered in Matty's ear and another croupier took over from him.

He hadn't been in the plush back office that often, just for the initial interview and to discuss a couple of big losses on his table. The casino's owner, Mr Mandelson, was watching a football match on Sky Sports. He was well-built, mid-forties, his face pockmarked from childhood acne. His hair was black, slicked back from the forehead, long at the collar. He always seemed to know what he was about.

'How's the table tonight?' he asked.

'Look, Mr Mandelson, I know we're not supposed to be too friendly with the punters, but Stevie and me were at school together. Haven't clapped eyes on one another since – not till tonight.'

'Easy, Matty, easy.' Mandelson motioned for him to sit down. 'Something to drink?' A smile. 'No alcohol on shift, mind.'

'Ehh . . . a Coke maybe.'

'Help yourself.'

There was a fridge in the far corner, stocked with white wine, champagne and soft drinks. A couple of the female croupiers said Mandelson had tried it on with them, plying them with booze. But he didn't seem upset by a refusal: they still had their jobs. There were seven female croupiers all told, and only two had spoken to Matty about it. It made him wonder about the other five.

He took a Coke and sat down again.

'So, you and Stevie Scoular, eh?'

'I haven't seen him in here before.'

'I think he only recently found out about the place. He's been in a few times, dropped some hefty bets.' Mandelson was staring at him. 'You and Stevie, eh?'

'Look, if you're worried, just take me off whatever table he's playing.'

'Nothing like that, Matty.' Mandelson's face broke into a grin. 'It's nice to have a friend, eh? Nice to meet up again after all these years. Don't you worry about anything. Stevie's the King of Edinburgh. As long as he keeps scoring goals, we're all his subjects.' He paused. 'Nice to know someone who knows the King, almost makes me feel like royalty myself. On you go now, Matty.'

Matty got up, leaving the Coke unopened.

'And don't you go upsetting that young man. We don't want to put him off his game, do we?'

# Four

It had taken a couple of days to get the tape from Gaitanos. At first, they thought they'd wiped it, and then they'd sent the wrong day's recording. But at last Rebus had the right tape and had watched it at home half a dozen times before deciding he could use someone who knew what he was doing . . . and a video machine that would freeze-frame without the screen looking like a technical problem.

Now he'd seen all there was to see. He'd watched a young man cease to exist. Of course, Hendry was right, a lot of people disappeared every year. Sometimes they turned up again – dead or alive – and sometimes they didn't. What did it have to do with Rebus, beyond the promise to a family that he'd make sure the Fife police hadn't missed something? Maybe the pull wasn't Damon Mee, but Bowhill itself; and maybe even then, the Bowhill of his past rather than the town as it stood today.

He was working the Damon Mee case in his free time, which, since he was on day shift at St Leonard's, meant the evenings. He'd checked again with the bank – no money had been withdrawn from any machines since the twenty-second – and with Damon's building society. No money had been withdrawn from that account either. Even this wasn't unknown in the case of a runaway; sometimes they wanted to shed their whole history, which meant ditching their identity and everything that went with it. Rebus had passed a description of Matty to hostels and drop-in centres in Edinburgh, and faxed the same description to similar centres in Glasgow, Newcastle, Aberdeen and London. He'd also faxed details to the National Missing Persons Bureau in

London. He checked with a colleague who knew about 'MisPers' that he'd done about all he could.

'Not far off it,' she confirmed. 'It's like looking for a needle in a haystack without knowing which field to start with.'

'How big a problem is it?'

She puffed out her cheeks. 'Last figures I saw were for the whole of Britain. I think there are around 25,000 a year. Those are the *reported* MisPers. You can add a few thousand for the ones nobody notices. There's a nice distinction actually: if nobody knows you're missing, are you really missing?'

Afterwards, Rebus telephoned Janis Mee and told her she might think about running up some flyers and putting them up in positions of prominence in nearby towns, maybe even handing them out to Saturday shoppers or evening drinkers in Kirkcaldy. A photo of Damon, a brief physical description, and what he was wearing the night he left. She said she'd already thought of doing so, but that it made his disappearance seem so final. Then she broke down and cried and John Rebus, thirty-odd miles away, asked if she wanted him to 'drop by'.

'I'll be all right,' she said.

'Sure?'

'Well . . . '

Rebus reasoned that he was going to go to Fife anyway. He had to drop the tape back to Gaitanos, and wanted to see the club when it was lively. He'd take the photos of Damon with him and show them around. He'd ask about the candyfloss blonde. The technician who had worked with the videotape had transferred a still to his computer and managed to boost the quality. Rebus had some hard copies in his pocket. Maybe other people who'd been queuing at the bar would remember something.

Maybe.

His first stop, however, was the cemetery. He didn't have

any flowers to put on his parents' grave, but he crouched beside it, fingers touching the grass. The inscription was simple, just names and dates really, and underneath, 'Not Dead, But at Rest in the Arms of the Lord'. He wasn't sure whose idea that had been, not his certainly. The headstone's carved lettering was inlaid with gold, but it had already faded from his mother's name. He touched the surface of the marble, expecting it to be cold, but finding a residual warmth there. A blackbird nearby was trying to worry food from the ground. Rebus wished it luck.

By the time he reached Janis's, Brian was home from work. Rebus told them what he'd done so far, after which Brian nodded, apologised, and said he had a Burns Club meeting. The two men shook hands. When the door closed, Janis and Rebus exchanged a look and then a smile.

'I see that bruise finally faded,' she said.

Rebus rubbed his right cheek. 'It was a hell of a punch.'

'Funny how strong you can get when you're angry.'

'Sorry.'

She laughed. 'Bit late to apologise.'

'It was just . . .'

'It was everything,' she said. 'Summer holidays coming up, all of us leaving school, you going off to join the army. The last school dance before all of that. That's what it was.' She paused. 'Do you know what happened to Mitch?' She watched Rebus shake his head. 'Last I heard,' she said, 'he was living somewhere down south. The two of you used to be so close.'

'Yes.'

She laughed again. 'Johnny, it was a long time ago, don't look so solemn.' She paused. 'I've sometimes wondered . . . ach, not for years, but just now and then I used to wonder what would have happened . . . '

'If you hadn't punched me?'

She nodded. 'If we'd stayed together. Well, you can't turn the clock back, eh?'

'Would the world be any better if we could?'

She stared at the window, not really seeing it. 'Damon would still be here,' she said quietly. A tear escaped her eye, and she fussed for a handkerchief in her pocket. Rebus got up and made towards her. Then the front door opened, and he retreated.

'My mum,' Janis smiled. 'She usually pops in around this time. It's like a railway station around here, hard to find any privacy.'

Then Mrs Playfair walked into the living-room.

'Hello, Inspector, thought that was your car. Is there any news?'

'I'm afraid not,' Rebus said. Janis got to her feet and hugged her mother, the crying starting afresh.

'There there, pet,' Mrs Playfair said quietly. 'There there.'

Rebus walked past the two of them without saying a word.

It was still early when he reached Gaitanos. He had a word with one of the bouncers, who was keeping warm in the lobby until things started getting busy, and the man lumbered off to fetch Charles Mackenzie, *aka* Charmer. It seemed strange to Rebus: here he was, standing in the very foyer he'd stared at for so long on the video monitor. The camera was high up in one corner with nothing to show whether it was working. Rebus gave it a wave anyway. If he disappeared tonight, it could be his farewell to the world.

'Inspector Rebus.' They'd spoken on the phone. The man who came forward to shake Rebus's hand stood about five feet four and was as thin as a cocktail glass. Rebus placed him in his mid-fifties. He wore a powder-blue suit and an open-necked white shirt with suntan and gold jewellery beneath. His hair was silver and thinning, but as well-cut as the suit. 'Come through to the office.'

Rebus followed Mackenzie down a carpeted corridor to a gloss-black door with a sign on it saying 'Private'. There was no door handle. Mackenzie unlocked the door and motioned for Rebus to go in.

'After you, sir,' Rebus said. You never knew what could be waiting behind a locked door.

What greeted Rebus this time was an office which seemed to double as a broom-cupboard. Mops and a vacuum cleaner rested against one wall. A bank of screens spread across three filing cabinets showed what was happening inside and outside the club. Unlike the video Rebus had watched, these screens each showed a certain location.

'Are these recording?' Rebus asked. Mackenzie shook his head.

'We've got a roaming monitor, and that's the only recording we get. But this way, if we spot trouble anywhere, we can watch it unfold.'

'Like that knifing in the alley?'

'Messed up my Mercedes.'

'So I heard. Is that when you called the police? When your car stopped being a bystander?'

Mackenzie laughed and wagged a finger, but didn't answer. Rebus couldn't see where he'd earned his nickname. The guy had all the charm of sandpaper.

'I brought back your video.' Rebus placed it on the desk.

'All right to record over it now?'

'I suppose so.' Rebus handed over the computer-enhanced photograph. 'The missing person is slightly right of centre, second row.'

'Is that his doll?'

'Do you know her?'

'Wish I did.'

'You haven't seen her before.'

'She doesn't look the sort I'd forget.'

Rebus took back the picture. 'Mind if I show this around?'

'The place is practically empty.'

'I thought I might stick around.'

Mackenzie frowned and studied the backs of his hands. 'Well, you know, it's not that I don't want to help or anything . . . '

'But?'

'Well, it's hardly conducive to a party atmosphere, is it? That's our slogan – "The best party of your life, every night!" – and I don't think a police officer mooching around asking questions is going to add to the ambience.'

'I quite understand, Mr Mackenzie. I was being thought-less.' Mackenzie lifted his hands, palms towards Rebus: no problem, the hands were saying.

'And you're quite right,' Rebus continued. 'In fact, I'd be a lot quicker if I had some assistance – say, a dozen uniforms. That way, I wouldn't be "mooching around" for nearly so long. In fact, let's make it a couple of dozen. We'll be in and out, quick as a virgin's first poke. Mind if I use your phone?'

'Whoah, wait a minute. Look, all I was saying was . . . Look, how much do you want?'

'Sorry, sir?'

Mackenzie reached into a desk drawer, lifted out a brick of twenties, pulled about five notes free. 'Will this do it?'

Rebus sat back. 'Am I to understand you're trying to offer me a cash incentive to leave the premises?'

'Whatever. Just slope off, eh?'

Rebus stood up. 'To me, Mr Mackenzie, that's an open invitation to stay.'

So he stayed.

The looks he got from staff made him feel like a football fan trapped on the opposition's turf. The way they all shook their heads as soon as he held up the photo, he knew word had gone around. He had a little more luck with the punters. A couple of lads had seen the woman before.

'Last week, was it?' one asked the other. 'Maybe the week before.'

'Not long ago anyway,' the other agreed. 'Cracker, isn't she?'

'Has she been in since?'

'Haven't seen her. Just that one night. Didn't quite get the nerve up to ask for a dance.'

'Was she with anyone?'

'No idea.'

They didn't recognise Damon Mee though. They said they never paid much attention to blokes.

'We're not that way inclined, sweetie.'

The place was still only half full, but the bass was loud enough to make Rebus feel queasy. He managed to order an orange juice at the bar and just sat there, looking at the photo. The woman interested him. The way her head was angled, the way her mouth was open, she could have been saying something to Damon. A minute later, he was gone. Had she said she'd meet him somewhere? Had something happened at that meeting? He'd shown the photo to Damon's mates from that night. They remembered seeing her, but swore Damon hadn't introduced himself.

'She seemed sort of cold,' one of them had said. 'You know, like she wanted to be left alone.'

Rebus had studied the video again, watched her progress towards the bar, showing no apparent interest in Damon's leaving. But then she'd turned and started pushing her way back through the throng, no drink to show for her long wait.

At midnight exactly, she'd left the nightclub. The final shot was of her turning left along the pavement, watched by a few people who were waiting to get in. And now Charles Mackenzie wanted to give Rebus money.

At three quid for an orange juice, maybe he should have taken it.

If the place had been heaving, maybe he wouldn't have noticed them.

He was finishing his second drink and trying not to feel like a leper in a children's ward when he recognised one of the doormen. There was another man with him, tall and fat and pale. His idea of clubbing was probably the connection of baseball bat to skull. The bouncer was pointing Rebus out to him. Here we go, Rebus thought. They've brought in the professionals. The fat man said something to the bouncer, and they both retreated to the foyer, leaving Rebus with an empty glass and only one good reason to order another drink.

Get it over with, he thought, sliding from his bar stool and walking around the dance floor. There was always the fire exit, but it led on to the alley and, if they were waiting for him there, the only witness would be Mackenzie's Mercedes. He wanted things kept as public as possible. The street outside would be busy, no shortage of onlookers and possible good Samaritans. Or at the very least, someone to call for an ambulance.

He paused in the foyer and saw that the bouncer was back at his post on the front door. No sign of the fat man. Then he glanced along the corridor towards Mackenzie's office, and saw the fat man planted outside the door. He had his arms folded in front of him and wasn't going anywhere.

Rebus walked outside. The air had seldom tasted so good. He tried to calm himself with a few deep breaths. There was a car parked at the kerbside, a gold-coloured Rolls-Royce, with nobody in the driver's seat. Rebus wasn't the only one admiring the car, but he was probably alone in memorising its number plate.

He moved his own car to where he could see the Roller, then sat tight. Half an hour later, the fat man emerged, looking to left and right. He walked to the car, unlocked it and held open the back door. Only now did another figure emerge from the club. Rebus caught a swishing full-length black coat, sleek hair and chiselled face. The man slipped into the car, and the fat man closed the door and squeezed in behind the steering wheel.

Like them or not, you had to admire Rollers. They carried tonnage.

# Five

Back in Edinburgh he parked his car and sat in it, smoking his eleventh cigarette of the day. He sometimes played this game with himself – I'll have one more tonight, and deduct one from tomorrow's allowance. Or he would argue that any cigarette after midnight came from the next day's stash. He'd lost count along the way, but reckoned by now he should be going whole days without a ciggie to balance the books. Well, when it came down to it, ten cigarettes a day or twelve, thirteen, fourteen – what difference did it make?

The street he was parked on was quiet. Residential for the most part with big houses. There was a basement bar on the corner, but it did mostly lunchtime business from the offices on neighbouring streets. By ten, the place was usually locked up. Taxis rippled past him and the occasional drunk, hands in pockets, would weave slowly homewards. A few of the taxis stopped just in front of him and disgorged their fares, who would then climb half a dozen steps and push open the door to the Morvena Casino. Rebus had never been inside the place. He placed the occasional bet on the horses, but that was about it. Gave up doing the football pools. He bought a National Lottery ticket when opportunity arose, but often didn't get round to checking the numbers. He had half a dozen tickets lying around, any one of which could be his fortune. He quite liked the notion that he might have won a million and not know it; preferred it, in fact, to the idea of actually having the million in his bank account. What would he do with a million pounds? Same as he'd do with fifty thou – self-destruct.

Only faster.

Janis had asked him about Mitch – Roy Mitchell, Rebus's best friend at school. The more time Rebus had spent with her, the less he'd seen of Mitch. They'd been going to join the army together, hoping they might get the same regiment. Until Mitch lost his eye. That had been the end of that. The army hadn't wanted him any more. Rebus had headed off, sent Mitch a couple of letters, but by the time his first leave came, Mitch had already left Bowhill. Rebus had stopped writing after that . . .

When the Morvena's door opened next, it was so eight or nine young people could leave. The shift changeover. Three of them turned one way, the rest another. Rebus watched the group of three. At the first set of lights, two kept going and one crossed the road and took a left. Rebus started his engine and followed. When the lights turned green, he signalled left and sounded his horn, then pulled the car over and wound down his window.

'Mr Rebus,' the young man said.

'Hello, Matty. Let's go for a drive.'

Officers from other cities, people Rebus met from time to time, would remark on how cushy he had it in Edinburgh. Such a beautiful place, and prosperous. So little crime. They thought to be dangerous a city had to look dangerous. London, Manchester, Liverpool – these places were dangerous in their eyes. Not Edinburgh, not this sleepy walking-tour with its monuments and museums. Tourism aside, the lifeblood of the city was its commerce, and Edinburgh's commerce – banking, insurance and the like – was discreet. The city hid its secrets well, and its vices too. Potentially troublesome elements had been moved to the sprawling council estates which ringed the capital, and any crimes committed behind the thick stone walls of the city centre's tenements and houses were often muffled by those same walls. Which was why every good detective needed his contacts.

Rebus took them on a circuit – Canonmills to Ferry Road,

back up to Comely Bank and through Stockbridge into the New Town again. And they talked.

'I know we had a sort of gentleman's agreement, Matty,' Rebus said.

'But I'm about to find out you're no gentleman?'

Rebus smiled. 'You're ahead of me.'

'I wondered how long it would take.' Matty paused, stared through the windscreen. 'You know I'll say no.'

'Will you?'

'I said at the start, no ratting on anyone I work with or work for. Just the punters.'

'Not even many of them. It's not like I've been milking you, Matty. I'll bet you've dozens of stories you haven't told me.'

'I work tables, Mr Rebus. People don't place a bet and then start yacking about some job they've pulled or some scam they're running.'

'No, but they meet friends. They have a drink, get mellow. It's a relaxing place, so I've heard. And maybe then they talk.'

'I've not held anything back.'

'Matty, Matty.' Rebus shook his head. 'It's funny, I was just thinking tonight about that night we met. Do you remember?'

How could he forget? A couple of drinks after work, a car borrowed from a friend who was away on holiday. Matty hadn't been back long. Driving through the town was great, especially with a buzz on. Streets glistening after the rain. Late night, mostly taxis for company. He just drove and drove and, as the streets grew quieter, he pushed the accelerator a bit further, caught a string of green lights, then saw one turning red. He didn't know how good the tyres were, imagined braking hard and skidding in the wet. Fuck it, he put his foot down.

Just missed the cyclist. The guy was coming through on green and had to twist his front wheel hard to avoid contact, then teetered and fell on to the road. Matty's foot eased off the accelerator, thought about the brake, then went back on the accelerator again.

That's when he saw the cop car. And thought: I can't afford this.

They'd breathalysed him and taken him to St Leonard's, where he'd sat around and let the machinery chew him up. Would it come to a trial? Would there be a report in the papers? How could he keep his name from getting around? He'd worked himself up into a right state by the time Detective Inspector John Rebus had sat down across from him.

'I can't afford this,' Matty had blurted out.

'Sorry?'

He'd swallowed and tried to find a story. 'I work in a casino. Any black mark against me, they'll boot me out. Look, if it's a question of compensation or anything . . . like, I'll buy him a new bike.'

Rebus had picked up a sheet of paper. 'Drunk driving . . . in a borrowed car you weren't insured to drive . . . running a red light . . . leaving the scene of an accident . . . ' Rebus had shaken his head, read the sheet through one more time and then put it down, and looked up at Matty. 'What casino did you say you work for?'

Later, he'd given Matty two business cards, both with his phone number. 'The first one's for you to tear up in disgust,' he'd said. 'The other one's to keep. Have we got a deal?'

'Look, Mr Rebus,' Matty said now, as the car stopped for lights on Raeburn Place, 'I'm doing the best I can.'

'I want to know what's happening behind the scenes at the Morvena.'

'I wouldn't know.'

'Anything at all, it doesn't matter how small it seems. Any stories, gossip, anything overheard. Ever seen the owner entertain people in his office? Maybe open the place for a private party? Names, faces, anything at all. Put your mind to it, Matty. Just put your mind to it.'

'They'd skin me alive.'

'Who's they?'

Matty swallowed. 'Mr Mandelson.'

'He's the owner, right?'

'Right.'

'On paper at least. What I need to know is who might be pulling his strings.'

'I can't see anyone pulling his strings.'

'You'd be surprised. Hard bastard, is he?'

'I'd say so.'

'Given you grief?' Matty shook his head. 'Do you see much of him?'

'Not much,' Matty said. Not, he might have added, until recently at any rate.

Rebus dropped him at the foot of Broughton Street, headed back up to Leith Walk and along York Place on to Queen Street. He passed the casino again and slowed, a frown on his face. At the next set of lights, he did a U-turn so he could be sure. Yes, it was the Roller from Gaitanos, no doubt about it.

Parked outside the Morvena.

# Six

'Mind if I join you?'

Rebus was eating breakfast in the canteen and wishing there was more caffeine in the coffee, or more coffee in the coffee come to that. He nodded to the empty chair and Siobhan sat down.

'Heavy night?' she said.

'Believe it or not, I was on orange juice.'

She bit into her muffin, washing it down with milk. 'Harry tells me you had him working a tape.'

'Harry?'

'Our video wizard. He said it was a missing person. News to me.'

'It's not official. The son of an old schoolfriend of mine.'

'Standing at a bar one minute and gone the next?' Rebus looked at her and she smiled. 'Harry's a great one for gossip.'

'I'm working on it in my own time.'

'Need any help?'

'Handy with a crystal ball, are you?' But Rebus dug into his pocket and brought out the still from the video. 'That's Damon there,' he said, pointing.

'Who's that with him?'

'I wish I knew. She's not with him. I don't know who she is.'

'You've asked around?'

'I was at the club last night. A few punters remembered her.'

'Male punters?' She waited till Rebus nodded. 'You were asking the wrong sex. Any man would have given her the once-over, but only superficially. A woman, on the other hand, would have seen her as competition. Have you never noticed women in nightclubs? They've got eyes like lasers. Plus, what if she visited the loo?'

Rebus was interested now. 'What if she did?'

'*That's* where women talk. Maybe someone spoke to her, maybe she said something back. Ears would have been listening.' Siobhan stared at the photo. 'Funny, it's almost like she's got an aura.'

'How do you mean?'

'Like she's shining.'

'Interior light.'

'Exactly.'

'No, that's what your friend Harry said. It's the interior lighting that gives that effect.'

'Maybe he didn't know what he was saying.'

'I'm not sure I know what *you're* saying.'

'Some religions believe in spirit guides. They're supposed to lead you to the next world.'

'You mean this one's not the end?'

She smiled. 'Depends on your religion.'

'Well, it's plenty enough for me.' He looked at the photo again.

'I was sort of joking, you know, about her being a spirit guide.'

'I know.'


He met with Helen Cousins that night. They spoke over a drink in the Auld Hoose. Rebus hadn't been in the place in quarter of a century, and there'd been changes. They'd installed a pool table.

'You weren't invited along that night?' Rebus asked her.

She shook her head. She was twenty, three years younger than Damon. The fingers of her right hand played with her engagement ring, rolling it, sliding it off over the knuckle and then back down again. She had short, lifeless brown hair, dark, tired eyes, and acne around her mouth.

'I was out with the girls. See, that was how we played it. One night a week the boys would go off on their own, and we'd go somewhere else. Then another night we'd all get together.'

'Do you know anyone who was at Gaitanos that night? Apart from Damon and his pals?'

She chewed her bottom lip while considering. The ring came off her finger and bounced once before hitting the floor. She stooped to pick it up.

'It's always doing that.'

'You better watch it, you're going to lose it.'

She pushed the ring back on. 'Yes,' she said, 'Corinne and Jacky were there.'

'Corinne and Jacky?' She nodded. 'Where can I find them?'

A phone call brought them to the Auld Hoose. Rebus got in the round: Bacardi and Coke for Corinne, Bacardi and blackcurrant for Jacky, a second vodka and orange for Helen and another bottle of no-alcohol lager for himself. He eyed the optics behind the bar. His mean little drink was costing more than a whisky. Something was telling him to indulge in a Teacher's. Maybe it's my spirit guide, he thought, dismissing the idea.

Corinne had long black hair crimped with curling tongs. Her pal Jacky was tiny, with dyed platinum hair. When he got back to the table, they were in a huddle, exchanging gossip. Rebus took out the photograph again.

'Look,' Corinne said, 'there's Damon.' So they all had a good look. Then Rebus touched his finger to the strapless aura.

'Remember her?'

Helen prickled visibly. 'Who is she?'

'Yeah, she was there,' Jacky said.

'Was she with anyone?'

'Didn't see her up dancing.'

'Isn't that why people go to clubs?'

'Well, it's one reason.' All three broke into a giggle.

'You didn't speak to her?'

'No.'

'Not even in the toilets?'

'I saw her in there,' Corinne said. 'She was doing her eyes.'

'Did she say anything?'

'She seemed sort of . . . stuck-up.'

'Snobby,' Jacky agreed.

Rebus tried to think of another question and couldn't. They ignored him for a while as they exchanged news. It was like they hadn't seen each other in a year. At one point, Helen got up to use the toilet. Rebus expected the other two to accompany her, but only Corinne did so. He sat with Jacky for a moment, then, for want of anything else to say, asked her what she thought of Damon. He meant about Damon disappearing, but she didn't take it that way.

'Ach, he's all right.'

'Just all right?'

'Well, you know, Damon's heart's in the right place, but he's a bit thick. A bit slow, I mean.'

'Really?' The impression Rebus had received from Damon's family had been of a genius-in-waiting. He suddenly realised just how superficial his own portrait of Damon was. Siobhan's words should have been warning – so far he'd heard only one side of Damon. 'Helen likes him though?'

'I suppose so.'

'They're engaged.'

'It happens, doesn't it? I've got friends who got engaged just so they could throw a party.' She looked around the bar, then leaned towards him. 'They used to have some mega arguments.'

'What about?'

'Jealousy, I suppose. She'd see him notice someone, or he'd say she'd been letting some guy chat her up. Just the usual.' She turned the photo around so it faced her. 'She looks like a dream, doesn't she? I remember she was dressed to kill. Made the rest of us spit.'

'But you'd never seen her before?'

Jacky shook her head. No, no one seemed to have seen her before, nobody knew who she was. Unlikely then that she was local.

'Were there any buses in that night?'

'That doesn't happen at Gaitanos,' she told him. 'It's not "in" enough any more. There's a new place in Dunfermline. That gets the busloads.' Jacky tapped the photo. 'You think she's gone off with Damon?'

Rebus looked at her and saw behind the eyeliner to a sharp intelligence. 'It's possible,' he said quietly.

'I don't think so,' she said. 'She wouldn't be interested, and he wouldn't have had the guts.'

On his way home, Rebus dropped into St Leonard's. The amount he was paying in bridge tolls, he was thinking about a season ticket. There was a fax on his desk. He'd been promised it in the afternoon, but there'd been a delay. It identified the owner of the Rolls-Royce as a Mr Richard Mandelson, with an address in Juniper Green. Mr Mandelson had no criminal record outstanding, whether for motoring offences or anything else. Rebus tried to imagine some poor parking warden trying to give the Roller a ticket with the fat man behind the wheel. There were a few more facts about Mr Mandelson, including last known occupation.

Casino manager.

# Seven

Matty and Stevie Scoular saw one another socially now. Stevie would sometimes phone and invite Matty to some party or dinner, or just for a drink. At the same time as Matty was flattered, he did wonder what Stevie's angle was, had even come out and asked him.

'I mean,' he'd said, 'I'm just a toe-rag from the school playground, and you . . . well, you're SuperStevie, you're the king.'

'Aye, if you believe the papers.' Stevie had finished his drink – Perrier, he had a game the next day. 'I don't know, Matty, maybe it's that I miss all that.'

'All what?'

'Schooldays. It was a laugh back then, wasn't it?'

Matty had frowned, not really remembering. 'But the life you've got now, Stevie, man. People would kill for it.'

And Stevie had nodded, looking suddenly sad.

Another time, a couple of kids had asked Stevie for his autograph, then had turned and asked Matty for his, thinking that whoever he was, he had to be somebody. Stevie had laughed at that, said something about it being a lesson in humility. Again, Matty didn't get it. There were times when Stevie seemed to be on a different planet. Maybe it was understandable, the pressure he was under. Stevie seemed to remember a lot more about school than Matty did: teachers' names, the lot. They talked about Gullane, too, what a boring place to grow up. Sometimes they didn't talk much at all. Just took out a couple of dolls: Stevie would always bring one along for Matty. She wouldn't be quite as gorgeous as Stevie's, but that was all right. Matty could understand that. He was soaking it all up, enjoying it while it lasted. He had half an idea that Stevie and him would be best friends for life, and another that Stevie would dump him soon and find some other distraction. He thought Stevie needed him right now much more than *he* needed Stevie. So he soaked up what he could, started filing the stories away for future use, tweaking them here and there . . .

Tonight they took in a couple of bars, a bit of a drive in Stevie's Beamer: he preferred BMWs to Porsches, more space for passengers. They ended up at a club, but didn't stay long. Stevie had a game the next day. He was always very conscientious that way: Perrier and early nights. Stevie dropped Matty off outside his flat, sounding the horn as he roared away. Matty hadn't spotted the other car, but he heard a door opening, looked across the road and recognised Malibu straight off. Malibu was Mr Mandelson's driver. He'd eased himself out of the Roller and was holding open the back door while looking over to Matty.

So Matty crossed the street. As he did so, he walked into Malibu's shadow, cast by the sodium street lamp. At that moment, though he didn't know what was about to happen, he realised he was lost.

'Get in, Matty.'

The voice, of course, was Mandelson's. Matty got into the car and Malibu closed the door after him, then kept guard outside. They weren't going anywhere.

'Ever been in a Roller before, Matty?'

'I don't think so.'

'You'd remember if you had. I could have had one years back, but only by buying secondhand. I wanted to wait until I had the cash for a nice new one. That leather smell – you don't get it with any other car.' Mandelson lit a cigar. The windows were closed and the car started filling with sour smoke. 'Know how I came to afford a brand new Roller, Matty?'

'Hard work?' Matty's mouth was dry. Cars, he thought:

Rebus's, Stevie's, and now this one. Plus, of course, the one he'd borrowed that night, the one that had brought him to this.

'Don't be stupid. My dad worked thirty years in a shop, six days a week and he still couldn't have made the down-payment. Faith, Matty, that's the key. You have to believe in yourself, and sometimes you have to trust other people – strangers some of them, or people you don't like, people it's hard to trust. That's the gamble life's making with you, and if you place your bet, sometimes you get lucky. Except it's not luck – not entirely. See, there are odds, like in every game, and that's where judgment comes in. I like to think I'm a good judge of character.'

Only now did Mandelson turn to look at him. There seemed to Matty to be nothing behind the eyes, nothing at all.

'Yes, sir,' he said, for want of anything better.

'That was Stevie dropped you off, eh?' Matty nodded. 'Now, your man Stevie, he's got something else, something we haven't discussed yet. He's got a gift. He's had to work, of course, but the thing was there to begin with. Don't ask me where it came from or why it should have been given to him in particular – that's one for the philosophers, and I don't claim to be a philosopher. What I am is a businessman . . . and a gambler. Only I don't bet on nags or dogs or a turn of the cards, I bet on people. I'm betting on you, Matty.'

'Me?'

Mandelson nodded, barely visible inside the cloud of smoke. 'I want you to talk to Stevie on my behalf. I want you to get him to do me a favour.'

Matty rubbed his forehead with his fingers. He knew what was coming but didn't want to hear it.

'I saw a recent interview,' Mandelson went on, 'where he told the reporter he always gave a hundred and ten per cent. All I want is to knock maybe twenty per cent off for next Saturday's game. You know what I'm saying?'

Next Saturday ... An away tie at Kirkcaldy. Stevie expected to run rings around the Raith Rovers defence.

'He won't do it,' Matty said. 'Come to that, neither will I.'

'No?' Mandelson laughed. A hand landed on Matty's thigh. 'You fucked up in London, son. They knew you'd end up taking a croupier's job somewhere else, it's the only thing you know how to do. So they phoned around, and eventually they phoned *me*. I told them I'd never heard of you. That can change, Matty. Want me to talk to them again?'

'I'd tell them you lied to them the first time.'

Mandelson shrugged. 'I can live with that. But what do you think they'll do to *you*, Matty? They were pretty angry about whatever scheme it was you pulled. I'd say they were furious.'

Matty felt like he was going to heave. He was sweating, his lungs toxic. 'He won't do it,' he said again.

'Be persuasive, Matty. You're his friend. Remind him that his tab's up to three and a half. All he has to do is ease off for one game, and the tab's history. And Matty, I'll know if you've talked to him or not, so no games, eh? Or you might find yourself with no place left to hide.'

# Eight

Rebus searched his flat, but came up with only half a dozen snapshots: two of his ex-wife Rhona, posing with Samantha, their daughter, back when Sammy was seven or eight; two further shots of Sammy in her teens; one showing his father as a young man, kissing the woman who would become Rebus's mother; and a final photograph, a family grouping, showing uncles, aunts and cousins whose names Rebus didn't know. There were other photographs, of course – at least, there had been – but not here, not in the flat. He guessed Rhona still kept some, maybe his brother Michael had the others. But they could be anywhere. Rebus hadn't thought of himself as the kind to spend long nights with the family album, using it as a crutch to memory, always with the fear that remembrance would yield to sentiment.

If I died tonight, he thought, what would I bequeath to the world? Looking around, the answer was: nothing. The thought scared him, and worst of all it made him want a drink, and not just one drink but a dozen.

Instead of which, he drove north back into Fife. It had been overcast all day, and the evening was warm. He didn't know what he was doing, knew he had precious little to say to either of Damon's parents, and yet that's where he ended up. He'd had the destination in mind all along.

Brian Mee answered the door, wearing a smart suit and just finishing knotting his tie.

'Sorry, Brian,' Rebus said. 'Are you off out?'

'In ten minutes. Come in anyway. Is it Damon?'

Rebus shook his head and saw the tension in Brian's face

turn to relief. Yes, a visit in person wouldn't be good news, would it? Good news had to be given immediately by telephone, not by a knock at the door. Rebus should have realised; he'd been the bearer of bad news often enough in his time.

'Sorry, Brian,' he repeated. They were in the hallway. Janis's voice came from above, asking who it was.

'It's Johnny,' her husband called back. Then to Rebus, 'It's all right to call you that?'

'Of course. It's my name, isn't it?' He could have added: again, after all this time. He looked at Brian, remembering the way they'd sometimes mistreated him at school: not that 'Barney' had seemed to mind, but who could tell for sure? And then that night of the last school dance . . . Brian had been there for Mitch. Brian had been there; Rebus had not. He'd been too busy losing Janis, and losing consciousness.

She was coming downstairs now. 'I'll be back in a sec,' Brian said, heading up past her.

'You look terrific,' Rebus told her. The blue dress was well-chosen, her make-up highlighting all the right features of her busy face. She managed a smile.

'No news?'

'Sorry,' he said again. 'Just thought I'd see how you are.'

'Oh, we're pining away.' Another smile, tinged by shame this time. 'It's a dinner-dance, we bought the tickets months back. It's for the Jolly Beggars.'

'Nobody expects you to sit at home every night, Janis.'

'But all the same . . . ' Her cheeks grew flushed and her eyes sought his. 'We're not going to find him, are we?'

'Not easily. Our best bet's that he'll get in touch.'

'If he can,' she said quietly.

'Come on, Janis.' He put his hands on her shoulders, like they were strangers and about to dance. 'You might hear from him tomorrow, or it might take months.'

'And meantime life goes on, eh?'

'Something like that.'

She smiled again, blinking back tears. 'Why don't you come with us, John?'

Rebus dropped his hands from her shoulders. 'I haven't danced in years.'

'So you'd be rusty.'

'Thanks, Janis, but not tonight.'

'Know something? I bet they play the same records we used to dance to at school.'

It was his turn to smile. Brian was coming back downstairs, patting his hair into place.

'You'd be welcome to join us, Johnny,' he said.

'I've another appointment, Brian. Maybe next time, eh?'

'Let's make that a promise.'

They went out to their cars together. Janis pecked him on the cheek, Brian shook his hand. He watched them drive off then headed to the cemetery.

It was dark, and the gates were locked, so Rebus sat in his car and smoked a cigarette. He thought about his parents and the rest of his family and remembered stories about Bowhill, stories which seemed inextricable from family history: mining tragedies; a girl found drowned in the River Ore; a holiday car crash which had erased an entire family. Then there was Johnny Thomson, Celtic goalkeeper, injured during an 'Old Firm' match. He was in his early twenties when he died, and was buried behind those gates, not far from Rebus's parents. *Not Dead, But at Rest in the Arms of the Lord.*

The Lord had to be a bodybuilder.

From family he turned to friends and tried recalling a dozen names to put to faces he remembered from schooldays. Other friends: people he'd known in the army, the SAS. All the people he'd dealt with during his career in the police. Villains he'd put away, some who'd slipped through his fingers. People he'd interviewed, suspected, questioned, broken the worst kind of news to. Acquaintances from the Oxford Bar and all the other pubs where he'd ever been a regular. Local shopkeepers. Jesus, the list was endless. All these people who'd played a part in his life, in shaping who he was and how he acted, how he felt about things. All of them, out there somewhere and nowhere, gathered together only inside his head. And chief among them tonight, Brian and Janis.

That night of the school dance . . . It was true he'd been drunk – elated. He'd felt he could *do* anything, *be* anything. Because he'd come to a decision that day – he wouldn't join the army, he'd stay in Bowhill with Janis, apply for a job at the dockyard. His dad had told him not to be so stupid – 'short-sighted' was the word he'd used. But what did parents know about their children's desires? So he'd drunk some beer and headed off to the dance, his thoughts only of Janis. Tonight he'd tell her. And Mitch, of course. He'd have to tell Mitch, tell him he'd be heading into the army alone. But Mitch wouldn't mind, he'd understand, as best friends had to.

But while Rebus had been outside with Janis, his friend Mitch was being cornered by four teenagers who considered themselves his enemies. This was their last chance for revenge, and they'd gone in hard, kicking and punching. Four against one . . . until Barney had waded in, shrugging off blows, and dragged Mitch to safety. But one kick had done the damage, dislodging a retina. Mitch's vision stayed fuzzy in that eye for a few days, then disappeared. And where had Rebus been? Out cold on the concrete by the bike sheds.

And why had he never thanked Barney Mee?

He blinked now and sniffed, wondering if he was coming down with a cold. He'd had this idea when he came back to Bowhill that the place would seem beyond redemption, that he'd be able to tell himself it had lost its sense of community, become just another town for him to pass through. Maybe he'd wanted to put it behind him. Well, it hadn't worked. He got out of the car and looked around.

The street was dead. He reached up and hauled himself over the iron railings and walked a circuit of the cemetery for an hour or so, and felt strangely at peace.

# Nine

'So what's the panic, Matty?'

After a home draw with Rangers, Stevie was ready for a night on the town. One–one, and of course he'd scored his team's only goal. The reporters would be busy filing their copy, saying for the umpteenth time that he was his side's hero, that without him they were a very ordinary team indeed. Rangers had known that: Stevie's marker had been out for blood, sliding studs-first into tackles which Stevie had done his damnedest to avoid. He'd come out of the game with a couple of fresh bruises and grazes, a nick on one knee but, to his manager's all too palpable relief, fit to play again midweek.

'I said what's the panic?'

Matty had worried himself sleepless. He knew he had several options. Speak to Stevie, that was one of them. Another was not to speak to him, but tell Mandelson he had. Then it would be down to whether or not Mandelson believed him. Option three: do a runner; only Mandelson was right about that – he was running out of places to hide. With *two* casino bosses out for his blood, how could he ever pick up another croupier's job?

If he spoke with Stevie, he'd lose a new-found friend. But to stay silent . . . well, there was very little percentage in it. So here he was in Stevie's flat, having demanded to see him. In the corner, a TV was replaying a tape of the afternoon's match. There was no commentary, just the sounds of the terraces and the dug-outs.

'No panic,' he said now, playing for time.

Stevie stared at him. 'You all right? Want a drink or something?'

'Maybe a vodka.'

'Anything in it?'

'I'll take it as it comes.'

Stevie poured him a drink. Matty had been here half an hour now, and they still hadn't talked. The telephone had hardly stopped: reporters' questions, family and friends offering congratulations. Stevie had shrugged off the superlatives.

Matty took the drink, swallowed it, wondering if he could still walk away. Then he remembered Malibu, and saw shadows falling.

'Thing is, Stevie,' he said. 'You know my boss at the Morvena, Mr Mandelson?'

'I owe him money, of course I know him.'

'He says we could do something about that.'

'What? My tab?' Stevie was checking himself in the mirror, having changed into his on-the-town clothes. 'I don't get it,' he said.

Well, Stevie, Matty thought, it was nice knowing you, pal. 'All you have to do is ease off next Saturday.'

Stevie frowned and turned from the mirror. 'Away to Raith?' He came and sat down opposite Matty. 'He told you to tell me?' He waited till Matty nodded. 'That bastard. What's in it for him?'

Matty wriggled on the leather sofa. 'I've been thinking about it. Raith are going through a bad patch, but you know yourself that if you're taken out of the equation . . . '

'Then they'd be up against not very much. My boss has told everybody to get the ball to me. If they spend the whole game doing that and I don't do anything with it . . . '

Matty nodded. 'What I think is, the odds will be on you scoring. Nobody'll be expecting Raith to put one in the net.'

'So Mandelson's cash will be on a goalless draw?'

'And he'll get odds, spread a lot of small bets around . . . '

'Bastard,' Stevie said again. 'How did he get you into this, Matty?'

Matty shifted again. 'Something I did in London.'

'Secrets, eh? Hard things to keep.' Stevie got up, went to the mirror again, and just stood there, hands by his sides, staring into it. There was no emotion in his voice when he spoke.

'Tell him he can fuck himself.'

Matty had to choke out the words. 'You sure that's the message?'

'Cheerio, Matty.'

Matty rose shakily to his feet. 'What am I going to do?'

'Cheerio, Matty.'

Stevie was as still as a statue as Matty walked to the door and let himself out.

Mandelson sat at his desk, playing with a Cartier pen he'd taken from a punter that day. The man was overdue on a payment. The pen was by way of a gift.

'So?' he asked Matty.

Matty sat on the chair and licked his lips. There was no offer of a drink today; this was just business. Malibu stood by the door. Matty took a deep breath – the last act of a drowning man.

'It's on,' he said.

Mandelson looked up at him. 'Stevie went for it?'

'Eventually,' Matty said.

'You're sure?'

'As sure as I can be.'

'Well, that better be watertight, or you might find yourself going for a swim with heavy legs. Know what I mean?'

Matty held the dark gaze and nodded.

Mandelson glanced towards Malibu, both of them were smiling. Then he picked up the telephone. 'You know, Matty,' he said, pushing numbers. 'I'm doing you a favour. You're doing *yourself* a favour.' He listened to the receiver.

'Mr Hamilton, please.' Then, to Matty, 'See, what you're doing here is saving your job. I overstretched myself, Matty. I wouldn't like that to get around, but I'm trusting you. If this comes off – and it better – then you've earned that trust.' He tapped the receiver. 'It wasn't all my own money either. But this will keep the Morvena alive and kicking.' He motioned for Matty to leave. Malibu tapped his shoulder as an incentive.

'Topper?' Mandelson was saying as Matty left the room. 'It's locked up. How much are you in for?'

Matty bided his time and waited till his shift was over. He walked out of the smart New Town building like a latterday Lazarus, and found the nearest payphone, then had to fumble through all the rubbish in his pockets, stuff that must have meant something once upon a time, until he found the card.

The card with a phone number on it.

The following Saturday, Stevie Scoular scored his team's only goal in their 1–0 win over Raith Rovers, and Mandelson sat alone in his office, his eyes on the Teletext results.

His hand rested on the telephone receiver. He was expecting a call from Topper Hamilton. He couldn't seem to stop blinking, like there was a grain of sand in either eye. He buzzed the reception desk, told them to tell Malibu he was wanted. Mandelson didn't know how much time he had, but he knew he would make it count. A word with Stevie Scoular, see if Matty really *had* put the proposition to him. Then Matty himself . . . Matty was a definite, no matter what. Matty was about to be put out of the game.

The knock at the door had to be Malibu. Mandelson barked for him to come in. But when the door opened, two strangers sauntered in like they owned the place. Mandelson sat back in his chair, hands on the desk. He was almost relieved when they introduced themselves as police officers.

'I'm Detective Inspector Rebus,' the younger one said, 'this is Chief Superintendent Watson.'

'And you've come about the Benevolent Fund, right?'

Rebus sat down unasked, his eyes drifting to the TV screen and the results posted there. 'Looks like you just lost a packet. I'm sorry to hear it. Did Topper take a beating, too?'

Mandelson made fists of his hands. 'That wee bastard!'

Rebus was shaking his head. 'Matty did his best, only there was something he didn't know. Seems you didn't know either. Topper will be doubly disappointed.'

'What?'

Farmer Watson, still standing, provided the answer. 'Ever heard of Big Ger Cafferty?'

Mandelson nodded. 'He's been in Barlinnie a while.'

'Used to be the biggest gangster on the east coast. Probably still is. And he's a fan of Stevie's, gets videotapes of all his games. He almost sends him love letters.'

Mandelson frowned. 'So?'

'So Stevie's covered,' Rebus said. 'Try fucking with him, you're asking Big Ger to bend over. Your little proposal has probably already made it back to Cafferty.'

Mandelson swallowed and felt suddenly dry-mouthed.

'There was no way Stevie was going to throw that game,' Rebus said quietly.

'Matty . . . ' Mandelson choked the sentence off.

'Told you it was fixed? He was scared turdless, what else was he going to say? But Matty's *mine*. You don't touch him.'

'Not that you'd get the chance,' the Farmer added. 'Not with Topper *and* Cafferty after your blood. Malibu will be a big help, the way he took off five minutes ago in the Roller.' Watson walked up to the desk, looming over Mandelson like a mountain. 'You've got two choices, son. You can talk, or you can run.'

'You've got nothing.'

'I saw you that night at Gaitanos,' Rebus said. 'If you're going to lay out big bets, where better than Fife? Optimistic Raith fans might have bet on a goalless draw. You got

Charmer Mackenzie to place the bets locally, spreading them around. That way it looked less suspicious.'

Which was why Mackenzie had wanted Rebus out of there, whatever the price: he'd been about to do some business . . .

'Besides,' Rebus continued, 'when it comes down to it, what choice do you have?'

'You either talk to us . . . ' the Farmer said.

'Or you disappear. People do it all the time.'

And it never stops, Rebus could have added. Because it's part of the dance – shifting partners, people you shared the floor with, it all changed. And it only ended when you disappeared from the hall.

And sometimes . . . sometimes, it didn't even end there.

'All right,' Mandelson said at last, the way they'd known he would, all colour gone from his face, his voice hollow, 'what do you want to know?'

'Let's start with Topper Hamilton,' the Farmer said, sounding like a kid unwrapping his birthday present.

It was Wednesday morning when Rebus got the phone call from a Mr Bain. It took him a moment to place the name: Damon's bank manager.

'Yes, Mr Bain, what can I do for you?'

'Damon Mee, Inspector. You wanted us to keep an eye on any transactions.'

Rebus leaned forward in his chair. 'That's right.'

'There've been two withdrawals from cash machines, both in central London.'

Rebus grabbed a pen. 'Where exactly?'

'Tottenham Court Road was three days ago: fifty pounds. Next day, it was Finsbury Park, same amount.'

Fifty pounds a day: enough to live on, enough to pay for a cheap bed and breakfast and two extra meals.

'How much is left in the account, Mr Bain?'

'A little under six hundred pounds.'

Enough for twelve days. There were several ways it could

go. Damon could get himself a job. Or when the money ran out he could try begging. Or he could return home. Rebus thanked Bain and telephoned Janis.

'John,' she said, 'we got a postcard this morning.'

A postcard saying Damon was in London and doing fine. A postcard of apology for any fright he'd given them. A postcard saying he needed some time to 'get my head straight'. A postcard which ended 'See you soon.' The picture on the front was of a pair of breasts painted with Union Jacks.

'Brian thinks we should go down there,' Janis said. 'Try to find him.'

Rebus thought of how many B&Bs there'd be in Finsbury Park. 'You might just chase him away,' he warned. 'He's doing OK, Janis.'

'But why did he do it, John? I mean, is it something *we* did?'

New questions and fears had replaced the old ones. Rebus didn't know what to tell her. He wasn't family and couldn't begin to answer her question. Didn't *want* to begin to answer it.

'He's doing OK,' he repeated. 'Just give him some time.'

She was crying now, softly. He imagined her with head bowed, hair falling over the telephone receiver.

'We did everything, John. You can't know how much we've given him. We always put ourselves second, never a minute's thought for anything but him . . . '

'Janis . . . ' he began.

She took a deep breath. 'Will you come and see me, John?'

Rebus looked around the office, eyes resting eventually on his own desk and the paperwork stacked there.

'I can't, Janis. I'd like to, but I just can't. See, it's not as if I . . . '

He didn't know how he was going to finish the sentence, but it didn't matter. She'd put her phone down. He sat back in his chair and remembered dancing with her, how brittle her body had seemed. But that had been half a lifetime ago. They'd made so many choices since. It was time to let the past go. Siobhan Clarke was at her desk. She was looking at him. Then she mimed the drinking of a cup of coffee, and he nodded and got to his feet.

Did a little dance as he shuffled towards her.